THEY RODE
GOOD HORSES

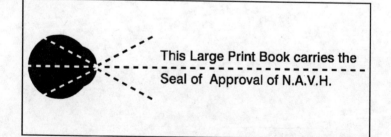

THEY RODE GOOD HORSES

D. B. JACKSON

THORNDIKE PRESS
A part of Gale, Cengage Learning

GALE
CENGAGE Learning®

Detroit • New York • San Francisco • New Haven, Conn • Waterville, Maine • London

GALE
CENGAGE Learning·

Thorndike Press® Large Print Western.
The text of this Large Print edition is unabridged.
Other aspects of the book may vary from the original edition.
Set in 16 pt. Plantin.

LIBRARY OF CONGRESS CATALOGING-IN-PUBLICATION DATA

Jackson, D. B.
  They rode good horses / by D.B. Jackson. — Large Print edition.
    pages cm. — (Thorndike Press Large Print Western)
  ISBN-13: 978-1-4104-5654-0 (hardcover)
  ISBN-10: 1-4104-5654-4 (hardcover)
    1. Life change events—Fiction. 2. Orphans—Fiction. 3. Large type books.
I. Title.
PS3610.A347T44 2013
813'.6—dc23
                      2012049293

Published in 2013 by arrangement with Cherry Weiner Literary Agency and Goldminds Publishing LLC.

Printed in the United States of America
1 2 3 4 5 6 7 17 16 15 14 13

With special thanks to the love of my life, my wife and best friend, Mary, without whose support and tireless help, Brady and Franklin would never have embarked on this epic journey.

These two men, their fast-running horses shall never carry them both back away from us, even though one man may escape.

— Homer, *The Iliad*

CHAPTER ONE

Madison River, Montana: 1891
Brady McCall grew up believing cowboys were the chosen ones, the privileged few consecrated by an ancient calling over which they had no control and, if they had, they would have chosen it anyway. McCall cowboys because that is all he ever wanted to do. By nature he is a horseman. Afoot he appears somehow incomplete, and in his presence the horse appears incomplete without him, as though the hand that created him created the horse with him in mind.

Age beset McCall before he knew he was old. First a few gray hairs. Then a few more, until that's all there were. The creases at the corners of his eyes set in gradually and soon enough he grew accustomed to seeing them there.

Now his muscles ache and he no longer remembers when they didn't. He does not accept old age and he allows himself no concessions because of it. Each morning he rises and his fingers fumble, stiff and gnarled, with shirt buttons that seem to grow more difficult each year. On cold mornings he is drawn to the heat of the stove. He washes up in a tin basin above which hangs a looking glass from wherein an old man stares back at him. The man in the looking glass is older than the man in the picture on the bureau who is his father.

But the old man who is Brady McCall walks erect and his back is strong and straight and in his eyes resides the unmistakable recklessness of his youth. Spring approaches and he grows restless. The days remain short and night comes early and the night air has yet to lose its chill. But winter has loosened its grip and now the old man's thoughts turn to spring and cows and long days in the saddle. Each year it's the same and each spring the restlessness within him returns, and this year it is no different.

He works by the light of a kerosene lamp and oils his saddle and repairs bridles and bits and broken spurs. Every scuff on the stirrup leathers and every scar on the saddle skirts holds a memory. McCall smiles at some and shudders at others, but memories are his life and he regards them all with respect. His cowdog lies at his feet as he does each evening, a ritual neither questions.

The smell of leather and mink oil and horse stir within the man an impatient spirit and the dog senses it. McCall puts up the saddle, hangs the bridle by the door and blows out the lamp. Neither he nor the dog sleeps much that night and before dawn the old cowboy sets off ahorseback.

The shadow of McCall and that of his horse preceded him over the rocks where once a creek ran. At a bend in the creek the horse turned and the shadow hurried to catch up. The riverbed narrowed and both horse and rider sensed more than they could see and more than they could discern from the meager trail they followed.

McCall leaned forward in the saddle and gauged the hoof prints leading out of the rocks and up onto the dirt bank. The tracks of the yearling bull that eluded them appeared to have been made as fresh as those that followed his horse. He glanced across the dry wash to a shallow bluff and a clearing where sparse brush and trees grew and the smoke from his branding fire spiraled upward in a thin column above which circled great eagles that lifted and disappeared into the clouds.

Up ahead in a willow break the bullock brushed up and waited and stared out at the horse and rider and waited motionless until they encroached upon the outer perimeter of his resolve, then he bolted. McCall nudged the horse into a trot and followed the yearling up a shallow bank then over the crest of a hill and down through the buckbrush and back onto the creek bed.

The bull trotted ahead, staying at the forward edge of his flight zone, and the horse followed without being asked to do so. McCall tied his catchrope on hard and fast and shook out a loop. In his left hand he carried the extra coils and the bridle-reins between his fingers. In his right the loop hung at the ready.

He followed the young bull and calculated the only shot he knew he would get. He rode up a flurry of upland game birds and the noise startled the bull to a stop and when it did McCall let loose the loop with a quick hand that made the rope sing and the bull turned its head as the loop settled over it and closed down around the thick neck. The bull spun away tossing its head, then lunged forward in a desperate attempt to escape its captors.

McCall jerked the reins and sat deep in

the saddle. The big gelding set back hard on its haunches, anticipating the coming jolt.

Sweat ran down McCall's face and he braced himself as the slack tightened and the rope stretched. He stood his weight in the opposite stirrup and turned the horse to face the bull. As he did so the bull swung around to face the horse then came back upon its own tracks and charged.

The bull crossed the horse's path at a full run, passed him on the off side, circled behind and, as it did so, the rope caught and jerked the horse's legs out from under him and laid him to the ground. McCall fell upon the rocks and took the full weight of the impact on his brittle ribcage. He lay in a pitiful heap, his body bent grotesquely over the boulder upon which he came to rest. His arm shook involuntarily and he gasped for air. He fought to clear his head and he fought to breath and he knew it was more than age that pinned his damaged body to the earth. He took short breaths, and he took a lot of them before his body parts began to rejoin the fight.

His instincts over-ran his sense of reasoning and McCall held tight to the slack rope he clutched in his left hand. The horse lay trembling, its sides heaving and its eyes wide and fearful. The rope remained tied to the

13

saddle horn. At the other end of the taut rope the bull lay choked down and confused. Its eyes filled with fear and rage and its nostrils flared red and large as everything in its nature rallied in its fight for survival.

The great beast stood and attempted to back away from the horse, but in so doing forced the noose to further cut off his air supply. Its eyes bulged, its tongue lolled to the side and the bull began to totter. It took a step forward and the rope around his thick neck loosened and the flow of air resumed and with each breath the fight within him swelled and he pawed the ground, sending rocks and dirt flying behind him.

McCall rose to one elbow and watched the bull and the bull watched him. The cowboy rose to his knees, maintained his hold on the rope and attempted to ease the horse up as he moved to regain his seat in the saddle. The horse gathered itself and rose quickly. The bull took another step nearer and McCall held onto the loosely coiled rope.

There was no look of reason in the bull's eyes, only the desperation of one about to be executed. And in that desperation the bull did the only thing he knew to do. He charged the horse and the horse did the only thing he knew to do, and when he bolted McCall was cast aside. Like the bull and the horse McCall did the only thing he knew to do, and he hung onto the rope while the circumstances in which he was cast played out like a scene in which he felt more like a spectator than a participant.

Then, as though summoned by a higher force, the bull and the horse sought their separate refuges and charged off in opposite directions. The coils in the rope began to disappear while McCall held on and watched, his brain unable to communicate to his hands as quickly as the impending disaster unfolded.

McCall cursed the bull and he cursed the horse and he cursed his misfortune. As quickly as he released the rope a coil twisted and trapped his thumb and the rope stretched tight, and when it did it severed the skin and flesh and tore the thumb from its socket in a bright spray of blood, and the thumb spun off into the air then tumbled to the ground.

McCall tottered and fell and the blood that sprayed his face felt warm against his skin and tasted sweet and heavy on his lips. He collapsed where he fell. He had no clear sense of his circumstances, but when he looked at the gaping socket of flesh and tendons he tried to vomit and couldn't, then he tried not to and couldn't stop himself.

He closed his eyes and attempted to dream away his circumstances. He held his hand under his arm and lay like that a long time before he looked again at the deformed claw that was once his hand.

The blood that ran from it soaked his shirt and trousers and pooled about the spot where he lay. He reached across his belt with his good hand and withdrew the skinning knife that hung there every day for half a century, and with it he hacked out the front of his shirt and fashioned two narrow strips of muslin which he wrapped and twisted over and around the thumbless hand. He tied it off and knotted it as best he could with one hand and his teeth.

If the dressing did any good, it was not evident as blood ran black and thick and dripped from his elbow into the widening pool where he sat. The hand appeared small and odd looking and McCall wished it wasn't his. His breathing was shallow but it gradually slowed and each breath came with more regularity. His mind wandered dull and senseless and he felt a detachment that made his pain and circumstances seem remote and unimportant. Some primitive voice deep inside him urged him. *Don't open your eyes and none of this will be real.* So he didn't.

A quarter of a mile to the east the smoke from his branding fire spun upward through the trees and bent with the wind, and had the fire been a hundred miles off it would have been no further out of reach for the old cowboy. Blood dripped from the elbow of his soaked shirt and if he heard any sounds at all, they were softly muted and deathly serene.

He had no sense of the time between when his eyes closed and when his head snapped back, but when it did the suddenness of it all awoke him in a fearful state.

He sat upright and cursed. He thought he had wet himself, and he looked down at his blood-drenched trousers then raised his eyes to the thumb lying between his boots. His eyes went back to the small rag-wrapped hand. He leaned forward to reach the dismembered thumb with his good hand but retreated when the bone fragments of his splintered ribs pressed into his lungs.

When the pain subsided enough for another attempt, he figured to drag the thumb closer with a willow switch lying within his reach. He tried again and again, failing to master the thin willow's flexibility. When he finally did, he took the thumb up and

17

regarded it with curiosity and revulsion, and his first thought was to cast it deep into the brush. He chose instead to tuck it into the pocket of his vest, which he did quickly before he might change his mind.

Light headed, McCall listed from side to side, the pool of blood spread and his sensibilities begun to unravel. In a moment of fleeting clarity and desperation he drew himself up to his knees, then rose to his feet and stood there wobbling and unsteady. He breathed and panted like a dog.

He turned and positioned himself at the wall of the creek bank and clawed his way up the loose rock and gravel high enough to see to the branding fire. He secured a hand hold on the grassy ledge and began to pull himself up. He grunted and dug his fingers in and failed to gain purchase as the loose gravel gave way and he plunged back to the bottom.

He tried again and again the gravel refused him. The third time he lacked the strength to rise to his feet and he lay there, back to the dirt bank, his senses taking their leave.

McCall's thoughts swirled about like a foggy mist that carried him into euphoria more satisfying than any dream; a place where no pain existed and where there was no sense of urgency or obligation. He felt warm and comfortable and light, as though he were dreaming a dream from which he could awaken at anytime had he chosen to do so.

Brady McCall resigned himself to his fate and he began to feel cold, but he lay quietly on his back and this time closed his eyes and settled onto the sand, with all the fight bled out of him.

CHAPTER TWO

St. Joseph, Missouri: September 1840

Brady McCall, ten years old on his last birthday, balanced himself behind the rough, wooden seat while his father, William, clucked the mule team out of a grove of hardwood trees and up onto the roadway at the eastern edge of St. Joseph. William McCall reined the mules in at the crest of a hill overlooking rows of plank-board buildings spread in imprecise uniformity along streets that pushed the city to the edge of the Missouri River. The city stopped there, abruptly and rudely, as though the river itself was the line of demarcation beyond which civilization ceased to exist.

Brady's mother, Elizabeth, sat on the seat beside her husband. Their new life in the west, which he convinced her was their destiny, was now as much a part of her commitment as it was his. William's vision was one of opportunity and adventure. Elizabeth shared that vision but hers was attended by a veil of grave uncertainty. She kept her reservations contained far below the surface and never voiced them to anyone.

Elizabeth gazed down upon the citizenry of St. Joseph with a mixture of interest and relief. It was good to see people with homes conducting day-today business. Already she realized how much she missed that on the trip from Virginia, but she smiled and took her husband's arm.

Her eyes danced and she wore her dark hair back, complimenting her strong, refined features. She looked up at her husband, smiled, and squeezed his arm. The smile and her reassuring touch were all the confirmation William needed and it pleased him.

Elizabeth turned back and called the children forward. Eight-year-old Rachael climbed up on the seat between her mother and her father. Brady lifted three-year-old Matthew from the soft bundle of blankets in the center of the wagon and brought him forward.

No one spoke and when they did speak, they all spoke at once.

For Brady, Virginia was now only a memory; vague and far removed — a place he thought about less and less, but already a place he was sure to never see again. Each day the memory became less clear and the destination loomed more and more real.

Beyond the outer reach of civilization, beyond the familiar, lay the vision only his father seemed to see with clarity. But, as the child walks in the steps of the father, Brady McCall advanced with confidence, his strength the strength of his father. He would listen to his father speak quietly over the evening fire and the Montana Territory of which he spoke gripped the boy in the same intoxicating way it did the father until it was unclear to the boy when the dream of his father became that of his own making.

He would later recall this point in his life for it was the crossroad beyond which everything changed. And he would wonder, if he could have changed it would he have left it as it was, or would he have altered the course.

Brady stood at his father's side. He watched him shake hands with wagon master James Garrett. He watched his father sign his name in Garrett's ledger book and he followed his father to a group of men waiting after the meeting in small clutches, reluctant to leave and talking amongst themselves as though they may somehow resolve collectively the growing layer of doubt that individually each felt.

Those of gravest doubt were those who professed the greatest confidence. William McCall mostly listened and Brady listened with him. The boy's head was filled with the names of rivers and mountains and what lay before them. The dangers, the opportunities, the overblown accounts of abundance were held in folded flyers and letters from those who had gone on before them. The grandness of it all overwhelmed him, but when he looked into the faces of those smiling men gesturing and pontificating in loud voices he was struck with great fear, for in those faces he saw something lacking that was far beyond his ability to comprehend. He had no way of knowing how inalterably their flawed assessment of their own cleverness would affect the course of his life.

Thomas and Emily Stilwell and their fifteen-year-old son, Franklin, arrived in St. Joseph from Georgia three weeks ahead of the Mc-Calls. Divested of everything they owned save the contents of their wagon, the Stilwells settled in for the winter. In the spring fifty-three families would cross the river, none expecting to ever return as each family created a new and better life.

Thomas Stilwell was tall, thick-wristed, raw-boned and direct. His eyes were penetrating and men regarded him with caution. But when he spoke his expression was friendly and disarming, and his easy manner led men to underestimate him.

He had a noticeable lack of regard for convention and authority but that, combined with his good nature, only added to his charm. These same traits ran clear in Franklin's make up. But those traits in the boy had somehow mutated to a level of reckless irresponsibility.

Franklin's handsome features came from his mother's side of the family, but there remained little doubt which side of the family should be held accountable for the personality that many foresaw as the downfall of a potentially good man. Whatever conclusions those that met him reached, none would regard Franklin Stilwell with ambivalence.

Thomas Stilwell was a hunter and a woodsman and he shared most of Franklin's fifteen years passing these skills on to the boy. Stilwell could overlook shortcomings in his son's social skills but he could never abide a lack of self-sufficiency, and it gave him great satisfaction to know his son commanded the skills of survival.

As Brady McCall would learn over the years, there was no clear line between Franklin's social skills and his survival skills, for as often as he appeared without equal in both disciplines, he just as often appeared devoid of any traces of either. But Franklin was adaptable. And for the short time he had been in St. Joseph, Franklin had scouted every inch of the town that might offer a young boy adventure and excitement.

Brady McCall was unsure what to expect as his father urged the mules between a long row of cabins and brought the wagon to a creaking halt near the door of the small utilitarian structure that would be their home until spring. The boy stood, looked up and down the narrow, rutted street then climbed down the wheel to the ground.

"What do you think?" his father asked.

Brady smiled up at him, "I don't know. It looks kinda crowded to me."

"It does to me too," his father said. "But, it'll get us through."

Rachael climbed down and waited while Elizabeth helped young Matthew to the dirt street and asked Rachael to take his hand.

After they surveyed the cabin, Elizabeth and the two younger children stayed inside to manage the cleaning and unpacking while Brady and his father unloaded the wagon.

Brady noticed a long-legged boy strutting across the street in their direction. His manner appeared cocky and self-assured and he wore a man's hat tilted to one side. Brady diverted his eyes but watched the boy as he approached.

Brady moved to the side to give the boy more space which, for some reason, he felt the new boy deserved as he walked up to the rear of the wagon where Mr. McCall unloaded an armful of quilts and blankets and handed them to Brady.

The new boy ignored Brady and looked up at Mr. McCall nodding and touching the brim of his hat. "Morning," McCall said, glancing the older boy's direction as he unloaded a bundle of bedding.

"How y'all doin'?" the older boy said with such grown up confidence that Brady couldn't take his eyes off him.

"I live over yonder," he said, nodding toward the cabin next door. "Can I give ya a hand gettin' unloaded?"

McCall looked at the boy for a moment. He was solidly built and, with the wide-brimmed old cowboy hat set back slightly on his head, looked older than he was. His cocky appearance was offset by innocent dark eyes and a polite manner.

The boy stood firm, still looking directly at McCall but trying very hard to make sure Brady was adequately impressed.

"Well, sure," McCall said. "We could use some help if you're not too busy. What's your name, son?"

"Franklin T. Stilwell, sir."

McCall smiled. "They call you Frank?" he asked.

"No sir. They call me Franklin."

McCall nodded and shook Franklin's hand. "Well then Franklin it is. Franklin, this here's my son, Brady."

McCall turned and gestured toward the younger boy, then backed through the door with his load and left Brady standing there, unsure of his next move. Brady hesitated then stepped forward and offered Franklin his hand.

"I'm Brady McCall. Brady C. McCall," he said as he stood up straight and tipped his head back to make up for some of the height difference.

Brady extended his hand. Franklin reached forth and grasped him about the wrist, leaving Brady's fingers nowhere to go but to grasp his wrist in return.

"This is how the Blackfeet do it, B.C." Franklin said. He didn't smile, and the look in his eyes was one of great seriousness.

"This will be our secret handshake," Franklin added.

"My name ain't B.C.," Brady said, not sure whether to be offended or flattered.

Franklin adjusted his hat and pulled it low over his eyes. He dropped Brady's arm and looked at him. His voice lowered and he put his face a little closer to Brady's.

"B.C. sounds more growed up then Brady. It makes you sound interesting . . . a kid your age ain't too interesting."

Brady bristled. "I never said I was interesting."

"Did you ever think about it?" Franklin asked.

"Well, no I didn't."

Franklin looked down at Brady. "I could tell," he said.

"Okay, then how about I call you F.T.?"

"No," Franklin said. "My name's Franklin and I'm already interesting."

Brady contemplated that a moment. "What do I gotta do to get interesting?" Brady asked.

"I ain't sure you're cut out to be interesting," Franklin said as he pushed Brady and laughed then picked up an armload of supplies and headed into the cabin.

Brady laughed and followed Franklin's

lead. He pushed Franklin back. "You ain't really all that interesting yourself," he lied.

Fall lost its color — the days turned gray, the nights grew long, the days short, and in the mornings the ground lay white with frost. Franklin and Brady were like a boy and his shadow. Where you found one, you found the other. By mid November there had been little snow, but a cold front from the north held temperatures below freezing day and night.

Wearing heavy gloves, a wool scarf and a thick jacket, Franklin was barely recognizable when he climbed up on the corral fence and waited for Brady to finish feeding the mules.

Franklin spoke and his words floated out into the freezing air in billows of white clouds of smoke and when Brady spoke it was the same.

"Hey, B.C.," Franklin yelled. "I got us a job."

"What do you mean?" Brady asked.

"You know . . . working . . . getting paid . . . that kind of a job," Franklin answered.

"Who'd pay us?" Brady asked.

"Mr. Hog would."

"Who?"

"Mr. Hog . . . you know . . . down at the livery?"

Brady looked up. "You mean Mr. Hogue? He said he'd pay us?"

"Yep," Franklin said, looking proud and just a little smug.

"We start in the morning. Fifteen cents a day . . . each," Franklin added.

"So what will we be doing?" Brady asked.

"This and that. You know, kind of be in charge when Hog's not there."

Brady shook his head. "Franklin, Mr. Hogue is always there."

"Yeah, well maybe," Franklin said sounding somewhat defensive.

"But it don't matter, 'cause we'll be in the money."

"You sure he wants both of us?" Brady asked.

"Uh huh . . . I, um . . . mentioned there was two of us," Franklin said.

Brady eyed him with a doubtful expression. "What do you mean you mentioned it?"

"Well, I mean I told him. He knows."

"And we start tomorrow morning?" Brady asked.

"Yep," said Franklin, with a silly grin as he puffed his chest and strutted with his thumbs hooked behind imaginary suspenders.

Brady never knew for sure when Franklin was lying, which was most of the time, but, as always, Brady found himself wanting to believe his friend. Whether it was a lie or an exaggeration, one thing was certain, Franklin would see it through to the end. And that meant excitement or adventure, and that was good enough for Brady.

Brady grinned.

"Knock on my door in the morning."

Franklin wet his fingertip and smoothed his eyebrows and gazed into his palm as though it were a mirror. He raised his eyes. "Try to look good," he said.

CHAPTER THREE

Brady was dressed and waiting when Franklin stepped up onto the porch and tapped on Brady's door just after daylight. "You ready, cousin?" Franklin asked when Brady opened the door.

Brady nodded. "I'm ready."

They could see their breath in the cold air as they walked down the middle of the street and turned at the edge of town along the rutted road that led to Hogue's Livery. A light shone in the barn and when they stepped through the heavy double doors, they saw Hogue's backlit form bending over a row of grain sacks.

In the darkened shadows of the barn the ominous figure appeared to both boys like some forbidding creature of the night. They hesitated and looked over at one another and Franklin nodded them forward.

Hogue ignored them as they quietly approached him. He looked larger and more intimidating than Brady recalled. And when he spoke his voice boomed and Brady's stomach knotted.

"What do you two piss-ants want?"

Brady looked at Franklin and Franklin continued walking towards Hogue. Brady kept pace and when they were close enough to discern Hogue's features, Franklin answered.

"Hey, Mr. Hog," he said as though he and the hulking man were close acquaintances.

Brady froze.

Franklin nodded an acknowledgment to Houge, which Hogue did not return.

"We're ready to go to work," Franklin added. "What can we get started with?"

Hogue stood to his full height. He shifted the wet cigar stub from one side of his mouth to the other without using his hands. He pushed his hat back and scratched his big stomach. He coughed and spat and wiped his mouth on his sleeve.

"I don't need no more help," Hogue said.

"Hey, Mr. Hog . . . it's me. Franklin T. Stilwell," Franklin said. "This here's B.C. McCall. I talked to you at church Sunday about me and him working for you and you said, that'd be fine."

Brady glared at Franklin for the mispronunciation then waited for Hogue's dismissal.

Hogue looked at Franklin then over to Brady. He walked up to Brady and lowered his face to his level.

"Yer kindly of a little squirt, ain't ya?" Hogue said.

"How old are you boy?" Hogue asked, shifting the soggy cigar stub to the other side of his mouth. Brady watched Hogue's lips and the cigar move together.

"He's thirteen and a half, Mr. Hog," Franklin lied before Brady could respond.

Brady shot Franklin a devastating look, but Franklin stood firm. Hogue shifted his eyes to Franklin, then back to Brady.

"Can you talk?"

Brady looked back into Hogue's red, watery eyes and lied, "Going on fourteen, sir."

Hogue straightened up and said, "Fair enough. You boys, you start now and work 'till I tell ye your done. If you do real good you can come back every Saturday and earn yourselves ten cents each."

Franklin looked over at Brady. Brady declined the look and cleared his throat.

"We gotta have fifteen," he said.

Hogue stood his full height again and glared down at Brady. "You what?

"Gotta have fifteen cents . . . each," Brady said, his voice steady and clear, but not challenging.

Hogue's eyes narrowed. He looked at Franklin. "You got a opinion on that?" he asked.

Franklin nodded. "Yes, sir. You said fifteen cents and we took you at your word. You'll get your money's worth."

Hogue pinched the cigar stub and held it between his fingers. He laughed and walked toward the office. "I always get my money's worth, boy. But, I think I'm going to like you two. You got your fifteen cents . . . but don't you be no slackers and you damn sure better take good care of my tools."

Hogue handed the boys each a double-bit ax and two manure forks, then sent them off to clean frozen stalls. By the end of that first day it was clear to both boys that Hogue would certainly get his money's worth. Hogue waved the boys over to his office, which was a wooden shipping crate turned upside down and a cane back chair next to it.

"I want you two peckerwoods to sign in and out each day so's we can keep a track of your time." He pushed a dirt-soiled scrap of paper across the crate. "You two can read, can't ya?"

Franklin looked over at Hogue. "Yes sir, we both read good. What do we put on here?"

Hogue pulled out his cigar and pointed it at the paper. "Where it says, start . . . write in the time you started. And where it says, end . . . write in the time you left. There's a clock up there on the wall by the hay hooks. Get yer time offa there."

On the way out the door, Franklin punched Brady on the shoulder and laughed. "Hey, B.C., we're working men now!"

The boys worked hard. Each day they tried to get a little more done than they did the time before. But, three weeks into the job, Franklin began to lose interest. He got distracted. He looked for shortcuts and diversions for entertainment. And the less Franklin did, the harder Brady worked to make up for it.

By the fifth week things froze up solid. The boys chopped horse manure until noon. The work went slower than ever. For all the work they did that day, there was little to show for it. If there had been any glamour to being employed, it had worn off.

Franklin leaned back in the dry hay, crossed his boots and laced his fingers behind his head.

"What are you doing?" Brady asked.

"Thinking," said Franklin.

"Is there any chance you'd be thinking about doing some work?"

Franklin set his hat on his knee and scratched his head. He sat up and looked directly at Brady.

"B.C.," he said in a quiet and serious tone. "You know the red haired lady I was telling you about that works over at the Silver Star? If I tell you something about her will you promise, on your mother's life not to never tell no one else?"

"Frank," Brady said.

"Franklin." The older boy corrected.

"Okay, Franklin . . . I told you before, don't never ask me to swear on my mother's life, 'cause I ain't ever doing it. If you don't want to tell me about the red haired lady, I don't give a dang."

"B.C., I seen her in the altogether," Franklin said.

"What do you mean, in the altogether?" Brady asked.

"I mean in the altogether. Four times." Franklin held up four fingers to make his point.

"You're lying." Brady laughed awkwardly, wanting to believe it was true but knowing

Franklin was making the whole thing up to divert his attention away from the job.

"I can prove it," Franklin said.

Brady wanted to believe it was true. With the exception of the one occasion when he walked in on his sister at bath time, Brady had never seen so much as a picture of the uncovered female body.

"Come on, Franklin," he said, "let's just finish up here so we can go home."

Brady was disappointed and had no desire to indulge Franklin's fantasy.

"Hey, B.C., I forgot to tell you, ol' man Hog said we could leave when this one stall's done."

"You're lying," Brady said.

But, even as he said it he knew something was brewing in his older friend's head that would probably get them both in trouble before it was over. It annoyed Brady that Franklin could stretch the truth so badly and still never feel responsible for the consequences. But more than anything it frustrated him that he always wanted to believe Franklin, even when he knew Franklin was lying. He guessed it was because Franklin was so masterful in mixing his lies with the truth that it was impossible to tell where one left off and the other began.

The rest of the day passed uneventfully as

the boys chopped away at the frozen horse manure, and Brady's thoughts turned to wondering what a nude woman really looked like.

That evening Brady had just finished dinner when Mrs. McCall responded to Franklin's trademark knock at the door.

"Evening, Mrs. McCall," Franklin said, nodding to Mrs. McCall as he stood on the porch with his hat held down at his side. "I was wondering if B.C. could come help with some of my studies. I'm starting to get a little behind in my numbers."

"Well, good evening Mr. Stilwell," Mrs. McCall said. She looked over at Brady. "Yes, that's fine, but you be home by 8:30. You still have your own studies to attend to tonight."

Brady already had his coat on and was heading for the door with Franklin right behind him. "I won't be late," he said over his shoulder.

Franklin and Brady walked towards the Stilwell house and as soon as they were out of sight they turned and headed downtown. Franklin put his hand on Brady's shoulder. He leaned down close to Brady and whispered, "Hey cousin, you ain't going to believe this."

Brady looked at him.

39

"When we get to the Silver Star we gotta be real quiet and when I give you this sign (Franklin made a slash across his throat with his finger) you can't make a sound, know what I mean?"

Brady's eyes widened and he shook his head. "No, I don't know what you mean."

"Well, it's a Blackfoot sign. Just remember . . . not a sound." He made the sign again.

Brady was not at all sure getting caught spying on a nude woman was worth it. His stomach tightened and his mouth was dry as he spoke.

"Franklin, what are you talking about?"

"You'll see soon enough," Franklin whispered as they stepped into the alley and picked their way over piles of discarded horseshoes, broken buggy parts and rusty pieces of iron that appeared to have been important at some point in time but now lay in waste.

Brady's heart pounded and he tore his sleeve on a protruding nail and knew his mother would question him about it and he would have to lie to her. As they made their way to the junk pile at the rear of the blacksmith shop, they heard music from the Silver Star and Brady could feel his heart throbbing in his ears.

Franklin led Brady to an old storage shed at the back of the saloon, carefully swung open the door suspended by the top hinge, then disappeared inside, leaving Brady standing in the dark.

Brady heard a soft whistle from inside the dark interior. Then he heard it again and Franklin stuck his head back outside. He motioned to Brady.

"Well come on in, but be quiet."

Brady's best judgment told him to leave. His sweaty palms and dry mouth and rapid pulse all confirmed that what they were doing was wrong and he wanted to just turn and go. Franklin gave him the Blackfoot sign and motioned him to follow. The anticipation and the look on Franklin's face overruled any idea he had of leaving and Brady stepped in behind Franklin.

It was cold and damp and Brady shivered.

"Now what?" Brady asked in a voice barely above a whisper.

Franklin whirled and slashed his finger savagely across his throat. Brady felt his heart go cold and his stomach tighten and his hands shook. Franklin motioned him forward and led him to the boarded up door that at one time was an outside entrance for the two rooms at the back of the saloon.

A thin beam of light shone into the dark

shed from the keyhole of the saloon door. On the lighted side of the door voices laughed and spoke in whispers. A man. A woman. Silence, then laughter and more talking. Brady could hear every word and he was mesmerized by the very thought of being this close to them and them not know it.

In the reflection from the light beam Brady could see Franklin had placed an old anvil stump before the door and the soil around it had been walked smooth by someone who had been there more than one or two times. This was clearly not Franklin's first trip to the stump.

Without further explanation Franklin took his seat upon the stump, cupped his hands around the keyhole and pressed his eye to it.

Brady's mind raced as he reflected back on his earlier conversations with Franklin. This was just like Franklin. What sounded like a lie turned out to be the truth and here was Brady McCall on the verge of his first real manly encounter and he had no idea what to expect. He just knew the attraction was more than he could deny and he tapped Franklin on the shoulder. Franklin ignored him and Brady tapped him again and Franklin shook him off.

"There she is. I see her. She's got a customer."

"Let me look," Brady said.

Franklin slashed his finger across his throat, but didn't budge.

"Her name's Anna Lee," Franklin whispered.

"Okay, get ready. Come on an' take a look, quick!"

Brady took his place on the stump.

"I can't see anything," he said.

"Get your eye real close, then look off to the right," Franklin said.

Brady drew a sharp breath and pressed his eye to the keyhole. He felt his jaw drop and squeezed his closed eye shut.

"Franklin, she's taking them off," he whispered.

Brady watched as her garments dropped to the floor one by one. He drew in another sharp breath when she exposed the smooth white skin of her shoulders and her large rounded hips. Her hair fell to her back. She whispered to the cowboy, then turned slowly. And there she was . . . in the altogether, just as Franklin promised.

Brady stopped breathing. His eye strained and his imagination ignited as she moved and her large breasts swayed and bounced. He imagined he could smell her perfume and he still hadn't taken a breath. She moved and his eye followed. He couldn't stop staring at her breasts. His face flushed red and hot and suddenly he grew dizzy and lost his balance and tumbled in a heap off the stump.

Franklin leaped past him, took over the position at the keyhole and scanned the room with his eye, hoping for one last look.

The yellow light in the room dimmed. "Damn," Franklin said.

Brady leaned against the wall and laughed. "Do you believe that?" he said. "She was naked as could be."

Franklin turned and leaned back against the door. "I told you," he said.

The boys slipped quietly away, left with only their imaginations and the creaking of the old bed. They talked and they laughed and they swore each other to secrecy. The agreed it was wrong and they vowed not to go back, but Brady and Franklin never missed a Saturday night at the stump after that.

CHAPTER FOUR

No two people were any more different than Franklin and Brady, nor more alike. They fought and they argued. They stood up for one another. They disagreed on almost everything, but through it all they never questioned their friendship.

Franklin cussed and chewed tobacco and his preoccupation with women's breasts made it impossible for him to carry on a conversation without some reference to the female endowments. And, as near as Brady could tell, Franklin had no established preferences. In Franklin's eyes a breast was a sacred jewel to be admired in any setting.

"B.C., did you ever wonder what it feels like to just touch one?" he asked.

Brady glared at Franklin, then looked away without answering.

"Well . . . did you?"

Brady shook his head. "Not really," he answered.

Franklin laughed. "I know you have. I saw you looking lots of times.

"Yeah, well it's not the only thing I ever think about like it is with you," Brady said.

Franklin was right and it aggravated Brady that he could no longer look at a woman without thinking about her breasts. Brady felt guilty about his preoccupation, but not bad enough to discourage him from the weekly pilgrimage to the Silver Star.

Franklin, on the other hand, took great pride in his mammary expertise. Franklin thrived on excitement and the greater the risk the better. Brady loved the excitement, but was bound by a higher level of conventional thinking and a sense of responsibility that never encumbered Franklin.

Their five-year age difference was never an issue. Brady looked up to Franklin — fascinated by his older friend's worldliness and his direct approach to reducing every decision down to terms of how much fun it might be.

Franklin admired Brady's sense of obligation and he took special pride in luring Brady off course at every opportunity, as though Brady's fall from grace gave them even more in common. Franklin saw it as his mission to liberate Brady from the constraints of society, but it was not lost on

Franklin that grownups trusted Brady and held him in high regard. And, on that rare occasion when they did get careless and got caught, it was a foregone conclusion that Franklin's bad influence was to blame. Their age difference worked in Brady's favor as well. Brady could be excused his indiscretions because of his age; Franklin should have known better.

The job at the livery stable proved to be a good outlet for the excess energy of the two boys. Brady's serious approach to the job began to influence Franklin and before long Franklin was working as hard as Brady. And even though he never mentioned it, Hogue was delighted at the transition, but he never expected it to last long with Franklin.

In late January a storm blew in from the Canadian north country. It started cold and slow and by mid-morning snow fell, light at first, with no indication of what was to follow. The temperature continued to drop. Brady and Franklin turned their backs to the wind and swung their axes hard and fast to break up the ice on the livestock watering troughs more than half a mile downwind from the barn. The trough lay along the perimeter fence line and the fence itself, a sturdy split rail affair, was banked with drifting snow half way to the top rail.

47

A layer of ice formed on the surface of the water as the boys chopped and lifted thick blocks of ice and threw them over the fence where they laid heaped in a growing pile, accumulated but never thawed from previous days.

Then the storm quieted, the sky darkened and the temperature plummeted. Brady pulled his collar up and shivered. Franklin looked up at the sky.

"Come on, Brady . . . hurry up. We're going to be in for it," he said.

Brady responded by chopping faster while Franklin threw out the ice blocks. Before they finished the wind picked up and howled. The sky broke open with awful speed and snow whipped across the field, first picking up from the ground on the wind, then working into a full-force blizzard until visibility disappeared altogether.

"B.C., I can't feel my toes," Franklin screamed over the roar of the wind. "We gotta get back." Franklin leaned into the wind and started across the white, featureless field. Brady caught him by the sleeve of the coat and pulled him back.

"That's the wrong way," Brady shouted. "We gotta stay on the fence line."

Franklin nodded in agreement and the two boys plunged into the waist-deep snow that would not support their weight. They forged ahead, pushing and lunging and struggling. Franklin fell, then forced himself up in a flurry of profanity. Brady waited.

"Keep going," Franklin shouted.

Side by side they plowed through the deep snow, following the fence line and finally reaching firmer footing.

"There it is," Brady said. "I can see the barn."

They stomped across the yard and Franklin laughed. "This ain't worth no damn fifteen cents to me," he said.

They approached the barn and the door swung open and Hogue stood there and waved them in. Hogue brushed the snow from their coats as they stepped past him.

"You're a pair to draw to," he said shaking his head. "Git you up next to the stove there and thaw out some."

Hogue reached out and took the ax from Brady's hand then looked over at Franklin.

"Where's your ax?" he asked.

Franklin caught the glare in Hogue's eyes and averted his gaze.

"I guess I left it," Franklin said in a low voice.

Hogue stood his full height. His expression grew cold and gave the boy no quarter.

"You left it? This boy here didn't leave

his, but you guess you just left yers?"

Hogue's face turned red and his teeth clinched down hard on the unlit cigar stub.

"When did you plan on fetching it back here . . . sometime this spring when it's warm and sunny and you don't have nothing else to do? Or do you suppose it's not your problem?"

"I dropped it. I'm sorry," Franklin said.

"Well sorry don't get that ax back here, now does it?" Hogue said, his voice loud and unreasonable.

Franklin gritted his teeth and he weighed his words carefully, and just before he said something he knew he would regret, he heard the door open and slam shut and Brady was gone.

Hogue glared at Franklin. "I suppose you're going to quit too," he said.

Franklin grabbed his mittens and pulled on his hat. "He didn't quit. He's going after your damn ax."

Franklin didn't wait for a response. He cursed under his breath and by the time he got out the door, Brady had disappeared into the swirling blizzard. Franklin followed the new outbound footprints rapidly filling with new snow and he called out to Brady as he plunged into the storm along the fence that now barely showed a single rail above the snow base.

Franklin pulled his coat up tighter around his face and he screamed Brady's name, but the wind blew the words back at him and muffled them to ineffectiveness. Again and again he called out and again and again the wind stole the sounds and killed the words.

Franklin's stomach turned. He called out louder and louder and pushed deeper into the storm until he wanted to cry. Franklin continued along the fence line, shouting and cursing and watching the snow drift and blow.

All this for an ax. He cursed Hogue and he cursed St. Joseph and he cursed the snow and the cold and the wind.

His legs ached. His heart pounded and his lungs burned. What daylight there was would be gone soon and the thought of Brady out there at night panicked him. He hooded his eyes and squinted into the fading light and shouted until his voice was gone and he continued shouting, for he knew nothing else to do.

Then he removed a mitten, put two fingers in his mouth and whistled in groups of three shrill blasts, a signal he knew Brady would recognize if he heard it. Franklin saw movement off to his left. He tilted his head for a better angle and tried to see into the driving snow. Now it was unmistakable. He stumbled through the snow and he whistled and he shouted a hoarse and raspy shout and the shape moved towards him.

Then nothing. No shape. No movement. No sound.

"Brady," he screamed. He cupped his hands to his mouth and his voice was lost to the wind. He stumbled toward the spot he saw movement and squinted into the heavy veil of snow but saw nothing. He had visions of Brady lying face down, snow drifting up around his coat and trousers and silently covering him.

He stopped and he listened, and beneath it all, he prayed. His hands shook and his body trembled and, for the first time since he set out after Brady, he felt the cold. The wind shifted and the top rail of the fence was all but covered with the blowing snow. Franklin felt hollow and the tremors that shook his body did so more out of fear than cold.

Franklin's voice was barely a low hiss. He sucked in the frozen air and he whistled and he trod in the direction of the movement he knew he saw earlier, and then he saw it again. This time there was no doubt. He plunged through the snow. The frozen air seared his lungs and he called out and when the shape struggled into view Franklin wept, then he cursed, and when the mule saw him, it stopped.

The tears froze on Franklin's face and he turned and plowed his way back to the fence line and when he did the mule followed.

Franklin turned and cursed the mule and when he turned back, Brady emerged from the half light, crusted with ice and snow, following what was left of the fence and dragging the ax behind him.

Franklin seized Brady by the arm, brushed the snow from his shoulders and away from his face and anger flashed in his eyes.

"Why did you do that, B.C.? Are you nuts?" Franklin asked through gritted teeth.

Brady shifted his eyes, but held his head as though it were frozen in place. He nodded and they both laughed. Then their expressions grew grave.

The light that was dusk now became almost dark and the snow that drifted up against the fence breached the top rail and, if the fence had been there at all, it was no longer evident.

Franklin slapped Brady on the arm. "Come on, we gotta get out of here fast," he said. Then he turned to leave and Brady caught him by the sleeve.

He shook his head. "That's the wrong

way. This way," he said, pointing with the ax handle.

Franklin looked right and left then back at Brady. "Are you sure, B.C.?"

Brady nodded. "I'm sure."

CHAPTER FIVE

Like the wail of a creature in the night, the wind screamed to a frenzied pitch, changed directions and slashed at the boys. The effect was disorienting and debilitating and with each new flurry the temperature dropped and the cold slowed them to a crawl.

Their chests heaved and their legs burned and the crystallized air clawed at their lungs. Each step they took felt like the last step in them. Fear gave way to exhaustion and exhaustion gave way to resignation and Brady dropped to the snow face up and Franklin fell to his back next to him.

"I gotta rest," the older boy said and he closed his eyes.

Just for a second or two, the younger boy said to himself and he closed his eyes.

For a moment, just a moment and no longer. The seduction of death on its best behavior; warm, inviting, unobtrusive.

The younger boy was jerked upright by the collar so abruptly it sent a shock running through his body with the suddenness of being jarred from a deep sleep. He was at first confused, then the older boy's voice cut through the fog with complete clarity.

"Wake up, B.C. Come on!" The voice boomed over the drone of the wind.

The he pulled Brady to his feet.

The younger boy was glassy-eyed and slow to respond, but he found his balance, reached for the ax and followed Franklin in mute compliance. Franklin took the ax from him and probed the snow for the fence rail and when he found it he continued probing until he established the line of the fence. "It's this way," he said, pointing with his frozen mitten.

When it was too dark to see, the soft light from the barn shone like a tiny beacon in the storm and the boys struggled forth, afraid to look away, afraid it might disappear.

Then the light of a lantern swung towards them and behind the lantern a man. From their positions buried waist deep in snow, the man on snowshoes loomed over them and when he extended his hand, Brady took it.

Hogue led them to the barn and when

they got inside, the boys shivered and Franklin glared at Hogue and set the ax against the wall with the other one.

"Here's your damn ax," he said.

Hogue ignored the remark and ordered the boys out of their frozen clothes. He gave them each a dry blanket and poured them both a cup of coffee and they held it between trembling fingers and tried to sip it but couldn't for the shaking.

Hogue opened the door of the stove and stoked the fire and put on another piece of cordwood and told the boys to warm themselves. And they did, and it was a long time before their hands steadied.

"I never meant for you to go back after that ax," Hogue said. He looked up, first at Brady, then at Franklin and neither boy spoke and if they had an opinion, it did not show in their expressions.

They drank their coffee and stared at the fire. Hogue stoked it again, then cleared his throat.

"That took some grit," he said. He wanted to say more, but didn't.

Franklin stood, reached for the pot and poured himself more coffee and offered to pour for Brady. Brady shook him off and he offered it to Hogue, who extended his cup in response.

"You was probably right," Franklin said. "I should oughtn't have left it."

Brady sat back and his eyes followed Franklin, then they shifted to Hogue.

Hogue took the cigar stub between his fingers and pinched the wet end of it.

"Look, you're good boys," he said. Hogue was silent and the boys waited, as though the silence itself demanded their attention. Hogue appeared to be in serious contemplation and Brady could see their careers coming to an abrupt end. Both boys watched Hogue and waited. Hogue cleared his throat and pointed into the air with his cigar stub.

"Look, I got me a couple a Indian ponies out back I took in trade," Hogue said.

Franklin nodded. "I know, we seen 'em." Then he looked over at Brady.

Hogue spat and the boys watched the spittle sizzle on the hot steel surface of the stove.

"How'd you boys like to have them ponies?" Hogue asked.

Brady looked at Franklin and Franklin looked back at him then over to Hogue.

"We ain't got the money to buy no horses," Franklin said

"No, I didn't reckon you did," Hogue said.

"Well, how much you want for 'em?" Brady asked.

"All I got in 'em is the feed," Hogue said. "A Frenchman . . . a trapper, left them here. Traded 'em for his feed bill. Didn't do me no favor though."

"How much?" Brady asked again.

Hogue thought a moment. "Tell you what . . . you work out the rest of the winter and take care of them horses. I'll take the feed out of your pay and the horses are yours. I'll throw in a couple of old saddles and blankets and you can make up the bridles from any spare parts you find laying around here."

"That's it?" Brady asked.

Hogue nodded. "That's it."

If there was a smile on Hogue's face, it only showed in his eyes.

The boys grinned and Franklin offered his hand to Hogue. "You done bought yourself two slaves," he said.

Brady stood, held the blanket around him with one hand and extended other.

"Thanks, Mr. Hogue," he said.

"Them's good buffalo ponies," Hogue said. "The Frenchman won 'em from the Comanche in a bet."

Brady looked over at Franklin and Franklin looked back. Franklin grinned and gave Brady his thumbs-up approval.

Franklin knew the horses and he knew the

story. He was there the day French trapper shared a bottle of whiskey with Hogue. He listened outside Hogue's office when the Frenchman bragged in his broken English how he won the horses from a Comanche called Little Crow. And Franklin remembered laying awake that night feeling the wind in his face as he imagined himself riding free and wild across wide stretches of plains and through stands of trees and across creeks and rivers. Franklin knew these horses.

He knew the stout paint gelding with gray eyes and he knew the uncut buckskin with the proud head and tail that flagged when he trotted along the fence line at the sight of new horses being turned out.

The next morning the boys were back at the barn surveying their new horses and it was Brady who grew quiet then asked the question: "Well, which one do you want?"

Brady tried not to show his desire for the buckskin. He hoped Franklin would pick the paint horse and that would be that. Brady knew if he showed any interest in the buckskin, Franklin may take him for himself. And, because Franklin was the older of the two, Brady automatically assumed that gave Franklin first pick.

"Hmmm, I don't know for sure," Franklin

replied. "Which one do you like?"

"Don't matter to me none," Brady said. "The paint's nice." Then, fearing Franklin might take that as a bid, he added, "So's the buckskin."

Franklin walked around the horses eyeing first the buckskin then the paint and back again. He scratched his chin just like he'd seen his father do when buying anything he would have to bargain for. He removed his hat and reset it upon his head, then walked the circle the other direction.

"Dang it, Franklin. Will you just pick one?" Brady said.

Franklin smiled and looked at Brady from under his hat brim.

"I have a better idea," he said. "Get out your folding knife and we'll play one game of stretch. Winner gets to choose."

Brady shook his head and reached into his pocket. "You can't make nothing easy, can you?" he said.

"This'll be easy if you still throw like a girl," Franklin said, then he laughed.

Brady gritted his teeth. "No throw over twelve inches."

Franklin agreed. "Go ahead," he said.

The boys faced one another, stood with feet together, and Brady held his knife by the blade and made a solid throw and stuck the blade to the hilt barely less than twelve inches out from Franklin's left foot. Franklin moved his foot next to the blade then pulled the knife from the dirt and looked back at Brady.

"Nice throw," he said, then he stuck his with great authority and Brady moved his foot to the mark and re-stuck his. Franklin moved his foot. Then Brady and back to Franklin. No misses.

Soon, Brady was stretched to the point of losing his balance and it was clear that Franklin's longer legs gave him an unfair advantage. Franklin saw the anger in Brady's eyes as Brady realized he'd been cheated, but before Brady could protest, Franklin reached forth and put his hand on Brady's chest and pushed him off balance.

Franklin laughed and ran as Brady came for him.

"Take whichever one you want," he said, "but please don't hurt me."

Brady's anger turned to laughter when he caught Franklin and got him in a headlock.

"Okay, I'm taking the buckskin," Brady said.

Franklin stood up. "The buckskin?" He laughed. "Are you nuts? The buckskin's a stud horse. He'll run your skinny ass ragged if he don't kill ya first."

"I don't care," Brady responded. "That's the one I want."

And it was settled. The two buffalo ponies took priority over everything in the boys' lives except the standing pilgrimage to the keyhole on Saturday nights. And for the rest of the winter they spent every free moment at the livery and worked harder than they had ever worked before. They sat their horses bareback in the barn and talked for hours without going anywhere. They rode in small circles inside and practiced backing and turning and one day Hogue produced two old and beat up saddles and bridles made up of spare parts and saddle blankets worn and thin and he gave them to the boys.

And when he shook their hands his expression was serious. "Them are good horses," he said. "Take care of them and they'll take care of you."

CHAPTER SIX

The weather turned and the snow melted. The boys rode deeper and deeper into the wilderness each day, exploring and hunting. Franklin turned out to be a good teacher and Brady learned to track and hunt and find water. Playtime turned serious when the boys began bringing enough game home to supply several close families. What was left over they sold to the local butcher.

It had been a long winter and it was Bill McCall who suggested the boys supply meat to the families around them. He sat them down one afternoon.

"Boys," he said. "The ribs are beginning to show on your popularity around town." He addressed them both but looked at Franklin.

"You might do well to mend a few fences with the neighbors. We got plenty and they could use the fresh meat."

That was all the boys needed to hear. The

enterprise was born and Brady took to it as quickly as Franklin did. Selling to the butcher shop was Franklin's idea and the extra money just made it better.

The two young hunters on their Comanche Indian ponies managed to attain the status of at least minor celebrities, a standing that they bore with a complete absence of humility.

Snow turned to slush, then to mud, and spring was evident everywhere. The transient neighborhood changed with the weather. The men checked and repaired the wagons. They assembled the mule and oxen teams and readied them for the trip. Women packed belongings and removed the children from school.

Garrett, the wagon master, inspected the teams and the drivers and their equipment. He organized new arrivals, and when the roster was full he called for a final meeting and announced to the assemblage they would depart St. Joseph at dawn the next morning.

Bill McCall loaded the last of his family's belongings on the wagon and walked back to Elizabeth as she stood on the porch of the cabin that had been their home that winter. He put his arm around his wife's shoulders as they both stood looking back towards the east and the direction from which they had arrived in St. Joseph the previous fall. Elizabeth put her arm around her husband and looked up at him and smiled.

"This feels so final," she said. "Now I'm anxious to get to our new home and get settled in."

Bill smiled. "Me too, Liz . . . me too," he said.

She held his calloused hands to her lips and kissed his fingertips.

He turned to face her and held her close and looked down into her eyes then tilted her head and touched his lips to hers. Elizabeth had her arms wrapped tightly around her husband's neck when Brady came out of the house.

"I'm going to Mr. Hogue's with Franklin to get our horses and say goodbye," Brady said.

Then he looked back over his shoulder. "Hey, Pa," he said. "If you two stand around mooning like that all day we might get left in the morning." Then he laughed as he ran off.

Bill McCall laughed. "Don't you worry about us. We'll be the first ones there," he said.

Elizabeth smiled at them. It warmed her

heart to see the close relationship between Brady and his father. Brady waved and ran towards the Stilwell cabin and Elizabeth shook her head. Then she looked back up at her husband.

"How did the meeting with Mr. Garrett go?" she asked.

"Well, he said the roster is full. We got fifty-three families signed on and all accounted for." Then he paused and his expression was weighed with carefully chosen words when he continued.

"Garrett is concerned about the fact we got so many inexperienced teamsters. He wants our wagon and the Stilwell wagon up front to start out. Seems to think we'll set a better pace."

Elizabeth looked at him with questions in her eyes that did not reach her lips and Bill knew she wouldn't be satisfied with an evasive answer.

"Garrett's real concerned about Indians and he's concerned about the Niedermeirs."

"You mean Horst Niedermeir's health?" Elizabeth asked.

Bill nodded. "Yes, that and them five little children of theirs."

"What did he say," Elizabeth asked.

"He put it to a vote," Bill said.

"And?" Elizabeth asked.

"We voted to let them come, but I'm not at all sure we done the right thing."

Elizabeth squeezed his arm. "Everyone has a right to their own dreams," she said.

"I guess," Bill said. "Garrett assigned Brady and Franklin T. to the drovers crew. Their heads are so big now I thought we'd wait to tell them about their new jobs."

Bill smiled and shook his head. "You don't suppose they'll be proud do you, Lizzie?" he asked.

"Proud?" she said, then she laughed too. "Unbearable is more like it."

That night no one slept much. Franklin and Brady pitched their bedrolls out near the wagons where their horses grazed hobbled and contented. Both boys were allowed to carry a saddle rifle and each wore a belt knife. With few exceptions, the other boys their age walked or drove. Those that had rifles or shotguns had them packed in the wagon and, of those that had a knife, they carried them folded in a pocket.

There was no possession among the boys of the camp to compare to the Indian ponies and the mystery assigned to those horses. And nothing incited the admiration of the young girls or the envy of the other boys more.

Brady and Franklin settled back on the ground leaning against their upturned saddles, watching the two Indian ponies grazing in the moonlight.

"You know, Franklin?" said Brady. "Them horses of ours probably already been to some of the places we're going."

"Probably," Franklin replied in a thoughtful voice uncharacteristic of him.

"We ain't never going back, you know?" Franklin said.

"What do you mean?" Brady asked.

"Home. We ain't never going back home," he said.

"I guess I knew that," Brady said. "Just never really thought about it like that."

"Well, cousin, think about it, 'cause it's the truth," Franklin said.

Brady shifted his weight and pulled his blanket up. "Does it ever scare you?" he asked.

Franklin turned his head to look at Brady, but Brady gazed up at the stars.

"Does what ever scare me?" Franklin replied.

"What's out there," he said nodding in the general direction where the sun had set earlier. "And that we ain't never going home again," he added.

"No. It don't scare me none," Franklin said. "Well, I do think about it some, and I wouldn't say I was scared but, yeah I do think about it and wonder."

"Me too," Brady said.

CHAPTER SEVEN

When the camp rose that morning, it was well before daylight and they arose, not well-rested, but tired of waiting for night to end. Brady and Franklin were saddled and waiting at the bedding grounds when the man in charge of the drovers arrived to assign them their positions for the day.

Bill McCall and Thomas Stilwell had their teams lined out at the river's edge when daylight blended up gray into the black horizon to the east and Garrett gave the signal to move out.

Elizabeth held her breath as Bill urged the skeptical mules into the swift flowing current of the river. The tongue of the wagon disappeared beneath the surface of the muddy water and the mules snorted and tossed their heads as the cold water inched up over their bellies. The river bottom was firm and relatively flat, and McCall was thankful Garrett had picked a good crossing. Elizabeth turned back in her seat to make sure Rachael and Matthew were bundled up against the cold morning wind that blew through the wagon from the west.

She turned and rose up in the seat to see if she could locate Brady. She saw the herd milling and wagons moving out of sequence, but nowhere in the confusion and the half-light did she see Brady or Franklin, and when she looked back at the broiling water eddying up around the mules and tugging at the wagon, she held McCall's arm and he looked over at her.

"They'll be all right," he said.

She smiled and it pleased her he understood how she felt. "I can't help but worry. He's still a baby, you know?" she said.

"He's a lot closer to being a man than he is a baby," McCall said in a reassuring voice.

Elizabeth held her breath and didn't exhale until she saw the lead mules step up on solid ground. And when the wheel mules emerged and the water drained off the wagon and ran down the sides of the mules, she looked back at Rachael and Matthew. "We made it," she said smiling.

The Stilwell wagon pulled up right behind the McCall outfit and McCall and Stilwell stepped down to survey the progress of the other wagons. Stilwell whistled and shook his head.

"Look at the mess, will you," he said. We're going to be here a while."

Wagons and teams crowded the track to the river and teamsters ignored their line order. Garrett rode up and down the line admonishing first one then another, and his face was red and his voice loud and his horse lathered. He gestured with his hands and he called forth his trail boss.

"Simpkins, I told you to hold them wagons up. Two at a time is all we can get across. Now get back up there and get them men back in position and keep them there," Garrett commanded.

Simpkins glared at Garrett. He wheeled about and spurred his horse out and Garrett watched him waving his arms and redirecting the inexperienced teamsters back into position.

The crossing took all morning and it took most of the day before the long line of wagons stretched out and assumed an acceptable traveling order that would eventually become part of each day's routine.

Brady and Franklin rode day herd and they rode night herd and when they weren't with the livestock, they rode their Indian ponies at the flanks of the great caravan and watched for strays. The horses set them apart from the other boys and freed them from the walking and the dust and the endless hours of being bound to the wagon where the scenery never changed and each day was the day past and the next day held no promise to be otherwise.

By the third day the delegation began to show signs of organization and the patterns established themselves into a routine that gave the travelers some small comfort in the familiarity of the wagons they followed and those that followed them. But inexperience and poor judgment were commonplace and Garrett found himself challenged time after time by those who would bicker and argue and question his decisions.

Each time a dray team weakened under the load of an over laden wagon and the owners discarded heavy furniture or stoves, the disappointment spread to other members, who reckoned they would be next.

When the reality of the delicate balance between success and failure began to set, in the attitudes of the settlers became increasingly self-serving and self-focused.

Early into the second week of the journey, Mr. Niedermeir's cough turned to blood. He traveled three more days propped up inside the wagon staring out through glazed eyes, and on that third night he died without making a sound.

Niedermeir's death was the first, and it was the most devastating. For the first time, the severity of what, to some, was nothing more than a grand adventure and the opportunity of a lifetime, had now been defined in clear terms. There was no turning back, no chance to re-think the decision or to reassess the risk. Every family in the company had gambled everything they had and now some finally realized the gamble included their lives, and the impact was frightful.

Quiet exchanges in guarded conversations wanted to find someone to blame, some way to mitigate the feelings that had they the opportunity to start all over again, they would have elected to stay home. But it was never said. Instead, an undercurrent of discontent developed.

Standing over the new grave, Mrs. Niedermeir and her children were a pitiful sight. Her slightly built frame draped in a dress too large and her thin arms holding her children to her betrayed her attempt to appear strong. Her fate rested in the hands of the other families and none among them wanted to be the first to say what they all thought. She had no hope to continue and none to return. It was as though the entire family died when her husband did. Every woman watching was Mrs. Niedermeir for that moment.

The preacher's wife was the first to step up. She enlisted her husband and together they approached every family for a contribution. Some gave willingly, some gave grudgingly, but all, save one, gave something.

When the preacher's wife approached Randolph Osborne, he turned and busied himself at the tool box mounted on the side of his wagon.

"Excuse me, Mr. Osborne." she said when he failed to acknowledge her presence. "Would you like to contribute anything to help the Niedermeirs?"

Osborne avoided eye contact with her.

"They shouldn't have been out here," he said. "They had no business putting their burden on us. I'm sorry. They'll get no subsidy from me."

The preacher's wife's eyes widened and she glared at him as she turned and hurried away without another word. She knew Osborne was an outsider and a dissenter, but she was not prepared for his cold and vile attitude and her hands shook as she returned to the gravesite, where the preacher addressed the others.

He asked for help and he asked for anyone

willing to take the children in and someone to help drive the Niedermeir wagon, and as he implored his tiny congregation he knew he asked the impossible, and it showed in his voice. He looked over at Mrs. Niedermeir and the children and his voice shook and he asked for bowed heads and he prayed. He then asked for silent prayer. And, when he raised his head, it was clear that Mrs. Niedermeir's hopes had died with her husband.

He didn't admonish the congregation and he didn't pass judgment and he didn't preach his way into anyone's heart to find a conviction based on faith and poor judgment. But he did wait and he did weigh his thoughts and his words and, when he spoke, it was a last plea.

"We need a volunteer," he said. "One man to take this family back to St. Joseph."

He looked out over the crowd of downcast eyes. He looked from man to man, from woman to woman. He saw tears and he saw men wringing their hands and others trying to remain inconspicuous.

He let the silence touch every man on the shoulder. None acknowledged the touch.

"I'm going to pray one more time," he said. "Then I want you all to join me in a verse of *Just as I Am*."

They sang and he prayed and no one moved. His voice started out soft and sweet and others joined in, as though the singing exempted each of them from personal conviction, and the preacher looked out over the crowd, his eyes imploring, his arms outstretched to heaven.

"We're going to sing the last verse," he said. And they did. And the long silence that followed that final verse was awful.

They waited a long time and no one looked up. The preacher refused to give in and he too waited, and the silence was heavy with conviction as Mrs. Niedermeir and her small children awaited sentencing.

Finally, a voice from the back of the crowd broke the long silence.

"I'll do it."

The crowd split and stepped back from where the voice originated. And there, with all eyes fixed upon him, stood a cowboy few had taken the time to meet. With leather chaps, Mexican spurs and a wide-brimmed hat pulled low over his eyes, he was an unlikely answer to anyone's prayers. His left arm rested over the butt of the pistol he wore cross-draw fashion. His right thumb hung hooked in the front pocket of his trousers. His expression was serious and he had the air of a man who was capable. Who he was and why he was there now seemed like very important questions none had bothered to ask earlier.

"Praise God," said the preacher as he looked skyward then back down at the cowboy. "Amen. What's your name, son?" he asked.

"Travis Kincaid, sir."

Kincaid stood firm and the preacher waited for him to advance. Kincaid held his position and looked down at his boots then back up at the preacher and the preacher stepped into the crowd and approached Kincaid and extended him his hand. Kincaid shook it and the preacher placed both his hands on Kincaid's hand and there were tears in the preacher's eyes. Kincaid diverted his eyes and cleared his throat and he appeared embarrassed.

"Bless you, Mr. Kincaid," the preacher said in a soft voice. "We can never repay your kindness."

"None expected, sir," Kincaid replied.

The preacher looked about and the congregation stood silent but relieved. No one spoke and no one moved. Then Garrett stepped forward and joined Kincaid and the preacher.

"Son, we appreciate what you're doing but

you know we can't wait for you," Garrett said.

Kincaid nodded. "I know," he said. "I've got two good horses and I'm traveling light . . . I'll catch up."

Less than an hour later, Travis Kincaid tossed his bedroll and saddle into the Niedermeir wagon, tied his horses on behind and touched his hat as he turned the team about and laid the wheels in the same tracks that had brought them there.

The company stood in silence and watched the solitary, canvas-topped vessel bob and tilt frighteningly insignificant across the immense landscape until there was nothing left to watch. And not a person watching felt exempt from the same fate.

Elizabeth McCall squeezed Emily Stilwell's hand and shook her head.

"How arrogant we are to challenge this inhospitable land with such meager resources," she said.

Emily nodded in agreement and said, "I dread to think how many of us would return with her if we knew what lay in store for us."

CHAPTER EIGHT

They followed the Platte west and the land was flat and on the best days they covered less than twenty miles; most days not even half that. There were sparingly few good days. The weather turned hot and dry and the terrain stretched out before them flatter and more monotonous than any among them had imagined. It rained seldom, but when it did rain, it rained without warning. The storm clouds blew in suddenly and the ground became a slick track of clay and mud that stuck to the wheels and to the feet and bogged the wagons until the teams tired and quit. On those days the going was slow and patience ran thin.

Dissension among the men lessened as the demands of each day grew and the routine they settled into became an exhausting list of chores that was never completed. But the unrest among a few continued to fester.

Brady C. McCall and Franklin T. Stilwell

rose above it all. Their horses gave them freedom and independence. They were mobile and not obligated to the common chores that kept other boys their age wagon-bound and conscripted into duty as wood gatherers and day laborers.

It was difficult to be inconspicuous and modest and neither boy tried. Franklin found it impossible not to be arrogant and he accepted his new station in life void of grace or humility. Where the young girls gathered at the noon stops he galloped by and touched his hat. When the young girls carried water up from the river he rode through at a deliberately slow walk. And he did so where the boys gathered wood and then he made sure his rifle was laid cross-saddle and he smiled as he nodded and trotted out of camp.

The attention Franklin received from the young girls was not lost on Brady and soon he, too, galloped through camp and the two of them were more than some of the other boys could bear. Franklin rode his reckless reputation to the point it crossed the blacksmith's son, a thick-chested boy with large knuckles and a short temper.

The blacksmith's son and his friends waited it out and one evening they caught Franklin alone watering his horse at the river's edge. The blacksmith's son called Franklin out and Franklin met him head on and struck the boy a powerful blow before the boy solidly beat him to the ground and laid him out and left him where he fell.

Franklin was up and leaning against his horse, his face bloody, his lips swollen and his right eye bruised and shut when Brady rode up.

Brady dismounted and approached Franklin.

"You okay?" Brady asked.

Franklin looked at him with his good eye.

"Do I look okay?" Franklin said through puffy lips.

Brady looked at him, his expression serious and concerned.

"No," Brady said.

"Well, I ain't."

"What happened, your horse throw you?"

Franklin squinted his good eye and paused before he answered.

"Carl Nelson jumped me."

"Who?" Brady asked.

"The blacksmith's kid. You know, that big-ass kid that's always tight-jawed about we got horses and he don't," Franklin said.

"Oh yeah, him," Brady said. "I'm surprised that's all he done to you."

"Yeah, well," Franklin said. "It ain't over."

"What do you mean?"

"I mean it ain't over . . . I gotta fight him again."

"Why?"

"Cause I didn't hurt him and he'll think he can do this anytime he pleases now."

Franklin spat blood and wiped his nose on his sleeve.

"He got the jump on me. Besides . . . he done this in front of all his friends. If I don't stand up to it, I'll be fighting them all before it's over."

Brady looked up at Franklin. He couldn't decide if Franklin was the bravest or dumbest person he knew, but he felt good for Franklin, knowing he was willing to take another beating just to prove a point.

Brady thought about that a long time.

Franklin waited. Almost two weeks later he rode up on Carl Nelson and his friends sufficiently far from the attention of the camp to go unnoticed. He swung down from his horse, let the reins drop and walked right into the center of them. The boys looked at him, curious and amazed.

Franklin stood before the blacksmith's son and smiled a half smile.

"Hey," Franklin said.

"Hey," the blacksmith's son said back to him, looking down at him with a questioning expression on his face.

Franklin drew back a shaking fist with a flat rock rolled up in his fingers and drove the fist hard, knuckles first, into the boy's throat. The boy's eyes grew large and red and he gasped for breath. Franklin drew back again and fired two awful sounding blows to the boy's eyes. The boy staggered backwards and Franklin followed, delivering blow after blow until the boy's friends pulled him off.

Franklin twisted and turned and cursed and fought and, in the short time it took him to break free, the blacksmith's son regained his breath and returned in a fury. He snatched Franklin around the midsection and wrestled him to the ground and pounded his face bloody raw. The boy stood and Franklin came up with him. Franklin lunged at the boy and the boy drove his head into Franklin's face, breaking a tooth and lacerating Franklin's lips against his teeth.

Franklin staggered and the boy rallied forward and laid his knuckles alongside Franklin's head until his ear bled. He hit him again and Franklin went down. The boy turned to leave and Franklin wobbled to his feet and tottered there.

"This ain't over," Franklin said though

swollen and bleeding lips.

"You're crazy," the boy said over his shoulder.

Franklin tried to walk, but stumbled and fell. He sat in the dirt a long time and when he could, he rose and went to the river and bathed his wounds and let the cold water run over his hands.

The following day, Franklin made his way down the row of wagons at the noon stop. He found the blacksmith's son and when their eyes met the blacksmith's son stood and his face went white and he watched Franklin approach without faltering. Franklin stopped directly in front of the boy and the boy stood his ground. Franklin opened his mouth to speak and he grinned a broken-toothed grin and stuck out his chin.

"I'm ready to pick it up where we left off anytime you are," Franklin said.

The blacksmith's son shook his head. "I'm good with it like it is if you are."

They never fought again.

After that the days all seemed to roll together, each one like the day before, and soon the pattern became a routine that never changed. At four each morning the night guard woke the wagon master, who in turn woke the camp. People emerged from tents and from under the wagons where

86

they slept. They tended the stock and hitched the teams. Smoke rose from the small fires throughout the camp as the smell of breakfast mixed with the smell of wood smoke. A baby cried. A dog barked. Harnesses rattled and men's voices carried through the darkness. Some argued and Garrett mediated meaningless quarrels and shouted directions at inexperienced drivers whose teams were fractious and disruptive.

By seven, the caravan of wagons formed into a moving tangle of disorder that somehow righted itself into a tedious convoy as it did day after day, inching along with no sense of harmony with the virgin land it lacerated with its steel wheels.

By midday the earth lay before them parched and dusty. Heat waves distorted the horizon and mothers put wet rags to the faces of their children to ease the burnt skin and swollen cheeks.

Garrett scouted ahead and when he returned, he rode the line of wagons and spoke to each he passed. "Cool water and shade another mile ahead."

They watered up from an artesian well and pulled the wagons into a stand of cottonwoods and scrub willow bordering the banks of the Platte. The water they filled the barrels with was sweet and clear and they all drank what they could and replaced the muddy river water they had carried since they struck the Platte.

They pressed on and the weather, which earlier had been unstable and cold, was now unbearably hot. With the heat came short tempers and a growing swell of criticism of Garrett's leadership. Osborne, who resented Garrett from the onset, grew more irrational and critical as he found others dissatisfied with the way Garrett commanded the company.

Two nights earlier Garrett stopped the convoy early to camp without water and with no shelter from a dust storm that developed and drove the immigrants to their wagons with no fires and little sleep.

By dawn the wind subsided and while it was still dark, Garrett put the camp on the march. The stock needed water and grazing and Garrett's maps and charts were more misleading than helpful, and Garrett realized he had only his own resources to rely upon.

Osborne complained to anyone who would listen and, after the dry camp and poor shelter, more listened than didn't. They whispered in the shadows and there were those among them who shared Osborne's misgivings.

Less than three miles from last night's dry camp the caravan arrived at a grassy site with good water and protected from the wind by a dense stand of trees and brush.

Osborne gloated. Had Garrett scouted further the day before, this would have been last night's camp. Most agreed with Osborne. Garrett's credibility began to erode and by the end of the following week the attitude of the malcontents bordered on mutiny.

Garrett warned of hostile Indians and admonished the men for their careless manner and lack of readiness. Over the next week they were approached on three separate occasions by Indian hunting parties who came and traded fresh meat for cloth and buttons and trinkets of little value. They came childlike and reserved and made no demands and turned their eyes to the ground when addressed, and the immigrants looked down upon them as ignorant and harmless and nothing Garrett said dissuaded them from that opinion.

Talk of Garrett's weak leadership grew to the point of raising doubt even among those who supported him. Garrett sensed the problem, but chose to deal with it in his own quiet way by not dealing with it at all.

Thomas Stilwell approached Bill McCall

as McCall fed the small cook fire near his wagon.

"Hey, Bill," Stilwell said. "Got another cup of coffee there?"

McCall looked up and nodded. "Sure do," he said.

McCall tapped the tin cup against his trouser leg, righted it and poured hot coffee from the pot hung over the edge of the fire. He handed it to Stilwell and offered him a seat at the log laying like it had fallen there for that purpose.

"How you all doing, Tom?" McCall asked.

"Good as can be expected, I guess," Stilwell replied. His expression was somber and McCall could see he didn't come just for the coffee and company.

"You concerned about this thing with Garrett?" McCall asked.

Stilwell looked over his cup, a little surprised.

"Well, yes, as a matter of fact, I am," Stilwell said. "How 'bout you?" Stilwell asked back.

"Yeah, I'm real concerned," McCall said. "If Garrett don't do something soon, he's flat going to lose control of this outfit."

Stilwell took a slow draw on the hot coffee and nodded.

McCall shook his head. "I don't know

about you, Tom, but good or bad, I don't see how we can make it without Garrett." Then he added, "Besides, I ain't sure all this is his fault anyway."

Stilwell stood up, tipped the last of the coffee down and looked over at McCall.

"It ain't his fault. He's doing what he knows to do." He paused, then splashed the last few drops from his cup into the fire.

"What worries me," Stilwell said in an uncharacteristically soft voice, "is what happens when we hit Indian Territory."

McCall nodded and started to comment as Garrett stepped into the light of the fire.

"Coffee?" McCall asked.

Garrett nodded. "If you got extra," he said.

Garrett took the cup and looked first at McCall, then at Stilwell. "I couldn't help but overhear you," he said and there was no malice or apology in his expression.

McCall began to speak but checked himself. Stilwell looked down at his boots then his eyes rose to meet Garrett's.

"It's not a secret we got a problem," Garrett said. "Look, I'll do what I can, but when it comes right down to it every man's got to decide for himself where he stands."

Stilwell nodded. McCall pondered a thought and Garrett waited.

"Seems clear to me," McCall said, "that the big issue is the Indians."

"That and clearing the Sierras before the first snowfall," Garrett added.

Stilwell looked at Garrett. "How serious is this thing with the Indians?" he asked.

Garrett half-smiled and shook his head. "I don't know how to tell you how serious it is. But don't let what you saw the other day fool you. Them Gros Ventres weren't here just for the buttons and mirrors and pretty ribbons."

"What do you mean?" McCall asked.

"I mean, they were sizing up our outfit," Garrett said.

"What do you think they want?" Stilwell asked.

"Pretty much everything we got," said Garrett. He stared into the fire and the flames reflected in his eyes and they appeared tired and troubled. Then, without looking up he said, "I'm a trapper. I know the mountains, I know the weather and I know Indians . . . but I don't understand farmers. I can tell you what I know. I can get you across them mountains . . . but I can't make you do anything you choose not to do . . . and I can't give good sense to anyone who doesn't already have it."

There was a long silence and McCall

weighed every word. It was clear to McCall that Garrett knew his business. The Gros Ventres treated him with respect. On the trail he never lost his bearings. He was a loner, but he took his job seriously and he never avoided an issue.

Garrett had good judgment and he made good decisions. But he never pretended to be what he wasn't. McCall knew when he signed on, just as did the others, that crossing the frontier was a gamble. There would be casualties; that was a guarantee. Everyone understood it. McCall wondered how many believed it.

What they didn't know was that Garrett was not the first choice for the job. With no previous experience, he was selected on the basis of his knowledge of the mountains when the man hired as the original wagon master declined the job. The company needed a wagon master, Garrett needed the money and there were no other applicants for the job.

Garrett was handed a few crudely drawn maps, the company roster and a handbook of vague rules of conduct that detailed things like the weather, the terrain and a short section advising on how to negotiate with the Indians.

McCall drew his own conclusions about

Garrett's capabilities and most agreed he was a good guide. McCall and Stilwell reckoned it was all the years hunting and trapping alone in the wilderness that accounted for the lack of leadership skills he demonstrated.

But more concerning than Garrett's unrefined leadership was the deep realization that most of the men in the company were ill prepared and refused to believe the Indians were a threat at all. And when the doubters became vocal and challenged Garrett's decisions and leadership, both McCall and Stilwell grew troubled over the divisiveness that weakened Garrett's control and influence.

Finally McCall spoke up.

"You know, Jim, there aren't more than a dozen men in this company going to be ready for any kind of trouble if it starts," he said.

"If that," Stilwell said looking up at Garrett.

"I know," said Garrett pushing his hat back and staring into the fire.

"So, what do you think?" Stilwell asked.

"You mean about the Indians?" Garrett said looking over at him.

Stilwell nodded.

"Here's how I figure it," Garrett said.

"Them Gros Ventres is a long ways from home. I expect they'll be back looking to run off some of our livestock . . . try to pick up a few horses . . . maybe catch a wagon or two straggling behind."

Garrett stopped talking and a long silence followed. He looked back up at McCall and Stilwell.

"They won't think twice about killing anyone," he said. "Best thing we can do is not give them an opening."

Garrett nudged a half-burned limb further into the fire with the toe of his boot. He pulled his hat down tight and strode to the center of the camp.

He stood near the big fire. The flames caused shadows to flicker across his eyes and as he stood there. His silence commanded the attention of those near him and soon all eyes were upon him and he began to speak in a voice soft but firm and cold.

"I signed on to try to get you all across the mountains alive. I'm not sure I can do that," he said.

Not a soul moved. Not an eye left his.

"If we do everything right some of you are going to die. That's a fact. What I can't do is allow you to keep going the way some of you are. Sickness and misfortune are beyond my control . . . being prepared for Indians isn't."

Garrett surveyed the crowd and the crowd grew uncomfortable. He let the words sink in. He nodded to the man nearest him.

"Where's your rifle?" Garrett asked.

The man looked down. "In my wagon."

"Is it loaded and easy to get to?" Garrett asked.

"No sir, it ain't," the man answered.

Garrett picked another man, asked him the same question and got the same answer. He asked three more and of those only one was armed and ready.

"The Gros Ventres will be back. When they do come back, it will be for higher stakes than the trinkets you sent them off with last time. They'll want horses and cattle and maybe more."

"More?" a voice asked from somewhere within the crowd.

Garrett looked out but didn't answer.

"Starting tonight we'll double the guard. Every rifle will be loaded and where you can get to it fast. And I don't mean just for tonight," Garrett said.

"How do we know there's anything to worry about?" Osborne asked from the shadows of the camp. Then two more voices seconded Osborne's question. Then another and another echoed the first.

"Because we're interlopers here and it's an Indian's nature to protect his land from interlopers. We have things he doesn't have. Out here they take what they want. But mostly, Mr. Osborne, they don't want us here so we have every reason in the world to be worried."

CHAPTER NINE

Garrett lost control over the company of immigrants a little at a time and nothing he said or did could change that. Those who opposed him resented his threats and discounted his warnings. Those who sided with Osborne did so openly and the camp began to split. Garrett couldn't see he was on a collision course but, by his own nature, he knew he couldn't adjust his thinking to that of the inexperienced company he commanded. He also knew he lacked the ability to force them to his way of thinking. The diseased organization consequently began to consume itself.

The company continued to fall behind schedule until Garrett's plan became no plan at all. He cursed the maps provided to him, not so much for their poor rendering, which made them crude in scope and scale, but for their absence of reliable detail. There was no water where water was promised, distances were neither accurate in terms of mileage or travel time. Landmarks appeared where none shown on the charts and those that were shown on the charts were inaccurately placed.

Finally, the wagon master put away his navigational aids and trusted his instincts. He considered the odds of engaging the Sierras late in the season. He worried about the weather. A September crossing was a gamble, but a gamble with fair odds. He would risk that. An October crossing was a fool's bet he sensed he may be forced to take.

Early snows came regularly in the Sierra and when they did come, they came with frightening speed. No contingency plan could offset a late start and an early snow, and Garrett felt himself cornered by the impossibility of his circumstances.

Each night he closed his eyes and vowed never again to captain a foolish mission, but each day he arose determined to get this company of ill prepared easterners delivered as promised, whatever it took to do so. He gave up explaining nature's unalterable timetable and simply pushed the immigrants as hard as he dared, pursuing the trail like a man possessed.

They stopped twice a day. At midday they

rested the stock. At night they collapsed into their bedding. All but a few of the settlers degenerated into a contingent of detached beings sleeping in their clothes and eating cold meals. The women were the last to give up, but even they lost the energy to keep their children clean or to maintain any family life beyond that which was required to manage through each day.

Sickness beset them and soon they buried first one, then another. Some fell to cholera, others to consumption and misfortune. Burial ceremonies were perfunctory exercises devoid of all but the briefest observance and shallow graves presided over by hard faces and expressionless eyes gone beyond the capacity for tears.

Garrett ran out of things to say to those who ceased trying, so he said nothing at all. He could scarcely contain his anger as he watched the men in the families put away their weapons and resign themselves to whatever consequences befell them. His stomach twisted at the thought of his own fate tied to theirs.

Three hours past dawn the temperature rose to stifling levels. Garrett and his scouts preceded the dust-embroiled wagons, riding into the sun, tentatively aware of two horsemen approaching, barely discernible from the landscape upon which they tracked.

Garrett stood in the stirrups. He could get no clear impression of the riders. He swung down from the saddle and dropped to one knee and sky-lighted the riders as they topped the next rise in the trail then disappeared in the swales only to re-appear, faceless silhouettes, dark and calm, lending them an appearance of innocence that was as threatening as it was reassuring.

Garrett stepped back up into the saddle. He kept his eyes fixed on the riders and signaled a scout rider back to alert the wagons and waited.

Like a hunter poised, Garrett quietly slid his rifle from its beaded scabbard and ratcheted the hammer back two clicks. He laid the long gun across the saddle in front of him and traced the curve of the trigger guard with his fingertip and he waited. His eyes never left the approaching horsemen.

He nudged his pony to the top of a brushy knoll and stood the horse among the cover of stunted scrub willows and buck brush and gazed across the void whereupon the two horsemen advanced. He knew they saw him and he knew they could see the cloud raised by the wagons. But still they closed the gap and their pace was neither urgent nor reticent, and by nothing more than their sunlit forms he reckoned them to be a white man and an Indian. A trapper and a squaw, he concluded.

Garrett relaxed some. When the riders were close enough he could discern the features of their faces, the man held up a hand and smiled a toothy smile.

"Hey," the trapper said, his voice resonating deep from within his big chest.

"Hey, yourself," Garrett said, regarding the trapper with a sideways look.

"Joseph Walker?" Garrett asked.

"Yes, sir," the trapper said. He squinted and looked at Garrett, then he grinned and nodded.

"Well, bless my heathen ass . . . Jimmy Garrett, how are ye, son? I thought sure they'd of buried you by now."

Garrett shook his head and the two rode forward and shook hands.

"No, not yet," Garrett said.

"I see that," the trapper said laughing.

"What business do ye have with them folks?" Walker asked, pointing with his thumb at the cloud of dust inching up on them from the east.

Garrett rubbed his eyes as though the act itself was an expression of some implied absolution.

"Trapping wasn't working out. I figured

I'd try my hand at this," Garrett said. "Winter of '36 and I just up and quit the mountains."

Walker nodded. He understood.

"What about you?" Garrett asked.

"Oh, I still trap some," Walker said. "You know . . . enough to get by is all. Mountains is in my blood. I don't know nothing else."

Garrett said nothing for there was nothing to say, but in his eyes resided a distant reflection of an ancient calling both men had answered a thousand years before they were born. And by their silence they acknowledged an unwritten pact of brotherhood, a fraternal covenant of misfits rendered in a deviant language known only to those who found solace in the absence of people.

Walker let the silence run over past the point of social comfort.

"Pardon my lack of manners," he said. "Jimmy, this here's my wife, Kit-ah-lay."

Garrett touched his hat and said good morning. She smiled but said nothing.

"She's a good woman, Jimmy. One of the best," Walker added.

Walker laughed. "She don't say much, but she speaks pretty good English when she's mad," he said.

Garrett recognized her Nez Perce outfit.

He spoke to her in her native tongue and said it was nice to meet her, and she replied back that it was nice to meet him too. She was not shy but had the reserve common to her people in the company of strangers.

The three dismounted and took up a place in the shade of a thin row of cottonwoods clustered at the runoff trickle of an artesian spring that surfaced from a rocky ledge above them and wet the ground where grass grew thick and trees grew as though to have come there for the water as the remainder of the surrounding landscape lay barren and parched.

Garrett spent two winters on the Bitterroot with the Nez Perce, he told Kit-ah-lay. He asked if she knew his friend, Spa-wa-khan, a Nez Perce shaman. Her eyes sparkled and she covered her smile with her hand. Yes, she knew him. He was her uncle she said. She spoke first in Nez Perce, excited and animated and mixing in English words among the lilting and guttural sounds of her own language.

When her speaking slowed and calmed she talked of her tribe and family and homeland. It pleased her that Garrett knew of the places she knew and knew of the people she knew and she stood and talked with her hands as she asked many questions and told stories as though they had been a long time waiting to be told.

Garrett asked them to stay the night. Walker hesitated then deferred the decision to Kit-ah-lay who said yes they would stay. Walker laughed and said he guessed they would be staying.

The trapper and his Indian bride were honored that night by every man, woman and child in the camp as they all turned out, as though the presence of Walker and his wife was somehow a good omen or, at the very least, an opportunity to hear firsthand news from the west.

The men gathered wood and built a large fire in the center of camp. They ate together and after they ate they talked. Then two men with fiddles tuned up and were joined by a five-string banjo player and a man with a Jew's harp.

One man sang. His voice, a sweet tenor voice hauntingly out of place in this frontier outpost, was clear and perfect and when he sang no one sang with him, so enraptured were they with the way the song transported their thoughts out of the wilderness and back to a civilization that now lingered as a memory that may only have been a dream that never existed anyway.

For that brief interlude there was no dust,

no doubt, no regret and no fear. It was a magical reprieve like a cool fountain from which they all drank freely.

A full moon rose amidst a sky thick with stars. And the night air grew cold and damp and the heat of the fire made the children yawn and some slept in their mothers' laps. The fire burned down and children and women, one by one, retired to their beds. The night guards excused themselves and retired as well.

More than a dozen men remained. They stoked the fire and a whiskey jug of uncertain origin circulated among them. There was small talk and there was man talk. There was talk of the past and some talk of the future, but there was no talk of substance as far as Walker was concerned. He stood and refilled his cup. Facing Garrett, he corked the jug and put one foot up on the log he used for a seat. He made no bid for the floor, but the talking stopped and Garrett and the others regarded him as though he had.

"We seen sign of thirty, maybe forty Gros Ventre on the trail the two weeks past," Walker said. "Heading your way. They split up and sent ten or twelve of them your direction. You should have met up with them a while back."

"We did," Garrett said. "Looked like a hunting party near as we could tell. We traded them some and they left."

Walker took a pull on his whiskey cup and nodded.

"Figure they was just sizing you up?"

Garrett nodded back. "I figure they was."

Walker took a seat nearer the fire.

"They'll be back," he said.

Garrett nodded.

An uneasy silence ensued and the men watched Walker. It was not lost on Walker that he had the full attention of the tiny congregation gathered about him. He spoke in a low, almost reverent voice.

"Ever seen a man scalped?" he asked slowly of no one in particular.

He looked around at the men over the rim of his cup and took another pull.

"It ain't a sight you'd soon forget."

He wiped the whiskey from his moustache with the back of his buckskin sleeve and continued.

"One time, me and a couple a them young heathens from the Northern Cheyenne was packing a muley deer back from a hunt. We broke a clearing and run up on a Crow boy all by hisself with his plaited hair greased and his face painted up. Him being no more than sixteen or seventeen and kneeling down and drinking from the river alongside a stole Cheyenne pony. He seen us and he run. They caught him, 'course. Took him down. Jerked his head back and cut his scalp right off a his head. I never heard so much screaming. Blood running in his eyes . . . his head bone showing through. Him, red with blood and no hair, stood up pounding his chest and cussing them Cheyenne."

Walker paused and stared into the fire. He looked about and his voice dropped to a whisper.

"They took him down. Spread him out like this. Made him watch. Then they cut that poor bugger's pecker off. He begged for his life like nothing I ever seen."

Walker stood and traced an imaginary line with his knife from rib to rib across his stomach.

"Then they cut him like this," he said. "Not too deep. His damn innards dropped out. It was just plain awful. He didn't beg for his life no more. This time he begged to be kilt."

Walker took another pull on the whiskey cup and cleared his throat.

"Did they?" someone asked.

"Did they what?" Walker said.

"Kill him?"

Walker shook his head.

"No. They left him. Down on his knees in the dirt. His blood running out. His insides falling out of his hands. We rode off and left him like that."

He tipped the cup again and sat down. No one spoke and he continued.

"Gros Ventres will do you the same way they get a chance," he said nudging a stick back into the fire with the toe of his moccasin.

"It don't seem right I know, but it makes good sense to a Indian," he added.

No one spoke and no one wanted to be the first to move. Garrett eyed the men, each of whom seemed to be trying to sort out what Walker had said as though he might find exemption for himself.

McCall and Stilwell carried on a brief, private conversation. They waited and looked to Garrett but he also waited. McCall then stood and contemplated his words before he spoke. All heads turned toward him and their shadows wobbled in the light of the flame.

"I'll say it straight out," he began. "I don't doubt what there's more that Mr. Walker hasn't told us. And I don't doubt for a minute that we'd be easy pickings for an Indian war party. Excepting for Mr. Garrett here, and Travis Kincaid, who ain't even here, I don't think there's another man among us who's fought Indians before or much understands their ways."

McCall gestured toward Garrett. Heads bobbed in agreement.

"I think it's time we let Mr. Garrett here do his job."

Walker nodded, but he had his say and that was that. McCall looked about, searching the shadowed faces for some sign, some righting of reason, but there was none. Not a whisper. They looked pitifully like the farmers and merchants and civilized citizens they were, ill prepared to defend their lives and feeling terribly threatened by the images of scalped and brutalized human bodies.

The circle of men drew in tighter. Some threw out what liquor remained in their cups, others took in deep breaths, but none spoke and all eyes fixed on Garrett.

Despite his lack of leadership skills, Garrett appeared confident and convincing as he stood straight and addressed his grave and uncertain congregation.

"Well, I didn't plan it this way, but we are where we are and there ain't two ways about that."

Garrett's eyes sought out those he could see directly and a few heads nodded in agreement. He let an uncomfortable silence make his point, then he continued.

"Look," he said. "You can choose not to follow my orders . . . that's up to you. But this ain't no place to argue about who does what. I'll say what and I'll say when. If that ain't good enough for you, I'll ask you to leave camp and you're on your own. I'll do my best to get the rest of you where you're going alive . . . that's my part of the bargain."

Garrett motioned the men in closer and snapped out orders to those he picked out of the group as he outlined his plan. Then he tossed the stick he used for a pointer into the fire and sparks crackled and the fire flared and flaming cinders rose up into the black sky.

"The easiest part of this trip is pretty much over," he said. "Here on out you got to assume everything wants you dead."

CHAPTER TEN

Garrett sat alone by the fire with Walker and the squaw. He pushed another log into the coals and the three of them talked into the night. They spoke of the mountains and of the rivers where the beaver and the muskrat and the mink and otter filled their traps . . . places they had been, places still not on any white man's map.

Garrett and Walker respected the Indian for his ability to live at peace with nature. And they admired the way nature provided for the Indian in ways that would leave a white man lost and wanting. Walker could not understand and Garrett could not explain how he found it in himself to guide a caravan of would-be landowners into the midst of a people who could themselves not conceive of the principle of land ownership.

In their hearts, Garrett and Walker were more Indian than white man and, while they believed philosophically in the Indian way of life, they were part of a culture that found them belonging to neither the Indian nor the white man. They were caught in the opposing evolution of the two lifestyles.

Neither man realized it, but both were trying desperately to adapt, each in his own way. Neither with any hope of success.

"You know," Garrett said. "My last winter on the Musselshell with the Piegans was the worst year I ever had."

His eyes seemed to age as he spoke.

"I remember the last trap I ever set just like it was yesterday. Me and three of them Piegans was working a trap line and we seen this old Pend d'Oreille warrior dressed in his best war shirt. His hair was greased up and he was sitting a war painted pony by himself on a rocky ridge high above the river. He was calling on the spirits. It made my hide crawl to hear him chant and sing like that."

Walker listened quietly and sipped from his whiskey cup. Garrett shook his head slowly.

"I rode on up to him thinking it would be alright," Garrett said. "He looked at me like he couldn't see me. If I didn't see him move I'd swear he was dead. I spoke to him and just kept on with his chant."

Garrett stared off into the night, then back

at the fire.

"That was the worst winter I ever had and I ain't never been back."

The squaw listened to Garrett's story but she neither spoke nor gave any indication she understood any of it. This dark eyed daughter of the earth, whose destiny was forged in ancient teachings whispered down from one generation to the next for more than a thousand years, was of a culture that stood teetered on the brink of extinction. And though it was never spoken, in her heart she understood and ventured forth into the white man's world alone and searching.

"Jimmy," said Walker in an uncharacteristically subdued voice. "Sometimes I get to thinking and I just don't know where this world's goin'."

They stared at the fire a long time. An owl glided quietly through the trees, a coyote yipped at the moon and somewhere a long way off, a Gros Ventre warrior prepared himself for battle.

At daybreak, the trapper and his dusky bride stopped at the crest of the trail and turned back long enough to see the last of the wagons lurching and creaking along deeper into Indian Territory.

Osborne quietly refocused his negative

influence when it was clear the settlers invested themselves in Garrett's leadership. Mr. Dixon, an unusual man not unlike Osborne himself, gravitated to Osborne and together they shared embittered criticisms and fed off each other's diseased sensibilities, departing further and further into the darkness of irrationality.

"Garrett put me on night guard tonight," Dixon complained to Osborne as the they unhitched their teams at the end of a long day. "I got two spare horses not worth ten dollars in that herd. They're not worth getting killed over and I, for one, don't plan on losing sleep over someone else's livestock."

"I understand," said Osborne. "It's your right to do as you see fit. If Garrett had his way we'd all be bowing down to him. He might think he is almighty important, but you damn sure don't owe him a thing."

At midnight, Dixon failed to report for his shift. Garrett waited twenty minutes. When Dixon did not arrive, Garrett headed back to Dixon's wagon. Garrett found Dixon asleep in his bedroll beneath the rear axle of the wagon. He nudged the end of Dixon's bedroll with the toe of his boot.

"Wake up," he said.

Dixon did not reply. Garrett reached down and grabbed the end of the bedroll and dragged Dixon and his bed out from under the wagon.

"Get up."

Dixon came to life in a fury and he threw off his bed covers and jumped to his feet. He drew his belt knife and charged Garrett. Garrett stood firm.

Dixon stopped face to face with the unflinching wagon master and shouted, "You no good son-of-a-bitch . . . get away from my wagon."

The knife trembled in his hand. Garrett didn't budge. The savage look in Garrett's eyes caused Dixon a brief moment of self-doubt. Before Dixon could slash out, Garrett slammed the barrel of his revolver hard against the side of Dixon's face, causing his jaw to shift and his teeth to grind.

"Don't make me take your head off," Garrett whispered. "I'll be back in five minutes and you best be mounted up and on your way out to relieve your man."

Dixon trembled with fear and anger. His eyes went wild and he pursed his lips and ground his teeth. He threw down the knife and left it where it lay and glared at Garrett. His expression reeked of frustration and confusion. He knew if he spoke, his words would be vile and inside he wept.

Garrett gave him the room he needed to

make the right choice and as he walked back into the night, Garrett turned and looked Dixon in the eye with neither hate nor malice.

"You got one chance to do this right," he said.

Osborne lay in his blankets and listened, quietly pleased with himself. Others overheard the incident and many thought Garrett harsh and unreasonable but no one challenged him and none comforted Dixon.

Dixon's wife watched from inside the wagon, horrified and unwilling to interfere. Dixon saddled up in silence, never acknowledging his wife and she not asking to be recognized by him. Dixon reported as directed and rode his post alone and brooding.

Before first call the next morning a wailing cry came from the Dixon wagon. Garrett was the first to get there and he found Mrs. Dixon staring out at her husband mounted on his horse where it stood tied to the rear of the wagon.

Dixon's head hung over his bloody shirt and his legs were bound to the saddle with rawhide strings. His throat gaped and his eyes lay fixed and hollow in their cold sockets.

Others came running, screaming hysterically and cursing and grumbling and speculating. Their rage spewed forth vile and contemptible. They blamed the Gros Ventres. All the evidence was there . . . the rawhide lacing that lashed Dixon to his saddle; his missing knife and pistol belt. They insisted Garrett dispatch a search party, but Garrett waved them off. He studied Dixon's outfit before McCall and Preacher Baldwin covered the body and carried it off.

"No Indian did this," Garrett said. "I can't tell you for sure what happened, but I can tell you this wasn't the work of the Gros Ventres."

"How can you be so sure," a voice asked from the crowd of faces pressed around Dixon's wagon.

Garrett looked to be sure Mrs. Dixon had been taken to another wagon.

"He still had his scalp," Garrett said. "This isn't the way an Indian thinks," he added.

"Well, then who did do this?" the voice asked.

"I don't know, but it wasn't them," Garrett said.

They buried Dixon and the preacher spoke over him amidst an undercurrent of dissension that made it clear to Garrett he hadn't been convincing, but he offered no further explanation and instead put the camp on full alert and doubled the guard.

For all the complaining and disagreement on the subject, the McCall's and Stilwell's and the majority of the others sided with Garrett. Osborne and those he influenced grew increasingly outspoken. The camp, divided and distracted, drove on into the wilderness more vulnerable than ever.

CHAPTER ELEVEN

Three days after they buried Dixon, just as the sun inched up over the ridgeline, Brady McCall exploded into camp at a full gallop, his coat blowing and his eyes streaked with tears, kicking and whipping the buckskin. The horse's nostrils flared, his ears lay pinned to his head and his hooves pounded the dry dirt up into clouds that flew about his legs.

"Indians," Brady screamed. "Hurry! They're killing everyone. Come on, you gotta help."

Brady charged recklessly into the throng of men and women and spotted his father among them. Bill McCall grabbed the reins and stopped the buckskin as it blew and pranced and tossed its head.

"Brady, are you all right?" he asked, his voice shaking.

"I'm okay pa . . . but I don't know what happened to Franklin. We gotta go back and help him. Please hurry," Brady pleaded.

"Get to the wagon now and look after your ma and the kids," McCall ordered.

"Mount up," he shouted to those around him.

Two dozen armed riders fell in behind McCall, whooping and yelling as they galloped wildly out of formation along the river, up through the brush and into the breech of battle with gunshots echoing all about them and no sense of who the enemy was or where they were. When they broke out of the trees and onto the grazing site it was a confusion of horse and man out of control. They scattered the livestock and rode up on four of the night guards defending positions in a deep ravine above the river. They located three others safely firing from positions in the rocks at the mouth of a small clearing. Five Indians and a riderless Indian pony escaped into the cover of the woods north of the trail and disappeared under cover of a coulee where the brush grew thick.

Cattle, mules, and horses stood scattered for three or four miles throughout the trees and it was impossible to make any sense of the confusion. What Indians they could see were out of range and had too great a lead for any of Garrett's riders to overtake them.

McCall located Stilwell and could see by
the expression on his face that he had not
yet found Franklin. They spread out and
Stilwell searched frantically for his son. He
turned his horse and rode into a thicket of
trees. No sign of Franklin. He emerged from
the brush onto the shoulder of a clearing
gently sloping away to a granite escarpment
at the distant edge of which lie a crumpled
body clad in denim trousers and pull-on
boots.

Stilwell paused. The fletchings of two arrows waved from the man's back. He
spurred his horse and dismounted on the
fly at the foot of the corpse. He prayed to
himself. *Please don't let it be Franklin.*

He gently lifted the man's head. "Barnett,"
he said aloud.

Stilwell pressed his fingers to the man's
jugular, then laid the man's colorless face
back onto the cool grass. He caught up his
horse and followed the hoofprints of cattle
and horses upward to the ridge.

While Stilwell searched the low meadow,
McCall circled high up into the rocks and
spotted Franklin's horse picketed in the
thick brush, but he saw no sign of the boy.

"Hey, Mr. McCall, up here," Franklin
shouted from his granite fortress.

"Franklin, are you all right?" McCall

asked as he dismounted.

"Yes sir, I'm fine," replied Franklin. "But I think they done got Mr. Barnett. I seen them run him yonder into them trees."

Franklin reloaded as they talked.

"They almost got Brady," he said.

"What happened?"

"Me and Brady was riding together over there. Mr. Barnett was over there by them trees. Some of the horses started acting funny, but ours didn't. We figured it was Indians so we started for these rocks."

He reached into his pocket and continued talking fast.

"We told Mr. Barnett we thought there was Indians but he didn't believe us. Then a arrow got him and he rode off with it stuck in his back. I told Brady to head for help and he lit out. I was up here. Then I saw a Indian going after Brady. I yelled, but Brady didn't hear. So I shot him. The Indian I mean."

McCall looked at Franklin. He wasn't sure how much of all that to believe, but he put his arm around Franklin's shoulder and thanked him.

"Let's go find your pa. He's mighty worried about you," McCall said.

The battleground was already buzzing

with flies. Dead cattle lay about in disarray, among them a saddle horse with his lifeless legs sprawled out before him. A mule stood gazing glassy-eyed with an arrow wobbling halfway through the crest of his thinly maned neck.

McCall and Franklin leveled out on the trail and turned toward the east. In the tall grass at the edge of the path lay a dark-skinned body with plaited hair adorned with otter fur and eagle feathers, his finely beaded buckskin shirt violated by a red hole in the back the diameter of a man's thumb.

"That's him," Franklin said, his voice apprehensive and uncertain. "Is he kilt?"

McCall dismounted and knelt beside the body, his back to Franklin.

"Yes he is, son."

Franklin dismounted, but wouldn't look at the body.

"I didn't have no choice, Mr. McCall. He was after Brady."

"You did the right thing, Franklin. That took courage."

McCall stood and led Franklin to the edge of the brush. He looked back up to the spot in the granite outcropping from which Franklin fired the fatal shot.

"That was at least a two hundred yard shot," he said. "That took a steady hand

and a sharp eye."

"Yes sir," said Franklin.

Franklin was expecting a speech or at least a few words of fatherly advice, but none came and Franklin began to feel more like a man than a boy, and the feeling suited him. He chanced a closer look at the warrior on the ground and nothing he could think of made him feel good about that.

"Franklin!" Mr. Stilwell yelled. "Franklin are you okay?"

He swung down before his horse stopped and grabbed Franklin and held him tight in his arms. Franklin hugged him back.

"I'm okay, pa."

"You had me worried."

"I'm fine."

Garrett rode up, followed by half a dozen others as they assessed the damage and tried to sort out the details of what happened.

"Who shot this one?" Garrett asked as he walked over to the warrior's body.

"Franklin T. Stilwell here," McCall said nodding toward the boy.

Thomas Stilwell looked amazed.

"Franklin, you shot him?" he asked.

Franklin nodded.

"He got a clean shot from up in them rocks by the tree line," said McCall pointing to the spot, two hundred yards from where they stood.

"He was after Brady and Franklin stopped him," McCall said.

Garrett shaded his eyes with his hand, looked back up the hill and then to Franklin. "That was some shot."

He stepped past Franklin, giving him a reassuring squeeze on the arm as he moved in and kneeled next to the warrior's body. Garrett untied the warrior's knife. He stood up and pulled the antler-handled blade from its beaded sheath. He slipped it back in as the men watched in silence.

"This is yours," he said, handing it to the boy. "It's Gros Ventre."

Franklin nodded. He hesitated, then reached for the knife, almost afraid to touch it. He took it anyway. The dead warrior seemed more real to him now. He wanted to cry. He killed a man, broke the sixth commandment and here they were congratulating him. Admiring eyes were upon him, glorifying him. Franklin felt ashamed.

He tried, but couldn't swallow the dry spit in his throat. He looked at his father and his father's expression was not one of approval. Franklin tucked the knife in his shirt and swung back up into the saddle without using the stirrups. He touched the horse with his heels and started back to camp alone. A mile from camp Thomas Stilwell caught up with his son.

"It's right to not feel good about killing a man," he said. And they rode the rest of the way in silence.

CHAPTER TWELVE

Brady met Franklin and Mr. Stilwell as they rode into camp. He waved and rode up next to Franklin. He sensed Franklin's somber mood. "Hey," he said.

"Hey," Franklin said back.

"You okay?"

"I guess," Franklin answered.

Brady looked over and Franklin stared ahead.

"I kilt one of 'em," Franklin said.

"You did not."

Franklin stared straight ahead.

"You didn't kill no Indian."

Franklin handed Brady the knife.

"That was his," he said.

"Is that true, Mr. Stilwell, did Franklin really shoot one?"

"Yes he did, Brady."

"Was it the one that was coming after me?"

"Yep," Franklin said.

"Franklin, I seen him. I thought I was a gonner for sure. I turned to look at how close he was and I seen him fall off a his horse," said Brady.

"I seen he was going after you when you lit out, so I drew a bead on him. When I could see past the smoke he was down and his horse was a running loose by hisself."

"Well take a look at this," said Brady pointing down to the rear of his saddle.

Franklin looked at the painted arrow buried deeply between the two layers of saddle skirting leather behind Brady's left leg.

"That's how close he came to getting me," said Brady, wide-eyed and indignant.

"That sombitch," Franklin said. He caught himself and looked over at his father.

"Sorry," he said.

"They would have kilt us all," Franklin said.

Mr. Stilwell touched his son's shoulder, "I know, son," he said. "No question about it."

Franklin balanced his feelings of guilt against the reality taking shape in his mind, and he began to recognize the compromises of principle he would spend a life time resisting.

"Pa," said Franklin. "What I done, I mean shooting that Indian and all . . . was I wrong for doing that?"

"No, Franklin, what you done today was not an easy thing to do. We always brought you up to believe in the Bible and God's word. It ain't never right to kill no man, but then again, it ain't right to stand by and let your friend die neither. You done the right thing."

"Yeah," said Brady, confirming Stilwell's approval, "that Indian would a had my hide for sure if it wasn't for you."

Franklin smiled. He began to feel a little prideful.

"Well, I did get a nice knife out of the deal," he said.

"Are you going to wear it?" Brady asked.

"Sure . . . why not?"

"Well, what if they come back and see you with it?"

"I don't mean I'll wear it all the time. I'll just wear it when I want to."

Franklin handed the knife to Brady.

"Look at them beads," he said. Then he leaned over closer to Brady and whispered. "This could have been the knife that scalped many a white man."

Brady felt a chill run along his back. His face drained of color and the knife felt big and heavy in his hand. The intricate bead-work and buckstitched leather made it feel personal and forbidden. He handed it back to Franklin.

Franklin whipped the knife from its scabbard and slashed the air in a reckless manner, then drew the flat of the blade across his pant leg and tested the edge with his thumb.

"No Gros Ventre getting this without a fight," he said with growing self-confidence.

They rode the rest of the way in silence and it was uncertain which of the two boys held Franklin's heroics in higher regard.

CHAPTER THIRTEEN

The overhead sun burned high in the sky by the time the wagons were ready to roll out after Preacher Baldwin said his piece over Barnett. A hastily prepared mound of freshly turned earth marked the trail where they buried him. For Dixon and Barnett the journey was over, but for their families the ordeal had just begun.

What Garrett failed to achieve in unifying the immigrants, the Indians accomplished with amazing efficiency. The men looked to Garrett for leadership and found him to be direct and unwavering. Even Osborne became less antagonistic and limited his criticisms of Garrett to private conversation unlikely to draw Garrett's attention.

Each day broke hot and dry and the wagons pushed steadily onward as Garrett worked under pressure to make up lost time. He called stops only to water the stock and force marched through the midday breaks.

If there was a common sense of urgency it was motivated more by the settlers' desire to leave behind the battleground than it was to make up for any time lost. Despite the dust and heat, the wagons traveled in close formation, banded together like buffalo falsely secure by their numbers and the proximity of one to the other.

The dust that rose about them obliterated the sun and obscured their visibility and, though they saw no further sign of Indians, they chose the tightly clotted formation instinctively and would not deviate from it.

Behind the first rank of wagons that made up the forward contingent, the secondary ranks were manned by teamsters covered with tarps and rag-covered faces and hats lowered against the dust amidst a cloud that hovered over them and extended for miles and hung in the air to the east long after they had passed over the land to which it eventually returned.

Drivers lurched hacking in their seats, coughing mute coughs while their children huddled blanketed in the heat with dry tears on their cheeks and their sweaty little faces red and parched. Mothers rationed water and passed wet rags up to their husbands and attempted to keep their babies cool and dampened their dry lips with spit-moistened fingertips, none of which offered any lasting relief.

At noon the McCall wagon rotated to the front rank. Bill McCall mounted his saddle horse and scouted forward with Garrett while Elizabeth took up the double-reins and clucked the mules forward into the clear sunlight. The breeze that passed through the wagon was hot, but clear and breathable and Elizabeth felt luxurious and privileged to be out of the dust.

McCall and Garrett rode five or six miles ahead of the wagons and found no sign of Indians. They relaxed some, but Garrett's eyes never stopped moving. He noticed everything.

"You know, Bill," Garrett said. "Them Gros Ventres was mainly only after horses. If they was looking for scalps they'd have taken all they wanted."

He stopped, dismounted and examined a slightly turned track Bill missed.

"Coyote," he said.

He stepped back up into the saddle and touched his horse forward.

"I don't know if them Gros Ventres will be back or not," he added.

"If you had to say, what would you say," McCall asked, not meaning the question to be taken lightly.

"I wouldn't say . . . but I'd be ready all the same," Garrett said.

McCall nodded and they rode for the better part of an hour before they spoke again.

"When do you expect we'll reach Fort Laramie?" McCall asked.

"Two weeks, give or take," Garrett replied.

A small spring bubbled up at the base of a stand of cottonwoods and they pulled up to water the horses. McCall was quiet. He pulled his hat off and ran his thick hair back with his hand, then pinched his hat back on.

"How much stock you put in Mr. Walker's talk of Comanche up this way?"

"Quite a lot."

"How so?"

"Well, for one thing, I heard them Texas Rangers is running the Comanche pretty hard. And maybe it's justified and maybe it ain't . . . all the same they're stirring up a hornet's nest and it don't make it any easier on folks up this way."

"Is there much chance we'll run across the Comanche this far north?" McCall asked. "I don't know a lot about 'em, but I do know this is a long way out of their territory"

"There's a chance," Garrett said. "We'll know more when we get to Laramie. I wouldn't expect to see the Comanche this far north, but you never know about a bunch of young, wild heathens when they get riled."

It was sunset when Garrett and McCall turned back toward the wagons and it was full dark when they got them circled for the night. A breeze picked up and cleared the dust that followed the wagons into camp. They watered the dray animals and loose stock and re-filled water barrels by the light of the moon. The water was cool and some stood belt-deep in it for a long time while the gently flowing river slowly soaked away the heat and the dust.

Brady and Franklin rode their horses up to their saddles into the river to let them cool and drink and both boys did likewise.

Despite the earlier attack and the concerns of their mothers, Brady and Franklin left their names on the night guard roster and when they pulled their blankets around themselves after dinner, both boys fell into an exhausted sleep.

At midnight the air was cold and Franklin kneeled beside Brady, careful not to wake the rest of the family lying nearby.

"Hey, B.C., come on, it's time to go," Franklin whispered.

Brady sat up and shivered and rubbed his eyes.

"Hand me my hat," Brady said to Franklin, as he pulled on first one boot then the other. "It's cold," he said, reaching into his bedroll for his jacket.

"It ain't bad once you been up," Franklin said.

"How come you're wearing that warrior knife?" Brady asked nodding toward it.

"Ain't you scared some Gros Ventre will see it?"

"Yeah, I thought about it."

"And?"

"Well, I don't figure I'll be seeing any Gros Ventres on any good terms anyway so it probably doesn't matter none."

Brady pulled on his jacket and admired Franklin's trophy knife as he slid his own old skinning knife on his belt. In the slow light from the campfire Franklin looked like one of the men standing there. He was almost as tall as his father and his shadowed silhouette was muscular and broad in the shoulders. And twice Brady caught Franklin practicing with his father's razor, carefully scraping away at the tender skin of his face and laughing in a voice that had grown deeper over the winter.

Brady liked the way the knife hung recklessly at Franklin's side and he liked the way the fringe and the beadwork attracted attention to it. His own knife, by comparison, seemed insignificant, but he wore it like Franklin wore his and, in some ways, it made him feel more prideful for owning it.

As he buckled his belt and pulled on his hat, Brady felt like a little boy next to Franklin, who stood six inches taller and outweighed him by forty pounds. Five years difference in their ages never seemed like much to Brady until now. In Brady's eyes Franklin couldn't have been a bigger hero. An Indian fighter at fifteen with a story to tell that he was asked to repeat over and over again to grown men who listened in awe and nodded to him when he rode past, or when they chanced to meet him walking through camp.

Franklin bent down and picked up Brady's rifle in one hand as he carried his own in his other.

"Ready to go?"

Brady reached over and took his bridle off the wagon wheel hub.

"Yep," he said. "I'm ready."

The boys caught their hobbled horses and led them to the picket line where they brushed them and saddled them in the lantern light. Other riders approached the picket. Some coming off, others going on. There was little talk and what talk there was brief and strained.

The moon was full and the sky was clear and the shadows in the bushes moved on an intermittent draft of cold air that settled in the meadows and rolled softly up from the river. The air smelled of damp grass and wet dust and everywhere the riders looked they imagined Indians harbored by the darkness and reeking of revenge.

The relief riders banded together as they rode out, making nervous talk and turning in their saddles at the sounds in the night and carrying their rifles across in front of them, cocked and ready. The tension among the men put Brady and Franklin on edge, and when they came upon the night guards they were to replace, they found them bunched in small groups huddled against their fears, waiting out the night.

The livestock grazed a high meadow bordered by the river to the north and lined with cottonwood trees and buck brush on the southern and western perimeters. The captain of the guard avoided riding into the exposed clearing on the tree side of the meadow where he ordered Brady and Franklin to take up their posts without a word of advice or caution.

Three Feathers and Buffalo Dancer stood calm and relaxed as the boys sat their horses side by side, facing in opposite directions, watching each other's back as they whispered.

"You know we'll be splitting up when we get to the Snake River, don't you, B.C.?"

"Yeah, I know."

"We probably won't ever see each other again."

"I know that too."

"We sure did have us some good times," Franklin said.

Brady laughed quietly and nodded. "The saloon was the best."

They fell silent.

Franklin leaned forward, his arms resting on the saddle horn.

"You could come on to California with us."

Brady looked at him. His eyes reflected the moonlight. He crossed his arms.

"I can't."

"Well you could, but I know you can't," Franklin said. Then he leaned back and put both hands on his horse's rump.

"Anyway, we'll still be blood brothers no matter what." he said.

Brady smiled. "Yep, we'll always be blood brothers."

CHAPTER FOURTEEN

The night passed without incident and the next two days were dry, hot and uneventful. By noon on the third day the sun bore down upon the shadowless earth until not a living thing save the immigrants and their livestock chose to stay out in the heat of it. And when the wagons rolled to a stop the small shadows they cast were crowded with camp dogs and children and elderly men and women, all competing for a chance to get out of the sun.

Brady rode up from the north side of the river. His face was flushed red and the crown of his hat soaked through with sweat. Trail dust clung to the buckskin's legs as high up as the river was deep, and flies swarmed about his face.

Brady swung his leg over the saddle and dismounted.

"Is that wheel broke, pa?" he asked, pointing to the massive rear wheel leaning against the sideboard.

"I believe it just needs a little grease. It started squeaking some shortly after we crossed the river the last time," his father said, holding up the grease pot to make his point.

"Where's ma?"

"She's bringing up some water. She'll have something for you to eat here shortly. You hungry?"

Brady smiled. "Starved," he said.

"Here, hold this for me," McCall said, handing the grease bucket to Brady. "You mind checking them single-trees and taking a look at that kingpin while I grease this up?"

"Sure, Pa."

Brady hobbled Buffalo Dancer, hung the bridle over the saddle horn and loosened the cinch. He crawled under the front part of the wagon where the tongue meets the kingpin and carefully checked it all around.

"Hey, Pa," he called out. "Better come check the sand bolster."

"What is it, son?"

"I don't know, but it looks like a crack to me."

McCall's expression was serious. He slid under next to Brady.

"Where is it?"

"See right there?" Brady said, pointing to a hairline fracture that ran half the length of it.

"Sure enough. Good eye," he said, laughing.

"It don't go all the way through, but I best wrap it just the same. It'd be a long walk if that broke down."

Brady smiled.

McCall wiped the area clean with his big, rough-skinned hand and wrapped it meticulously with wire in smooth, even turns which Brady admired for their symmetrical perfection. He wondered how men learned to do things like that so well.

"Pa?" Brady said quietly.

McCall looked over at the boy as they both lie on their backs in the dirt.

"When do you think we'll get to the Snake River?"

"Oh, five maybe six weeks if we keep going like we been. Why do you ask?"

"Well, no reason really."

"What's bothering you, son? You starting to think about leaving ol' Franklin when we split up there?"

Brady smiled a weak smile. It always surprised him when his father seemed to know what he was thinking.

"Yeah, I guess," Brady said.

McCall stopped what he was doing and sat beside Brady. He was quiet and gave Brady time to think.

"Pa, Franklin's the only best friend I ever had."

"No question you two are as close as any two boys I ever saw."

He pushed his hat back and patted Brady on the leg.

"Your ma will keep in touch with his ma . . . I expect you two ain't seen the last of each other yet. Things happen and good friendships endure," he said.

His eyes were confident and the corners wrinkled when he smiled and that was enough for Brady. He tried not to think about it past today, and having it officially on record with his father gave it a sense of reckoning and credibility of a higher order and that made it better.

Back on the trail and less than three hours later, the terrain began to change and trees and brush appeared scattered before them. An hour after that the wagons spread out and stopped along the cut of a violent river. Its banks denied them access and its current spit and swirled in contempt as it crashed through rocks and boulders and carried with it debris and whole trees uprooted and turning slowly like prehistoric carcasses of unknown origin.

Garrett held up the wagons and, as the teamsters crowded their rigs in closer, tempers ran short as the men contemplated the long delays and a treacherous crossing. Garrett sent two scouts upriver and he rode down river in search of a crossing.

Osborne strode through the clutch of men gathered at the river's edge, ranting and cussing. And, while some thought him irrational, others nodded approval.

Half a dozen men avoided the gazes of the others as they slunk about and drew into a delegation with Osborne presiding over them, his eyes consumed in hatred and his expression restrained but malevolent. He reckoned Garrett to be an Indian sympathizer and he said so, and others concurred. From there it was a small step to condemn Garrett's actions as those of a man in whose judgment they had grave misgivings.

By the time Garrett and his scouts returned, the mutinous deputation had adjourned and only Osborne remained at the meeting site.

Garrett assembled the drivers and addressed them from atop his lathered mount.

"Boys, we've been up and down this river four miles in each direction, an' there ain't but one place to get these wagons across.

But it ain't gonna be easy and it ain't gonna be fast. The river is higher than it's ever been the last three times I come through here. The bottom is loose rock and sink holes that'll swaller a wagon. We got no choice but to float 'em, and it'll take the better part of a week."

Garrett sat up straight in the saddle and waited for a response. People grumbled and shook their heads. There wasn't much talk, but the talk there was bordered on dangerous, and Garrett chose to disregard it. He could never reconcile his thinking to the arrogance he saw in some, and he had no tolerance for complainers and whiners, but the well-intentioned he knew among the others were a dilemma for him. They listened and worked hard, and they learned and tried to improve but, for all their good intentions, they were no better off than those who trod blindly forth right alongside them.

The weak delegation of would-be adventurers bent under the load. Less than halfway through their journey they had travelled for over two-months, and the road back was no longer an option. It showed on their faces and their hands and the way they shuffled along. It showed in their dress and it showed in their disregard for cleanliness and conversation.

There were a few among them who held up, but even they lost the will to carry the emotional load of those who broke earlier. But for all their failings and misgivings, the inexperienced travelers were remarkably resilient.

The women of the company bore the greatest burden, for their lot had been cast by their men and was not a thing of their own doing. They tended the morning fires and they tended their children, thin and raggedy and pale. They stoked the evening fires, and were the first to rise and the last to rest. When they had nothing left to give, they gave more. Their skin, blackened by dirt and sun, and their hands looked no different than the hands of the men. Vanity and fastidiousness died early. And when the women withdrew for their own self-preservation, the vitality of the company bled into dust.

James Garrett felt like an observer of a great pantomime in which the players deteriorated before his eyes. He saw it in them all, but he saw it in the women in a way that was disturbing. The fair-skinned ladies who joined the company in St. Joseph had about them a delicate manner and refined appearance, each trying not to look too much like the other, similar but unique.

He now saw before him hollow-eyed creatures, one indiscernible from the other, who seemed to have mutated into leather-skinned beings of uncertain age mechanically moving through each day. Most made no attempt at changing into fresh clothes. Many slept in the clothes they wore.

The men walked and rode. At night they collapsed onto their blankets, some without removing a boot.

Garrett never expected the news of the week-long river crossing to be received well, but he was unprepared for what followed.

A voice, loud and irrational, exploded from the fringe of the crowd. It was Osborne, spit dribbling from the corners of his mouth, his fist pounding the air. He railed at Garrett. Nothing he said made sense, but his words were vile and accusing and, in the end, it was his fear of dying on the trail that pushed him past his limit.

He stood silent and surveyed the crowd, then he looked up at Garrett.

"Garrett, you misfit, heathen, son-of-a-bitch," he said calmly. "You just wouldn't listen. Because of you people are going to die."

There was a frightening presence about this inconsequential man that everyone saw and Garrett's instincts made it personal.

"Dixon should have killed you when he had the chance," Osborne added in a soft voice.

Garrett dismounted and started for Osborne. McCall pushed his way through the crowd and wrestled Osborne out of the crowd and dragged him back to his wagon. Osborne did not resist.

Three men intercepted Garrett.

"Hold on, Jim," one of the men said. "He doesn't know what he's saying. It was just a bit too much for him. He'll be better in the morning. Please don't take this personal."

Garrett was calculatingly well-controlled. The atmosphere was explosive and everyone was fearful that Garrett would not be as forgiving with Osborne as he had been with Dixon. The strained anticipation was almost unbearable and finally Garrett defused the tension.

"Let's get these teams moving. There's a place about two miles upstream where we can ready the wagons and make camp. We'll start across as soon as we get the first one set up," said Garrett.

Garrett remounted and turned his horse upstream to lead the wagons to the crossing.

When the first of the wagons was in position, Garrett barked out orders to the four drivers in the lead.

"You men, start unhitching them teams and start unloading them wagons. We're going to have to float 'em across."

Garrett took the end of one of the long ropes and secured it to his saddle horn then plunged his horse into the swift current and started for the other side of the river. A dozen feet into the current, both horse and rider disappeared below the surface. The men on the bank froze. The two men holding the loose end of the rope watched as the submerged section of the rope on Garrett's saddle started drifting downstream. They pulled the rope hard against the current and Garrett and his horse popped back to the surface. The horse was in a panic and snorted loudly, pawing the air wildly with his front feet, fighting to get to the opposite side of the river. Garrett lost his hold on the saddle and was now gripping the horse's tail with one hand as he reached for the rope with his free hand.

Every eye in the camp watched until the exhausted horse reached the river bank, emerged from the water with Garrett in tow, and stood there shaking. The horse's sides heaved in and out as he greedily sucked in the fresh air. Garrett came out of the water the same time his horse did and calmly walked over to untie the rope from the saddle horn.

He tied the rope to a large tree near the edge of the water, then shouted to the men on the other side.

"Alright, boys, I need two more of them ropes like this one over here. Tie them on one at a time and I'll pull 'em across."

Once all three ropes were in place, Garrett returned to the wagons and this time made it back across the river without mishap. He proceeded to get the four teams across, then had the first wagon stripped of its wheels and pulled down to the water. One rope was secured on the far side of the river and ran through the center of the wagon, then secured to a tree on the opposite side of the river. The center rope kept the wagon from drifting downstream and prevented it from turning midstream and getting out of control. The first rope was then tied to the front bolster and hitched up to one of the teams on the other side. Using a tree as a fulcrum, the team strained in their traces as the first wagon entered the water. As soon as the floating wagon was in the mainstream of the river the force of the water pushed it heavily against the center rope, but the pulling power of the team moved it easily across with its load of two men and the wheels from two wagons.

The first wagon made several trips back and forth, transporting people and belongings, until the contents of the four lead wagons, including the wheels, had been safely deposited on the western side of the river. The first wagon was then pulled out of the water, after completing its final trip, and was reassembled to be moved to the new campsite on the west bank.

This process was repeated until darkness made it too dangerous to continue. By nightfall, five wagons had been taken across.

"Mr. Garrett," said Preacher Baldwin, as the men and women gathered on the east bank of the river to assess their progress, "How long do you think it will take for us to get the rest of the wagons and the livestock across the river?"

"If things go like they done today, I expect we'll be done in about four days," said Garrett. "Right now we got us other problems to think about. Our camp is split and we're good bait for them Indians."

Garrett turned to address the men waiting.

"By the time that sun cracks up in the morning I want you four wagons unloaded and nothing left inside but the wheels and jacks," said Garrett pointing to the drivers of the next wagons in the four-abreast line up.

Garrett continued with his orders for the next day's work and assigned men on both sides of the river to work the ropes and help with the heavy work of dismantling and reassembling each of the wagons.

It would take the better part of a week to move the company less than a mile closer to Fort Laramie. The fear of getting so far behind schedule as to lose the race for the Sierras to the winter snows was on every man's mind.

CHAPTER FIFTEEN

The river crossing was something upon which the immigrants had not counted. Supplies ran low in some wagons, and the shortages caused concern for the larger families who couldn't carry enough surplus for extended contingencies.

Osborne had taken refuge in his wagon after McCall dragged him forcibly back there and did not come out to unhitch his team. It was well after dark when McCall walked by Osborne's wagon and heard him in muffled conversation. McCall resisted the urge to tell Osborne to turn his team out for feed and water and debated whether or not to stop at all.

McCall continued on past the wagon, but was struck by the peculiar sound of Osborne's voice and by the fact that there was no light in the wagon. Contrary to his nature, he decided to go back closer to the wagon to try to hear what Osborne was saying. Osborne spoke in a voice that at times sounded like the voice of a child and at other times was deep and angry. McCall listened but never heard a response to the one-sided conversation. Then the voice changed, and it was neither that of Osborne nor anyone McCall recognized.

McCall listened and chills ran up his back when he realized both voices belonged to Osborne. Twice, then a third time, McCall stopped himself from throwing back the canvas fly at the back of the wagon. The voices stopped, and McCall stopped breathing as he listened. Then the softer of the two voices hummed, repeated a lullaby, then stopped.

A pistol shot lit up the inside of the canvas and the explosion rattled the framework that held it up. Black smoke belched out of the small opening at the rear of the wagon.

McCall threw the canvas back. His eyes adjusted to the dark, and the reflection of the campfire light on the gaping red hole at the back of Osborne's head made him turn away. When he did look back inside it was an awful dream in shades of red and black, and McCall could only stare.

They laid Osborne out on the ground on a bloody sheet, and when they pulled a woolen blanket from the wagon to cover him, they found Dixon's knife and pistol belt and strings of rawhide, the same as those that bound and tethered Dixon to his horse.

Garrett waited for the protests, waited for the accusations, and waited for the gasps of disbelief, but as he looked out upon the downcast eyes of the company before him, all he saw were men and women exhausted of energy and drained of emotion. Standing with expressionless faces, they were no longer willing to invest in the right or wrong of Osborne or Garrett, or the loss suffered by Dixon's wife.

They dug the grave. They buried Osborne and bowed their heads with open eyes while the preacher said words no one heard. They returned to their blankets and in the morning, after they allocated Osborne's provisions, they turned his team in with the free stock and never moved his wagon from where it stood near his grave. And his name was never mentioned again.

CHAPTER SIXTEEN

Six days later the last wagon crossed the river. Eight days after that, Garrett rode out in the morning. When he returned, he rode the line up and down and waved his hat, and when he told them they would reach Fort Laramie by mid-day the next day, there was whooping and hollering as the news passed down the line.

That night they built a large fire, and they ate together. The men wore clean shirts and the ladies wore fresh dresses. Young girls tied their hair up in ribbons and young boys gathered around the fire with hair combed and parted wet and left to dry in place.

They ate and they visited, and the men passed a whiskey jug. Preacher Baldwin played the fiddle while some danced and others repaired to small groups to talk. Talk had been spare for a long time, but tonight they put aside their concerns and their differences. For tonight there was no journey;

upon that there was unspoken and unanimous agreement.

Bill McCall and Tom Stilwell shared a cup of whiskey. Neither spoke much, but when they did it was of what lie ahead. It was hopeful talk and it was uncertain talk. It was left unsaid, but both men secreted thoughts of doubt that had no place in a course set with no provisions for turning back. Bill passed the jug to Tom, and in that brief meeting of their eyes a pact was drawn and agreed to, and by that mere acknowledgment both men were sworn to the blindness of pressing ahead at all costs.

No such covenant existed between Elizabeth McCall and Emily Stilwell, for when they spoke, the conversation was of home and friends and lives given over to the kinds of dreams men dream. And both women, each in her own way, looked back at what they surrendered with a divine strength and a resolution to go forward on faith alone.

Fort Laramie was a milestone, the first real measure of success . . . an outpost once thought so remote and distant as to be unreachable when calculated by the progress of each day's journey, but now it was there. Less than a day's ride, and the thought of it renewed the spirits and brought light back to the eyes of those now gathered about the campfire.

Tom Stilwell raised his eyes and looked to the shadows at the clearing where the preacher stood and tapped his foot and played the fiddle to a group of young people gathered around him. He looked back at McCall, half smiling.

"Wonder where them boys of ours got off to?" he said.

McCall nodded in the direction of the music.

"Looks like them over yonder drawing straws to see who asks that pretty little Granger girl to dance," Bill replied.

Stilwell laughed.

"Yeah, sure enough," he said. "At the rate they're going about it, this could take a while."

McCall smiled and shook his head.

Franklin and Brady stood off to the side, just at the fringe of the firelight but near enough the center of the activities to be easily noticed. They wore their shirts tucked in and buttoned to the top. Both boys combed and slicked back their hair . . . Franklin's suggestion, and his first order of business in explaining to Brady how to impress the girls.

"Girls like boys with smooth hair," he said.

Franklin moved into the perimeter of the firelight. He slid his Indian knife more

159

towards the front of his belt than he normally wore it and turned to Brady.

"How's it look, B.C.?"

"How's what look?" Brady asked.

Franklin pointed impatiently at the knife.

"It looks good," Brady said. Then his expression clouded.

"What's wrong with you?" Franklin asked, as though he didn't care if he got an answer or not.

"Well, are you going to ask Allison to dance or not? She keeps a looking over here," Brady said.

"I ain't decided if I want to ask her or the other one," Franklin said. "If I ask Allison, the other one will get mad and if I ask the other one, Allison will get mad."

Franklin looked at Brady and Brady tightened his jaw and fumed, but didn't say anything.

"It ain't easy deciding," Franklin said.

Just as Brady was about to respond, Allison and her friend approached them. Allison smiled at Brady and said, "Well, would you like to ask me to dance?"

Brady felt his face burn, and his mind raced to find the right thing to say. While he fumbled for the right words, Franklin stuck out his arm and Allison's friend hooked her hand in it, and off they walked, laughing and talking as they headed into the dancers' circle.

Brady looked down at his boots then back up to Allison, who stood there smiling and waiting.

"Umm, well, yeah I would," Brady said softly.

Allison smiled and waited.

Then she said, "You may."

Brady laughed. Then he smiled.

"Would you like to dance?" he said finally.

Allison took his hand. "Yes I would, thank you."

They danced and they laughed, and every time the couples passed, Franklin tipped Brady's hat or pushed him off balance. The longer they danced, the more the boys disrupted the patterns, until the square dance became a test to see which couple could stay on their feet the longest.

Emily and Elizabeth watched their sons from the chairs they sat on at the far side of the fire. Both women smiled as they talked.

"Will you look at those two boys of ours," Emily said. She laughed. "Sometimes I don't know whether to be embarrassed or grateful."

Elizabeth shook her head and laughed. "I'm sure if we knew everything they did, we'd have every right to be embarrassed.

But I can't imagine a finer friendship."

"No," Emily said. "It's a rare gift those two have. They argue all the time, but I've never seen two boys look out for each other like they do."

"Yes, I think it's wonderful they found each other," Elizabeth said. "I'm just worried what will happen when we go our separate ways."

"I think about that every day now that we are so close," Emily said.

They fell silent, then Elizabeth spoke.

"We will only be in Fort Laramie long enough to get supplies and repair the wagons," she said, "but I hear there will be hot baths available." She smiled at Emily.

"Oh, I can't wait to sit and soak in a steamy hot bath," Emily said. "And if I'm not out by the time you all get ready to leave, just leave me there." She laughed and Elizabeth nodded in agreement.

Elizabeth looked down at Matthew sleeping in her arms and Rachael nodding off at her feet. She stood slowly. "I think I better get these two off to bed," she said to Emily. Then she bid Emily and the others goodnight and walked back to the wagon.

One by one the lanterns went out at each wagon. Tree frogs and crickets answered one another's calls, and somewhere deep in the night an owl called out. A hawk screeched from somewhere very high overhead, and the soft breeze that floated across the plain carried with it the lonesome sound of a distant coyote. The flames of the campfire slowly subsided, and only the glowing embers persisted, and the camp slept.

CHAPTER SEVENTEEN

"Brady . . . wake up," Bill McCall whispered, as he touched the boy's shoulder. McCall stood in the light of the moon that hung bright and low, and the boy raised his head from the blankets and looked about. He watched his breath as he spoke.

"What time is it?" he asked in a voice still husky from sleep.

McCall smiled. "About two hours before dawn. You said you wanted to get up early."

"Thanks, pa," Brady said as he shivered and dressed and saw the camp was busy with people already up and readying themselves for an early start.

Elizabeth had breakfast ready by the time Brady pulled on his last boot. She looked up from the cook fire as he ran around the end of the wagon on his way to catch up his horse.

"Brady McCall, you hold it right there

young man," she called out in time to stop him before he was out of earshot.

Brady turned and walked slowly back to the fire.

"Yes, ma'am," he said, shifting impatiently from one foot to the other.

"Brady you have to sit down and eat breakfast. You can't expect to be out there all day on an empty stomach."

"But ma, I ain't hungry," Brady pleaded. "Everyone else will get the good spots and I'll get stuck in the back again riding drag." He looked up at her from under his floppy hat with pleading eyes.

"Well alright," she said, "but take these along to eat on the way." She handed him two hot biscuits. He stuffed one into his mouth and the other into his pocket. Then he turned on his heel and ran off.

"Thanks ma," he called back, his voice muffled by the biscuit held between his teeth.

Late in the afternoon Garrett's scout rider trotted his lathered horse among the wagons and announced Fort Laramie lay just over the next set of hills. Judging by the tracks the many horses and wagons lay before them, this was a much used roadway, and that alone gave cause for excitement and anticipation.

Drivers clucked their teams up, tightened the formation of the wagons and hurried along, eager to see anything again that even remotely resembled civilization. The first wagon was close behind Brady and Franklin as they crested the last rise and saw the timbered structure of the fort. They stood in amazement at the activity in and around the compound that was neither as large nor as elaborate as either of the boys imagined. It was not a city or even a village, and whatever military value the place had was lost on the boys. But the number of horses and riders and men walking about was far beyond their expectations, and the teepee's grouped around the stretch of plains to the west left them staring wide-eyed as they sat their horses and watched without speaking.

Finally Franklin stood up in his stirrups for a better looked and whistled as he exhaled to make a point.

"Damn . . . I mean dang, B.C. You see all them Indians?" he asked.

Brady stood in his stirrups as well and then sat back down and looked over at Franklin.

"What if they're Gros Ventres?" Brady asked

"What do you mean?" Franklin asked.

Brady nodded toward the beaded knife on

Franklin's belt.

"One a his relatives could be among 'em," Brady said.

Franklin unbuckled his belt and slid the knife off as Brady spoke. He reached back and tucked it deep inside his saddle bag. Then he smiled at Brady.

"I ain't worried about it, cousin," Franklin said. "Then again, there ain't no point looking for trouble neither."

Brady laughed. "Well, if anyone asks . . . I don't know you," he said.

Garrett halted the wagons and rode on in. When he returned he waved the drivers on and led them to a bivouac area in a grove of sparse cottonwoods at a broad and grassy bend in the Chugwater River, a mile or so west of the fort. As the last of the wagons arrived and formed up, a committee of curious Indians and an army captain and his sergeant rode up and asked the whereabouts of the wagon master.

Garrett rode out and presented himself.

The captain saluted, then dropped his hand crisply to his side without dismounting his horse. The sergeant sat his horse straight-backed and unsmiling.

"I'm Captain John Lewis. Welcome to Fort Laramie," said the blue uniformed soldier. His expression was friendly and his manner easy, but beyond the outward appearance of professionalism lay a sense of fatigue in his bearing, and his eyes were the eyes of a man who was aged far beyond his years.

"Captain," Garrett said, as he nodded in response to the officer's salute.

The captain anticipated the next question and said, "We got plenty of hot water for baths, the quartermaster's stores are full and the blacksmith can fix you up on wagon repairs."

Then he added, as though it were a necessity and not an option, "You'll want as much ammunition as you can handle and the armory has a few good rifles for sale if you're interested."

"Much obliged, captain," Garrett said as he looked across the faces of the drivers and their families gathered and standing within hearing distance. If they had a response to the captain's suggestion it did not show in their expressions, and Garrett dismissed it at that.

The officer paused, as though expecting questions and, when none came, he continued.

"After you folks get settled in, General Gibson would like to meet with you in his quarters . . . say five o'clock?"

"That'll be fine," Garrett said. "It will be me and a few of the men."

"Very good, sir," the captain said. "Enjoy your stay and let me know if there is anything I can do for you while you're here."

He snapped another salute and turned his horse back through the line of Indians who had followed him there and returned to the fort.

That evening Garrett and a group of men that included McCall and Stilwell rode back to the fort and found their way to the general's office. General Gibson greeted them and invited them to sit.

The general was pleasant, but short on words, and his patience balanced between obligation and intolerance. His voice was heavy with the responsibility of his station, and his manner suggested he was a man who had spent too much time assigned to wilderness outposts like this one. He carried an unlit cigar in his fingers as he paced across the room. Then he stopped talking and surveyed the company of civilians assembled before him. His eyes were alert and hard and filled with authority.

He gazed from one man to the next, not at all uncomfortable with the direct eye contact and lack of dialogue. The civilians grew ill at ease and some shifted in their seats while others diverted their eyes.

"This is South Pass," the general said, pointing to a spot on the large map that dominated the wall behind him. He used the cigar as a pointer and didn't look too check for accuracy as he tapped the spot on the map with the end of the cigar.

"And here," he said, moving the cigar eastward, "is where we are."

"In between," he added, as he waved the cigar over the expanse of map between the two spots, "is Indian Territory."

His eyes moved from man to man and he examined the men one at a time as though he was searching for something or waiting for a response, but none came. He stood with his cigar hand in front of him and rolled the cigar between his fingers. The men watched the cigar.

"For the most part these are hunting grounds to the Crow and the Blackfoot and some of the Sioux tribes." He paused again. Then he threw the cigar down on the desk and there was nothing left to watch but him, and he moved a step closer to the assemblage.

"They tolerate us," he said. "But they don't change for us . . . and they're not sure yet what to think of all these white people and their wagons. Up till now we've not had much trouble with them."

He touched his forehead and his voice softened, and the men sat up and raised their eyes to him.

Garrett stood to speak and the general ignored his motion for the floor. He walked back to the map and Garrett sat as though commanded to do so, and the general identified an area southeast of the route between Fort Laramie and South Pass.

"We have information that a war party . . . maybe two-hundred or more renegade Comanche are on the move north from here. The U.S. Army has yet to engage them, but this is, as near as we can tell, a loosely organized band of young warriors out killing just for the sake of killing. It doesn't make sense that they would be this far north, but we don't get paid to figure out what makes sense and what doesn't."

Any relief the settlers felt at reaching this stage of the journey now hung like a millstone on the backs of each man in the room and, after a long silence, Garrett once again took the floor.

"General," Garrett said, with an air of directness that caught the general off-guard, "we couldn't be less prepared to defend ourselves against a bunch like that. We don't have the arms, the ammunition or the experience. I want you to tell me what you think we're going to be up against . . . we can't wait and we can't turn back, so we got to take our chances one way or the other."

The other men remained silent and most moved to the edge of their seats.

"Look, I can't tell you for sure what they'll do or where they'll go, but I can tell you, you all would be a primary target if they get this far north. Now, there is a slim chance they won't get up this far. The Comanche generally stay to the south . . . but that's not a guarantee."

The general looked over at Captain Lewis, and if the captain had an opinion about the situation, it did not show in his expression.

"What are chances of getting an Army escort?" Garrett asked.

"I'm prepared to offer you an escort," the general said, "but I can't spare enough men to do you any good in the event you encounter hostile activity from a bunch this large."

"We'll take what we can get," Garrett said with genuine gratitude in his voice.

The general nodded as though to acknowledge the implied thank you. Then he waved the captain over to his desk.

"Captain Lewis," he said, as he wrote out a brief set of orders and handed the document to the young officer, "Select fourteen of your best men and draw mounts from the stock we've had under training . . . you'll want good horses."

"Yes, sir," the captain said. He stood erect and held a sharp salute until the general returned it, then his hand cut away smartly, and the captain turned and walked briskly out of the room.

The general's expression was grave, and he turned to Garrett. "I would strongly advise that you lay in whatever ammunition and rifles your party can afford to properly arm themselves. In the meantime, we do have plenty of provisions available and we'll do all we can to get you all back on the trail as quickly as we can." He stuck out his hand and Garrett shook it.

The layover at Fort Laramie took eight days; five more than Garrett planned on, and the prospects of an early snow now troubled him as much as the thought of an encounter with the Indians. When they departed the fort and their last acknowledged link with civilization, Garrett set about pushing the company at an ambitious pace.

Behind them, wheel ruts lay across the plains and converged on the horizon, where they disappeared and made their homes seem impossibly distant. Before them lay the foothills and beyond that the mountains, and the closer they got the further they seemed to have to go. Garrett grew unrelenting in his efforts to drive them onward.

CHAPTER EIGHTEEN

When the Platte River narrowed and changed, the terrain became rocky and inconsistent, and the livestock showed the strain of the extra effort required to traverse it. The pace slowed, and wagons queued up along a linear course and spread out even further, from front to back.

They left the Platte and followed the Sweetwater. And each day the going grew more difficult, and each day the range of mountains and its intimidating peaks grew more prominent. They camped in a high meadow at the base of the mountain, and the mountain itself stood before them, and the trail they saw etched upon the ground rose up and into the trees. The full magnitude of the task before them struck them with an awful sense of impossibility that left no man among them untouched.

After supper, Garrett stopped by to talk to a small group that had gathered near the

175

campfire where the McCalls and the Stilwells ate together.

"Evening folks," he said. "You all ready
for the big climb up them mountains?" The
question came in the form of small talk, but
his tone suggested an underlying concern
and a seriousness that did not invite a
rhetorical response.

Bill McCall looked up at Garrett's sun-
darkened and deeply lined face. He forked
in another mouthful of beans and swallowed
slowly before he spoke.

"Jim, my mules are dog-tired . . . we're
working them into the ground."

"That's a fact," said Stilwell. "Most of
these teams are running thin, mine included. We either got to slow the pace a bit
or give them a day to rest up."

Garrett nodded as though he understood
then said, "Simple truth is, we can't rest or
slowdown, neither one. We got to get over
South Pass before them Comanche do."

He paused, looked up the trail in the
direction of the mountain, then back at the
fire.

"You never seen it snow up there. If we
ain't over when the snow comes, that's all
there is . . . everything ends right there."

Emily and Elizabeth listened and, though
neither spoke, they were both thinking the

same thing. If the teams didn't keep pace the loads would be lightened and that meant the heaviest items would be discarded first. Stoves, bureaus, chairs and all but the barest of essentials would be sacrificed. The trail below them was littered with the daily reminders of those who preceded them with teams that weakened, and every piece of furniture or heavy cookware or stack of books from someone's personal library stood as a testimony to the lengths to which they would go to get up the mountain.

The men talked and the women silently prayed and when McCall looked over at Elizabeth he saw in her eyes a willingness to do whatever had to be done, and he knew he could not ask her to sacrifice even one more piece of what little she had left. Their eyes met in mutual understanding of a situation they both knew was beyond their control.

Garrett reached down and peeled a piece of bark off the log and threw it into the fire as if to emphasize his point.

"We got no choice," he said, shaking his head and staring into the fire. "Every day we use up on this side of the mountain we'll pay for on the top."

Garrett's words shot through the heart of the matter. No one argued, no one offered another point of view, and the expressions looking back at him were those of resignation more than determination. He excused himself and walked on.

For the next three days the wagons moved slowly up the eastern side of the pass. Behind them the trail lay littered with furniture, trunks and equipment, discarded as the first of the weaker teams began to fail. Up ahead the trail narrowed. On the north side a steep, rocky cliff formed a rough wall reaching nearly two-hundred feet to the top. The south side was boxed in by a thick stand of aspen trees growing so closely in formation that a man on horseback could not navigate a direct route through any part of it.

The trail snaked its way through the narrow passage between the rock wall and the trees and the wagons were forced into a single file for the better part of it. Garrett sent extra scouts out, and Captain Lewis deployed his men front and rear. His instincts and military training converged in a chilling realization that their position was not only un-defendable, but it compromised every advantage they might make for themselves. He watched his forward contingent ride up then drop over the first rise before them, disappearing from sight as though the mountain itself had taken them. The captain ordered his men to seek the high ground where ever they could, but there was none to be had, and they pressed on against every instinct he possessed as a man and a soldier.

Storm clouds gathered and rolled over the highest granite peaks to the west. The sky grew dark and overcast and the air was sultry. The earth took on the musty smell of new rain before it rains. The darkness of the sky hung low over them like a premonition of something uncertain and every man, woman and child of them felt its cold presence. They bundled and tucked the babies deep inside their blankets like fragile porcelain dolls and the children gathered about mothers without being asked to do so. There were no sounds save that of the wind and the creaking of the wagon wheels. The unnaturalness of it all weighed heavily on man and beast.

McCall's mules crowded the steep north side wall with their ears cocked forward, their heads tilted and their nervous eyes fixed on the dark, shadowed trees. The mules mouthed their bits and tossed their heads and refused to settle into their normal rhythm.

"I don't like the feel of it, Elizabeth," said McCall, as he jumped back onto the moving wagon and climbed into the seat next to his wife. "Check them rifles and make sure we got plenty of shot and powder close by."

Bill had felt trapped and exposed from the time they were forced to run the wagons into a single line. Elizabeth looked shaken.

"What is it, Bill? Did you see something? What's wrong?"

"I ain't sure. I didn't see anything, but I've got a real uneasy feeling I can't explain. Maybe it's just the weather or this crowded trail we're on. I don't know for sure."

Bill watched the mules. He trusted their sixth-sense ability to detect danger, but nothing he could see or hear justified their nervousness. He knew it was probably just the change in the weather, but he couldn't help feel there was more to it than that.

For the next three hours the wagons slowly penetrated deeper and deeper into the confines of the mountain. The aspens bent in the wind, the dark clouds tumbled lower and dropped down to treetop level. The air turned cold.

Captain Lewis stopped to talk to each of the drivers as he made his way back along the trail from the lead wagons. He approached the McCall wagon and drew his horse in closer. McCall handed the reins to Elizabeth and leaned over to hear what

Lewis had to say. The captain's troubled expression betrayed his professional demeanor, and Bill could sense the anxiety in the soldier's voice.

"Mr. McCall, no cause for alarm, sir, but we're pretty spread out on this trail, and I want to make sure you have your firearms ready . . . just in case."

Bill reached down and lifted the barrel of his rifle so the captain could see it.

"Good," the captain said. Then he looked across at Elizabeth.

"Ma'am, if you got anything inside you can use as cover against this side canvas, you should get it moved right away. Anything that will offer a little protection would help."

McCall looked at the captain and his voice was noticeably uneasy when he spoke.

"Captain, you seen any sign of Indians since we been up here?" McCall asked impatiently.

"No sir, we haven't. But if they're out there, we couldn't have picked a worse place to . . ."

The captain's voice trailed off and for a moment he sat there with no expression on his face. He listed from side to side slightly, and his eyes dropped to the arrowhead dripping blood where it protruded from his shirt. Bubbles frothed at the wound site, and the young officer appeared apologetic as he pitched forth from the saddle.

CHAPTER NINETEEN

Bill and Elizabeth stared in stunned disbelief. They watched the captain's body drop to the ground. As quickly as McCall contemplated going to the aid of the captain or grabbing his rifle, the hideous sound of screaming warriors echoed forth from the darkness in the trees on the downward side of the trail, and the world exploded in fire and the sounds of gunshots and dying animals and mothers shrieking to protect their children.

There was no plan and there was no organization, and the number of painted warriors swarming from the aspen cover was terrifying. Men died watching without ever raising a rifle or lifting a hand in self-defense.

Confused horses took flight and crowded the narrow trail in a milling mass. Riders dropped like shooting gallery targets with every volley of arrows and rifle shot that belched from the trees.

The wagons stood in disarray. In those few brief moments death and disorder spread from the lead wagon to the last wagon. Panic set in. The company of settlers fired blindly into the trees, and they fired blindly in the direction of the massing of warriors, but few of their shots were true, and few got off a second shot.

McCall's mules made no attempt to run, but, instead, stood trembling. A quick volley of arrows from the nearby trees and the nearside mules dropped in unison. The offside mules stood with traces pulled down by the fallen mules. McCall looked up in time to hear a close-range rifle shot slap into the hide of the wheel mule, and bone and hide scattered where the bullet hit, and he dropped as though his legs had been pulled out from under him.

"Elizabeth, get under cover," Bill shouted, as he pushed her into the wagon. In the same motion he brought his rifle up to his shoulder and looked down the barrel at a warrior running straight at his wagon. He squeezed the trigger and the lead ball tore a path through the Indian's chest, catching him mid-stride and taking him off his feet.

He threw the rifle back into the wagon and Elizabeth handed him a loaded one, then slammed powder, shot, and wadding down the warm barrel of the first rifle.

Two warriors assaulted the rear of the wagon ahead of the McCall's, and as they drug the lifeless body of Mrs. Baldwin out over the end board, McCall fired a shot that shattered the skull of one of the warriors and covered the other with bone and blood. The second warrior turned with no regard for his fallen comrade and charged at McCall like a frenzied animal.

There was no time to wait for a reloaded rifle. McCall unsheathed his knife and stepped forward to meet the warrior who lunged up on the wagon tongue and was at the front foot board when a rifle shot boomed from inside the wagon. A cloud of black smoke followed. The warrior crumpled to the ground and McCall turned to see Elizabeth lower the weapon from her shoulder and sit back down to reload.

Behind Elizabeth, Matthew and Rachael huddled together, shaking and sobbing. McCall saw the terrified expressions, and his stomach knotted and he felt ashamed. And for the first time he could remember, he felt fear.

Elizabeth looked over at him as she slammed the ramrod down the bore of the rifle. He thought of Brady and his hands shook. Elizabeth screamed and McCall turned to see a warrior halfway up the front of the wagon. McCall's fear turned to rage.

He met the warrior at the foot board and reached forth and took a handful of the greasy hair and jerked the warrior toward him. The warrior groaned when his chest crashed against the seat. Then, quietly and swiftly, the warrior plunged his knife its full length into McCall's groin.

Elizabeth and the children watched in horror. McCall showed no reaction to the knife, as he mechanically raised his own blade over his head with both hands grasping the wooden handle. With his full force he drove the blade deep between the shoulder blades of the young warrior. He withdrew the bloody blade then slammed it home a second and third and fourth time. The warpainted body went limp and McCall pushed it back over the side.

McCall slumped to his knees on the floor of the wagon, his trousers soaked with blood and hemorrhaging from a severed femoral artery. He looked up at Elizabeth. His eyes apologetic, his expression helpless and ashamed. She reached out to him but they never made contact. An arrow, silent and errant, ripped through the canvas and lodged itself deeply into her back. The impact took her off her feet and she stared at her husband as she fell forward and watched as another arrow tore blindly through the canvas and struck him squarely in the chest. William and Elizabeth McCall died before the savages overtook the wagon and dispatched the two children.

In the confusion of the attack, Thomas Stilwell was able to get Emily out of the wagon and near the cover of the trees when the attackers over-ran them. Stilwell fired his last shot, stood between Emily and the warriors converging upon them and took the barrel of the rifle in his hands and swung viciously at the first of the Indians to come into range. The warrior fell and behind him a flurry of arrows hissed through the air and left Stilwell and his wife standing there momentarily stunned at the number of feathered, wooden shafts protruding from all parts of their bodies. They slumped to the ground and Stilwell hovered over Emily's body as he felt a knee driven into his back.

Stilwell reached behind him and grabbed a handful of hair and pulled his attacker over his shoulder and pinned him to the ground before him. His hands clenched around the warrior's throat and the warrior twisted and writhed and fought for his release until he could fight no more, and his eyes rolled back and he lay calmly in Stilwell's grip.

Stilwell's head snapped back, and he felt the weight of a man upon his shoulders and felt his hair being pulled. He struggled, but had not the strength. Blood ran into his eyes and he could smell it and taste it on his lips, and when he sensed his scalp lift away in a violent ripping sound, he felt the earth grow quiet and dark, and he died before he felt the burn of the knife on his throat.

A Comanche warrior stood. His victory cry rang out loud and he held his trophy high, blood running down his bare arm and his eyes filled with hatred and triumph.

CHAPTER TWENTY

Brady and Franklin rode a narrow draw to the upper trail shortly after they left camp that morning, leaving the scouts and other outriders to the trails below. High on the upper rim they could ride undetected and still have a good view of the lower trails much of the time.

They rode carefully through the brush and granite boulders, and they rode slightly back from the forward positions of the two army scouts. The weather was unnerving and they both shared a sense of uneasiness. They rode out upon a lightly treed escarpment to check their positions.

The army scouts sat their horses far below them and appeared to be checking for sign.

"What do you suppose they're doing?" Brady asked.

Franklin stood in his stirrups for a better look, then replied in a soft voice that made Brady uncomfortable.

"They seen something on the trail . . . I don't know what."

They heard no sounds and they saw no movement below them. Then, as though it were being played out in slow motion, the two scouts lurched convulsively in their saddles in rhythm to the arrows that ripped into their backs. Their shirts ran red with blood and the two scouts fell silently to the ground. The horses sidestepped them but did not bolt. And there were no other sounds and there was no other movement.

Brady and Franklin looked at each other. Franklin made a frantic sign for silence, then pointed back to the cover of the brush and boulders, and they wheeled their horses around and secluded themselves out of sight from the trail below. Franklin drew his rifle.

"What are you doing?" Brady asked.

"We gotta warn the others," he said, and before the words were spoken and before he could squeeze the trigger, the awful sounds of gunfire and war cries and screaming echoed up the canyon, and both boys fell silent.

They waited, then Franklin screamed "Let's go."

Brady looked down the steep trail and they spurred their horses out of the heavy brush in the direction of the gunfire. The sounds resonating off the canyon walls painted a horrible picture in the boys' minds. Brady's hands shook uncontrollably, and Franklin cursed and pounded the horse's sides with his heels and fended off the brush with the hand that carried the rifle.

The trail was narrow and in places the gravel so loose the horses slid on their haunches to stay upright. Brady rode in the lead, and at a wooded bend pulled his horse up abruptly and turned to Franklin, his eyes wide, as he signaled Franklin to get off the trail and into the brush.

Their horses stood with sides heaving and gasping for air. Brady dismounted, and Franklin swung down beside him.

"What's wrong?" Franklin asked, his chest pounding.

Brady dropped his reins and dropped to his knees and motioned Franklin to follow. They crawled out to a rock outcropping and Brady pointed down the slope where a Comanche warrior stood his post mounted on a painted horse not a hundred yards before them. Concealed above the main trail, the warrior waited to intercept any who may slip through below him.

"What are we gonna do now?" Brady asked, in a voice shaken with childlike uncertainty.

Franklin put his index finger to his lips to signal Brady to silence. He paused for a moment, then handed his hat to his young friend. Franklin cradled the rifle in his arms, dropped to his belly and snaked his way thirty-yards closer. He rose partly up to look over a fallen tree, then lowered the rifle down to the dry bark and rested it against the notch of a broken limb and set his sights.

Brady was mesmerized and barely breathed as Franklin slowly drew back the hammer. It seemed an eternity. The warrior turned his horse slightly, exposing the broad view of his back to Franklin, and Brady saw Franklin's jaw tighten and saw his finger apply pressure. He held his breath and when the shot exploded, he flinched and his eyes widened at the big, red hole gaping along the warrior's spine as he lifted from the horse's back and lay in a grotesque heap on a twisted leg, with an arm turned up behind him.

Franklin rose to his feet and took a final look at the dead warrior. He stood there for a moment like he was going to speak, then a second warrior rode out onto the trail, reining his flighty horse with one hand and brandishing a bloody war ax in the other.

The warrior spotted Franklin before he

could move to cover and let out a terrifying battle cry. He urged his fiery mount up the trail at a gallop. The awesome spectacle of the painted warrior on his painted horse destroyed the boy's confidence.

Franklin had no time to reload. He looked back at Brady. His eyes widened and he didn't make a sound as he watched the youngster brace his rifle against the side of a slender pine tree. Brady pulled back the hammer and waited. Franklin watched helplessly as the shrieking warrior galloped closer and closer.

Franklin turned to run. The Comanche brave covered fifteen more yards. Brady didn't move a muscle. Ten more yards and Franklin broke for cover, yelling at Brady as he ran. "Run," he shouted.

Brady could now see every detail in the warrior's face. The dark Indian pony never broke stride as he bore down on Franklin. Moving in for the death blow, the warrior raised the long-handled ax over his head.

Brady closed his eyes and squeezed the trigger. Black smoke and fire belched out of the muzzle of Brady's rifle, and the deafening roar of the shot reverberated through the trees. The Comanche brave's head twisted violently. The impact of the big gun blew the warrior off the back of his horse as the heavy, lead ball tore the flesh away from his face.

His war-painted horse bounced to a stop, then calmly walked a short distance away and quietly dropped his head to graze.

Franklin ran back to Brady. He picked up his hat and he motioned to Brady. Brady nodded back and his expression was hard. He set the rifle on its butt plate and packed in another load.

"Reload and let's go," he said hoarsely.

Tears threatened to betray Brady's manly demeanor, the little-boy look in his eyes was that of a lost child and Franklin patted him on the arm.

"We better hurry," Franklin said.

With their rifles reloaded, the boys mounted up and made their way slowly along the rim of the trail, careful not to reveal themselves and watchful to avoid another surprise. The going was slow and the sound of battle raged at a feverish pitch. The boys both knew, as long as there was gunfire there was hope. The game trail they followed turned and dropped sharply down to the right, and the boys began the final descent.

War cries and anguished screams and rapid fire gunshots were close when half a dozen mounted warriors saw the boys and opened fire on them. Bullets chewed up the ground all around them and arrows hissed overhead, but neither boy was hit.

The frenzied Comanche whipped their horses up the hill and Brady and Franklin spun their horses around and lunged back up the trail. A quarter of a mile up the granite break they left the path and took cover in a tangle of heavy brush among the boulders where their horses left no sign. The boys breathed heavily as they moved deeper into the concealment of a narrow ravine. They listened intently, gasping for air and shaking involuntarily. The warriors clattered by in the rocks, whooping and yelling until their frightening voices faded beyond the next crest in the trail.

The boys dismounted, tied off their horses and slipped into a shallow fortress of granite with only one way in and one way back out. They rested and they waited. Smoke columns rose high into the air overhead from the trail below, and the sounds of gunfire and war cries became more sporadic. Now only an occasional shot cracked the still air, and the voices they could hear were voices speaking a language they didn't understand.

They looked at each other and wept.

For the third time, the searchers rode within fifty yards of their position without detecting the location where the boys had left the trail. The Indians' voices were loud and angry as they rode back in the direction of the wagons.

The smoky air turned cold and faded to darkness and when the moon and stars came out, the smoke rose up to meet them, and the boys lay huddled and waiting. Not a shot was fired for more than two hours and not a word was spoken between the two boys, but both understood the only thing left for them to do was to try to stay alive.

In the clearing half a mile below them, Brady and Franklin could see burning cinders rise up from the massive fire in the Indian's camp. The warriors gathered up bags of sugar and jugs of whiskey and sat about the fire eating the sugar off their wet fingers and drinking until they vomited or passed out. They couldn't see well from their position, but the boys heard the screams of women and had only their imaginations and the pitiful cries to tell them how unfortunate the women were to not have died in the battle.

Brady winced each time a female voice cried out. The boys felt sick and empty and prayed the voices did not belong to their mothers or to Rachael. Long into the night the cries continued until one by one they too were silenced and the only sounds were those of the warriors who argued and fought among themselves. Eventually even those voices surrendered to the whiskey, and there were no sounds at all.

Brady stared into the darkness. He tried to remember exactly how his mother looked when he last saw her. He remembered his father's smile and his strong hand on his shoulder. He saw clear images of his sister and his little brother, and tears swelled in his eyes.

Franklin sat with his head in his hands and his face was streaked with tears. He looked over at Brady.

Brady looked back at him with an almost pleading expression.

"You think they killed them all?" he asked quietly, and slightly shaking his head from side to side as though to prompt the right answer.

Franklin nodded. "I think they did."

Franklin choked back the tears and stood up. Brady stood with him. He put his arms around the boy and held him like a father holds a son, and they both cried.

Brady cleared his throat, then pushed himself away.

"We can't let 'em get away with this," Brady said, as he wiped his arm across his nose, and dug his knuckles into his eyes to clear away the tears. He picked up his rifle, made sure it was loaded, then reached down to check his knife.

Franklin spoke through gritted teeth.

"We'll leave the horses and go on foot."

Staying close to the rocky path in the darkness, the boys picked their way toward the spot where the renegades had dragged their prisoners. The wind had scattered the cloud cover and small patches of moonlight broke through, giving the boys enough visibility to see the trail and to see the shapes of several warriors stretched out in the dirt near the campfire.

Franklin assessed the situation as best he could in the poor light. He took Brady by the arm and whispered.

"B.C., all we can do is get as many as we can before they get us."

Brady nodded in agreement and they sat to wait out the cloud cover for better light.

CHAPTER TWENTY-ONE

The moon slipped out from behind the clouds, and the light it gave cast long shadows and in the shadows lay warriors, some in their own vomit, others on the bare dirt, and all with blood dried in finger stripes across their skin.

A few others sat wobbling over whiskey jugs between their legs, and some talked in low voices, and there were too many to count.

Brady and Franklin waited quietly at the edge of the Indians' camp, searching the dark ground and hoping to catch the small band of warriors by surprise. Brady's heart was filled with hatred and fear. Franklin was unusually calm, and both boys felt unprepared for what they had to do next. Brady grew impatient and inched forward for a better look. As he did so, he momentarily lost the grip on his rifle and caught it just as the steel-plated butt struck a loose rock.

The sound was insignificant, but it occurred when all else was silent, and two warriors posted as sentinels heard it and immediately stopped to listen. Brady held his breath and Franklin froze in place, then the rock slid and began to roll slowly over the edge of the trail. When it plunged over a steep ledge and took more rocks with it, the warriors sprung to their feet. They woke those they could and charged toward the source of the sound.

"Brady, up there," Franklin said, pointing to a small opening just above the path. They scrambled up and concealed themselves as best they could among the large rocks. They would not be visible from the downward side of the trail but they would be partially exposed once the braves were abreast of their position. The boys slunk behind the cover of the rocks and readied their weapons. Their hands shook as they watched the renegades pounding up the steep embankment toward them.

For all they had to drink, the Indians moved quickly. They split up just before they reached the boys' position, then the frightened youngsters lost sight of them. Brady stood fast with his rifle trained on the narrow opening between the rocks, facing the trail. His heart hammered and his chest heaved as somewhere in the cold darkness, death stalked him.

Then, as if by some supernatural force, the evil, painted face of one of the Comanche braves filled the space in front of Brady. He was so close Brady could smell his foul, liquored breath.

Brady cursed between clinched teeth and squeezed the trigger. The shot exploded into the forehead of the warrior, entering through a hole the size of a man's finger and exiting amidst a handful of bone and tissue. The muscular body slumped back out of sight.

"Over there," Franklin shouted, as another warrior swung his rifle around the far side of the rock and pointed it directly at him. Franklin jerked the trigger of his rifle without aiming, and the shot ricocheted off the face of the rock and buzzed out into the open night air then made a splattering sound when it tore a ragged path into the renegade's mid-section. The warrior spun off his feet, dead.

Franklin's heart hammered. Brady was trying to reload, but was shaking so badly he couldn't get the ramrod down the barrel. Franklin's hands shook but he did manage to get partially reloaded. He hastily reached for the ramrod.

"B.C.," he whispered in a gravelly voice, "There's still one more out there. Hurry."

The unmistakable double click of a rifle hammer ratcheted menacingly in the darkness of the rocks above them. Franklin felt a chill and the hair on the back of his neck raised up as he anticipated a shot crashing into his back. Brady whirled and looked up as he feverishly tried to get his shot packed.

There above them stood the renegade, his legs braced and his rifle pointed down at them. For a moment the moon shone from behind the dark clouds and the light reflected off the barrel of the warrior's rifle. He stood calm and deliberate. He brought the rifle to his shoulder, and Franklin pushed Brady out of the line of fire just as the warrior slumped backwards and his rifle rattled down the rocks and into the darkness.

Franklin grabbed Brady by the arm.

"Let's get out of here," he said, as he turned to retreat through the narrow passageway between the rocks. They pushed through the heavy brush, and Franklin reached the opening first. He glanced back to make sure Brady was behind him. When he turned back to the opening, the dark outline of a man blocked the exit. The dark figure moved toward him. Franklin drew his knife and jumped back in fear.

"Hold on, I'm on your side," the voice said in a reassuring whisper.

Brady and Franklin looked at each other and moved further back into the rocks. The man slipped in beside them.

"Take it easy, boys. It's me, Travis Kincaid."

Brady and Franklin were stunned. Both boys started talking at the same time. Finally, Brady stopped to let Franklin continue with the questions.

"How did you find us?"

"It's a long story," Kincaid said. "Right now we got other things to think about."

The boys agreed.

"What are we going to do?" Franklin asked.

"Look, boys I'm real sorry," Kincaid said. "But there's not much chance they left anyone alive down there, you know that don't you?"

They nodded again.

"But we can't let them get away with this," Brady said.

"What are your names?" Kincaid asked.

Franklin looked at him; his first thought was, *this ain't much of a time for small talk.*

"I'm Franklin T. Stilwell. This here's Brady McCall," he replied.

Kincaid stuck out his hand and they shook.

"All right, Brady, listen to me," Kincaid said. "There's a good chance none of us will get out of here alive if we don't use our heads."

"What do you mean?" Franklin asked.

"Bad as you think of those Comanches, they been pushed hard, and now they're pushing back the only way they know how. If it's up to them, they won't leave any of us alive."

The boys held their heads down.

"I know you're looking for revenge. I don't blame you a bit. But right now we got to be thinking about how we're going to get ourselves out of here."

"How much of what happened down there did you see?" Franklin asked.

"Not much. I saw the smoke from way down the trail. Saw Indian sign early on. By the time I got close enough to see anything it was almost dark."

"And?" Brady asked.

"It's bad," Kincaid said. "Real bad."

CHAPTER TWENTY-TWO

Dawn was less than two hours away and the camp was still and quiet. The wind died down to a soft shifting of the air currents, and the earlier gunfire failed to arouse the rest of the warriors from their drunken sleep.

Kincaid and the two boys crept single file back up the narrow trail. Kincaid sensed the boys' uneasiness and turned to speak over his shoulder as they continued silently through the brush.

"Don't let the quiet bother you. All that whiskey finally caught up with them. Keep your eyes and ears open. It won't take much to set them off again."

Kincaid tied his horse with Buffalo Dancer and Three Feathers, then the three men started back up the trail, away from the direction of the wagons and the main war party.

Within a hundred yards of the camp, four

renegades snored in a drunken stupor on the bare ground where they had passed out earlier. Kincaid and the boys looked for any sign they might find to tell them if any of the white captives were still in camp. There were none.

On their hands and knees the three crept cautiously through the tangled brush. Twenty yards in front of them one warrior lay apart from the others, wheezing and sleeping deeply. Kincaid drew his knife and motioned for Franklin and Brady to stay under cover off the side of the trail. He handed Franklin his rifle then dropped to his belly and snaked his way into the enemy camp.

As he made his way through the brush, a warrior they had not seen sat bolt-upright no more than three-feet in front of Kincaid. Kincaid made no sound as he raised himself and pulled the warrior back down and drove his knife upward between the soft V of the Indian's rib cage.

Kincaid held the muffled and writhing warrior until he stopped struggling. He twisted the knife and drove it home twice more before he gently lowered the body to the ground. Brady and Franklin looked at each other nervously. Kincaid crawled back to them. He was all business now, and no emotion showed in his face.

"I'm not sure how many of them are out there," he said. "I counted seven last night. We got three, there are still four laying out there in the dirt, and this one makes eight, so my count was wrong, and there could be more. I'm going to try to slip into camp without waking anyone. I'll try to get to the other side of that clearing to see if any of our people are there. Franklin, you cover that side," said Kincaid, pointing to the left edge of the clearing. "Brady, you cover the other side," he whispered.

"But Travis," said Brady. "Even if me and Franklin don't miss we can only get two of them. There'll still be two more left."

Travis squeezed the handle of the pistol hanging at his side and said, "Just make sure you don't miss, and I'll take care of the other two."

Kincaid turned, dropped flat to the ground, and inched his way slowly across the clearing. As he approached the first drunken renegade, Brady and Franklin watched in awe. Without a sound or so much as a scuffle, Kincaid hunkered over the warrior and, in one smooth motion, covered the Indian's mouth, then plunged his knife blade deep in the center of the renegade's chest. Then, with deadly silence, he worked his way towards the next snoring, war-painted bodies.

Brady's mouth went dry, and he could hear his own heart pounding. The moon slipped from behind the clouds and cast its silvery light onto the clearing, exposing Kincaid as he continued methodically on in the direction of the other three warriors. When Kincaid was within striking distance, he felt his stomach knot. The renegades' hands were covered with dried blood, and the one nearest him had two fresh, blonde-haired scalps tied to his wrist.

Less careful now, Kincaid rose up and drove his knife violently into the chest of the sleeping Indian. With his last breath the Indian groaned loudly, waking the warrior next to him. Kincaid was taken by surprise. The still-groggy Indian rolled sideways with the speed and agility of a cat. The warrior was on his feet, facing Kincaid, who was still on his knees.

Franklin saw Kincaid's predicament and raised his rifle, looking for a clear shot, but Kincaid was in the line of fire. Before Franklin could set up a shot, Kincaid lunged toward the warrior. His quickness caught the young warrior off guard, and Kincaid laid him open with a violent slash across the abdomen that spilled the warrior's intestines out at his feet. Franklin was repulsed by the sight, and in one merciful, reflexive action he squeezed the trigger. The report from the rifle echoed off the canyon walls, and the heavy slug sent the renegade twisting off his feet.

The warrior hadn't hit the ground before Kincaid rose to his feet and shouted, "Let's get out of here."

The fourth renegade sat up in a stupor, confused and uncomprehending. Kincaid dispatched him with his pistol and ran back to where the boys waited.

Franklin shook his head. "Damn, Travis, I'm sorry. I wasn't thinking," he said.

Kincaid grabbed them both and spun them around.

"Don't worry about it now. Head back up into the brush."

No sooner had Kincaid said that, then the fury of hell broke loose back in the direction of the wagons. War whoops and loud, angry voices filled the canyon in response to the unexpected sound of gunfire. Already, the rumble of galloping horses could be heard pounding the rocky trail towards them.

"Get up that hill and under that brush," Kincaid ordered.

All three dove for cover, and the ground shook and it sounded like every warrior in camp was mounted and charging after them.

The rim of the skyline turned a dull shade of gray as dawn approached. All night long the boys had prayed for daylight. It couldn't have come at a worse time.

Travis and the two boys lay hidden less than twenty feet from the trail. Their cover was thin but, with no time to move into a better position, they knew their only chance was to remain absolutely still and to hope the Comanche would move through fast enough not to notice them.

Dust billowed up from the hooves of scores of horses that had slowed to a trot on the crowded trail. War whoops and loud voices mingled with the sound of the horses as they drew nearer.

"Don't make a move, and don't make a sound," whispered Travis. "Even if they look you right in the eye, stay still. If they do spot us, wait for me to make the first move, then make your shots count."

Their eyes filled with horror and both boys nodded. Brady was emotionally drained. Fear, guilt, uncertainty, hate and sorrow galvanized his senses to the point of numbness.

The first of the riders passed directly in front of them without slowing. At this point the trail was narrow and, as the warriors filed past, Brady was sickened by the blood spattered bodies and the many scalps he saw hanging at their sides. Brady counted silently to himself and tried to remember the faces as they passed. He stopped counting after a hundred . . . and still they came.

Kincaid watched as each group of warriors rode by. They carried their dead and wounded with them, and Kincaid realized they were leaving. They were not looking for them, and he prayed neither of the boys would give their position away. Five warriors rode apart from the rest. They pulled their ponies to a halt on the trail and stopped directly in front of Kincaid and the boys. They were so close Brady was sure they saw him. He held his breath and waited with his eyes riveted to the faces streaked with war colors and sweat. The warriors talked loudly back and forth but they did not see the three white men hiding in the bushes, almost under their feet.

Brady's rigid muscles ached but he sat frozen, trying to memorize every feature of the faces before him. These five were different from the others that had ridden by. Their hair was not the same as the others.

Their headdress was different, and they wore beautifully decorated deerskin shirts. The other Comanche warriors were bare-chested. Brady tried to remember the horses and the painted marks they bore.

Brady listened to their voices. He hated the careless demeanor of the killers who had slaughtered people the day before and now sat talking as though it were just a game they played.

The guttural, rhythmic sound of their voices sounded hard, and cold. One young warrior spun his big gray horse around and stood facing Brady. From his neck hung a locket, and it shone in the early fragments of dawn and reflected above everything else he wore.

Brady bristled and his expression was careless and vengeful. He recognized the locket and Franklin pleaded with his eyes for Brady not to do anything. Brady half-rose and Franklin stopped breathing.

Kincaid touched Brady's leg with the toe of his boot and the boy let it go.

CHAPTER TWENTY-THREE

Digging their heels into the sides of their horses, the five warriors loped off to join the others. Dawn brought color to the thin gray day and the sun rose warm and red. Ground squirrels scampered across the trail, birds twittered, and two-hundred men rode away victorious and laden with treasure. Behind them three young men contemplated revenge.

Kincaid and the boys did not move until they were certain the renegades were a safe distance down the trail. Kincaid relaxed, sat back and looked toward Brady.

"Did that gold necklace belong to your mother?" he asked.

Brady stared blankly at the ground and nodded. His lip quivered and a tear fell, wetting the back of his dirt-stained hand as it made a tiny trail across his knuckles and dripped down onto the wooden stock of his rifle.

"Yeah, it did. I'll get it back," Brady said, looking up at Kincaid with a cold expression.

Franklin stared into the dirt. His eyes narrowed. He looked up at Brady.

"I'll help you . . . we'll find him," Franklin said.

Brady stood and Kincaid stood in front of him and placed his hand on the boy's shoulder. "Some things are better left alone," he said.

"Not this one," Brady said. "It ain't even my choice to make, Travis."

Kincaid stood silent. Brady nodded towards Franklin.

"Me and him are blood brothers, and he don't have no choice neither," Brady added.

"I understand," the cowboy said. "I'm just asking you to think about it, that's all."

Kincaid and the boys collected their horses and stood in the warm morning sunlight before they mounted up. They were tired and wrung out, and the thought of returning to the site of the massacre hung heavily over them.

With one foot in the stirrup and the other still on the ground, Kincaid hesitated. He stepped back down.

"Why don't you boys ride on up the trail and water your horses? Give them a chance

214

to graze some? I'll ride back to the wagons to get a look at things first." Travis knew it was a weak attempt, but he hoped he could save the boys from what he knew awaited them.

"Forget it, Travis," said Franklin. "We're going back."

"We're coming with you," Brady said.

Kincaid spat and pulled his hat down as he stepped back into the saddle.

"I figured as much," he said.

CHAPTER TWENTY-FOUR

The three riders descended the rim in silence. The hoof prints of unshod horses lay before them where the trail had been ridden to dust, and the brush was littered with books and pots and shoes and a child's doll. Further down, a broken rocker and a twisted steamer trunk, and for the next two miles, pages from Bibles and old photos and dishes, shattered and slung about with great disregard. A mile more and the woods were thick with debris and clothing and personal belongings that, a few hours earlier, seemed so valuable, yet now so worthless.

They walked their horses and no one spoke. Brady's face was pale and drained. Franklin's eyes were red-rimmed, and he clenched his jaw. Kincaid rode two horse-lengths before the boys. The trail rose, then fell and turned at a shallow bend.

Kincaid raised his hand and all three halted.

"There's a wagon up ahead," he said.

He looked back at the boys and Brady nodded him onward. They rode together, and when they approached the wagon, flies buzzed and the smell of death assaulted them. A young team of oxen lay grotesquely tangled in their bloody harness, their bodies bloated and pockmarked with bullet holes and pin-cushioned with arrows. The wagon rested on its side with its wheels in the air, and its contents strewn about from both ends.

When they rode by, Kincaid dismounted and checked inside. Both boys waited. Kincaid stepped back into the saddle and shook his head. They rode on.

Before them, another dead team, with eyes gone and buzzards tearing flesh from the empty sockets. The birds hissed and gorged themselves, tearing at the bullet holes and spreading their wings, but not leaving. Blood stained their wretched faces, and they were heavy from their feeding orgy.

Kincaid checked inside the second wagon then, before they reached the third, he pulled his horse up.

"Wait there," he said over his shoulder. He dismounted and moved down into the brush below the trail. The boys waited, their faces ashen, their eyes dark and hollow. Kincaid was gone a long time, and when he climbed out of the brush he dropped his eyes and his voice was low and faulty.

"It's not your families," he said. "I think it's the Turners and the Eastmans and some I don't recognize.

"Dead?" Franklin asked.

Kincaid nodded. "Looks like nine of them, including the babies."

Franklin dismounted.

"Don't," Kincaid said. "They're scalped and cut up bad. You don't need to see that."

"You sure they're all dead?" Franklin asked.

"They're dead."

Kincaid remounted and Franklin followed suit.

They rode slowly, and the bodies appeared. First a few here and there then more, until they had to dismount and walk, so littered was the trail with human remains. From a slight rise in the trail Franklin recognized the Stilwell wagon. Four of the six mules stood waiting. The two wheel mules lie heaped in dark pools of dried blood.

"You don't have to do this, Franklin," Kincaid said.

He held the boy's arm. Franklin jerked free. Brady stood beside him.

"I'll go with you," Brady said.

Kincaid let the boys go ahead, and he fell in behind them.

They found Emily Stilwell first. The wide skirt of her dress fluttered in the wind and she lay face down, her arms twisted behind her and her feet turned at unnatural angles. Her dress was soaked in blood, and when Franklin saw her he collapsed to his knees before he could approach her, and he cried.

Brady stood next to him with his hand on Franklin's shoulder, and he cried.

Kincaid said, "I'll get her a blanket."

He found a quilt near the wagon and before he covered her he straightened out her arms and fixed her feet. At the edge of the trail he found Mr. Stilwell, his scalp torn away and his shirt missing, and his body cut many times with gaping slashes. Kincaid wrapped him in a wool blanket and placed his body next to that of his wife.

Franklin and Brady watched and sobbed.

Kincaid returned and stood over the boys.

"You two go back down the trail to one of them other wagons and fetch us three good shovels. Do it now." His voice was firm, and the boys did not question him.

They returned with the shovels, their faces streaked and all the fight whipped out of them.

"Yonder's a clearing," Kincaid said, pointing to a small meadow off the trail. "Go on down there and start digging."

"Travis," Brady said. Travis cut him off. "I know Brady . . . you stay with Franklin. I'll let you know what I find."

Kincaid found the McCalls where they fell. He wrapped Bill McCall in a canvas wagon sheet, found a quilt for Elizabeth and blankets for each of the children. He fashioned a travois and carried the bodies back to the meadow then returned for more and more.

By the end of the day they had buried twenty-three bodies and marked each grave with a board and a name. The remaining bodies they couldn't name and couldn't bury.

Kincaid built a great pyre and upon it they placed the bodies, each one wrapped and soaked with kerosene.

They caught up their horses and Kincaid sent Franklin and Brady on ahead. He returned, said a prayer over the massive arrangement and set it afire. He waited until the heat and stench of burning flesh drove him away.

He circled the graveyard meadow and saw wild flowers on six of the graves. The McCall grave markers were carved with knife point, *Love, Brady.*

Brady retrieved the McCall family Bible and spare clothes from his wagon. Franklin did likewise, and they rode with their Bibles clutched beneath their arms and tears running from their eyes.

They waited up the trail and watched the massive billow of black smoke rise from the forest until it formed a column and the flames followed it skyward.

CHAPTER TWENTY-FIVE

They rode in silence for the better part of an hour, each leading a pack horse loaded with supplies. In front of them, the trail cut its way up toward the summit. Behind them, the narrow column of smoke rose up from an insignificant dot on the landscape that would remain fixed within the minds of two young men for as long as they lived.

It was Kincaid who finally broke the silence.

"I don't like to be the one who brings this up, but you boys are going to have to give some thought to what you want to do next," he said. "I'll get you to Fort Hall, but after that I leave the trail and head north from there."

"Well, Travis, what are me and B.C. supposed to do?" Franklin asked.

Kincaid hesitated. He thought of his own circumstances and could find no way to include two young boys in his plans. He looked over at Franklin.

"Look," he said. "You boys are in a fix, but look at me. I'm one man living in a shack so poor the dog won't stay in it. Every dollar I had is in a bunch of Texas cattle that may not even make it through the winter. I'm worse than no help at all."

"We can work," Franklin said.

"Yeah, we can help out and we ain't that much trouble," Brady said.

"I didn't say you were any trouble, I just don't have any way to take care of you. I'll get you to Fort Hall. You can get a ride back to Fort Laramie with the next Army patrol going that way. Then they'll help you all get back home," Kincaid said.

Brady and Franklin stared up at him.

"We don't got no home to go back to," Franklin said.

"I guess I got my pa's place in Montana Territory. Help us get there and me and Franklin will make it on our own," Brady said.

"You know what, Travis? Forget it," Franklin said. "Me and B.C.'s going after them Indians anyway. And when we get done with that we're going to the Gallatin and live on our own ranch."

"You sure about that?" Kincaid asked.

"I am," Brady said.

223

"Me too," Franklin snapped back.

Kincaid shook his head.

"Tell me how the hell two snot-nosed kids are going to go up against two-hundred Indians."

"We ain't," said Franklin. "We're just going after the one."

Kincaid spat. "Well ain't you a pair to draw to."

He pulled his horse up, looped the pack horse's lead rope around the saddle horn and stepped down from the saddle. He paced back and forth, kicked the dirt every time he turned and spat again.

"And just exactly what the hell do you expect me to do about it?" he asked.

Brady looked down at Kincaid.

"Just help us find the one who killed my family."

Kincaid threw his hat in the dirt. He leaned over the saddle, draping his arms across the cantle. He looked sideways at Brady and then over his shoulder at Franklin. Two dirty-faced boys looked back at him.

"Damn me," he said. "I'll do it on one condition. We find him and whatever happens, happens. If we don't get killed, we part company and you two are out of my life forever."

Brady grinned and Franklin smiled. Franklin stuck out his hand.

"Deal," he said.

They shook. Kincaid picked up his hat and remounted. They started up the trail behind the fresh hoof prints of hundreds of horses.

Kincaid was quiet. The boys rode one on either side of him and neither spoke.

"For starters," Kincaid said. "The one we're looking for is a Sioux, not a Comanche."

"How do you know that?" Franklin asked.

"Their dress, their ponies, the way they did up their hair and war paint. Then we heard them talk. I don't know the language much, but it was Lakota Sioux . . . no doubt about that."

"You think we can find them?" Brady asked.

"We'll sure try. Just hope they don't find us first."

The talk stopped and they rode another twenty minutes, then Franklin bristled and gave Brady the Blackfoot high-sign. At the same time Kincaid dismounted and circled the brush at the bend in the trail with his pistol drawn and cocked.

Franklin and Brady held the horses and stood by with their rifles ready. Suddenly a scream ripped through the afternoon quiet and the boys jumped for cover. The brush moved and Kincaid's muffled voice drifted forth.

"Hold your fire boys."

Kincaid pushed the branches aside and emerged with a tattered white girl and a ragged woman in a blood-soaked dress.

"It's Allison," Brady said. "And her mother."

"B.C., get me a blanket off my bedroll," ordered Franklin, as he rushed out to assist Mrs. Granger.

The girl appeared unhurt, but the woman had lost a lot of blood. When they laid her on the blanket she looked at them through glazed eyes, then collapsed into unconsciousness.

"Franklin, bring me the canteen off my pack horse," Kincaid ordered.

He stripped the scarf from around his neck as Franklin returned with the water. He quickly checked the woman for injuries.

"We're in luck. Bullet went clean through her arm. Missed the bone, but she's been bleeding some."

Allison sat blank-eyed and still, her focus somewhere inside her for she regarded neither her rescuers nor her surroundings. Franklin draped his blanket over her shoulders but she gave no sign she noticed or cared.

"We can't stay here," Kincaid said. "There's a place back the way we came, about a mile or two. It's got grass, a small creek and a few trees for protection. Let's get these two back there before it gets dark."

"Franklin, you go cut two strong saplings about fifteen feet long. We're going to have to make up a travois for that pack horse of yours. Brady, you get some of that rope out and then repack as much of Franklin's load onto your trail horse as you can."

The boys hurried about while Kincaid tried to speak with Allison, who refused to say anything or to look directly at him. He checked to make sure she wasn't injured then left her to help the boys get their outfit together.

It was almost dark when they settled into camp. A small, clear stream ran nearby. They had protection from the wind and were hidden from the trail. Kincaid insisted on a cold camp that night out of fear the renegades may have left behind a small band of warriors to protect their flanks and to return to investigate the funeral fire he was sure they saw.

They cleaned Mrs. Granger's wound, treated and bound it, and when she regained consciousness Kincaid gave her water from a tin cup. She drank and coughed then drank again.

"Not too fast." Kincaid held the cup in her hands. "How you feeling?"

"Allison?" she said, her eyes wild and darting.

"She's right here, ma'am," he said pointing to the girl.

The woman calmed and she drank again. "My husband?" she asked.

Kincaid shook his head. Her eyes were cold and there was no expression in them. She pushed herself up and managed to get to her knees. She took hold of her daughter and held her face and turned it to hers. For a moment there was nothing, then they hugged and both began to weep.

"It's all right, sweetheart. It's all okay now," she said. "We're okay now."

Allison buried her face in her mother's matted hair. "Who's here?" she asked between sobs.

Her mother patted her back and rubbed it and spoke softly. "It's Brady and Franklin and Mr. Kincaid," she answered.

Allison pulled back and looked around. She saw Brady first, then Franklin and then Kincaid. She reached an arm out without releasing her grip on her mother and each of them embraced her.

Brady's mind was numb. Neither he nor Franklin or Kincaid had slept in the last thirty-eight hours, and it was all he could do to summon a clear thought. He looked at Allison. In a certain way he was jealous. At least she still had her mother. He had no one. It was a fleeting thought and made him ashamed for thinking it.

Brady moved around to sit in front of Allison and gently lifted her chin to look directly into her eyes. He spoke to her in a slow, quiet voice.

"Are you all right, Allison?"

She nodded. He touched her arm.

"I'm okay," she said in a whisper so soft Brady could barely hear her.

"Do you know if my father and my brothers are all right?"

Brady looked at Kincaid then over at Franklin.

Kincaid gave him a nod. Brady's eyes were red-rimmed and his soft voice cracked when he tried to speak. She looked at him and he wanted so badly to tell her they were fine. He cleared his throat and spoke with such a gentle manner she began weeping before he finished.

"We put them next to mine. They weren't as bad as most. We put markers on them, and Travis prayed some over them."

Mrs. Granger listened and her body lurched as she held herself back, and when she could resist no longer, she held Allison and they wept until there were no more tears.

They made their beds and Kincaid walked to the edge of the clearing as the others slept. He sat, his back to a tree and his thoughts a spin, and crossed his feet and watched the stars. Of all the stars in the sky and all the people on earth he wondered about the order of it all. He stared a long time contemplating the circumstances that had beset him.

CHAPTER TWENTY-SIX

Kincaid let them sleep more than an hour past daybreak. He built a fire and started the coffee and cleaned the fish he caught while they slept.

Brady awoke first. He looked out from his blankets, his hair mussed and his face puffy. He stumbled to the fire in his stocking feet, his boots in his hands and his hat set back on his head.

"Morning," Kincaid said.

"Morning."

"Sleep good?"

"I guess . . . I don't remember."

"Still sleepy?"

"Uh huh."

Kincaid handed the boy a cup. "Hold this, I'll pour you some coffee."

"Thanks."

"Are you going to be this worthless all day?" Kincaid asked.

Brady smiled. "No, I'll probably get worse."

Brady sat back and sipped the hot coffee. "You know, Travis, I feel like I just dreamed all this. It feels like we can go back to the wagons and everything will be like it was."

Kincaid turned the fish and nodded. "Yeah, I know," he said.

"It wasn't no dream, was it?"

"No, it wasn't. Go wake the others," Kincaid ordered.

They ate breakfast. Talk was spare and Franklin was unusually quiet. Kincaid stood and scraped his plate into the fire.

"Mrs. Granger, do you feel like you're strong enough to travel again?"

She didn't answer immediately, and Kincaid hoped her spirits were in better shape than the rest of her. He remembered her from the first few weeks on the trail. She had fine features with sunshine eyes and a friendly smile. To look at her now it was impossible to recognize her as the same woman.

She looked at him. Her face was swollen and cut and her eyes were dark and lined and her hair was matted with blood and dirt. She tried to smile.

"Yes, I think so," she replied. "But we have

to go back to the wagons."

Kincaid knew that was coming.

"Yes, ma'am, we will," he said, knowing it would do no good to try to dissuade her. He dreaded the thought of how she and the girl would react when they came face to face with the massacre site.

"Thank you Mr. Kincaid, that's very kind of you," she said with resignation. Then she stood up slowly and walked nearer where Kincaid was busying himself packing up the camp.

She spoke quietly, hoping to be out of earshot of the youngsters.

"What will become of Allison and myself? We can't possibly make the trip on to California alone and we can't go back." With that, she began to cry.

Travis wanted to put his arm around her and comfort her but felt awkward about it and decided not to.

"Do you have anyone in California that you know?" the cowboy asked, as he began to lay the groundwork for what was quickly beginning to feel like a thinly constructed solution to her dilemma.

"Yes, my sister and her husband live near San Francisco, and we had planned to stay with them until . . ." the tears started again and ran down her cheeks as she paused to compose herself. She continued, "until . . . John could find work and we could get our own place." She took in a deep breath, held it for a moment then exhaled as she closed her eyes. Looking back up at Kincaid, she said, "I'm sorry."

"Ma'am, you've been through a lot. It's all right," he replied, admiring her courage.

"If we push steady we can make it to Fort Bridger in about two weeks. I passed two other companies coming up behind us on my way back from St. Joe. They should both be through Fort Bridger within a week or two of the time we get there. Maybe you can join then and go on to California like you planned."

Diverting to Fort Bridger was not what Kincaid wanted to do, but Mrs. Granger and her daughter were a new set of obligations he hadn't counted on, and he knew he had to get them to Fort Bridger, or he might find himself promising to take them all the way to California.

Heading back down the trail to the wagons, Allison rode double with Brady on Buffalo Dancer. Mrs. Granger refused to be carried on the travois and chose to ride one of the pack horses instead.

The trail was fresh and dusty and well traveled by the hooves of many Indian ponies, and the thought of the renegades traveling here only a day earlier un-nerved Allison. She clung to Brady and he patted her hand where it gripped his shirt.

In an upper clearing grazed oxen, mules, and horses left behind by the Indians. Further along the trail the bloated carcass of a slaughtered oxen lay stiff-legged and pocked with bullet holes. When Allison saw it she turned her head and buried her face into Brady's back.

Brady looked back at Mrs. Granger when they encountered the first of the litter of personal effects and clothing scattered about in a chaotic manner. She covered her mouth with her hand. Brady turned his head back and dreaded every step the horse took.

As the riders approached the first battered wagon, a large buzzard, gorged on the rotting flesh of a half-eaten mule, stretched his wings to lift off. Annoyed that his greedy feeding orgy had been interrupted, he set down heavily on another fly-infested carcass thirty feet away.

The air was still. The smell of rancid flesh and evacuated bowels hung over the area, gagging Allison, who held her hand over her nose as she complained to Brady.

Brady reached into his back pocket and

withdrew a dirty rag.

"Put this over your nose," he said. "It'll cut down the smell some."

"Oh Brady, this is awful," she said.

At that point they turned off the trail and followed Kincaid through the trees. The smell of death was now downwind from them, and they entered the welcome shade of the tall aspens. They continued through a break in the woods and emerged onto the graveyard meadow.

Kincaid dismounted. The others did likewise. The sun crossed the trees at a mid-morning angle, casting long shadows across the clearing and lighting the makeshift wooden markers at the end of each fresh grave.

Kincaid showed Mrs. Granger and her daughter to the Granger markers then nodded and returned to where the boys stood the horses.

Franklin handed Kincaid his reins. He took off his hat and walked to the far end of the meadow and stood at the foot of the graves he had dug for his parents. He bowed his head and his body shook. He stood there a long time, then walked off in to the trees to be alone.

Brady, who the night before appeared so much older to Kincaid, looked like a little boy, kneeling and crying on the graves. Kincaid watched him. He spoke, but Kincaid could not hear him. Kincaid turned away, pushed his hat back and put his face in his hands.

Brady stood and wiped his nose on his sleeve and thumbed the tears from his eyes, then he walked to the sunny end of the meadow and picked a thick handful of wild flowers. He returned to the graves and stopped, first at his mother's, then his father's, then those of his sister and brother and laid fresh flowers on each one. Then he did the same for the Stilwells and the Grangers. He turned to leave, but the graves with no markers stood lonely and unattended, and Brady returned to the meadow where the wild flowers grew and collected a great many of them and distributed them to each of the anonymous burial plots and said something over each one before he returned to the horses.

Brady and Franklin stood by the horses with Kincaid for more than two hours before Kincaid went into the graveyard and convinced Allison and her mother to leave.

They rode in silence to a grove of trees where a creek ran through and Kincaid made the ladies comfortable and instructed them to wait while he and the boys made a final trip back to the wagons.

They located the Granger wagon and righted and reloaded it as best they could. They caught up a mule team and hitched it up, then employed a team of oxen to clear the trail to allow the wagon to pass. Kincaid and the boys, with their well-stocked outfit, re-entered the grove by late afternoon. Clouds piled against the mountain peaks, and the sun disappeared and the air grew cold.

Mrs. Granger shivered as she and Allison climbed into the wagon. She recognized the wagon, but not the team and, apart from a weak smile, she showed no interest in the contents nor the order in which she found things. Mrs. Granger held her arm around her daughter, and Kincaid climbed up into the seat beside them. He clucked the mules on and when they passed the scattered livestock, the animals slowly milled and fell in behind them as they had done every day since they left St. Joseph. The last of the funeral pyre still smoked and they passed it without slowing.

Franklin and Brady rode a mile ahead watching the trail and sharing no talk. What was on their minds was private and neither would breach the privacy of the other.

For the next two weeks the solitary wagon

tilted and bumped along like a detached ship lost at sea. On the fifteenth day, after they left the killing grounds, the tiny remnant of the Garrett wagon train limped into Fort Bridger.

Chapter Twenty-Seven

At Fort Bridger the heavy gates stood open and the single wagon proceeded through, attracting more attention for the oddity of its singularity than had it been a full company.

Kincaid led his party across the parade ground and a solemn reception of soldiers and on-lookers could only imagine what had befallen this unlikely arrival. Kincaid located the post commander and made a full report of the massacre. He secured accommodations for the Grangers and made provisions to sell the extra livestock on their behalf.

He told the boys they would layover one day, trade what stock and provisions they had for those they needed, then they would set out after the Comanche war party.

The boys settled in as best they could, and just before dark a trapper trotted his pony and packhorse through the gates. Brady and

Franklin watched from the quartermaster's doorway as the trapper greeted first one then another and another of those he knew by name. He seemed to know everyone as he rode across the grounds and stopped at the hitch rail where the boys stood.

He touched his hat. "Boys," he said.

They touched their hats and Franklin said, "sir."

Brady nodded.

"Name's Charles Du Mer," he said, in a big but gentle voice.

"I'm Franklin T. Stilwell," Franklin said, as he stuck out his hand.

"My name's Brady McCall," Brady said, and he stuck out his hand too.

"And what brings you boys way out here?"

Franklin nodded towards the wagon conspicuously out of place among the military and trade wagons.

"We come out from St. Joseph," Franklin said.

"Were you part of the Garrett outfit I heard about?" the trapper asked.

The boys both nodded.

The trapper turned and undid the first knot on his pack load.

"I'm sorry for what happened to you lads . . . you're lucky to be alive."

The trapper untied two more knots and

looked over at Brady.

"Will you hold this while I set my rigging down?"

He handed Brady his Hawken rifle, and Brady handled it with great reverence.

"Life can be hard on a man out here," he said. "But if you got it in you, there ain't no better life anywhere."

He set his pack down and reached for the rifle. He tied the rifle onto his saddle and then turned to face the boys.

"What are your plans now?"

"We're going to kill the Indian who killed my ma," Brady said in a voice flat and hard.

"Ever kill a man?" the trapper asked.

Brady and Franklin looked at each other. Franklin looked down at his boots then looked the trapper straight in the eye.

"Yeah, we both did," he said, his eyes unflinching and no brag or regret in his voice.

The trapper looked them both over, looked at Brady, then at Franklin.

"It's no concern of mine," he said. "But I can tell you, no good ever came of letting revenge get control of your life."

"Well, that's fine for you," Franklin said. "But you ain't us."

The trapper smiled.

"No, I know I ain't. But if you're dead set

on it, maybe I can help some."

"How can you help us?" Brady asked.

"Well, I can tell you where to start looking for the ones you're after."

Brady's eyes widened. Franklin asked the trapper to wait and ran off to fetch Kincaid. When they returned, Kincaid introduced himself and told the trapper what he knew. The trapper put that together with what he saw and concluded the war party he encountered was the same one.

"They was packing dead and traveling slow when I came up on their camp at Sandy Creek," the trapper said. "Maybe half a dozen Sioux rode with them. Renegades for certain by my thinking."

"How much of a lead do they have on us?" Kincaid asked.

"Maybe a week," the trapper said. "But three men traveling light could make that up. And if you was to take the June Pass, you could maybe catch them on the Ottertail."

Can you tell us how to get there?" Kincaid asked.

"Yeah sure. I'll draw you out a map."

Brady watched the trapper talk and looked at the broken fingernails and rough hands and buckskins and moccasins. The trapper's blue eyes shone from skin darkened by the sun and, when he smiled, deep creases made them come alive. Brady couldn't figure him out, and when the trapper left to tend his other business, Brady followed him.

"Mr. Du Mer?" Brady began.

The trapper interrupted. "My friends call me Charlie."

"Charlie?"

"Yes, Charlie."

Brady smiled.

"Okay, Charlie. What's it like up in them mountains where you trap?"

"Sit down," Charlie said, pointing to the bench on the plank-board walk in front of the commander's office. "Up in them mountains is places no white man has seen. It's like it was when the good Lord left it. Lakes blue and clear so's you can see clean to the bottom. Every manner of game and fish . . . if you take to fish, which I seldom do."

"What about the Indians?"

"Some's good, some's bad . . . pretty much like folks everywhere. I always found them to be fair and generally they treat you like you treat them."

Brady looked up at him with a skeptical expression and a little anger stirring in his eyes.

"Don't hate them all because of what happened. If you got to hate someone, which I don't recommend, hate the ones that did it, but don't hate every one because of it."

They talked of the weather, and Charlie made the weather come to life as though it were a person, and Brady understood the meaning of what he said. He talked of nature and creatures and freedom, and Brady asked many questions.

They talked late into the night and Brady's head was filled with grand images and a longing planted like a tiny seed waiting for the right time to germinate.

The next morning, Kincaid and the boys stood their saddle horses and well-provisioned packhorses at the livery where Amelia and Allison Granger met them to bid them farewell.

The post commander assured Kincaid the Grangers would be looked after and would join the next wagon train bound for California.

"Travis," said Amelia Granger, "I cannot tell you how indebted Allison and I are to you and the boys. We owe you our lives and I will never forget your kindness. I sincerely hope we meet again someday."

Mrs. Granger hugged the cowboy, then she thanked Brady and Franklin, and kissed each of them on the cheek.

Franklin pulled down his hat, "You take

care, ma'am." Brady just blushed.

Allison thanked Kincaid and threw her arms around him. He wrapped her up in his arms and said, "You'll do just fine in California."

Allison walked over to Franklin. She stood there a moment, then gave him a hug.

Franklin stammered, "Uh, maybe we'll see you some day, Allison."

Allison got to Brady. He braced himself for a hug. Allison took his hands in hers and held them to her cheek. Her eyes welled with tears.

"Brady McCall, I will never ever forget you . . . ever."

Brady felt a knot in his throat. He clinched his teeth and swallowed. He touched her face with his fingertips.

"Allison," he began, then he stopped. "I won't forget you either."

Brady looked over his shoulder a long time and Allison stood there waving and he watched until he could see her no longer.

CHAPTER TWENTY-EIGHT

They left Bridger, and Travis Kincaid set out on the trail of the renegades at an exhausting pace. With a singularity of purpose as lethal as that of a timber wolf on a blood scent, he pursued the tracks of the war party with relentless determination. His eyes missed nothing, and what talk he did make was spare, and he made no concessions to the inexperience or young age of the boys.

Kincaid was frighteningly serious. Every ounce of his energy was drawn together and concentrated on the task of reading the trail left by the Comanche. He was like a man the boys no longer knew, and neither boy dared question him or divert his attention away from the signs of the renegades as they bore deeper into the wilderness.

They watched him with sideways glances. They strained to see the invisible signs that caused him to drop unexpectedly from his horse to the ground, where he would examine bent grass, an overturned stone, or an obscure impression in the flinty earth.

Then, with no noticeable reason for his action, he would stand and he would raise his head and look about. Without uttering a word he would remount, and they would be off again. Each day the pattern was the same. The cold, lonely nights were spent in restless sleep with meager sustenance, and before dawn they were mounted and waiting for daylight.

On the sixth day they rode high where the air was thin and the timberline was a clear demarcation between the forested slopes and the barren granite summit. The trail turned sharply up along a rocky butte where the aspen trees grew thick, then it dropped abruptly down into a high-mountain meadow and showed evidence of having been trodden by the hooves of many horses as it disappeared into the shadows of the close-growing pines. Beyond the stand of Ponderosa pines lay Sandy Creek, a snow-fed flow deceptively gentle with treacherous holes and poor footing for the horses.

From Charlie's description, Kincaid recognized the broad meadow where the river widened and formed a clear, deep pool. The river tumbled gently over the rocks, and green grass grew up to the water's edge. Kincaid raised his hand to signal the boys. They halted and held the horses. Kincaid dismounted.

"This is it," he said softly. "This is where Charlie saw the war party."

His eyes searched the trees below. The late afternoon shadows stretched across the clearing, making it difficult to distinguish the real from the imagined.

"The old Frenchman must have been back up in there," Kincaid said, pointing to a thin line of trees high above that rimmed the clearing and angled off back to higher ground to the southwest.

"By the time he got from here to Bridger it had to have been a week or better," Kincaid said, thinking aloud. "We gained ground on them."

Brady's heart pounded in his chest. He was preoccupied with vengeance to the point that he refused to think of the consequences when they did overtake the renegades. His stomach churned. Charlie's warning rang in his ears.

"Always keep the edge. If you lose it out here, you're a dead man."

Brady wasn't thinking about the consequences of what they were doing, but Charlie's warning and Kincaid's caution made his nerves come alive, and he leaned down from the saddle and tilted his head toward Kincaid.

"Hey, Travis, do you think any of 'em's still around here?"

"I don't think so, but you boys stay put. I'm going down for a look."

Kincaid was gone almost an hour. The air turned cold. The sun dropped behind the jagged peaks that rimmed the western edge of the meadow. The bright colors that surrounded them turned to gray shadows before Kincaid walked out from the lower stand of trees. He approached with his rifle resting in the crook of his arm.

"They were here all right. Just like Charlie said. They rode out heading due north, and they aren't more than two, three days ahead of us," Kincaid said, catching his breath.

"We'll rest the horses and be on our way at first light."

Franklin hobbled the horses while Kincaid set up camp and started a fire.

Brady stood knee deep in the numbing-cold creek. He stood motionless, poised with a spear he had cut from a nearby willow. Suddenly he thrust the sharply-pointed shaft into the water and lifted out a glistening rainbow trout.

In one easy movement he cast the fish up

away from the water in the direction of the camp. In another quick motion he penetrated the brilliant surface of the water and brought out a larger fish that twisted and thrashed to free itself. When he had more than a dozen of the small trout piled in the tall grass he waded out of the creek and set to cleaning.

That night they sat hunkered and staring, silently devouring the fish like primeval hunters before the light of the fire that projected their gaunt shadows against the trees behind them.

For the next three days they followed the trail from Sandy Creek and, just as the trapper supposed, the Indians changed course and headed east, making their way with no regard for covering their trail.

Kincaid knew this route would detour South Pass, cross the summit through the rugged mountains on treacherous game trails, then exit the eighty-mile long bowl at Muddy Gap. The fresh tracks of the renegades hammered the ground into a clear path that headed in a direct line up the western slope of the Divide. The three searchers swung their horses out onto the trail in pursuit.

Sweat foamed on the breast collars of the pack animals, and the headstalls of the saddle horses ran wet and shiny. The horses' sides heaved as they sucked in the thin air and plodded upward. Kincaid gauged the spent horses' stamina and finally pulled off the trail and dismounted.

"Get off and let 'em blow," he said.

Franklin drank from his canteen and wiped the back of his hand across his mouth to catch the dripping water as it ran down his chin. He offered the canteen to Brady. Brady shook him off.

Standing next to Buffalo Dancer, Brady loosened the stallion's cinch, then walked him in the shade to cool out. The buckskin snorted as he dropped his head to nip the tops off the tender clumps of grass that grew where the sun warmed the ground between the thick stands of trees.

Brady moved slowly around, checking his horse's feet and legs, then did the same with his pack horse. The load was secure, there was no galling from the rigging, and both horses were now breathing easily. He re-tightened the cinch on his saddle and looked impatiently over at Kincaid.

"Travis," he said, with annoyance in his voice. "Can we get going before we get too far behind?"

"Brady look at these damn horses. They're plumb wore out."

Kincaid paused.

"I know what you're thinking," said Kincaid. "But you gotta understand something. Everything's got to rest, even those renegades. Those Indians don't know we're after them, and they're in no particular hurry. And you can bet on one more thing. If they did know, they wouldn't try to outrun us. They'd double back and finish our sorry asses."

Kincaid was right and Brady knew it, but that didn't make it any easier.

By nightfall they had climbed to a point just below the summit. Darkness forced them to stop.

They made no fire. The three trackers gave in to exhaustion, wrapped themselves in thin wool blankets, and slept with hunger gnawing at their insides, while the cold brought on convulsive shivers. They collapsed into unconsciousness.

An hour before daybreak Kincaid had the pack horses loaded and his own mount saddled when he woke the boys. The moon was low in the sky and there was only the slightest suggestion of dawn behind the sharp ridge to the east.

In minutes they were headed up the steep grade. The horses plodded and their breath steamed out in smoky trails in the frosty air.

Brady's teeth chattered and he held his arms tight against his chest. If Franklin was cold, he didn't show it.

They hadn't eaten in almost a day, and the food they packed was gone except for a small sack of salt and a handful of beans. Now, in the half-light of dawn, Brady watched for the movement of anything, bird or beast, suitable for sustenance.

Gradually the sun shone in their faces from an oblique angle. The horses lunged up the last steep grade of the trail, and the riders emerged from the forest to gaze down onto the Great Divide Basin.

The air was cool and the rich colors of the early morning splashed across the landscape in spectacular beauty. In the shade of a blue spruce a young buck raised its head and sniffed the breeze, switching its tail and searching the highlands with nervous, darting eyes.

Kincaid decided to risk a shot, calculating the Indians were still too far ahead to hear it. He raised his rifle slowly and took careful aim. He would not risk a second shot.

His finger eased down on the trigger, and as quickly as the loud report of the shot echoed down the mountain, the deer's heart exploded in his chest, and he dropped where he stood.

Kincaid built a smokeless fire. The three trackers crouched in a small circle around the fire and silently gorged themselves on the fresh meat. The trail had become their obsession and eating only a necessary inconvenience that delayed and hindered them. This morning the meat tasted especially sweet.

With full stomachs and tired muscles they emerged from the east end of the basin and followed the trail north where it crossed the mountains at Muddy Gap then crossed the Sweet Water River before heading east once again.

Splashing up onto the north bank of the Sweet Water River, they followed the trail where it led them for almost three miles before Kincaid pulled his horse up abruptly.

"Damn," he grunted.

He leaped from the saddle and paced back and forth across the horse tracks, kneeling and touching the impressions of the hoof marks, then getting up and walking with long strides to both outside edges of the tracks left by the Indians.

"What is it, Travis?" Franklin asked.

"They split up on us. Twenty or thirty of them never came out on this side of the river. I should have caught it sooner. I just didn't figure it out until we got to this stretch of softer ground. Head on back to the river. If we don't find that other trail, we could have half the damn war party breathing down our necks before we know it."

Back at the river, Kincaid left Brady to mind the pack horses while he sent Franklin west along the river's edge and he rode east. Brady waited nervously. As anxious as he was to overtake the renegades, he did not count on the possibility of them doubling back and attacking.

Thirty minutes later Kincaid galloped back.

"All right," he said. "We got it. They used the river to cover their tracks and rode out about two miles downstream. They're riding northeast and it doesn't look like they're on to us."

Brady was visibly angry and frustrated. Now they had two trails to follow and he knew they couldn't track both bands of fleeing warriors. He was certain their quarry had out-smarted them.

CHAPTER TWENTY-NINE

"Well now what?" Brady said to Kincaid. "We can't follow all of 'em, and how we gonna know which way them damn Sioux went?"

"Brady, I'm betting the Sioux went with this bunch," said Kincaid, pointing in the direction taken by the smaller group.

"They're heading east toward Sioux territory. If I'm right, the big part of the war party will turn south and start back to their own country once they reach the flatland."

Brady clinched his jaw and gritted his teeth.

"Well, that's a lot of tracks and we didn't see that many Sioux with the Comanche. Why would they all leave and go this way?"

"I don't know for sure," said Kincaid. "Ride on upriver and fetch Franklin. If we lose track of them now, we may never find them."

They descended the mountain and crossed

the foothills. The smaller war party made no effort to cover their tracks, but as the land leveled out it was dry and hard and rocky and the trail became more difficult to follow. When sign was clear it showed the tracks of twenty-three, maybe twenty-four horses, all headed east and moving at a brisk pace. Not hurried, but deliberate.

The temperature at the lower elevations turned hot, and Kincaid and the boys tied their coats on behind their saddles, and as they rode they squinted into the sunlight and sweat ran down their backs.

The treed foothills flattened into a broad plain of golden grass, and the only trees that grew were those at the creek banks and springs. The trackers pressed on, stopping only to rest the horses or take water when they could. They ate salted strips of venison and never made a fire. Rest came only as a necessity, and they did not stop long in one place.

Kincaid rode ahead. Brady and Franklin followed with the packhorses. At the top of a shallow bluff Kincaid waited and surveyed the terrain. The boys approached and Kincaid walked back toward them, leading his horse.

"Well boys, looks like this is it," he said, as he paused and looked over the broad expanse of earth that lie before them. Travis's voice sounded resolute, and he looked over at the younger boy.

Brady bristled. "What do you mean this is it?"

He shook his head. "We ain't quittin'," he said, setting his jaw and glaring back at the cowboy.

"Yeah, come on Travis, we done come too far to give up now," Franklin added.

Kincaid looked up at the boys and shook his head.

"We're not quitting. Get down off your horses, I want to show you something."

With puzzled looks on their faces, the boys followed Kincaid to a nondescript patch of bare ground. The hard, red, dirt was rocky and dry, but it didn't look any different than a hundred other places they passed that morning.

"See them brush marks?" Kincaid said, pointing out barely visible lines among the many sets of hoof prints.

As they walked on, Kincaid showed the boys where, one by one, five sets of brush marks left the trail in a northerly direction.

"What does that mean?" Brady asked.

"Well, it looks like the Sioux are heading home, and the Comanche are covering the trail for them."

"Travis, that don't look like nothing," Franklin said. "All them horse tracks go this way," he said, whipping his hand straight down the trail.

"That's how they want it to look," said Kincaid.

"It's an old Comanche trick. The lead riders tie onto loose brush and drag it behind while the others ride over the trail. When the brush-draggers pull out they don't leave a mark, and everything else looks pretty much the same. Next thing you know, there's one less set of tracks in the bunch and a fella won't even miss them in the count," Kincaid said.

"Now, look at this," he said, walking along an invisible line where he claimed the brush-dragger rode.

"This one got a little careless, or maybe the brush rolled over, but he left a mark."

Sure enough, one unshod hoof print stood out just as clear as if someone had left a road sign.

"These marks are your Sioux heading for home. The rest of these tracks will head straight down the trail far enough to cover the cut-offs, then they'll turn south to join up with the rest of the band."

Kincaid counted five sets of brush tracks, and he knew they belonged to the Sioux.

The prospect of catching up with five Sioux renegades was far more reassuring than the long-shot odds of surviving another encounter with a full war party.

"Boys, it looks like things are starting to fall our way," Kincaid said. "We got a chance if we can catch up before they run in with the rest of their tribe out there somewhere," he added, with a broad sweeping motion that took in thousands of miles of prairie.

CHAPTER THIRTY

Five Sioux warriors rode the Medicine Root River deep into Sioux territory, and three white riders followed.

The young Sioux warriors carried many scalps and rifles and bullets, and they would brag late into the night upon their return, and they would be honored among their tribe. It would be a time of celebration and joyful reunion.

In their haste the prideful young warriors left behind an uncovered trail, for they feared no reprisal.

Kincaid and the boys pushed their horses unrelentingly through the heat of the day. By late afternoon, Franklin's packhorse pulled a tendon. They stopped, unpacked the panniers, stripped the horse of his rigging, pulled its shoes, and turned it out to fend for itself. Cursing their bad luck they rode hard to make up for the delay.

At dusk the trail turned and headed out

across a rocky, alkaline flat. The hard ground and long distance finally got the best of Kincaid's packhorse. The poor beast stopped and hung his head, unable to go any further. Kincaid split up the ammunition and venison between the other horses and left everything else behind. They continued on until there was no light by which to ride, then they stopped the horses and dismounted, exhausted and hungry.

In the dark Kincaid located a small spring, and by the light of a full moon saw horse tracks and moccasin tracks, and he knew by the freshness of the tracks the Sioux now rode no more than a few hours ahead of them.

They watered the horses and dropped the saddles, then wrapped in thin wool blankets and curled up to sleep. They slept for two hours. A full moon stood high in the starlit sky.

Kincaid got up and walked out into the dry flats without saying anything to the boys. Time was running out. They were well into Sioux territory, and Kincaid knew they had to overtake the warriors before they rejoined their tribe. He awoke the boys.

Brady and Franklin sat up, looked at each other through tired, red eyes and said nothing.

Kincaid reached down for his saddle. He glanced over toward the boys. "Mount up," he said.

The boys moved stiffly. The horses stood with their heads hung low and protested with a groan when the boys threw on the saddles and pulled the cinches tight.

Moon shadows were sharp and the extra light gave Kincaid the advantage he needed to stay on the trail and close the lead on the Sioux. Brady and Franklin watched carefully for the signs that led Kincaid through the rocks and over the hard ground. Falling behind with Franklin, Brady pulled his horse in closer and whispered.

"How can he tell where we're going?"

"I don't know," said Franklin. "He learned it from the Indians, I guess. He's acting strange, ain't he?"

Brady didn't reply. He just watched as Kincaid leaned low over the side of his horse's neck and read the trail. The Big Dipper rotated to a vertical position in the northern sky, and when it did, Travis and the boys rode out of the alkaline flat and onto a gentle roll of brush-covered hills. The trail continued due east and down the precipitous slope of a steep ravine.

Kincaid started down first. Just below the rim the loose rock gave way. He fought it, but his horse's front legs buckled, and the horse plunged downward head first, rolling, sliding, and tumbling, end-over-end.

Kincaid was helpless as the horse rolled over on top of him. Instinctively he was able to kick free of the saddle, but before he could roll clear the horse crashed down upon him a second time. This time Kincaid did not move, and the horse continued the long slide down the embankment.

Brady and Franklin watched as the horse rotated limp and unmoving, then came to rest at the bottom of the washed-out draw.

They leaped from their horses and slid down the steep bank to where Kincaid lay face-down. Franklin rolled him over on his back. In the bright moonlight they could see his face was covered with blood, and his nose was badly distorted.

Franklin pulled him up by his shirt and shook him.

"Travis, please don't be dead," Franklin pleaded. Kincaid did not respond.

"Brady, get me a canteen," he shouted to his young friend, who knelt beside him. Brady scrambled up the hill.

Franklin held Kincaid, praying the cowboy was not dead. Then Kincaid moaned, and blood oozed from his mouth when he tried to speak. Kincaid's eyes were glazed and unfocused. He did not try to move as he struggled to regain his senses. Brady returned with the canteen and a rag.

"Is he alive?" Brady asked.

"He's hurt bad, but he's alive. Give me that water," Franklin said, as he reached for the canteen.

Franklin poured the water carefully over Kincaid's face, and the cowboy pulled himself up slowly into a sitting position. Diluted blood ran freely from his nose and mouth.

Kincaid reached out and clutched the canteen. He took a small amount of water into his mouth, then spit it out, thick with blood. He did this repeatedly, until the bleeding subsided.

Then he tried to blow his nose, but it was swollen and painful and plugged with broken cartilage and bloody mucus.

"Son-of-a-bitch broke my nose," Kincaid mumbled through puffed lips.

"Travis, it sure enough looked like you was killed the way that horse of yours came down on top of you," Brady said.

"Did he get back up?" asked Kincaid.

"He's still laying down there," Franklin said, nodding toward the bottom of the draw.

"Brady, take your knife. Go down and

check him out. If he's still alive, cut his throat. If his neck isn't broke, his leg is. Either way, this is as far as he goes," Kincaid said, sitting up straighter.

Brady looked at Kincaid. He hesitated, hoping Kincaid would reconsider and send Franklin.

"Brady, we can't risk a shot. This is something you need to do," Kincaid said, noting the boy's reluctance.

Brady nodded and checked his knife, then started down the steep incline. At the bottom of the ravine Brady could make out the dark form of the saddle horse stretched out in the rocks. He moved closer, hoping the horse would be dead. Brady saw no sign of life so he crouched lower to see if the horse was still breathing.

Suddenly the frightened animal lurched, and Brady jumped back. Startled and shaken, he waited for the horse to calm down. The horse thrashed and rose up on his forequarters, but could get no support from the hind legs, spread uselessly out at odd angles. The horse tried once more, then gave up.

Brady watched the horse, whose bewildered eyes didn't understand why his legs no longer responded. The boy moved in closer to the horse and dropped to his knees near the head. His hands shook as he ran his fingers down the groove in the horse's neck, seeking out the jugular vein. His fingers stopped when they reached a spot where the pulse was strong.

Brady bit his lip, covered the animal's near eye with his left hand, and carefully placed the sharp edge of the knife close to the skin. He closed his eyes and cut as deeply as he could.

The horse flinched. Brady felt the warm blood run thick across his hand. The animal relaxed, but he breathed a long time before his chest stopped heaving, and his muscles jerked a long time after his eyes turned cold, and Brady waited.

The boy stood up, walked a few steps, then vomited. He spat to clear his mouth of the foul taste, then returned to the horse to retrieve Kincaid's saddle and bridle.

He dragged Kincaid's gear to the top of the escarpment and they made camp there. Exhausted and drained, they rested until morning.

When they rode out at dawn they traveled light, carrying only what food and ammunition would fit into their bedrolls and saddle bags. Kincaid rode Brady's packhorse. He was miserable. Both eyes were black and his nose was swollen into a shapeless, purple bulb. The skin from his eyes to his upper lip was stretched tight and shiny from the swelling.

For the first two hours he repeatedly snorted and spit up gagging wads of mucus and coagulated blood. Kincaid's eyes puffed to the point the narrow slits barely let in enough light for him to see. He rode in great pain. He struggled to keep his eyes open, and for the next four hours the trail set a straight course due east. Then, somewhere in the shadow-less heat of midday, the tracks of two unshod ponies joined those of the five Sioux warriors.

CHAPTER THIRTY-ONE

The endless flatness of the country converged with gently rolling hills barren of trees and woody vegetation except where a creek ran or a spring surfaced. The three riders rode up out of a long ravine, and Franklin pulled the gray-eyed paint up sharply.

"Travis, ain't that a fire up yonder in them trees?" he whispered.

Kincaid tilted his head back and squinted through puffy eyelids.

"Damn sure is," he said.

He paused and looked at the boys. They stared at him without speaking.

"Look," he said. "We don't have to go through with this."

Brady's expression hardened and Franklin's jaw clinched.

"Sometimes enough killing is enough," Kincaid said.

The boys looked at him a long time. Kincaid coughed, snorted, and spit out a bloody wad.

"I say we finish what we started," Brady said.

Franklin nodded. "We're here. It wouldn't be right to back down now."

Kincaid drew a deep breath.

"Well, all right then," he said. "Only chance we got is to take them by surprise."

He dismounted and motioned the boys down. He nodded to a low spot in the ravine.

"We'll leave the horses down there and go in on foot."

They tied off the horses and took stock of their weapons and ammunition. Each carried a rifle, a handgun and a belt knife. They checked the weapons.

"Won't be no time to reload," Kincaid said. Then he stuck out his hand to Franklin.

"Whichever way it goes, you boys done your families proud."

Franklin shook his hand and Kincaid turned to Brady. They shook hands.

"We won't know what to do 'til we get there," Kincaid said. "So stay low, keep quiet, and shoot straight."

They followed a shallow draw into the trees, then followed the small, fast-moving stream toward the campfire smoke. Further upstream in a meadow beyond the campfire, seven Indian ponies stood hobbled in the grass near the water.

Kincaid and the boys inched up through the tangled brush to the edge of a shaded clearing where the Sioux camped and slept through the heat of the day.

Kincaid signaled the boys, pointing and holding up three fingers. As Kincaid searched the camp with his eyes, Franklin held up two fingers and pointed to a partially concealed spot in the brush where one of the braves and a young girl lay bare-skinned.

Brady spotted the other two nearby in the brush to his left, not far from where the horses grazed. A copper-skinned Indian girl lay peacefully in the arms of her young warrior. Their eyes were closed and their bare bodies lay in deep sleep on a settler's quilt spread out on the ground.

Kincaid signaled to Franklin to cover the pair nearest him and made his way to an advantaged position over the three sleeping warriors. He signaled Brady to cover the sleeping girl and the brave on the quilt. From where he stood, not ten yards away, Brady had a clear line of sight on the girl and her sleeping warrior companion.

Brady's heart pounded, his mouth went dry and his breathing was short and rapid. His hands shook. He checked his handgun and looked down to make sure the hammer was cocked on his rifle.

One of the hobbled ponies raised its head and tested the air with flared nostrils. Then another head and another came up. The lead pony pawed the ground and snorted, and when it caught the full scent of the white men, it tossed its head and whinnied.

Then everything happened at once. Gunfire echoed out in volleys from downstream where Kincaid and Franklin were positioned. There were too many shots fired. Brady knew the renegades were returning fire. Instantly, all the memories of the long night of the massacre came back to him, and Brady seethed with fear and anger.

He stepped into the clearing and screamed at the warrior and the girl as they sat rigid and stared up at him with terror-stricken eyes.

Brady hesitated. Before him sat a young girl, not much more than a child. Her face was one of innocence and she covered herself, and for a moment Brady felt embarrassed. The warrior wore no war paint and held no weapon and he was no more than sixteen or seventeen years old. His expression was fearful and the vile appearance he struck in Brady's mind the night of the massacre seemed out of place, looking at him now.

The young brave gazed at Brady with the same soft-eyed innocence he saw in the girl. *They're just kids,* Brady thought to himself. He relaxed his grip on the rifle, but stood unmoving. Two more shots rang out, then he heard Franklin call out.

"B.C. where are you?"

"Over here," Brady called back.

Franklin crashed his way through the brush and into the clearing. When he beheld the unclothed pair, he tilted his head in the direction from which he had come.

"Travis wants you to bring them two over to the fire." He pointed in the direction of the smoke.

"What happened?" Brady asked.

"You should of seen it. They fired on us, and Travis got all three of them."

They motioned the girl and the young warrior to stand and move toward the fire.

"We got the other two that was over there," Franklin said. "They ain't hurt."

Brady again motioned with his rifle for the boy and girl to stand up. When they did, the boy stepped out to the side in full view. Brady's expression ran cold and his hands trembled. Franklin looked at Brady then back at the Sioux.

The young brave's face drained of all expression and his eyes filled with fear. He reached to his throat and tore away the gold chain and necklace and dropped it at Brady's feet. The girl recoiled and held her arms tight around herself and the renegade warrior pleaded for his life.

The girl sobbed and held her hands to her mouth, and she too pleaded.

"Come on B.C., let's get them back to Travis," Franklin said in a soft voice.

Brady relaxed his grip on the rifle, and tears threatened his red-rimmed eyes. The warrior made a sign of gratitude with his right hand and when he brought his left hand up to his face it was adorned with men's rings. On his thumb he bore the one that Bill McCall had worn as long as Brady could remember.

A deafening report caused Franklin and the girl to recoil and the fifty-caliber ball from Brady's rifle split the boy's chest and sent him twisting to the ground.

Brady straddled the boy's back, jerked his head back by the hair and reached for his knife.

"No," Franklin screamed as he wrestled Brady off the warrior's back.

"He's dead. That's enough."

Franklin stood back. He looked at Brady and there was no remorse in the young boy's eyes. Brady sheathed his knife. Franklin picked up the locket and removed the rings from the dead hand. Brady stood over the body and glared, and his breathing was heavy and his heart was full of hate.

The girl wailed hysterically and stood quivering with her hands covering her mouth. Franklin was visibly shaken. He stepped forward and handed her the deer-skin dress near her feet.

"Come on B.C.," Franklin said, as he led his friend and the young girl back to the campfire.

When only the girl came to the fire the last warrior bolted for his life. He disappeared into the heavy brush along the creek, and Franklin was right behind him.

"Brady, cover the trail. I'll get the other side of the creek," Kincaid shouted as he splashed across the water and navigated the slick rocks.

Thorny brush and whipping branches tore at Franklin's clothes and slashed his skin as he charged blindly after the Indian and lost him in the heavy undergrowth. Franklin stopped to listen. All he could hear was his heart pounding in his ears and the sound of his own breath cutting sharply into his lungs as he gasped for air.

His eyes darted back and forth. Suddenly, his head snapped back and the impact of the Indian's knee in his spine drove his body forward. Franklin tried to scream for help but no air came.

Franklin's throat burned, and he reached up to get his fingers under the berry vine the warrior pulled tight around his neck Franklin dropped his pistol and clawed frantically at the choking vine. The warrior fought to pull it tighter.

Franklin grappled for the knife at his side. His bloody fingers found the handle. He jerked the knife out and slashed wildly at the boy behind him. He felt the knife penetrate and he slashed again and again. His lungs burned and he desperately choked for air.

He reached over his head and grabbed a handful of hair and pulled the warrior upon his back and drove him to the ground. He gasped for air and sucked in breath after breath, and when he turned to the warrior, the renegade held Franklin's handgun and thumbed back the hammer. He took aim, but his hands shook, and in that moment of hesitation Franklin set upon him in a wild frenzy until the young warrior lay limp and bloody and unmoving.

Franklin staggered to the creek, and when he reached the water he dropped to his knees and he submerged his hands and watched the blood turn the water red. He stayed like that until the water ran clear and Kincaid walked in beside him.

Kincaid laid his hand on Franklin's shoulder.

"Are you okay?" he asked.

Franklin looked up at him. His expression was old and ancient and, he shook his head.

"No, I'm not," he said.

Kincaid understood and together they walked out of the water and back to the camp where Brady presided over the two young girls who huddled together trembling and unable to comprehend the brutality of the three white men who invaded their camp and killed without reason.

Brady and Franklin stood mute and hollow-eyed and expressionless. Kincaid addressed them in a solemn manner.

"You boys fetch their horses . . . all of them."

Brady tilted his head to look at Kincaid, his jaw set and defiance in his eyes. Franklin stiffened.

"We're going to let these two go and take their dead with them. We got no further quarrel here."

Brady looked over at Franklin and Franklin nodded. While the boys caught up the horses Kincaid bundled each of the bodies in a blanket. He tied them off, and when the boys returned they secured each of the lifeless bundles to a horse and handed the lead ropes to the girls.

Hatred burned in the eyes of the girls but fear kept them from speaking out. Kincaid tried to explain to them, but he didn't have the words, and they stared blankly as he spoke. He stopped mid-sentence and waved them off.

Kincaid and the boys watched for a long time and when there was nothing left to watch, Brady cried.

"Why did it have to be like this, Travis?" he asked.

Kincaid shook his head. "I don't know, Brady, I just don't know."

CHAPTER THIRTY-TWO

Kincaid and the boys never spoke again of the massacre or the bitter revenge they wrought upon the five young Sioux warriors whose blood stained the sand around an un-named creek in a place they would never see again. There was no pride in what they had done and no satisfaction and no remorse. They let the nightmare end there.

Now, as they rode the trail back toward Bridger, there was an absence of purpose and, for Franklin and Brady, there was nothing left but uncertainty. Kincaid sensed it, for he felt it himself. He agonized over their circumstances but convinced himself the boys would be better off in California. He knew he could arrange accommodations for the trip once they reached Bridger. He would return to Montana to fulfill his own plans. The boys would grow up with more opportunity in California than he could offer them on a start-up ranch in the remote

Montana Territory. Then it was settled. He decided to tell the boys first thing in the morning.

The sun was full-up when the boys awoke to the sound and smell of their first campfire in more days than either could recall. Franklin and Brady pulled on their boots and stood with Kincaid near the heat of the fire.

"Morning."

"Morning, Travis."

"Morning, Travis."

"I worked out a plan last night," Kincaid said.

"So did we," Franklin said.

"Well, here's mine," Kincaid said. "And it's the one we're going with."

Brady listened, and Franklin pretended to.

"I'll get you back to Bridger, get you lined up with someone heading to California, and that'll be it," Kincaid said, as he splashed the last of his coffee into the fire.

"And that'll be what?" Brady asked.

"That will be the end of my obligation to you two," Kincaid replied.

Franklin stood up to his full height and looked Kincaid straight in the eye.

"That ain't a good plan, Travis."

"We're coming with you to Montana and help you with your ranch," Brady said.

281

"Like hell you are," Kincaid responded.

"We already decided," Franklin added.

"Seems like I ought to have some say in that," Kincaid said.

"You do. Just say, yes," Franklin said.

"Come on, Travis. You don't have no one either," Brady said. "We'll be good help."

Franklin looked at Kincaid. His expression softened, and he smiled that rogue smile of his.

"Try it for the winter, Travis. If it don't work out, me and Brady will line out for California come springtime."

Kincaid took off his hat. He wrung his face in his hands and picked his hat up and slapped the dust off on his leg.

"Look, it's hard work. It gets lonely . . . and damn cold. There ain't even a decent place to live in there. The answer has to be no."

Brady watched Franklin's expression turn to the whipped puppy look he was so familiar with when Franklin would find himself with his back against the wall and he was out of options.

"Okay, we understand," Franklin said softly.

"I'm sorry, boys. There's just no other way," Kincaid added.

"You know we got no one and nothing

waiting for us in California," Franklin said, after an uncomfortable silence.

Kincaid didn't respond. He studied the two young faces. *These boys have already seen the bottom end of it,* he said to himself. He packed his cup in his saddlebag and looked back over his shoulder.

"You saying I'm stuck with you?" he asked.

Franklin grinned. "That's pretty much it," he said.

Brady stood and Kincaid smiled.

"What the hell," Kincaid said. "Let's give it a go. If it works, it works. If it don't, it don't."

It wasn't much of a ranch. A one-room cabin stood at the far end of the valley, against the base of a gentle-sided mountain. It was built sturdy, but the chinking was in poor repair and it needed a new door.

In the wide meadow a river made up two sides of a small pasture and a lodge pole fence enclosed it. The grass grew green and tall and the valley laid at an east-west tilt, protecting it from the prevailing north wind and lending itself to mild winters. Kincaid defined the ranch in terms of the area it covered, from one mountain peak to another, and it covered an area more than a man could ride in three days.

The first day at the ranch Kincaid stood on a flat area of clear ground and used a pointer he whittled from a pine branch to sketch his plans in the dirt for Brady and Franklin to see. He showed them winter pastures and summer feeding grounds and corrals and barns and he filled it in with cattle and good horses, and when he had finished his vision was clear to the boys.

Then Kincaid smoothed a spot in the dirt with his boot. He used the branch to draw three circles at the corners of a triangle.

"This will be our brand," he said. "We'll call it the Triple Dot and burn it into the hides of the best cattle and the best horses in the territory."

And so it began. For the next six years they put all their time and energy into building one of the largest cattle operations north of the Canadian River. With windfall profits from army contracts and the cooperation of the Blackfoot Indians, the three cattlemen were able to expand the ranch, which included two divisions: the Gallatin, and the Ennis Lake Ranch.

With a growing demand for more good horses, Kincaid brought broodmares up from Texas and crossed them on Brady's stud, Buffalo Dancer. Soon, the buckskin and dun-colored offspring of Buffalo Dancer established a reputation for speed and stamina that made them the most sought after horses in the territory. No outside mares were bred to Dancer. Only mares and geldings were sold off the ranch, insuring that the topside bloodlines would remain within control of the Triple Dot.

When the boys decided to stay on that first year, Kincaid promised them each a one-third share of every new calf and every foal that hit the ground from that point forward. A nod in agreement and a handshake cemented the partnership.

Cold Montana winters and short mountain summers forged the boys into men. Travis Kincaid galvanized their youthful minds with a discipline for hard work, a sense of honor in their business dealings and more horse and cow knowledge than most men learn in a lifetime.

Franklin and Brady threw themselves into the business and, when he was fourteen, Brady was sent by Kincaid to negotiate an army beef contract, which he was sure they had little or no chance of getting. Brady, more out of naive optimism than good business skill, brought back an agreement to supply not only beef, but horses as well and at prices that virtually guaranteed the success of the ranch.

By the early spring of '47, the boys could no longer deny their restlessness. Franklin was almost twenty-two, and Brady had just turned seventeen. It was time to see what the rest of the world had to offer.

It was an agonizing decision for both the boys. They owed everything to Travis Kincaid. Their love for the man and the ranch they grew up on pulled at them with a force so strong neither boy could be the first to verbalize the feelings that now ran deeply in both of them.

Brady and Franklin sat in the mid-morning shade near the corrals where they had been since daybreak, branding, castrating and doctoring the new crop of calves. While they waited for the cowboys to bring in the next bunch, Brady put his hat on his knee and wiped the sweat from his forehead with the back of his gloved hand. He kept his head down, but directed his eyes toward Franklin.

"You'll be about twenty-two here in a few weeks won't you, old-timer?" he said casually.

"Damn sure will, what's it to you?" Franklin said, sticking his chin out defiantly.

"Oh, I was just thinking," Brady responded, leaning back against the tree.

Franklin refused to give him the satisfaction of his curiosity, and Brady finally broke the silence again.

"I'd give just about anything to see some of them places Charlie talks about, where he traps up north."

"Not me," said Franklin. "I want to see the ocean and eat off of shiny glass plates in one of them fancy hotels in San Francisco like Travis told us about."

"Do you think we'll ever do any of that?" Brady asked in a serious tone that told Franklin this was more than one of their wishful-thinking discussions.

That conversation got both young men thinking and talking, and soon the talk turned into planning, and the next thing they knew they were trying to find a way to tell Travis they had decided to answer the call.

Unable to let the uncertainty continue, Franklin and Brady agreed they would not let another day go by without telling Kincaid of their plans. At dinner that night conversation was awkward and uncomfortable. Kincaid pushed his empty plate away, got up, walked over to the big, stone fireplace and retrieved three long cigars from a box on the mantle.

He handed each of the boys a cigar and sat back down. Brady and Franklin looked at each other in confusion. This was not like Kincaid. He would occasionally enjoy a cigar himself, but early on he laid down the law and absolutely forbid the boys to smoke or chew.

Kincaid passed the light around then leaned back in his chair and let a billowy, blue cloud drift up toward the massive logs that made up the cross beams in the ceiling.

"Boys," he said. "We always been able to talk out any problems we ever had. And, we never kept anything from one another. Ain't that right?"

The boys both nodded.

Franklin managed to produce a red-hot ash at the end of his cigar and, with his natural flair for showmanship, made a big circle with his mouth and released a lop-sided smoke ring that floated irreverently across the room. Brady kicked him under the table, and Franklin looked back at Kincaid.

"That's right," Franklin said. "We always come right out and say what's on our minds."

"Well," said Kincaid, "It's natural for a young man to want to see a little more of the world."

Brady looked up at Kincaid.

"It's not like we wouldn't be back," he said.

Franklin stood. "Yeah, Travis. We figure things are caught up good here. We got good help, so's it's not like you'd be left high and dry. We'd expect the cost of the help to come out of our shares."

"Franklin, you know it's not the money. Hell, we got more than any of us ever figured on, and we never did it for the money anyway."

Kincaid moved to the fireplace and sat on down in his big chair and crossed his boots on the hearth.

"There's no good time to do what you boys need to do . . . and I guess there ain't no bad time either. But you know this is your home. Don't lose sight of that. And don't feel like you ever drifted so far or so deep you can't come back."

Both boys stood and moved to the fireplace to stand near where Kincaid sat.

Franklin spoke first.

"Travis, we owe you everything. This is home. And you're family." He reached out and squeezed Kincaid's shoulder.

"We'll be back, Travis," Brady said. "You pretty much raised us to be how we are, so you're stuck with us."

Kincaid laughed. "I figured that from the start . . . just took me a few years to get used to the idea."

Kincaid pulled his feet down and leaned forward. The boys sat on the hearth and Kincaid took a pull on his cigar.

"So, tell me about your plans."

"Well," said Brady, looking over at Franklin for reassurance, "I figured on riding north with Charlie and trapping for a while. I got in my mind a picture of all the places he talks about."

"I did pretty much the same thing when I was about your age," Kincaid said. "And you know something? I never regretted a minute of it."

"Have you given any thought to what it will take to get yourself outfitted with a decent trap line?"

"I have," said Brady. "I'm going to need to draw about two-hundred dollars and a good pack horse. I'll take Dancer for my saddle horse, if it won't weaken our breeding plans too much."

"Brady, don't you worry about that. You take Dancer. He's done his job here. We've got two of his sons that throw spitting image babies of that horse of yours. He's put his stamp on them so strong that long after he's gone, you'll see his blood in every good horse in this territory."

Brady's face shined with a look of gratitude and pride.

Kincaid turned toward Franklin. By now, Franklin had fully mastered the art of blowing smoke rings, and he proceeded to put six perfectly formed circles into the air, one right behind the other.

"Franklin, you're a natural," Kincaid said, laughing. "Why is it I get the feeling your plans won't include a trap line?"

"You know me, Travis. I never did mind a little privacy, but I don't believe a man should go too long without having someone better looking than Charlie to talk to."

Kincaid smiled.

"You got a point there," he said.

Franklin continued.

"I thought I'd try my hand in San Francisco." He laughed. "Might be a good idea to send someone ahead to tell them Franklin T. Stilwell is coming to town."

"No doubt they'll find out soon enough," said Kincaid.

"I guess you're right," said Franklin, grinning. "But I figure I'm going to need about eight-hundred dollars, a pack horse, that stripped-legged mule and Three Feathers for my saddle horse."

"It's as good as done," said Kincaid. "Do

291

you know what you are going to do when you get to California?"

"Well, I can't rightly say that I do, but I figure that'll kind a work itself out when I get there," Franklin replied.

From there, talk ran late into the night, and the lantern wick was burning low when the three friends finished reminiscing about the past six years together. A week later the boys were packed. They shook hands all around and outside the gate Franklin turned his outfit to the southwest, while Brady and Charlie took the trail north.

Just before the trail dropped away toward the river Brady turned in the saddle and waved for the last time to Travis, who was now barely visible, standing alone on the porch of the cabin.

Charlie was quiet, and Brady felt an emptiness settle over him. He wondered if he would ever again see Franklin and Travis. His thoughts were filled with a mixture of anticipation and apprehension. This was a glorious turning point in his life, and Brady could hardly contain his excitement, yet he felt he was riding away from the closest thing he may ever have to a family and a home.

The frantic sound of hoof beats pounded up the trail behind them. Brady and Charlie turned their horses, puzzled and a little un-nerved. Charlie swung his rifle to the other side of his saddle in the direction of the approaching horseman.

Through the intermittent breaks in the trees, Brady could make out the unmistakable sorrel and white markings of Three Feathers. Franklin waved his hat and yelled as he galloped toward them.

"B.C., hey B.C., hold up."

Franklin was out of breath when he bounced to a stop alongside Buffalo Dancer.

"Give me your knife," he said to Brady.

"What?" Brady asked.

"Just give me your knife, will you?" Franklin asked.

Brady slipped the knife out of its sheath and started to hand it to Franklin.

"No, I mean the whole thing," Franklin said. "I need the cover too."

Brady handed it to him. Then Franklin reached inside his shirt and handed Brady the Gros Ventre knife with the beaded sheath.

"Here," he said. "I want you to have this."

"I can't take your knife," Brady said, trying to pass it back.

"Yes, you can. It'll bring you good luck and I'd feel a whole lot better if I knew you had it. Besides, I like yours better anyway."

Franklin slid Brady's knife under his pistol belt, turned back down the trail, and waved his hat as he called back over his shoulder.

"Charlie, you take good care of B.C. or you're going to have to answer to me." Then he laughed a big laugh like his father used to and disappeared into the trees.

CHAPTER THIRTY-THREE

Charlie and Brady trapped and hunted the mountains and streams in an area that ranged from the Musselshell River in Montana Territory to the tip of the northern Rockies in the Canadian Territories.

It was a time of magnificent discovery for Brady. Under Charlie's subtle guidance he learned how to find food and shelter in a land that appeared to be inhospitable. He learned how to read the signs of nature and how to anticipate and adjust to the ever-changing weather. He learned to balance the brutal necessity of survival with the gentle tranquility of the unspoiled wilderness. He learned to take nothing for granted except his own insignificance.

Most importantly, Charlie helped Brady to understand the close relationship the Indians had with the earth, and he taught Brady the delicate balance that existed in their way of life.

The old trapper held a high respect for the Blackfoot, Nez Perce and other tribes that allowed him to hunt their lands in peace, and Brady soon developed his own high regard for these people, who would give them a place by their fire and share their last food with them and make him feel like they were honored to do so.

Brady adapted quickly and the first year of trapping was good. He loved the solitude of the wilderness and eagerly looked forward to the time he spent with his friends in the Blackfoot tribes. In quiet, thoughtful moments, Brady could not imagine himself living his life any other way.

During the second winter the two trappers put lines out in a swift, unnamed river far up in the north country. They were working out of a deserted miner's cabin where they agreed to rendezvous by the end of the week. Brady waited, but Charlie never returned.

Concerned for Charlie's safety, Brady set out on snowshoes with only a light pack and his rifle. It was not unusual for Charlie to be a few days late, but this time Brady had a bad feeling — a premonition like the ones the Blackfoot medicine men claimed were a message from the Great Spirit.

Early on the third day Brady, reached the river where Charlie had set his lines. He searched for signs of his friend, but the snow-covered ground showed only the small footprints of snowshoe rabbits, birds, and deer.

Down river he found Charlie's mittens hanging from a tree branch near the water's edge, swinging by the rawhide thong that lashed them together. Half a dozen of Charlie's traps lay in a careless heap in the rocks near the water.

Brady started downstream, and the sky began to darken with storm clouds. He searched for signs of Charlie, but found none. Then ahead, at a wide bend in the river, the water eddied in a pool around an ancient aspen shrouded in ice where it lay in the current, and embraced in its bony arms the frozen body of a man.

Bile rose in Brady's throat, and his heart pounded, and his hands trembled. He stopped at the base of the giant tree, removed his snowshoes and crawled out to retrieve the body, which had become frozen to its branches, and it took him a long time to hack away the ice to free it.

Brady pulled the body to the bank, laid it on its back, and brushed the snow from its face. The crystallized eyes were those of a stranger and the frozen skin distorted the features, but the gray beard was that of the old trapper and when he saw it, Brady wept.

He said a prayer and built a travois and rigged the frozen body to it, then lashed it to his shoulders and began the trek out.

The snow was deep, and by nightfall Brady had barely covered a mile. He ate, built a shelter in the snow, and slept. When he awoke it was still dark, and the wind blew and the snow fell and the temperature dropped. He huddled in his snow cave and looked upon the out-stretched arms and bent legs of the frozen body now covered in a thick blanket of snow so that all the angles and features of the body were lost.

At daybreak Brady brushed the snow from the body, hooked up the makeshift harness and pressed on. He stopped to drink and stopped to eat once. At night he fashioned another snow cave but this time was unable to sleep.

For three more days Brady inched his load forward. His strength left him, and his reason for hauling the body was no longer clear to him. Only his determination drove him, and on the fourth day he had nothing left to give, and his legs quit him. He sat in the snow and fought off the drowsiness. He stood and fell. He stood again and pulled the body forward a step then another and another, and this time he went down and did not get up.

He crawled to the leeward side of the frozen body and hunkered down. He did not remember going to sleep, but when he felt a hand on his shoulder, he awoke and sat upright and had no clear recollection of where he was or why he was there.

His snow-blind eyes did not recognize his Blackfoot friends, but when he heard their voices he stumbled to his feet. They insisted he leave the body. He refused and they argued, but so strong was his conviction, they finally agreed to help him return the body to the cabin.

Superstition kept the Blackfoot hunters from staying with Brady at the cabin, and they left him there with the frozen body and bid him farewell. Brady positioned the cadaver outside the door, covered it with a tarp and spent the next ten days snowed in until the storm finally broke.

Brady was rested and had his strength back, and for ten days he thought about his life, and he was not satisfied. The weather cleared, and Brady gathered dry brush and piled it high around the cabin. He carried the frozen body inside and said a brief prayer over it. He ignited the kindling and watched the cabin burn a long time.

He watched cinders flare and rise from the ashes and swirl high in the column of heat before they fell to earth. He looked around, humbled by the magnificence of his surroundings. Tall pines and spruce and aspens towered above him, reaching up to a sky shimmering blue, with delicate white clouds where once a storm ruled. He heard the wind and watched a fox watch him. But today there was an emptiness that made everything look different to him.

Watching the smoke from the cabin rise in a narrow column made his stomach knot and, at that moment, he knew he would never again set a trap or see this place the way he did when he and the old trapper presided over this wooded kingdom.

Brady watched the fire until only the ashes smoldered, then he turned Buffalo Dancer to the south and rode straight through to the Blackfoot camp on the Cut Bank River.

Brady spent the rest of that winter living among the Blackfoot. They accepted him because of the old trapper and because one among them, a shaman, saw a young white man in a vision who would bring good fortune to their tribe.

He was young and inexperienced, but Brady learned quickly. He had the natural instincts of a hunter and, thanks to the old trapper, he knew the mountains well. The Blackfoot respected a good hunter, and Brady would never return from a hunt empty handed.

Brady's dress changed and his appearance changed and his hair grew long, and he plaited and greased it and adorned himself with Blackfoot trappings. He learned the language, and he moved with the tribe and hunted with them and fought at their sides. He was more Blackfoot than white, but there was an invisible line drawn, and Brady was never invited to cross it.

They were excluded from tribal rites ceremonies of a high-religious order and they forbid him access to the medicine lodge of the Blackfoot. His closest friends, two young warriors near his age, Shy Wolf and Otter Tail, were embarrassed at his exclusion and made attempts to minimize the importance of the rituals. But it was not lost on Brady that Shy Wolf and Otter Tail took great pride in the scars they carried upon their chests from the rites of passage in the medicine lodge.

Late in the spring of 1850 the weather was warm and dry, and the tribe followed the buffalo to their summer feeding grounds as they gathered along a grassy stretch of Birch Creek. After a long winter it felt good to be on the move again. Women and children scurried about camp making preparations for the hunt and anticipating the night-long celebration that always followed a successful harvest of the buffalo.

Outside the teepees, buffalo ponies stood painted and feathered. They pawed the ground and waited impatiently. Inside, the hunters passed the pipe and the medicine man prayed for a safe and bountiful hunt.

Brady sat with the hunters, his first ceremonial participation among the elders of the tribe. He drew from the pipe, exhaled the smoke and watched it drift upward, slowly spiraling toward the slash of daylight, where it exited at the top of the lodge.

The strong tobacco dizzied him, and he heard a rumbling and felt the ground move beneath him. He looked about and the others felt it as well. They paused momentarily, and the rumble intensified and the hunters rose to their feet and scrambled for the opening.

Outside, the horizon rose and fell like a giant ocean wave of black, shaggy buffalo, amassed in a cloud of dust so immense it blocked the sun, and of such breadth there was no discernible definition to it at all.

Mothers panicked. Dogs yelped. Horses tore loose from their tethers. Children scattered out of control as the tribe scrambled for safety across the creek to higher ground, and the massive black herd bore down upon the camp.

There would be no turning the blindly stampeding herd. No stopping them and no way to save anything in its path. The dust cloud closed on the camp at a frightening speed.

From the safety of the high ground, a mother's voice screamed. Her baby, a child of three or four years of age, stood crying and immobile, out of reach and in the path of the charging buffalo.

Brady and three other warriors saw the child at the same time. All four fought their panicked horses on their lead ropes. Buffalo Dancer spun and pulled back, then calmed enough for Brady to throw a leg over the horse's back. Beside him the other three men could not get their horses under control. Two pulled free and ran off, the third circled and bucked and threw his rider.

Mothers watched and screamed. Old men and horseless warriors stood helpless, and no one attempted to cross the creek. Brady held Buffalo Dancer. The stallion pranced and tossed his head and switched his tail.

Brady dug his heels into the horse's sides, and he exploded across the creek, splashing water and riding headlong into the shaggy herd.

He engaged the outer edge of the buffalo herd and rode hard to outrun them to the spot where the child stood. Dancer was at his best. He threw himself against the first heavy-bodied buffalo to gain position, then lightly switched leads to slip out of range of the curved, black horns. He side-stepped their tossing heads, and his hooves flew over the ground, touching down only long enough to launch each powerful stride.

They cleared the herd, and Brady could see that the leaders were as close to the child as he was, boring down upon him with terrifying speed. Brady kicked Buffalo Dancer with both heels again, and the stallion lunged forward, eating up the distance in great strides.

Brady was barely able to stay ahead of the herd. Close behind he could hear their heavy breathing and smell the musty odor of their sweaty bodies. Up ahead, less than twenty yards away, the ground dropped away into a steep-sided draw.

The horse plunged down the embankment and across the draw, never breaking stride. Brady laced the fingers of his right hand into the thick mane of the horse, gripped tightly with his legs and leaned low to the ground as he thundered towards the boy.

The crying boy saw him coming and took two steps backward, then a third, and Brady nudged the horse closer with his left knee. Brady's mind raced, and he knew if the boy sat or fell or stepped back, he would have no second chance. The boy wept and Brady prayed he would not move. The ground behind him shook, and he could almost feel the hot breath of the buffalo on his back.

He closed the distance. The boy stood firm, faltered and stood, then raised his arms. Brady stretched as far as he could. The horse corrected and, when he was upon the boy, his hooves missed him by inches. Brady leaned further and reached forth and caught up a handful of the boy's hair and, with one quick motion, snatched him off the ground and up behind him crosswise on the horse's back. Brady sat upright and held the boy firm and asked the horse for more as the terrible beasts closed in behind them.

Brady prayed for the strength to hold the boy, whose weight shifted and put him off balance as the horse lunged hard to outrun the herd. Brady couldn't hold the boy. He slipped away. But when he dropped, Brady held firm onto the boy's shirt and let him swing free, and brought him back up and laid him across the horse's neck. He held him tight and looked back. Off to his right and to his left, dark, humped buffalo stretched like an endless stream of ghostly images that appeared to go on forever. It was impossible to outrun the herd. Brady took the only chance he had and set the buckskin on an oblique course in front of the charging buffalo.

The buckskin gasped for air but refused to slow. They pounded up a gentle hill that flattened to the creek, and the creek followed the contour of the land and bent away to the right. Brady counted on the buffalo following the creek. He turned the buckskin hard to the left and down across the water. He kicked the horse onward. He didn't look back until he heard the rumbling subside, and he knew the herd had turned.

It was a time of rejoicing in camp that night. The buffalo had come to them. The hunt was good, and many believed the shaman's prophecy and embraced the white man among them. Some were reluctant and some were skeptical, but none doubted that McCall was good medicine.

As the tribe celebrated, the medicine men secluded themselves in the vision pit. They stayed there for three days seeking guidance and illumination. When the eldest and most respected among them told of his dreams, he told of a white eagle and where the white eagle flew there were buffalo, and he believed the white man among them was a good omen.

The elder shaman then caused much concern among the other warriors when he told his people the white man must be given the opportunity to prove himself in the ritual of the medicine lodge. The chiefs and great warriors of the tribe deliberated throughout the night. Some protesting, others unsure. They passed the pipe and by the early hours of morning agreed that if McCall was the good omen sent to them by the great spirits, he could prove himself worthy in the sacred rituals of the medicine lodge.

For weeks McCall prepared himself. He saw the scars and pride worn by those who had succeeded before him, and he saw the shame and disgrace suffered by those who had tried and failed. From what he could learn from those who would speak to him, there were many mysteries associated with the secret rites.

Otter Tail confided in Brady, and told him the most difficult part of the ritual was the one in which those who succeeded took the highest level of pride. He showed Brady the massive chest scars he carried above his breasts and showed Brady how skewers pierced the heavy muscle there, one on each side. He demonstrated how the skewers were secured to long rawhide thongs hung from the reinforced braces at the top of the tall lodge. He tried to explain the pain and the need to block out all conscious thought as the lashings were drawn tight. He would be raised high above the floor of the lodge and suspended there until the muscles ripped free, or he begged to be let down. And he told of how he endured and Brady must endure.

McCall was apprehensive. This was the Blackfoot way of life. The boys spent all their waking hours developing and preparing themselves to become warriors. Their games were games of war and hunting and weapons and bravery. From childhood they prepared for the rituals in the medicine lodge, each believing he would not fail.

Then McCall was told it was time. He readied himself and entered the dream pit. If he were to be chosen, the great spirits would come to him in a dream and the shaman would interpret the dream and, if it was a good dream, McCall would be considered. For three days and three nights he hunkered without food or water or light and for the first day he had no dream. On the second night his dreams were nightmarish images with no connection and they appeared randomly throughout the day and night and next day.

When he emerged from the dream pit on the fourth day, Shy Wolf and Otter Tail and the elder shaman awaited him. The shaman took him to his lodge, and told him not to speak. Inside he prepared McCall a strong tea and lit the pipe, and they drank and smoked and the shaman asked McCall to tell him of his dream.

McCall told him he dreamed of a bird with no wings and the bird was left on a cliff high above a great river, and the river was inhabited by creatures that waited for the bird to attempt to fly. And McCall told the shaman he dreamed the dream from inside the bird's body, for when he stepped off the high perch, he felt the wind in his face as he plummeted earthward, and the creatures waited hungrily below.

Then McCall stretched out his arms to demonstrate, and he told the shaman the bird grew wings and he could fly, and when he flew he saw the earth and he saw the buffalo and the deer, and he had the feeling of great vision and great freedom.

The shaman nodded, but did not speak. He built a small fire and in the fire he placed leaves and grasses and colored powder McCall did not recognize. The fire smoked, and he waved the smoke about the darkened interior of the lodge with the wing of a hawk, and he chanted.

Then he became still and appeared to have left his body and when he returned he sang and chanted and told McCall his dream was a good dream. He told McCall that, for a white man, he was blessed with the favor of the spirits, and he told him it was the spirits who gave him the power to pull the baby from the certain death the buffalo herd intended for him.

"You will rest, and at the next new moon you will be tested."

The night of the new moon the elder shaman entered McCall's lodge and told him to follow him. McCall followed him to the medicine lodge, and when he stepped inside he saw nine young men stripped to their breechclouts, their skin painted and a shaman attending to each.

The elder shaman motioned a hideously decorated man to attend to McCall, and soon McCall was stripped and painted and stood with the others. All ten stood and waited, and there was no bravado about their demeanor and no fear, but when the ritual began there was a great amount of wailing, and the night wore on with no reprieve. The day came and passed, and the second night came, and McCall remained among the six who persevered.

Throughout that night McCall quit many times in his mind, but he would not give in and, when they hoisted the six into the air and he could feel the muscles detach from his bones, he forced his mind to exit his body and if there was pain, he felt none.

Sunlight shone through the smoke hole, and McCall did not remember being lowered to the ground. He did not remember the pain and the blood and the moaning and the pounding drums that never stopped beating. But for the rest of his life he never forgot the faces of Shy Wolf and Otter Tail when he stepped out of the medicine lodge into the daylight, and they addressed him by his Blackfoot name.

CHAPTER THIRTY-FOUR

By the time McCall turned nineteen he had ridden with the Blackfoot so long he could hardly remember when he hadn't. Both Shy Wolf and Otter Tail had taken wives and McCall began to feel like an outsider.

He spent more and more time with the Pend d'Oreilles, who sometimes hunted with the Blackfoot, and he met a girl among them. She was young, and her bashful smile and playful ways attracted McCall to her the first time he saw her.

Otter Tail said her name was Little Deer, and he introduced McCall to her. McCall was awkward and uncomfortable in her presence, but he felt warm and good when he was with her, and when he was not, she was in his thoughts constantly.

He asked Otter Tail for advice and Otter Tail asked him if he wanted to court Little Deer. McCall wasn't sure; all he knew was that she stirred feelings deep inside him and he wanted to spend time with her.

"Then you must talk to her father," Otter Tail said.

McCall went to her father with two good horses and a Henry repeating rifle. Her father was pleased, and Little Deer and her sisters stood outside and giggled, and they chided Little Deer because McCall was a white man, and they whispered how handsome he looked in his fine buckskin shirt.

That afternoon McCall called on Little Deer for the first time. They walked to the river, and the grandmother went with them. They sat in the grass near the water and the grandmother sat with them. She never spoke, but always watched and listened.

That night McCall sought out Otter Tail and Otter Tail assured him it would not always be so. But each time it was the same. When it wasn't the grandmother, it was the mother or an aunt. After McCall and Little Deer began to feel comfortable with one another, they would steal off and spend many hours talking and laying together in the tall, sweet grass in a secluded meadow high above the encampment.

Little Deer would lean on her elbow and touch McCall's face with her fingertips as he lay in the grass and tried to pronounce the Pend d'Oreille words she taught him.

She would lay in his arms and slowly repeat every English word she learned from him. She was captivated by her white warrior, and he hungered for her attention. In her presence he was calmed and gentled.

By the end of summer McCall couldn't remember ever being happier. Little Deer had grown more beautiful, and she carried herself with great pride, the envy of every young girl in camp. They spoke of marriage. The grandmother no longer accompanied them, and McCall was welcome in her father's lodge, where he provided much game and ate many meals. In the spring they would talk of marriage, McCall decided.

Fall came quickly and by late September the snow began to fall. The Blackfoot people left for their winter camp and McCall stayed on with the Pend d'Oreilles. The days became short and McCall spent more time hunting and less time with Little Deer, as it was with all the men in the tribe.

Little Deer appeared to lose her unstoppable enthusiasm for everything she did, and when McCall asked her about it, she said it was nothing. She developed a cough, only slight at first, but noticeable. McCall stayed with her more, and each day she seemed to weaken.

One morning she was unable to rise from her bed, and McCall arrived at the lodge of her father to find her attended by her mother and grandmother and the shaman.

"Will she be all right?" McCall asked.

"I think so," said her grandmother. The shaman was less sure.

For six days she lay, unable to rise, and McCall never left her side. He spoke to her and held snow packs to her fevered head. She smiled at him and spoke softly. McCall held her hand and lay his head on her breast, and they talked of spring. She squeezed his hand and told him she would be very proud to be his wife. She laced the fingers of her other hand in his hair and rubbed his head weakly as they talked into the night.

McCall told her to rest and sleep some, and she said no. She asked him if he would like a son, and he said he would. She asked if he would like a daughter, and he said a daughter would make him very happy.

In English she said very softly, "Little Deer loves Yellow Horse with all her heart."

McCall rose to look into her eyes and tell her how much he loved her, but when he looked down at her, she was gone.

McCall mourned for Little Deer a long time. He watched them offer her to the heavens, and he wept. And when he finished mourning, McCall lashed out in anger. Hatred seethed within him and he sought someone or something upon which to wreak revenge.

He returned to the Blackfoot and rode with their warriors against their enemies. He painted his face, greased his long hair, tied it up and adorned it with eagle feathers. He painted his body, and when he rode into battle he did so with a fearful vengeance and suicidal disregard for caution.

In time, the white warrior known as Yellow Horse became the subject of many conversations whispered around campfires in both the Blackfoot camps and those of the enemies who came to know him. He carried the scars of many battles and distanced himself even from those close to him. When Shy Wolf or Otter Tail tried to talk to him he shook them off, for he harbored a lifetime of hatred not even he understood.

At twenty-one he was a seasoned warrior; more Blackfoot than white man. His three-year quest for vengeance no longer had meaning. He thought often of Little Deer, but in his heart he knew the demons he fought were not the ones who had taken her.

He watched Buffalo Dancer grazing, always alone and never with the other horses. The buckskin was badly scarred. His gait showed some stiffness, especially on cold mornings when he hadn't been ridden for a few days.

When spring came and the snow began to melt, McCall announced it was time for him to leave. They understood. That evening they passed the pipe and celebrated. Otter Tail and Shy Wolf and McCall talked well into the night. They had grown up together, and as close as McCall felt to Franklin, he shared similar feelings for these two.

When McCall stepped out of his lodge the next morning, the entire tribe waited for him.

Broken Wing, the wife of Otter Tail stepped up first. She held his hands and she hugged him and she presented him with a deerskin pouch which she placed about his neck. "Keep it close to protect you," she said.

One by one they came by, and when they finished they stood quietly as he swung easily up onto the buckskin's back. McCall had earned the respect of the Blackfoot people, both as a warrior and a man of honor. He rode out with grave misgivings.

Young men on horseback solemnly rode

alongside McCall to the river. Each touched him as they peeled off when he turned to cross. At the water's edge, McCall turned to take a long, last look. He wanted to remember forever the friendship and acceptance he had experienced with the people who he respected and loved.

He turned away, and Buffalo Dancer plunged into the fast moving water, and they rode for miles before Brady turned his head to look back.

Chapter Thirty-Five

Buffalo Dancer sensed this journey would be different. There were no other warriors with them, no hunting party and none of the wild energy he had come to expect each time they rode out of the Blackfoot camp. Instead, the man in the saddle was quiet and subdued, and there was no urgency to his commands.

McCall took a deep breath and tried to remember the day he and Charlie pulled out from the Triple Dot. He glanced at the Gros Ventre knife that never left his side. He thought about the old trapper and back in the far reaches of his mind he remembered two young boys he was no longer sure ever really existed.

McCall was tired. He wanted to hear English words. He wanted to see Kincaid and he wanted to hear how Franklin was doing. He wanted to see the ranch and smell the hay and drink strong coffee.

He wondered how Kincaid looked. *Would his hair be gray? Did he ever marry? Was Franklin back yet? Was Franklin still alive?*

His mind wandered and his thoughts began to make the transition to the life he knew before the Blackfoot. A lot had changed. McCall had changed; he hoped Kincaid had not.

He traveled south and the sun was warm, but a sharp, north wind nipped at his back. He dropped down into the valley at the tip of Flathead Lake, then crossed over and followed the South Fork of the Flathead River until it petered out. When he crossed the Madison Mountains and looked down into the green Gallatin River Valley, he knew he was home.

Brady pushed Buffalo Dancer to a trot as they turned up the long, narrow road leading to the ranch house. Before he realized it, Brady stood apprehensively on the porch of the log house he and Franklin had helped build. It appeared as he had remembered it and it felt good to be there.

He knocked on the heavy wooden door. There was no answer. He knocked again, and Kincaid swung the door abruptly open. Both men stared at each other uneasily. Five years had made a lot of changes. Each waited for the other to speak.

Summer sun and the winter winds had etched deep lines at the corners of Kincaid's eyes. Gray showed through his hair and he appeared smaller than Brady had remembered. Kincaid's eyes narrowed and he stared at the young man standing before him.

"Brady?" he asked.

"It's me," McCall replied and the corners of his mouth moved into a weak smile.

McCall offered his hand and Kincaid grasped it with his knotted fingers and squeezed hard. He looked Brady up and down.

"What the hell happened to you?" he asked laughing and hauling the rugged looking young man into the cabin.

Brady grinned. He loved hearing the English language, and he especially loved hearing it spoken in a voice so vaguely familiar.

Kincaid studied the moccasins on his feet and the long hair. Brady had filled out. His shoulders and chest showed great strength. His manner was shy and Indian like.

"Look at you," Kincaid said. "If we weren't standing face to face, I'm not sure I'd recognize you, Brady . . . but you look good," Kincaid lied.

Brady looked at his feet, then back at Kincaid and smiled.

"You never could lie worth a damn," Brady said, then he threw his arms around Kincaid and held him very tight. Kincaid put his arms around Brady and they stood that way.

"It's so good to be home, Travis," Brady said, still holding Kincaid to him, not wanting to let go, not sure if this was real or a dream.

Kincaid patted him on the back grabbed the back of his head and pulled it to him.

"Well, you're home now. That's all that matters," he said.

Then they pushed back and stood at arm's length, their hands still on one another's shoulders, as if both thought the other would somehow disappear if he broke contact.

A knot swelled in Brady's throat as he looked Kincaid over. He tousled Kincaid's hair then ducked back and laughed.

"You don't look bad for an old man," he teased.

Kincaid took a swipe at him.

"You might have been some big deal with the Blackfoot, but you're still a snotty-nosed kid around here . . . and besides that, your work's piling up."

Brady looked around the room. His eyes took in all the changes he could see in Kincaid's appearance. Travis looked good. The years had treated him well and, even though there was some age showing on him, Kincaid hadn't changed much.

"I sure missed this place," Brady said. "Even thought about you a time or two, Travis. After all these years, I wasn't too sure you'd remember who I was."

"Well, I'll have to admit you have changed some since the last time I saw you," Kincaid said, as he laughed and shook his head.

"Come on and sit down." Kincaid said.

"I can't tell you how good it is to be here," Brady said. Then he added quickly, "Have you had breakfast yet?"

"No, I was just fixing to though. You hungry?"

"Yeah, I'm hungry. I'm always hungry."

"Well then, you pour us a cup of coffee and I'll heat up the skillet."

The two men had a lot to catch up on. Brady listened intently to every word Kincaid said and, in his excitement to tell Kincaid of the events of the past five years, he found himself using Indian sign language and substituting Blackfoot phrases for

English words that didn't come readily to mind.

"Whoa, slow down," Kincaid said. "My Blackfoot's a little rusty."

"Sorry, Travis. I guess my mouth's outrunning my brain."

Kincaid laughed. He refilled their coffee cups. The fresh smell of biscuits drifted over from the stove and two huge steaks sizzled in the frying pan. Brady's stomach rumbled.

"What do you hear from Franklin?" he asked.

Kincaid laughed.

"That kid," he said and shook his head. "He's real good about staying in touch."

He looked askance at Brady. Brady smiled and shrugged his shoulders.

"He owns a big hotel in San Francisco," Travis replied.

Brady laughed.

"Franklin T. Stilwell owns a hotel?"

"That's what he said. He started with a used up gold mine he won in a faro game. Struck a fair vein the second week he was in it, figured that was too much work for him and traded it to two Irishmen for the hotel."

Kincaid set the steaks on the table, then took the biscuits out of the oven.

"The first thing he did was change the

name of the hotel to the Gold Nugget . . .
for good luck I guess."

McCall laughed.

"I don't know, Travis. I can't picture
Franklin running a hotel."

Kincaid smiled.

"Neither can I."

"Have you been to see him?" Brady asked.

"No, never have," Kincaid said.

They ate and talked and finally Brady
said, "Let's go see him."

Kincaid looked over his coffee cup at
Brady.

"I'll make you a deal, Brady," he said.
"You stick around here long enough to help
us get through the spring branding and
drive a small bunch of army cattle over to
Fort Smith, and you and me will head out
to California."

Brady held up a fork full of steak to make
a point and said, "Travis, you got yourself a
cowboy."

The following day, Kincaid and Brady and
three ranch hands set out for what should
have been an easy gather. By evening bad
weather set in, and the cattle scattered. It
was four weeks before they got them gathered, and two more weeks before they
delivered the herd to Fort Smith.

The calves had been branded, the herd

was delivered to the army and things were back in order at the Triple Dot. With nothing left to delay them, Kincaid and McCall packed their saddle bags and turned in right after dark to get a good night's rest before they set out on the journey to California.

By the time the sun was high enough to cast a shadow, Kincaid and McCall had already put ten miles behind them.

CHAPTER THIRTY-SIX

San Francisco: 1853

By midmorning the San Francisco fog had cleared and the sun shone warm and bright over the east bay hills, with their groves of Eucalyptus trees and manzanita brush and fields of golden poppies coloring the landscape.

They rode bayside, and both men stood awed by the activity of the embarcadero, where ships docked and cargo lined the wharf and incoming vessels rocked empty and riding high on the tide, awaiting crews holed up in the bawdy backrooms of dark establishments presided over by women with no last names.

Kincaid inquired of a local businessman who directed he and Brady to the Gold Nugget. They stood beneath a sign that read, *Gold Nugget Hotel and Saloon.* From its outside appearance it was more saloon than hotel. It was located at the corner of an alley that looked as uninviting in the daylight as it must at night. Down the partially cobbled street lay the bay, and from where they stood, two islands were visible, but the view to the Pacific was obscured by a lingering haze that clung to the water.

Brady just shook his head.

"After you," Kincaid said, holding one half of the swinging doors open.

Brady stepped inside; Kincaid followed.

Two men sat at the bar and, by the looks of them, they had not succeeded in drinking off last night's drunk. A bartender busied himself behind the mahogany bar, and in the reflection of the mirror a once attractive woman smiled into the glass at them.

Kincaid smiled back, and Brady did likewise.

She tucked in a wisp of hair, smoothed the front of her dress and approached them.

"First time in town?" she asked, smiling pleasantly and assessing them both with her eyes.

Kincaid removed his hat and nodded. "Yes, ma'am, it is," he said.

He nudged Brady and Brady removed his hat, and when he did the lady looked at him surprised and with a curious expression that begged some sort of explanation. Both the look and the explanation escaped Brady, and she looked back at Kincaid.

"We're from Montana Territory, ma'am. Not much need for city clothes where we come from," Kincaid said.

She smiled and Kincaid stuck out his hand. She took it and he said, "I'm Travis Kincaid and this here's Brady C. McCall."

"Oh my gawd," she exclaimed. "B.C?"

She looked back at Kincaid. "Travis?" Then she laughed and put her arms around them both.

"Is Franklin ever going to be surprised." She pulled them over to a table. "I've heard so much about you two I feel like I've known you both all my life."

Brady and Travis looked at each other and smiled.

"What can I get you boys? Franklin had to run an errand, but he'll be back soon, and there is no way I'm letting either one of you out of my sight before he gets back."

She sat them at a table in the corner with a view of the bay and introduced herself.

"I'm Maggie," she said. Her face glowed and the beauty of her youth shined brightly in her eyes.

"Pleased to meet you, Maggie," Brady said, as he stood and smiled.

"Sit down, sit down . . . we're not formal here."

She shook Brady's hand and looked back at Kincaid.

"And you," she said, "are the handsome devil I've been dying to meet."

Travis beamed. "Well, Maggie, if I'd have known you were here, I wouldn't have waited so long to make the trip.

"Beer?" she said pointing to Brady. He nodded.

"Travis?"

"Same here."

Maggie hurried to the bar and returned with two beers and a cup of coffee for herself.

She sat next to Kincaid with her eyes looking directly into his.

"So how long are you here for?" She inquired with a look of courtesy at Brady to include him in the conversation.

Kincaid's eyes sparkled and Brady smiled, watching the two.

"Well," he said. "I'm thinking from what I've seen so far, we may be around a while."

He winked at Maggie, and she seemed to blush, although Kincaid knew better.

"Then I would just love to show you around anytime. Both of you," she said with a genuinely friendly smile that couldn't have uninvited Brady any more quickly.

They talked and waited and Maggie served them lunch and they had another beer. Maggie was alive with enthusiasm and wit and soon all three were laughing and talking like old friends. She apologized for Franklin, and they both assured her they knew Franklin well enough to not hold him to any kind of a timetable. Besides, she was much prettier than Franklin, Kincaid pointed out, and Brady agreed.

Outside someone thumped around and banged against the doors and shouted out, "Hey, someone give me a hand with these doors."

It was Franklin's unmistakable voice. Brady held his finger to his lip and motioned to Kincaid. Together they rose, and each held one side of the doors open while Franklin backed in with his arms loaded down. He was dressed in a striped suit and wore a bowler tipped back on his head.

"Thank you gentlemens," he said, as he nodded to Brady and turned towards Kincaid and started for the back of the bar. He turned back to Kincaid and stared.

Kincaid stared back and refused to help him out.

Franklin smiled, and he slapped the table next to him with both hands.

"Travis Kincaid! Man, what are you doing here?"

He laughed and advanced toward Kincaid as Kincaid smiled and reached out for him.

Franklin picked the old cowboy up and spun him around, ignoring the stranger who stood quietly and said nothing. Both Franklin and Kincaid laughed.

"Just came to check up on you," Kincaid answered, to the question that seemed like it was asked too long ago to still be relevant.

"Man, you look good, Travis," Franklin said, pushing himself back and taking a long look at the cowboy.

"You look pretty fancy yourself," Kincaid replied, snapping the brim of the bowler with his finger.

"So, what do you hear of B.C.?" Franklin asked.

Kincaid shook his head and laughed. Maggie could barely contain herself behind the bar, and Brady stood like an invisible cigar store Indian looking at Franklin expressionless and dying to say something.

"Well, last time I heard, Brady was in San Francisco," Kincaid said.

Franklin's eyes widened.

"San Francisco? What's he doing here?" Franklin asked.

"Why don't you ask him yourself?" Kincaid said, nodding toward the stoic figure to his right.

Franklin turned his head and stared. Then he shook his head but couldn't speak. Tears welled up in his eyes. He took a step toward Brady and all he could do was cry.

Brady moved forward and they embraced. There were no words spoken, but tears ran down their faces, and neither man made any attempt to conceal the fact.

Maggie held her hands to her mouth. She smiled and her makeup tracked dark streaks down her cheeks. Kincaid couldn't have been prouder.

Brady was the first to stand back.

"You sure don't look like any cowboy I know," he said, grinning.

Franklin laughed and slapped Brady on the shoulders and flipped his long hair with his fingertips.

"No, maybe not, but look at you."

They laughed and both began talking at once. Franklin noticed the two men at the bar watching with disapproving eyes.

"Hey," Franklin shouted as he advanced on the two men and picked them from the bar stools by their collars. "You two drunks get out of here."

"Whoa, whoa, whoa," one protested.

Franklin laughed again.

"No whoa, whoa, whoa. I'm tired of buying you drinks. Go get a job."

The two men dusted themselves off outside the doorway and Franklin shouted after them.

"Come back when you know how to act right."

Maggie took Brady and Franklin by the hand and led them to the table.

"Here, you two sit down and visit," she said. "I'm going to show Mr. Kincaid around town."

She deposited the boys and stood close at Kincaid's side.

"Mr. Kincaid," she said as she took his arm. "How would you like to see San Francisco?"

"I can't think of anything I'd like better," Kincaid replied.

As the couple left arm in arm, Maggie stuck her head back in the door, put her hand to her mouth and whispered to the boys.

"Don't wait up for us."

Franklin and Brady visited through most of the night, and the next morning at breakfast Kincaid sat between the two boys with a smile on his face and nothing to offer beyond a "Good morning." Franklin smiled.

"Well, Travis," Franklin said. "I hope you're proud of yourself, keeping my help out all night."

Brady laughed. Kincaid raised a hand in protest but didn't argue the point.

"There's lots you didn't tell us about you, Travis," Brady said. "And here we thought you were all about fixing fences and working cattle, and now look at you."

Kincaid grinned. "Maggie was just showing me the sights . . . there's a lot to see in San Francisco."

Brady looked at Kincaid then back at Franklin. "I think Travis here saw all he wanted to when he saw Maggie, judging by the way he was falling all over himself," Brady said laughing.

The next evening they stood on the cliffs watching the moon float at the end of a bright silver trail leading out across the breaking waves of the ocean. Franklin turned the conversation and thought he saw Brady's face flush.

"You remember Allison Granger?" he asked, looking at Brady and Kincaid.

Brady nodded and Kincaid said, "I'll never forget those two."

Brady waited, his heart racing, and his curiosity almost uncontainable.

"I see them from time to time," Franklin

continued. "They stop by every now and then, and I call on them whenever I'm down their way."

"How did things ever work out for them?" Kincaid asked.

Brady felt the warmth rise in his face, and he felt confused. He wanted to hear more about Allison, but at the same time he did not want to learn that she might be married and have a family of her own. He wasn't sure why, but he felt like she owed him some loyalty, or at least the first-right-of-refusal if she wanted to take a husband. It was non-sense and he admonished himself for thinking it.

"Mrs. Granger, her name's Mrs. Hayes now, got married. Her and Mr. Hayes run a dry goods store about a half a day's ride south of here," Franklin explained.

"Well, what about Allison?" Brady asked impatiently.

"I'll tell you straight away B.C., she ain't the same kid you remember," Franklin said. "She turned out pretty good. In fact, she turned out damn good."

Brady gritted his teeth.

"Damn it, Franklin will you get to the point? Is she married or not?"

His words echoed back to him in the silence that followed, and Brady would have given anything to retract them. His frustration and embarrassment exposed, Brady stuck out his jaw defiantly, and his expression dared one of them to say a word.

Kincaid casually threw down his cigar stub and kicked sand on it as he turned away to look up the coast line, struggling to suppress the laughter building up inside him.

Franklin grinned. The moonlight lit up his mocking smile. When Brady realized how much fun Franklin was having with him, he laughed.

"No, she ain't married, and she asks about you every damn time I see her," Franklin said.

"I don't know what she ever saw in you anyway, but she drives me crazy."

"She asked about me?" Brady asked.

"Yeah, but don't ask me why," replied Franklin. "You never let me know anything, so I never had much to tell her."

"How about the three of us taking a ride down to see them?" Brady asked.

"I think that's a fine idea," said Kincaid. "It would be nice to see them again, and to give this town a chance to rest up for a day or two before we look for some real excitement."

"I don't know," Franklin said, hesitating.

"That might not be a good idea."

"Why wouldn't it be a good idea?" Brady asked.

Franklin shuffled uncomfortably from one foot to the next.

"Well," Franklin began, "I never thought you'd ever come to California. I was getting tired of never having anything to tell them, so I told them you were, uh, well, you know."

'No, Franklin, I don't know. What?"

"I think I told her you were sick."

"What do you mean, sick?"

Franklin searched for the right words.

"I didn't want her to think you just forgot about her, so I told her you were . . ." he paused.

Brady waited. Kincaid watched, slack-jawed.

"I was . . . ?"

Franklin held up his hands. "Look, B.C., I was in a tight spot here."

"Franklin?"

"All right, all right. I told her you went insane. I told her you and that crazy-ass trapper went off in them mountains and, with just each other for company, you just took to drooling and babbling."

Kincaid had to walk down the beach to hold back the laughs.

"Was that all you told her?" Brady asked.

"Yeah, pretty much."

"Pretty much?"

"There might have been more."

Any hope Brady had of salvaging anything from this disappeared.

"What more?"

"You know, little things . . . extra details . . . she just kept asking all the time."

Brady sat on a sawed-off tree stump and slumped.

"Tell it all to me."

"I don't remember it all. I do remember about you getting snowed in and living on mice you caught and ate. Oh, and you and Charlie, you know, spending too much time alone together."

Brady exploded to his feet. Kincaid caught him and stood between he and Franklin.

"Easy, easy, easy boys," he said. Then he chuckled. "I'm sure we can get it all straightened out tomorrow."

Brady's expression eased. "Just let me shoot him once, Travis."

Kincaid laughed. "I don't think that's a good idea."

Franklin looked at Brady in his most innocent of expressions.

"I don't know what you're getting all huffy about," he said.

They walked back along the dark streets that dropped sharply to the embarcadero and the smell of the ocean and the cool air seemed strangely out of place to Brady and Kincaid. By morning the foggy streets swirled in a misty haze of damp air that, in the half-light of dawn, gave an eerie cast to the place. The clatter of the horses' feet on the cobblestones echoed into the empty corners of the alleys they passed, and Kincaid and the boys rode south.

Brady thought about Allison off and on over the years, and now the prospect of meeting her again rekindled boyhood memories as vivid as though they occurred yesterday. Somehow, in his mind, the image of her as a child matured with the years and he could see her as a woman, but her features were unclear, and all he recalled with clarity were her eyes.

His thoughts drifted aimlessly, but always returned to Allison and, the more he thought about her, the more apprehensive he became. He rode up quietly alongside Franklin.

"Franklin," he said. "You suppose there's somewhere along the way we can stop and get me a haircut?"

Franklin looked at him. "I don't know, cousin. We can keep an eye out for one of these cantinas where you might could talk someone into taking a shot at it."

Brady nodded and dropped back.

Kincaid fell in beside him but didn't speak.

"Hey, Travis."

Kincaid turned his head.

"Shouldn't I maybe a get a new shirt in town before we go visiting?"

"Don't you like the one you got?"

"I like it fine."

"Then why get another one?"

Brady laughed.

"Come on Travis. I haven't seen Allison in a long time. I think I ought to look decent."

"You look just fine."

"Are you sure?"

"I'm sure."

"All right. I just don't want to be embarrassed."

"Brady, you look fine."

Brady felt uneasy. What if she didn't remember him? What if she was simply indifferent and this entire unspoken bond between them was all in his head? Exactly what did he expect from a woman he last saw as a child?

The more he thought about it, the more he regretted the entire idea. He watched Franklin and Kincaid riding ahead, talking, enjoying the trip, laughing.

It was all too complicated.

Finally, Brady resigned himself to his fate, whatever it may be, and settled into the rocking rhythm of the saddle. The trail led through dark-green forests of broad-leafed ferns and tall redwoods and stands of eucalyptus with bark shredded and hanging. Occasionally the thick vegetation opened up onto wide expanses of wind-blown sand where the damp breeze carried in off the Pacific Ocean, and waves crashed against the shore and rolled up on the beaches.

Then the trail turned inland and dropped down into a valley protected on two sides by the rolling hills of the coast range. They encountered two Mexican vaqueros riding high-stepping horses of good breeding and, when they were within talking range, Kincaid touched his hat and said, "Buenos dias."

The vaqueros returned the greeting and all five horsemen stopped mid-trail while Kincaid carried on a brief conversation in Spanish, and then they rode on.

"Well, damn, Señor Kincaid. I didn't know you could talk Mexican. What'd they say?" Franklin asked as he looked over his shoulder to watch the two riders disappear up the trail.

Brady listened curiously.

"They said there was a big fiesta tonight in San Gregorio. Said we'd be welcome there."

"Ain't we the fortunate ones?" Brady said, grinning widely.

"We'll see about that tonight after you wash down some tortillas and beans with mescal tequila and a couple of cervezas," Franklin said, with the authority of previous experience.

Kincaid laughed. "If tequila is the only word you boys learn in Spanish, I'll guarantee it won't be one you soon forget."

They rode for the better part of an hour then the road turned eastward, and as they reached the top of a low round hill, Franklin called out. "There it is. San Gregorio, gentlemens."

The earth-colored adobe buildings with red-tiled roofs looked oddly foreign. From their position overlooking the small valley stretching to the south, the three horsemen could see people moving about the zócalo, around which the town was built.

In the center of the zócalo stood a fountain, and around it the plaza was cobbled and trellises shaded the tables. On the east end of the square, outside an adobe cantina, a charred beef lay on a bed of hot coals. In the fire pit in the corner grease dripped and sizzled from the hides of several pigs attended by young, dark-skinned girls in colored dresses. The grease flared on the hot coals, and the flames scorched the slick-skinned carcasses hung there with gaping mouths and beady eyes bulging from the heat.

Kincaid and McCall followed Franklin into town. They dismounted near a well-kept store with a neatly painted sign that read, *Hayes Dry Goods & Freight Co.* Franklin stepped down and the others followed suit. They wrapped the horses reins around the hitch rail and loosened their saddle cinches.

Franklin and Kincaid stepped up on the wooden sidewalk. Brady was still at Buffalo Dancer's side when the door exploded open and a woman's excited voice caused the surprised horses to set back. Franklin and Kincaid whirled toward the sound and Brady looked down at the leather latigo still in his hand, not daring to look up.

"Franklin T. Stilwell," Allison said, as she ran up and threw her arms around him.

"Allison T. Granger," Franklin said, holding her at arm's length to get a better look at her. "You're still skinny as ever, I see."

Then he smiled.

"Hey, I want you to meet someone," he said, as they turned toward Kincaid.

Allison smiled but did not recognize him. She stuck out her hand.

"Hi, I'm Allison," she said.

Kincaid smiled.

"I'm Travis Kincaid," he said.

Her hand covered her mouth and tears streamed forth.

"Oh my gosh. Travis."

She threw her arms around his neck and squeezed him tight.

"I didn't recognize you . . . I'm so sorry. It's so good to see you."

She stepped back, but held his hands. She smiled.

"You're even more handsome than I remembered," she said.

Kincaid smiled.

"California has been very good to you I see," he said.

Her eyes were bright and still teary.

She finally managed to compose herself and stood with her arms around each of them.

"What are you two doing here in San Gregorio? And what about Brady? Tell me about Brady."

Travis smiled and nodded toward the

horses where Brady stood half hidden by the big buckskin. "Maybe he should tell you himself," he said.

Brady stepped forward, and Allison let out a shrill scream.

"Brady!"

She ran into his arms, laughing and crying at the same time. He held her close and smelled her soft hair as it pressed against his face. His emotions whirled, and his senses converged in confusion. The years rolled away and Brady laughed with pleasure and relief. He had dreaded and looked forward to this moment with intense apprehension and misgivings. Now, he held her in his arms and any doubts he had disappeared.

Allison breathed in the earthy smell of Brady's deerskin shirt. She squeezed her arms around his well-muscled back and buried herself next to his chest. She raised her face to look at him. Her eyes explored his features. Her fingers gently touched an old scar that had healed roughly along his jawbone. His skin was dark from the sun, and there was an unmistakable seriousness about him and a hardness that she hadn't anticipated. But the gentle look in his eyes and the soul-revealing smile that she remembered in him as a young boy were still there.

He moved his face closer to hers. "There was hardly a day went by that I didn't think about you," he said quietly.

"Brady, that day you left us at the fort I prayed so hard that you would come back someday. Now here you are. It's so wonderful to see you . . . all three of you."

Allison wiped the tears from her cheeks, looked over at Franklin and Kincaid and then, smiling joyfully, took Brady's hand and walked over and put her other arm around Kincaid.

"Mother will be so surprised to see you. Come inside, I can't wait to see the look on her face. And I want you to meet my stepfather. He's been so wonderful to us," Allison said, as they walked together.

Allison reached over and tipped Franklin's hat over his eyes.

"Stilwell, I'll get even with you," she said in mock anger. "And when I tell Travis and Brady all the awful things you've been telling me about them, you'll be in big trouble."

Franklin leaned around Brady to look at her.

"You love me and you know it," he said, laughing.

CHAPTER THIRTY-SEVEN

By early evening the zócalo was crowded and noisy. Young vaqueros outfitted in finely tailored jackets and tight pants studded with silver conchos salted their hands and traded tequila shots, man for man. Their eyes were red, and they became loud and reckless.

The smoky smell of fried pan bread and roasted meats hung over the square in the still air of the night. Old men talked and dipped tortillas in plates of refried beans and ate hot peppers until their eyes watered. They quenched their thirst with beer from bottles with no labels and watched with desire the young girls, who danced before them, and flirted with the young men, who passed the tequila from one to the other.

The young ladies taunted and teased the young vaqueros with their eyes and their flagrant smiles as they raised their skirts and flaunted their bare legs. The vaqueros competed for their attention, taking straight shots and addressing the ladies with lewd remarks and obscene gestures that made the girls giggle and carry on as they encouraged the young men.

Kincaid and the boys said goodnight to Allison and her mother and her step-father and returned to the zócalo. They walked through the narrow streets crowded with Mexican soldiers and many vaqueros, who eyed them darkly and disparaged them with quiet remarks among themselves.

They found a table outside the cantina where music played and intoxicated young ladies danced and attracted a gathering. Franklin stepped into the cantina and returned with six bottles of beer he placed on the table before them.

"Welcome to California," he said as he raised his bottle and touched it to the bottles raised by Kincaid and Brady. They drank and talked and watched the young ladies, and when the beer was gone, Brady went inside for more.

When he returned, a beautiful young girl sat in his place and held Franklin's hands as she kissed his face and whispered to him and laughed as her eyes mocked a young vaquero who watched with a hateful expression and clinched teeth.

She sat back in her chair. Brady set the

beer on the table and stood away. She leaned forward, whispered to Franklin, then leaned back and slowly unbuttoned her blouse. First one button then another and another. Franklin smiled. He reached forward and let his fingers trace a line from her throat to her cleavage. She caught his hand there and brought it to her mouth and pressed his fingers to her lips.

Brady slipped back into the shadows, uneasy and on edge.

Franklin took another pull on the beer bottle and Kincaid turned to address the two ladies who pulled their chairs in next to his.

Kincaid danced with one, then the other, and he bought them beer and laughed and they made suggestive advances toward him, playful and teasing, and very noticeable. Kincaid spoke to them in Spanish, and they laughed and giggled. One wore his hat, the other whispered to him and asked him to dance again.

Brady watched Franklin as his young lady moved to his lap and kissed him while his hands openly explored her bare breasts beneath her loose blouse.

Brady looked at Kincaid, but Kincaid seemed unaware of anything beyond the two young ladies he entertained. It disturbed

Brady that Kincaid would let himself become distracted.

Franklin was loud and reckless, and it was his recklessness that ignited the passions of the young girl with him. Her teasing began in fun, but in the arms of this handsome gringo cowboy it became more than that, and now she was as void of caution as he.

Kincaid laughed and carried on with the girls at his side. But he never lost sight of the festering circle of intoxicated vaqueros, whose expressions were grave and dangerous as they watched Franklin openly challenge their pride.

Kincaid saw trouble coming and looked over at Brady. Brady nodded and shifted over to a better position near the arched adobe wall. Kincaid reached across and loosened the revolver hanging at his left side. He excused himself abruptly from his surprised female companions, then stood with his back to the cantina wall.

Five or six of the drunken vaqueros pushed through the crowd and advanced on Franklin's table. Kincaid called to Franklin, his voice muted by the loud music and drunken singing.

Kincaid turned, and Brady was gone. Kincaid pushed and shoved through the mass of people, trying to reach Franklin before the vaqueros did. The vaqueros rushed Franklin, waving their pistols and cursing him.

There was a loud report and a bright muzzle flash from one of the vaqueros before Kincaid or Brady could reach Franklin. Kincaid looked directly at Franklin and watched the blood spurt from the side of Franklin's head, while his body twisted and fell backwards from the chair. The girl screamed and ran, and the vaquero's second shot slapped into her back and took her legs out from under her.

Another shot cracked and the young vaquero, with his pistol still hot in his hand, lurched sideways and fell to the ground, his tailored jacket wet with blood, and his eyes gazing empty and skyward.

Brady got to Franklin the same time Kincaid did. Franklin lay on his back, his eyes closed, his expression vacant and bloody, his legs twisted beneath him. Brady dropped to his knees. He looked up at Kincaid.

"He's still breathing," he said.

Kincaid knelt next to Brady and held his fingers to the arterial groove alongside Franklin's neck. He turned Franklin's head gently in his hands and examined the wound.

"The bullet just took off some skin and

part of his eyebrow," he said.

"Hand me that bottle," he said to Brady, nodding toward the half-empty tequila bottle on the table next to them.

Kincaid turned Franklin's head and splashed tequila on the wound.

Franklin jerked his head, and his eyes opened. They darted about wildly. He shook his head and tried to sit up. He rolled his eyes, and stared up at Kincaid. When his eyes focused, he lay back down and tried to put his hand to his head.

"Who hit me?"

"No one hit you. You been shot," Kincaid said.

"Who shot me?"

"That fella over there," Kincaid said.

Franklin sat up and looked at the bloodied vaquero whose lifeless body lie at the feet of those who attended him.

"What happened?" Franklin asked.

"The Mexican was watching you and the girl, and I guess he didn't like what he saw. He came at you and got off one round before Brady stopped him," Kincaid answered.

Franklin looked up at Brady, his eye was bloodshot and discolored, and he held his finger over the raw hole where half an eyebrow once resided.

"Sorry, B.C. I never meant for anything like this to happen," Franklin said, with as much sincerity as Brady had ever heard from him.

The law came. The vaqueros were ushered out of town to the south, and Kincaid and the boys were escorted out of town to the north and asked not to return. They rode two hours in the dark and followed their moon-cast shadows up the coast trail. They looked for a place to sleep, and when they decided on a sheltered cove where the ocean waves could be heard in the distance, Brady did not dismount his horse.

"I'm going back," he announced.

"What for?" asked Franklin.

Kincaid looked up from the spot where he threw down his saddle and bedroll. He smiled and addressed Brady.

"Leave too many unsaid things with Miss Allison, did you?" he said smiling.

Brady smiled back. "Yeah, I did, Travis. I promised myself I'd never do that again. You boys be okay without me for a few days?" Brady asked.

Franklin touched the edge of his missing eyebrow. "We'll try to manage," he said. Then he stuck out his hand and Brady shook it.

"I owe you one for back there, cousin.

Stay out of the way of those vaqueros, and we'll see you when you get back."

"Take care, son," Kincaid said, and his tone was one of deep concern.

Brady looked at Kincaid, then at Franklin. "I'll catch up with you as soon as I get this sorted out," he said, then he turned his horse and rode south.

For the next two weeks Brady and Allison were together every day. At first their conversations were congenial and impersonal. They hinted often in that direction, but never spoke directly of their feelings, and neither brought up the massacre at South Pass.

Their relationship was natural and warm, and it confused Brady. He knew how he felt, but he never expressed his feelings to Allison. He was, at times, completely sure she had strong feelings for him as well, but other times he wasn't sure. In the end he just left it alone.

One afternoon they walked on the sand of a quiet stretch of beach. Allison put her hand in Brady's as they walked barefoot at the water's edge. Brady held her hand, and the touch of her felt electric, but Allison made it seem very matter-of-fact, and she talked as they walked.

"Have you thought about South Pass much?" she asked.

Brady looked at her. Her eyes were soft and vulnerable.

"I think about it all the time," he said.

He looked over at her and she looked back up at him. Neither had ever discussed the events at South Pass with anyone. Brady and Allison shared a hunger to find intimate common ground between them, and there was none more personal or more private than that nightmarish day.

They found a quiet place and stopped to talk. And when they did, it felt right and Brady opened every wound for her, and she shared hers with him. They spoke in great detail of their nightmares and fears and regrets. They relived that wonderful winter in St. Joseph, and they shared stories of the months on the trail after St. Joseph. They shared their feelings, and when Brady spoke of his baby brother and his sister and his mother and his father and their graves, he wept. And when he did, Allison wept. And they held each other.

Finally, Allison looked up at Brady and wiped the tears from his cheeks with the backs of her fingers. She touched his scars and traced the long one on his jawbone.

"Brady, I love you so much," she whispered.

Brady smiled. He felt he had always known Allison. He felt at peace when he was with her. When he was alone she was always in his thoughts, and when they were together he found himself falling in love with her a part at a time.

He loved the profile of her face with its high cheekbones and soft smiling lips. He loved the curl that fell loosely in front of her ear and her strong feminine hands. But most of all he loved the way she looked at him, as though no one else in the world existed.

Allison accepted Brady for everything he was and was not, and hers was an unselfish love that she expressed freely and openly. She never questioned her love for Brady and never thought for a moment that he could love her any less than she loved him.

Brady held Allison's face in his hands and spoke to her in a language she did not understand. She smiled.

"What does that mean?" she asked.

"It means your smile is my sunshine. Your tears are my tears. Your soul has come to rest in my heart forever."

"That's beautiful, Brady."

"I am so in love with you, Allison."

She lay in his arms for a long time.

"You know," she said. "I was almost married four years ago."

Brady rolled onto his side to see her face. "Almost?"

"Yes . . . to a very nice man who owns a bank in San Francisco. I met him through my step-father."

"What happened?"

Allison turned her face to Brady. Her eyes searched his, and she chose her words carefully.

"His name is Waddell Stuart. He offered me everything, Brady . . . a nice home, commitment, security . . . everything."

She dropped her eyes.

"I don't know what happened. I let us get all the wedding plans made, he bought a house for us . . . it was all set."

"But you didn't do it," Brady said as a matter of fact, but it sounded like a question.

"I couldn't. I was waiting for something and that wasn't it. I didn't know at the time what I was waiting for. I just knew I couldn't go through with it."

She smiled and her eyes shined.

"Now," she said. "Being here with you . . . feeling like I do, this wonderful feeling that just overflows my heart . . . now I know I was waiting for you, Mr. McCall."

Brady touched her face. He smiled, but his eyes were sad.

"What's wrong?" Allison asked.

Brady looked away, and he agonized over his words.

"I was in love once, with a girl I would have married," he said softly.

Allison felt a shudder course through her.

"Who was she?" Allison asked delicately.

"Her name was Little Deer. She was a Blackfoot."

Allison took Brady's hand.

"Tell me about her," she said.

Brady took a deep breath.

"Well, she made me feel like I was worth something. Our life was simple . . . it was hard, but it was simple. And I had this hole inside me that I couldn't fill. It's like part of me was always empty, Allison. No matter where I went or what I did, I couldn't fill it. And I did things I'm not proud of. Little Deer made all that go away for me."

Allison rubbed his hand between hers as he talked. Her eyes never left his, and she neither passed judgment nor asked him to explain.

Then he got very quiet, and she sat with him without speaking. He put his arms around her and held her very tight and kissed her hair where it brushed his lips, and he felt her arms around him like she never wanted to let go.

She closed her eyes and smelled him and touched him. She kissed him with great passion and held his face and finally looked at him.

"You're leaving, aren't you?" she asked, her eyes welled with tears.

Brady nodded and very quietly said, "Yes."

He pulled her close. He wanted to remember how she felt. He needed her.

"Why? Why are you leaving?" she asked.

He searched her eyes with his. He searched his heart for an answer she would understand, but in the end he didn't even have an answer he understood. He held her hands tight in his.

"I don't know who I really am, Allison," he said. "I just feel so lost inside sometimes, and I let things get away from me. I don't even remember being a kid, and now, every time things start to feel comfortable to me, I feel like I need to move on. I won't be any good to you or anyone else until I can settle these feelings up."

"And you think running away will do that?" she asked, her eyes soft and her expression one of delicate concern.

He shook his head.

"I don't know. I hope so," he said. "I don't want to lose you."

"Brady, I can't make you any promises, but you do what you need to do."

She kissed him, and they held each other a long time and, when he left, neither understood why.

Kincaid had left for Montana by the time Brady rejoined Franklin in San Francisco. He told Franklin he didn't expect Brady would be coming back to the ranch for a while, and he asked Franklin to look out for him where ever he went. Franklin told Kincaid he would.

Franklin could tell Brady was uneasy as they talked that night. Finally, setting aside the small talk, Brady stood up looked over at Franklin.

"I'm going to Texas," he said. "You coming with me?"

"Texas?"

Franklin scratched his head.

"You do mean Texas?"

Franklin shook his head.

"No, I ain't. B.C., there's nothing in Texas."

"I'm looking to join the Texas Rangers," Brady said.

Franklin laughed.

"The Texas Rangers," Franklin said with a sarcastic tone in his voice.

"Why the Texas Rangers?"

"It's something to do," Brady answered.

"There's lots of things that are something to do, but they don't all involve getting shot at," Franklin said.

"I know, but it would be like old times, Franklin. You and me. A new place every day. It beats sitting around a hotel counting your money."

Franklin surveyed the place with his eyes and with a broad sweep of his hand said, "I happen to like this hotel, and I don't mind counting my money and buying supplies and keeping it repaired and hiring people . . . in fact I like it."

Brady didn't respond.

"It's respectable," Franklin said, then he was quiet.

"Maggie," he said. "Would you bring us two more beers."

Maggie returned with two mugs of beer and turned to leave.

"Maggie, sit down here with us a minute . . . we need to talk something over with you."

Brady was puzzled, but not surprised.

"Maggie, how'd you like to buy The Gold Nugget?" Franklin asked.

Maggie smiled. "I would like that just fine, Franklin . . . and I would like to be twenty-years younger, but neither are likely to happen."

She stood and Franklin caught her arm.

"I have a proposition for you, Maggie," Franklin said.

"Well I am flattered dear but I am old enough to be your mother."

Franklin smiled.

"I didn't mean it like that," he said.

He looked over at Brady.

"Me and B.C.'s going to Texas, and I don't know when we might be back."

Brady looked at Maggie and shrugged.

"Look, Maggie," he said. "I've got more than enough money to take care of my needs."

Maggie sat down. Her expression was hopeful, but doubtful.

"This is a good place," he said gesturing broadly. "It makes money . . . and you already run it top to bottom."

Maggie listened. Brady pushed his chair back and grinned.

"You set aside ten percent of your profits after you pay all the bills. Deposit it in my bank each month, and when it gets to ten-thousand dollars, the place is yours. I'll sign the deed and leave it with the bank," Franklin said.

"Franklin, this place is worth a lot more than that and you know it," Maggie said.

"Maggie, you were the first friend I met when I got here . . . you put me up, fed me and never asked for a nickel," Franklin said.

Maggie's eyes lit up. She pinched his chin and laughed. "How could a girl turn down a face like this," she said. "I did that as much for me as I did for you."

"Maggie, you never change."

Maggie leaned back in her chair. "Say we do make a deal. How much are you going to need for a down payment?"

"Sweetheart, you just give me a kiss and pack me and B.C. a lunch and that's all the down payment I need."

Maggie stood and Franklin followed suit. She threw her arms around him.

"Franklin T. Stilwell, you have just made me the happiest girl in the world."

Franklin and Brady rode for the better part of the day and Franklin pushed back his hat and looked over at Brady. "Texas, huh?" he said.

Brady nodded. "Yep, Texas."

Franklin laughed. "Okay, if you say so, cousin."

CHAPTER THIRTY-EIGHT

Austin, Texas: December 19, 1853

The cold wind that followed them across Texas now rattled the office windows where Brady McCall and Franklin Stilwell stood with upraised right hands and vowed to uphold justice and the tradition of the Texas Rangers.

There were no uniforms, the captain told them, and not many rules. They would use their own weapons and anything they acquired along the way. Their badges were government issue and everything else was up to them. The pay was poor and, from what the boys could see by their surroundings, there wasn't much to look forward to at the other end. But the work was steady, and there wasn't a man among them who didn't wear his badge with pride.

Rangering was fighting fire with fire. Most times it was impossible to tell the rangers from the outlaws. They traveled in ones and twos and in small companies as needed, but they were loosely organized and unstructured, which suited the boys just fine.

It took a while for Brady and Franklin to adjust to following orders, but they settled quickly into the rough, fast-moving life of a ranger and quickly learned that staying alive was a full-time job.

For nearly two years Brady and Franklin hunted down and brought in wanted Comanche fugitives, they led retaliatory raids into Mexico against border outlaws and they thrived on the excitement. In many ways, the Texas Rangers were little more than organized outlaws themselves, but there was a glory and pride about them that stood firmly in the path of criticism. Brady and Franklin rode the wave of public admiration, and before they knew it, the myth collided with reality.

Eastern politicians and local officials tried unsuccessfully to control the reckless style of the rangers. But everywhere, Texans rallied around their rangers. The rangers got things done the Army couldn't. They operated in a swift and final manner and, as often as not, justice was carried out in the field.

The reputation of the rangers along the Texas-Mexican border became legendary, and every Ranger worthy of the badge did everything he could to live up to the legend.

Brady's skills as a scout and tracker put him at a level above all others. No one could pick up a trail and follow it like he could. His days with the Blackfoot taught him things few white men knew. He could lead a company of men through the prickly pear and cholla without leaving a sign or making a sound. His talents put him in great demand, and soon he found himself leading missions that engaged the hostile Indians from one end of Texas to the other.

In the meantime, Franklin's recklessness and courage earned him a wide-spread reputation throughout the border towns, where he found himself continually assigned to cases dealing with the worst of the criminal lot. His mind worked like theirs. He was uncanny in his ability to locate and bring to justice, any way he could, outlaws so corrupt even the Army gave up on them.

Franklin rangered like he did everything else, with style and to excess. He refused to compromise any assignment, and his ruthless pursuit of bringing criminals to justice at any cost narrowed down the number of those who would ride with him to but a handful of men no less impassioned than himself. Recklessness and courage were the trademark of the Texas Rangers, but Stilwell operated at a level beyond even the most dauntless of the lot.

Fourteen months after he and Brady were sworn in with the rangers, Stilwell was promoted to captain. By then only eight men in the company would ride with him, but there wasn't a man among them who wouldn't follow him to hell if he asked them. And he did. And they followed.

In south Texas they became known as Stilwell's Boys, a name which rose above that of the rangers and, except for the badges and the backing of the law, they were considered no less dangerous than the outlaws they pursued. The Mexicans called them *Los Tejanos Diablos* and, while they were loved by some and feared by others, even those they protected regarded them with gratitude, but watched them with eyes grave and full of caution, for they reeked of violence.

The territory they policed was governed by violence and ruled by violent men, and the most violent among them was Miguel Zaragoza. For a year and a half, Zaragoza and his men rode up from Mexico, eluding the army and raiding at will along a stretch of border one hundred and fifty miles long. He stole horses and cattle and killed indiscriminately, and when he returned each time to Mexico he was harbored by the people, for he was one of them.

When neither the army nor the rangers could effectively protect ranchers from Zaragoza, Stilwell was clandestinely given the assignment to pursue without restriction and without sanction. He accepted. And when he asked for volunteers among his men all eight stood, and by morning they were across the Rio Grande, badge-less and up against impossible odds.

Less than a day into Mexico, across stretches of desert and rocky, treeless ground, Zaragoza knew of Stilwell's mission. And the federales knew of the breach of jurisdiction a day after that, and both Zaragoza and the federales sent men to intercept and eliminate Stilwell and his men.

For nearly three months Stilwell's unmarked Rangers rode through northern Mexico like ghost riders, leaving no trail and only whispered references to their presence as they passed through villages in ones and twos, and no one knew how many they were or from whence they came. But what the people knew, Zaragoza knew, and in time Zaragoza grew reckless.

Then one night, returning to Mexico with over eighty-head of Texas horses, Zaragoza rode into Stilwell's carefully set trap. One by one the Mexican guards were eliminated and replaced by one of Stilwell's men. When Stilwell and his four remaining rangers slipped into Zaragoza's camp and demanded Zaragoza's surrender, a short flurry of gunfire ensued, leaving Zaragoza with a shattered arm and a bullet through his jaw.

A week later Zaragoza died in a U.S. Army medical tent through the doorway of which he could see the horses for which he had given his life.

In October of 1854, Brady McCall and six seasoned rangers pursued a Comanche war party west out of Texas and deep into Arizona Territory. The Comanche fled with two young white girls stolen from a family in a bold daylight raid, deep into the safe domain at the outskirts of San Antonio.

The kidnapping outraged Texans across the territory. By the time the news reached Washington it was exaggerated and volatile beyond reason, making it an issue of national proportion that few politicians could resist. With the outpouring of public attention against the Comanche and in favor of extreme measures to eradicate the Indian threat to citizens of Texas, great political pressure was brought to bear upon the U.S. Army and the Texas Rangers.

By the time the assignment got to McCall he was offered a company of U.S. Army regulars, his pick of the division of rangers, and virtually unlimited resources to support the mission. McCall selected six men he knew and trusted and hand picked the horses they would ride. He refused the soldiers and asked that all other pressure against the Comanche in the area be withdrawn. McCall was making this a personal mission and, contrary to the popular judgment at the time, he was given the approval to proceed on his own terms.

McCall and his rangers picked up the trail and rode day and night, stopping only long enough to rest the horses and eat. He remembered the single-mindedness of Travis Kincaid, and pushed his men the way Kincaid pushed him and Franklin. At a military outpost they traded for fresh horses, slept for a few hours, then set out on the trail.

At the base of the Peloncillo Mountains they crossed the Gila River and caught up with the Comanche war party in a wooded meadow where they rested. The Rangers circled the camp to the north and south to set up a crossfire. A fierce battle ensued, and the air was heavy with the smell of gun smoke, and the noise that echoed off the trees was awful. When the fighting subsided the meadow grass was red with blood, and there remained the carcasses of unshod horses. Three Rangers lay dead and one lay hobbled with a shattered leg and bone fragments protruding from the hole in his trousers. But there were no Comanche, alive or dead. And there was no sign of their leaving, only the reddened grass and the lifting smoke and the noticeable absence of the chittering of birds.

McCall bound the wounds of his comrade, gave him extra water, lashed him to his saddle and turned his horse in the direction of the military outpost from whence they came. They bid him farewell and he tipped his hat and they all knew his horse would carry a dead man before the day was out.

The Comanche turned to the south through the deserts bordering the Pedregosa Mountains. The land was parched and formidable and, except for the Apache, no human eked a living out of this wasteland. The Comanche made no concessions to the heat, and the pace they kept never slowed. McCall and his men pushed hard throughout the day.

For the next three days they pursued the Comanche. On the fourth day they found hastily made graves where the war party unburdened themselves of their dead. The trail became difficult to follow as the war party crossed the granite rock and shale scree to obscure their tracks. But McCall followed their tracks as surely as though they had left them with the intention of guiding him to themselves.

At the peak of the mid-day heat on the fifth day they overtook the small band of Comanche kidnapers. Surprised and unprepared, the Comanche put up a vicious fight. But the battle was short, and all but one of the Comanche lay dead.

The survivor was captured but he refused to talk, and McCall set to questioning him with deliberate patience that soon wore thin. The children were no longer with their captives, and McCall knew there was little time left to find them. The prisoner refused to talk and McCall's patience ran out.

Brady unsheathed the Gros Ventre knife. He grasped the Indian's ear roughly with his left hand.

The Indian's eyes widened. McCall slashed upward with the knife and took the Indian's ear off in one quick cut. The Comanche warrior writhed in pain, but still refused to talk.

The two rangers held the Comanche while Brady severed the rawhide lace that secured the brave's loincloth, allowing it to drop to the ground and expose the Indian's genitals.

McCall unhesitatingly reached forward and took the warrior's testicles in his left hand and raised the knife upward with his right hand. The warrior's courage and determination crumbled, and he spoke freely.

He told McCall the girls had been given to the Apaches. McCall knew what he had to do. The only way to deal with the Chiricahua in their territory was on their terms. He had to go the rest of the way alone. He argued with the other two rangers. They protested and refused to listen to his reasoning. McCall was unyielding, and finally they agreed. When he stripped down and dressed himself in the breechclout and moccasins of one of the dead Comanche braves, they knew there would be no further discussion.

McCall rode into the desolate Apache homeland armed with only the knife he carried. He ate what the Apache ate and slept where the Apache slept.

And when it was all done McCall would never reveal the details of the time he was gone, but two weeks later McCall rode down off the mountain with the children in tow. He was gaunt, exhausted and wretched looking as he descended the mountain, hunkered over the neck of his horse and leading an Apache pony carrying two confused white children.

He rejoined his men in a dusty border town where life hovered around a dimly-lit, adobe-walled cantina. He turned the children over to the two men he left behind, and they carried the rescued children and followed McCall to the cantina.

At the hitch rail two horses stood with their heads drooping, ignoring the heat and the buzzing flies that gathered at the corners of their vacant eyes. In the shade of the doorway a bare-ribbed mongrel slept, blocking the step. He whimpered, and his hind leg twitched spasmodically as McCall stepped over him.

Inside the door the men hesitated, while their eyes adjusted to the darkness. A short, wide, Mexican woman approached them. McCall spoke to her in broken Spanish. She took the children, cleaned them, fed them, and made a soft bed for them in her own crowded sleeping quarters. The children were bewildered and exhausted. They slept the rest of the day and night without waking.

In the morning the three rangers and the rescued children rode homeward to San Antonio.

The rangers received a rousing welcome when they rode down the long street that led to the San Antonio sheriff's office. News of the rescue traveled with blinding speed, and before McCall and his men could comprehend what was happening, the entire affair developed into a major political event. Aspiring politicians drew in reporters and writers, all clamoring for McCall's story and attempting to share the glory by association.

The details of the rescue had been told and retold so many times by so many different people, each adding his own colorful embellishments that McCall became an overnight celebrity.

Franklin, not to be outdone by any eastern Johnny-come-lately reporters, fueled the fires of fiction with stories of McCall's exploits that challenged the imaginations of even the most eager writers. So engaged were they with his tales, they followed him all over town relentlessly, furiously taking notes and asking questions.

At first, Franklin would humor himself by telling brash lies, not really expecting anyone to believe them. When he realized the entourage of journalists took him seriously, he gave them plenty to write about. They gathered around him and he leaned back in his chair and rattled on as they wrote. Hours later the journalists departed with cramped hands and mountains of notes.

If the legend of the Texas Rangers needed a lift, it got it that day. Deep down, Franklin felt satisfied with himself. He knew he had left his mark.

A month or two passed quietly. The excitement of the rescue had run its course, and the politicians had pretty much milked it for all it was worth. McCall's life, much to his relief, had returned to normal.

Chapter Thirty-Nine

Several months and many missions later, McCall and Stilwell saw discouraging changes in the way the rangers had begun to operate. It was progress. Paperwork grew, and the company governed itself more through regulation and procedure than it did through field operations.

In the beginning they made up the rules as they needed them and changed them when it suited the situation. Now it was different. The rules were printed and posted and every ranger better damn well adhere to them.

The days of three or four rangers cleaning out a town full of outlaws on their own were gone. The raids into Mexico had ceased altogether. The Comanche were dying off as the white man killed off his food supply, settled on his land, and attacked his villages. Lawmen had been brought in to take care of the outlaws, rustlers and thieves. The reputation of the Texas Rangers would live forever, but the excitement of the early days was consumed by progress.

Their boot heels echoed on the wooden sidewalks of Austin where McCall and Stilwell walked together one warm summer evening.

"It's not the same," said Brady. "I'm filling out more papers and doing less work every day. And the commander said the rangers were making progress."

"Well, if that's progress, he can keep it." Franklin said with disgust.

McCall got that look in his eye and glanced over at Franklin as they continued walking. Stilwell knew the look, and a grin started slowly across his face as he shook his head and waited to hear the details of McCall's next plan.

"What do you say you and me take a ride up north and see if we can't make a go of it hunting buffalo?" McCall said. "They're paying a lot of money for hides, and there wouldn't be any paperwork."

"We need to do something different . . . no question about that," Franklin said.

Then he looked over at McCall. "Where'd you come up with the buffalo idea, anyway?"

McCall returned Franklin's look. "It's dirty work," he said.

"I know it is . . . so what made you think of it?"

"I've been thinking about it awhile. Ever since I talked to a man who buys the hides. He said he'd buy every good one we could bring him. It'd be like picking money up off the ground."

Franklin laughed. "Well, not exactly, but I never heard of anyone getting shot by a buffalo, so I'm in," he said.

They resigned their commissions with the rangers and that fall they pooled their money, bought four Sharps fifty-two caliber rifles, a wagon, a team of mules, and enough paper cartridges to kill five-hundred buffalo each, providing neither of them ever missed a shot. They traveled north to set up their first camp on the Canadian River.

The buffalo moved in massive herds and, when encountered from an upwind position, would stampede for miles at the first sign of the hunters. Franklin learned quickly from McCall and soon discovered that, when caught and under attack, the huge, shaggy beasts would stand and circle, becoming easy targets as they refused to run.

Franklin also learned it was possible to bring down a hundred or more buffalo a day, but the limit wasn't how many they could shoot, it was how many they could skin. In the hot sun the flesh turned quickly. Wet hides were heavy, and the work of skinning was slow and tiring.

Franklin never missed a shot, and it didn't take him long to figure out that it only took a few minutes to sight in and bring down a dozen bull buffalo, but it took forever to peel off the one hundred-fifty pound hides and load them in the wagon.

It was dirty work. It was hard work. And, except for the money, there was nothing gratifying about any of it.

Greasy, exhausted and reeking of the smell of blood and black powder, Franklin stared into the fire as Brady hung the coffee pot on the iron hook over the flames one evening.

"Damn."

"You say something?" Brady asked.

Franklin looked up at Brady, pursed his lips, and repeated slowly. "Damn."

Brady ignored the remark. He was counting out loud as he walked among the hides piled up just beyond the light of the campfire.

". . . seventeen, eighteen, nineteen. Twenty hides salted, and I counted thirty-six buffalo still laying out there. I should have said something when I saw you pouring canteen water down your rifle barrel to cool it off. I just figured you knew how long it takes to skin a buffalo," said Brady.

"It don't matter none," said Franklin. "I'm a shooter, not a skinner."

"Come morning we'll both be skinners," said Brady. "We gotta get as many of them hides off as we can before they turn and start to smell."

Franklin turned his eyes toward Brady. "Fact is, B.C.," he said, "They smell bad before we even shoot 'em."

Then he paused, and his expression brightened. "I was wondering, if we doubled up our loads and shot them in the ass, if they wouldn't be skinned before they hit the ground."

Brady laughed. "Maybe . . . but to be on the safe side you might want to keep an edge on your knife."

Franklin pulled out his belt knife and held it up to examine.

"You know, I'm still carrying that knife I got from you . . . it ain't cut nothing since you gave it to me."

Brady smiled. "Well, I'm not altogether sure that's the knife's fault," he said.

They started before sunrise and worked through the day. The sun worked fast, and the smell became intolerable before they finished, forcing them to abandon many hides. After that, they were careful to regulate what they shot by what they could skin out. By the end of the week McCall and Stilwell had nearly two-hundred good buffalo hides ready for market.

McCall had been careful to show Franklin how to select only those bulls and cows whose coats were in full fur. He knew from his experience with the Blackfoot hunters that poor hides made poor robes.

For every buffalo that hit the ground, Brady felt guilty. For every carcass they left rotting in the sun, he felt that he betrayed everything in which he believed.

Franklin proved to have an excellent eye, and between the two of them they were able to pick through a herd and harvest the choicest animals at will. The other hunters they encountered simply set up their shooting stakes and killed anything that crossed their sights.

In town the buffalo hunters gathered with their hides, dickering with buyers and trading for everything from whiskey to gunpowder.

The buffalo hunters were an unsavory lot, most of them being rough spoken and crude, and with a low regard for life, human or animal. They were easily recognizable by the odor of death that preceded them. Their buckskin clothing had been rendered slick and shiny by blood and buffalo fat.

They worked in crews. Those with good rifles and a wagon would have a following of three or four skinners . . . misfits and drunkards who would endure the hard labor and offensive task of pulling the hides from the monstrous buffalo carcasses.

The pile of prime buffalo robes heaped on the McCall-Stilwell wagon attracted the attention of Edwin Farnsworth, a representative of a large furrier in England.

Farnsworth stopped and introduced himself, and explained that his company wanted to contract for all the number-one quality hides they could supply up until the spring of the following year. He paid top dollar and took every hide McCall and Stilwell had on the wagon. They signed a deal to deliver a thousand more by April.

Using the money from the sale of the first hides, McCall and Stilwell bought more wagons and hired on extra skinners. They headed north, following the migrating herds.

The hunting went well. McCall's uncanny tracking ability repeatedly led them to the largest herds. Round after round pounded into the midst of the thick-necked, milling beasts as the lead-balls crashed through the tough hides and tore through the lungs and heart. The shock of the impact dropped the enormous animals to the ground instantly. When the killing was done the skinners moved in and the rest of the herd thundered away to graze quietly in a distant meadow, where their tracks would eventually lead other hunters who pursued them.

Frigid north winds reminded Brady that soon the heavy snows would come and the hunt would be over. Dried buffalo hides filled two of the four wagons. A few more days and the other two wagons would be full, the contract would be satisfied, and McCall and Stilwell could pay off their five skinners.

Franklin pulled his horse up near one of the wagons. The skinner standing in the wagon loading the new hides was a quiet, powerfully built Mexican by the name of Jesus Martinez. Two razor-sharp skinning knives hung from the back of his belt. He wore a bandana tied over his head; no hat. Hard times and trouble had left their mark on him. Martinez was quiet and stayed to himself, and his expression warned others to do likewise.

"Hey, Martinez," Franklin shouted up to him. "When we get this one full, we're going to send Brank, Stokes and Guthrie on ahead with the three loaded wagons. You and Tio will stay with us until we finish up the last one."

"Bueno, but you tell that lazy Mexican he better not slow down. I don't want to be here when the snow comes," said Martinez, looking down but not stopping as he talked.

Franklin grinned. "Don't you be too damn hard on Tio, or I'll send him out and leave Stokes with you."

Willard Stokes was a self-proclaimed outlaw from some undisclosed town in Missouri. He bragged that he was on the run from the law for shooting two men in a gunfight. He was prone to talk to excess and grated on the nerves of every one in camp. Martinez, particularly, had a low tolerance for his dishonesty and his lack of integrity. Stokes got by, and it made no difference to him at whose expense he did so.

"I'll tell you, Señor Franklin. You leave Stokes with me, and you will have one skinny, little gringo hide to sell when we get back to town," said Martinez, as he held up a gleaming knife blade.

Franklin laughed. "I don't have no doubt about that. If there was a market for him, I'd leave him with you."

Franklin rode back to the loaded wagons.

John Brank tightened the last knot as he tied down the tall stack of hides. Guthrie was hitching up the mules.

"Brank," Franklin said loud enough to get everyone's attention. "You and Guthrie and Stokes are going' to take these loaded wagons and start back today. Me and B.C. and the two Mexicans will meet you in Chama after we finish getting enough hides to finish out the contract. Shouldn't be more than two, three days behind you."

John Brank was hired on as a skinner and driver after the McCall-Stilwell outfit had already started the hunt. He rode into camp one night looking for a warm fire and something to eat. He was obviously a buffalo hunter but never made it clear exactly what he was doing out there all alone. He was a big man, friendly enough, and a hard worker.

Brank had a vocal loathing for redskins and greasers, but Franklin found him to be an entertaining diversion from the monotony of the prairie. Brady, on the other hand, felt uneasy about Brank but figured it was his hateful talk that made him dislike the big man. But this was business, they needed the help, and as long as he did his work, no one much cared what he believed in. The boys gave him a job and he more than carried his share of the work load.

Guthrie was barely seventeen years old. He had left a broke farm in Ohio and headed west to relieve the family of one extra mouth to feed. He wanted to work and earn enough money to send a little home to help his family.

Franklin found Guthrie in town, leading the old plow horse he left home on and looking for work. He was indebted to Franklin for the job. He was a good-natured, strong boy, willing to work hard. He followed Franklin around like a puppy and hung on every word Franklin said to him. It was always, "Mr. McCall," and "Mr. Stilwell," and he couldn't break himself of the habit.

"Hey boss," Brank said to Franklin. "Maybe it would be a good idea for us to pack any extra supplies and ammunition along with us so you can travel lighter, if you're going to be along that soon."

Franklin thought that was an unusual suggestion for Brank to make, but said, "Good idea, Brank. Load all you can, but be out of here by mid-day."

CHAPTER FORTY

On the second night after Brank, Stokes, and Guthrie left with the three wagons for Chama, Brady was preparing for the last day's hunt. He rummaged around through the supply boxes as Franklin and the two Mexicans warmed their feet and hands by the fire.

The weather had taken a turn for the worse, and freezing temperatures made the skinning job almost impossible. The buffalo hides had to be stripped free of the carcasses while they were still warm, or they became too stiff to handle, and they would be lost.

Brady called out to the three men standing by the fire.

"Any of you seen the extra cartridges we had stored in this box?" Brady asked. "We had two-hundred and fifty rounds in here day before yesterday, and there ain't a damn one in here now."

The three men looked at each other and

shook their heads. Franklin jumped up. He checked the extra food. It was gone too.

"That sombitch," Franklin muttered through gritted teeth. "B.C., it was Brank. He cleaned us out."

All four men realized instantly what had happened.

Martinez spoke up first. "It was Brank and that little gringo weasel, Stokes."

"Load up. We're leaving tonight," said Mc-Call.

They traveled through the next day and night, stopping only to rest the horses and mules. On the second day a light snow dusted the ground, and the temperature dropped.

"Franklin, we're going to have to cover more ground, or we'll never catch them," Brady said.

"No question," said Franklin. "Martinez, hold up there. B.C., we'll need the fresh horses and we gotta travel light."

They stopped, dismounted and led their tired horses to the rear of the wagon where their spare horses were tethered. Brady ran his hand over the old scars that reminded him of the many battles and hunts he had been on with the big buckskin. Buffalo Dancer put his soft muzzle against Brady's arm, smelling the familiar scent.

Franklin hoisted the saddle in place on the back of Three Feathers, while the gray-eyed horse stood patiently.

Snow piled up against the wagon wheels in small drifts from the wind that cut at them from the north. Brady felt a twinge of apprehension in his stomach as the two friends mounted their old buffalo horses.

"Martinez, we'll catch up with you in Chama. Give them hides to Farnsworth and buy you and Tio a hot bath and a bottle of good whiskey. Wait for us there," said Franklin, as he and McCall spurred their horses away.

Martinez waved them away and the two riders disappeared into the blowing snow.

Three loaded wagons made an easy trail to follow. Just before dusk, the trail split. Chama was to the south, but the wagons headed east. The tracks showed one wagon started south but circled back around onto the easterly route.

McCall pointed to the confusion of wagon tracks and footprints in the snow where the trail forked.

"There was trouble here Franklin," said Brady.

McCall's eyes followed a lone set of boot tracks to where they led up the trail, the drifting snow made them appear as smooth indentations. He turned Buffalo Dancer and walked the same path. Less than a hundred yards up the trail, he called back to Franklin.

When Franklin got to him, Brady was on the ground next to a frozen body.

"Who is it?" asked Franklin.

McCall brushed the snow from the bullet hole between the dead man's shoulder blades. He turned the stiff body over and gently whisked the snow from the crystal-laden features of Guthrie's face. The gaping hole left in Guthrie's chest where the bullet exited was frozen . . . red and ragged.

"It's Guthrie," said Brady. "They shot him with a buffalo gun. Let him run this far down the trail then shot him in the back."

"Let's go B.C., we can't help him now. Martinez and Tio will pick him up. We gotta get Stokes and Brank before they unload the hides. They're heading for Dumas, and they'll damn sure sell the hides first thing."

They pushed their horses east, traveling hard into the night until the cold and dark forced them to stop. The flat terrain offered them little protection, but the refuge they took in a coulee attended by a thick growth of brush and trees provided a suitable windbreak and enough deadfall for a fire. They watered the horses from the spring that fed the delegation of willows that presided over it. They picketed the horses then hunkered down over the fire wrapped in their heavy coats and saddle blankets, but neither slept, and morning was a long time coming.

At dawn they shook off the snow and threw the stiff saddles over the backs of their horses standing butts to the wind and heads to the ground.

The trail they followed was no trail at all, and all that remained was the snow that covered it. They rode their instincts and pushed ahead, trusting the thieves had done likewise.

They rode into Dumas from the north, and when they located the wagons, they cursed the misfortune of bad timing. Brank and Stokes had been there the men told them. They sold the hides and wagons, they said. They did not take time for negotiating, but took what they could get, and no one could tell them how long ago they left or in which direction they travelled.

McCall and Stilwell rested the horses, and they themselves rested the day and the night.

The next morning they rode back to Chama. Martinez and Tio were there, as agreed. They abandoned the pursuit with grave reservations, and neither said it, but they both understood the business with Brank and Stokes was not over.

McCall and Stilwell sat with Farnsworth over dinner.

"Gentlemen," said Farnsworth. "You chaps have done an exemplary job in supplying very fine hides. It appears, however, that you have under-performed the terms of our contract. Our count shows you're one hundred and thirty-eight hides short."

Franklin looked over at Brady and smiled as he forked in another mouthful of beef and chewed with serious intent. He held the empty fork up as to call for the floor, swallowed slowly, then spoke.

"Eighteen hunnert and sixty-two out of two-thousand's pretty damn good, ain't it?"

Farnsworth was silent

"Franklin, I don't think that's what Mr. Farnsworth is getting at," said Brady.

"Mr. McCall is correct. I'm sorry, but unless the contract is fulfilled in its entirety, the provisions of paragraph four, item number three, automatically reduces our purchase price twenty-percent over the total number of hides you deliver," said Farnsworth, genuinely disappointed at the misunderstanding.

Franklin stood up and bent over Farnsworth, who sat back in his chair.

"Do you have any idea at all what we went through to get you them hides we got?" he asked, but it was no question, and Farnsworth didn't answer it.

"A good man died for them skins. Two men who ain't dead yet stole the rest. Me and B.C. left enough meat out there to feed this town for the winter, and we been sleeping out in the snow to get you your hides. And now you want to cheat us out a what's coming to us?"

This time it was a question, and Farnsworth was searching for an answer when McCall spoke up. His voice was deliberate and unsettlingly calm.

"Mr. Farnsworth, we agreed to two-thousand good hides before spring. We're still short by a hundred and thirty-eight, and it's not spring yet. We'll get you the rest of your hides," he said.

Franklin stared at Brady, and he looked at Farnsworth, and he knew not to speak, for all he had to say was hot-tempered and hateful.

Martinez and Tio returned to the frozen prairie with McCall and Stilwell. It took them the better part of a month to get the hides they needed. They all suffered frostbite, snow blindness and exhaustion. Tio stepped through the ice on a deep-water creek and couldn't attend to the foot before it froze, and he lost all the toes on that foot. But they delivered the remaining buffalo robes and shook hands with Farnsworth.

Tio took his share of the money and went back to his family in Mexico. Brady and Franklin mailed Guthrie's share to his family in Ohio, along with a note that broke a mother's heart. Martinez simply said "adios" to his friends and rode out of Chama quietly, as was his nature.

CHAPTER FORTY-ONE

El Paso, Texas: January 1857

McCall and Stilwell decided to spend the rest of the winter in California. Brady thought often of Allison but, except for one letter from her, they had not corresponded in almost three years. Franklin was ready for a change of weather, and they both agreed California was a good idea.

In a dirty, west-Texas cantina on the outskirts of El Paso, the two friends drank cerveza and talked. McCall fell silent, and his expression was one of serious contemplation and revelation. He stared into his beer and his eyes lifted to look up at his friend on the other side of the table.

Franklin stared at Brady. Then he sat back in his chair and raised his hand in protest.

"B.C., don't even say it. Whatever it is, I don't want to know nothing about it."

Brady looked indignant, as though he was unsure what Franklin was talking about.

"Look, B.C., every time you get that look it goes with an idea that ends up with me getting froze, shot at, or having to keep a promise you made that I never wanted anything to do with. So just forget it. I'm out. Done."

"Frank," started Brady.

"It's Franklin, thank you," said Stilwell, as he waved at the bartender. "Señor! Can we get two more beers over here?"

"Franklin, I was thinking."

"Yeah, I know you was."

"I don't feel right about killing buffalo the way we been doing. I mean, everything about it's wrong, except maybe the money, but that's not the point," Brady said. "There's a lot of people need the meat just to make it through each winter, and we're out there leaving it to rot. That ain't right, and I'm thinking we sell off our outfits and call it quits."

"Well hell," Franklin said, relieved and smiling. "If that's all that's bothering you, forget about it. Maybe you didn't notice, but that was my Sharps Martinez carried when he left Chama. When Tio pulled them black toes out of his sock, I had already done decided my days as a buffalo hunter was over."

McCall paused thoughtfully, took another

long drink of beer, and wiped the foam from his moustache with his sleeve.

"You know, we could join the army," he said.

Franklin looked at him like Brady had just lost his mind.

"Yeah, we could," Franklin drawled. "We could go lookin' for trouble just about anywhere, but why would we want to?"

"For one thing," Brady said, "We would take our rank from the rangers right in with us . . . both start out as captains. Army officers are treated pretty good. Unless, of course, you're ready to head back to the Triple Dot and finish digging all those post holes we never got to."

"I don't know," said Franklin. "I gotta think on that one. Let's go to California first. I can't remember the last time I was warm, and I would like to think about this one first . . . if you don't mind too damn much."

Chapter Forty-Two

San Francisco didn't suit Brady. The city had grown. New buildings were crowded in next to one another, and there were just too many people for his taste.

Not like Texas, Franklin thought, as he and Brady turned down the familiar street that led to Maggie's hotel.

They pulled their horses up in front of the place, and it looked pretty much the same, but well cared for, and it now included the small place next door, which Maggie had converted to a respectable restaurant.

Franklin smiled. "Looks like Maggie's done alright for herself. Let's go inside and see if she'll buy us a beer."

Franklin dismounted and Brady sat his horse and leaned forward in the saddle.

"Listen, Franklin, I think I'm going to take a ride down to San Gregorio to see how things are with Allison. How about if I meet up with you back here in a couple of days?"

"That didn't take as long as I thought it might," Franklin said, grinning. "You go on down and, if she's still talking to you, give Missy Granger a squeeze for me."

Brady laughed. "Will do . . . don't drink the place dry while I'm gone."

McCall visited with Allison's mother a long time. She explained how hard it was on Allison to lose him a second time, and how she waited until she finally gave up hope of seeing him again. She finally gave in and married Waddell Stuart. She was content. She and Waddell and their daughter, Elizabeth, lived in San Francisco. She told him she didn't think it was a good idea for him to try to see her. Then she held him, and he thanked her.

He went to his saddlebags and pulled out a deerskin sack from which he gently removed a Navajo silver and turquoise bracelet and a woman's ring, also of Navajo turquoise. He thought of the many times in his mind he played the scene in which he would present them to Allison, and in none of them did he envision the scene in which he now found himself.

He asked Mrs. Hayes to give the bracelet to Allison's daughter, then he tucked the ring back in the sack and returned it to his saddlebags. She said she would, and when he turned to leave she told him she wished him well, and in her eyes he could see she meant it. But, he also saw the torn expression that told him she was relieved that he would not interfere with Allison's new life.

And when he turned his horse to the trail north, he rode empty and devoid of purpose. His thoughts ran dark and vengeful, but there was nothing and no one to strike out at, and the light in his eyes ran cold.

After that, McCall and Stilwell parted ways. Franklin joined the Army and was assigned to a cavalry unit stationed in the western plains to help keep the Cheyenne and the Arapaho under some semblance of control. He proved to be a strong leader and a master strategist and was promoted to the rank of Colonel.

McCall drifted at loose ends. Instead of enlisting in the army as he had planned, he saddled Buffalo Dancer and headed for Montana. He wasn't sure what he was looking for or what he expected, but after less than a month at the Triple Dot, he knew he couldn't stay.

The ranch was still home to him, but things had changed. Kincaid had met Laura Spaulding three years earlier. She was the widow of an army officer who had been assigned to Fort Smith. They became close friends, eventually fell in love, and in the spring of 1858, they were married.

Laura treated Brady like a son. Brady confided in her and trusted her with his thoughts. Both Laura and Travis went out of their way to help him feel comfortable, but Brady could not get on even terms with his feelings.

Brady never questioned why Allison didn't wait for him. He replayed his decisions over and over in his mind and wished it weren't so, but it was. He wanted to blame someone or something, and every time he tried it came back to him, and he was the worse for it.

Late one night after the others had gone to bed, McCall sat outside on the porch, staring out at the darkness. The door opened and closed softly behind him, and he turned, expecting to see Travis. Laura smiled and handed him a cup of coffee then sat down on the step beside him without speaking. They sat like that a long time.

Laura put her hand on his arm and spoke very softly.

"You know, Brady, love can be a hurtful thing sometimes. We never know for sure what God has in his plans for us. You just have to do the best you can."

Brady didn't look at her, but he nodded his head in agreement.

"I'll tell you what I do know," she said. "I know that you must be careful not to let that hurt get in the way and make you do things you know are not right."

Then she put her arm over his shoulder, and just for the moment he let himself feel like a small child, and with all his heart he wished it was Bill McCall asleep in the house and his mother here with him on the porch. He closed his eyes and wished it hard, and when he opened them, Laura smiled gently and patted his back.

"Miss Laura," he started, then caught himself.

He cleared his throat and collected his thoughts.

"I just feel like I'm going out of my way to give up everything that means anything to me, and I just can't seem to do anything about it. And I don't understand why me and Franklin are left, and everyone else is gone."

Laura wanted to cry, wanted to comfort this small boy, but all she could do was pray for the right words, and she knew there were none to be prayed for, and that alone made her feel empty and helpless.

If Laura had any strength to offer this boy it was gone, and she crept quietly over her next words.

"Brady, you're a wonderful young man, with so much to offer and so much to look forward to. I know you have a good heart, and I beg you to please listen to it."

Brady looked over at her and smiled. He turned and hugged her and thanked her.

The next morning, Brady went to the barn before the sun came up. He gave Buffalo Dancer an extra ration of grain. He spent a long time brushing the buckskin. His fingers touched the roughly healed scars that reminded him of so many different places they had been together. He thought of the battles the big horse had carried him through, and he wondered where all the years had gone since the young buckskin buffalo pony splashed across the Missouri river with a ten-year old boy on his back.

Brady felt more alone than he ever had before. His heart was heavy as he spoke to the stallion, who flicked his ears and nuzzled the grain bucket. Buffalo Dancer raised his head, stopped chewing, and watched Brady intently as the cowboy continued talking. The proud, old buckskin seemed to understand something was different this time.

Finally, McCall slipped the halter up over

405

the buckskin's head and led him out to the gate of the big, tree-shaded brood mare pasture. McCall dropped the halter from the buckskin's head and stood there holding the loose lead rope. The horse stood without moving. Then he sniffed McCall's hand and snorted. He raised his head, then trotted off a distance.

Brady watched the stallion strike a noble pose then thunder majestically off to claim his mares.

"I owe you everything, old friend," McCall said. He felt insignificant and alone as he watched the horse disappear over the ridge of the hill, and he stood there a long time staring out across the meadow.

CHAPTER FORTY-THREE

McCall left Montana and drifted for the sake of drifting. He traveled south, and by the time he reached Arizona Territory, he had attracted trouble in more places than he could remember. He didn't consciously look for trouble, but he went where trouble went and something inside him began to feel comfort in conflict. Soon enough he gravitated closer and closer to those things that allowed him to feel pain or to inflict pain, until it became his nature.

On an evening in late July, McCall sat alone at a small table at the back of a smoky saloon in Tucson. He started to get up to leave when the doors flung open, and three cowboys pushed their way to the bar. McCall poured himself another drink and sat back in his chair.

He reached across and checked the pistol hanging at his left side. He let it drop lightly back into the holster and waited. The loudest of the three was a slightly built man, whose courage was re-enforced by the two well-armed friends who drank his whiskey and laughed at his crude badgering of the bartender as they took over the place.

McCall's heart pounded as the familiar sound of the intruder's voice finally matched a name. The man turned and caught McCall's stare. For an instant he froze and fell silent.

"How's the buffalo business, Willie?" McCall asked.

Willie Stokes was motionless for a moment, then in a panic he reached for his sidearm. He drew and his first shot went wild, tearing into the wall behind McCall. McCall got off a shot and it caught Stokes in the chest with a hollow slap. The impact lifted Stokes off his feet and slid him back against the bar, where he stood suspended in time, then slumped to the floor.

The two men who came in with Stokes un-holstered their pistols and gauged their odds against the single spoiler now standing alongside his table.

McCall shouted, "Don't do it. It ain't your fight."

Before the words were fully spoken lead whined across the air at McCall, carelessly drawn and off-target, just enough to give

McCall an edge. He dropped to the floor as he fired twice in rapid succession, and his bullets ripped through the shirts of both men, who bled out and stopped breathing before they could be attended to by those who watched in silence.

The next morning McCall watched the sunrise through the bars of the Tucson jail. He was absolved of any criminal responsibility, but the judge declared him an undesirable and a troublemaker and ordered him to leave the territory.

Outside the courtroom, McCall stared blankly at the distant Sierrita Mountains. There was nothing about himself he was proud of; no redeeming quality to balance against the men he killed the night before, and if he had thought of Allison, he would have been ashamed. But as it was he felt neither guilty nor ashamed.

He earned his living crossing the border into Mexico at night and stealing horses to sell in Texas. Knowing the horses came from Mexican outlaws who had stolen them in the first place brought no honor or pride to it. To McCall it was simply a game that he played better than those from whom he stole.

He thought of Kincaid and the Triple Dot

less and less. He did wonder about Franklin, but even that seemed like a memory belonging to someone he no longer knew, and he gained no pleasure from thinking it.

McCall knew his last trip across the border was his last, and he was done with it without even thinking about it. He gazed up the street one direction and back down the other, and if he had a preference, it was no preference at all.

From across the dusty street, a soldier in a blue officer's uniform walked his direction. The soldier called out to him.

"Captain McCall," said the uniformed officer as he approached.

"Captain, it's me, Clayton Parmelee. I served under you in the rangers."

McCall stuck out his hand, happy to see a friendly face for a change.

"Clay, it's good to see you again."

There was a moment of awkward silence, as they looked each other over.

"It appears they call you Major Parmelee these days," McCall said, nodding toward the gold braid on the soldier's uniform.

"That they do, captain. Has kind of a nice ring to it compared to some of the things they called us in Texas," said the major.

"How do you happen to be in Tucson?" asked McCall.

"Well sir, we're down here on a little Apache business, and I heard you were going to be the main attraction at our local judiciary here today. Thought I might persuade you to take a job with the army as a scout, if they didn't hang you."

"I don't know Clay. I'm not really looking for anything too structured right now."

"You might like this job. It puts me to mind of the way we operated in the rangers before it got too civilized. Be your own boss. Just help us track a few outlaw Apaches that have been raising so much hell around here."

It didn't take McCall long to think it over. He decided anything was better than the prospect of one day dying face down on the dirty floor of a saloon where he would be tended to by lost souls who didn't even know his name.

"Well, I could use a change of scenery. There is one thing though," McCall said.

"And what's that, captain?"

"I have to work alone," McCall said, with no room for compromise in his voice.

"I pretty much guessed that," the major replied. "I ran that by the commanding officer just in case it came up, and he's in complete agreement. This isn't a typical Army job. The Apache don't do things the

411

way we do. We figured it was time to meet them on their own terms."

McCall listened and paused a long time before he spoke.

"When do we start?" McCall asked.

The major looked relieved, and he offered McCall his hand.

"We can go write up the papers now, and you'll be on the United States Army payroll effective today, if that's acceptable to you," the major said.

"Suits me just fine," McCall said.

McCall adjusted to Army life slower than he thought he would. But, for all that was in him that resisted the structure of an obligated existence, he found solace in the sense of purpose the military gave him. Discipline was rendered equally, and despite the immunity he had as a military employed civilian, they called him on his infractions and showed no tolerance for his disrespect for convention, and he adapted.

They redirected his aggression and frustration to a common enemy, and McCall took to it with great vengeance. Outlaw Mescalero and Chiricahua Apache raiders felt the wrath of a new breed of army scout. McCall was a patient hunter and a relentless tracker, who took his prey one at a time.

If they saw him he, was a shadow, if they heard him, he was a whisper. But, mostly they never saw him nor heard him and that made him a force more feared than the army itself.

McCall respected the Apache. They were tough and elusive and able to survive in a land never meant for the living. In them resided an instinct for cruelty and an endurance for hardship unlike anything McCall had ever seen before. He knew them as a young ranger, and he knew there was no give in them. He had no personal hatred for them, nor they for him, but both understood there was no negotiation for an accord between them.

In due time, McCall took one, then another and another of them, until the offenders retreated further and further into the wastelands of the high desert, where they vanished without a track or any sign they had ever existed in the first place.

McCall felt a familiar pattern in his life repeating itself. Scouting had run its course. He lost his taste for that which had driven him there, and he found himself thinking more and more of the rode he traveled and those whose faces now seemed like the faces of strangers he dreamed in a dream. He sat alone at a dark table with the glass of whisky he never touched and wondered, *If I could go back and change any part of my life, what would I change?* And he had no answer.

The next day he quit the Army.

He stood his horse at the edge of the world and gazed out at the end of it where it dropped off, and nothing beyond it was visible. Like a small ship with a meager sail and no rudder, he set forth upon the great plain, bobbing and waiting for the current to push him along.

Brady C. McCall. Twenty-nine years old, and he felt as though he had already lived two lifetimes. Allison Granger remained his greatest regret and the one failure for which he could find no way to forgive himself. He carried three month's pay in his saddlebags and rode north, only because Mexico was to the south, and he had no reason to go there. He skirted the tall mountains to the east and set a course which was no course at all, but it took him onto the prairies that stretched before him, and his insignificance was measured by his smallness in comparison.

The air smelled sweet and for the first time in as long as he could remember nothing hung over his life. No obligations, no responsibilities. When he came to a fork in the trail, he gave his horse his head. He ate when he was hungry, slept when he was tired, and each day was a magnificent re-awakening in which he was thankful to be a part.

At day's end he stopped and watched the sun set in a resplendent red sky, like a prairie fire at the edge of the world. He couldn't remember ever feeling more alive. He listened to the leaves of the cottonwood trees whisper in the wind. He heard a multitude of bird sounds he didn't remember hearing the day before. The water in the creek tasted cool and sweet, and not since his days with the Blackfoot people had he felt so close to the earth. And it felt good.

At night, when he pulled his blanket up to sleep, the sky was crowded with stars. Owls called gently to their mates, and McCall could close his eyes and rest. And when the moon was up, coyotes bent their heads heavenward and called out to it. In those moments of consummate solitude, Allison Granger never failed to slip into his thoughts.

Chapter Forty-Four

Kansas: Late May, 1859

The open land before McCall stood empty, and the vastness of it gave it a sense of foreboding. But to McCall it represented freedom. Freedom from obligation and freedom from his memories and, he hoped, freedom from himself. He rode easy in the saddle, and the horse he rode stepped out at a relaxed pace that suited him, for neither the man nor the horse saw anything before them but more of the same, and there was no hurry about them.

In the early morning hours he could smell the sweet smell of fresh dew on the buffalo grass that grew where he lay. At night the sky seemed to move further away to make room for the stars that shone, and he remembered the Blackfoot names for many of them. He watched the stars move, and he lie there breathing slowly.

If I could, he thought, *I would change a*

few things.

There would have been no killing. There would have been no move from Virginia, then there would have been no Franklin and no Allison and no Kincaid. Nothing that was part of his life would have existed. No Buffalo Dancer and no scars on his chest. There was more of him on this side of South Pass than there was on the other. He tried to imagine his father and his mother growing old, and he couldn't.

For all he had become, good and bad . . . for all he had seen and done, he couldn't imagine it any other way. For as many times as he had wished it different, he had no picture of how it should have been. He lay there a long time before he completed the thought.

You can't change one thing without changing the rest.

He looked skyward and imagined the stars were angels, and in his mind he reconciled himself to a universe of a much higher order than man alone. He didn't name it, he just accepted it as a reaffirmation of his own insignificance, and he understood.

Maybe where you're going and how you get there is all that matters. Where you've been is gone, and there's no way to change that, he said to himself, or maybe it was to the horse

or to the stars, but when it was said, he left
it at that.

By the time McCall reached the Arkansas
River he began to encounter other riders.
They traveled in ones and twos and in large
companies. Some looked to settle, some
pressed on, and those that came to settle
did so in unlikely places. He wondered
which of them stopped and settled where
they did because they had nothing left in
them and stopped because of it, and which
stopped because their dream was small and
they accepted the first offering presented
them.

*Do they have any idea what's on the other
side of them mountains?* he asked himself.
And if they did, would they move on or stay?
He knew they would stay just as easily as he
moved on.

He saw signs for towns with splendid
names like Emporia and Great Bend, and
when he passed through them, they were
small clusters of modest buildings presided
over by visionaries who planted the seeds of
civilization just as the farmers who followed
them planted seeds of corn and wheat. And
together they stood waiting and hoping that
others would follow. It looked to McCall as
a futile effort born of vanity and nurtured

418

by arrogance, and he continued riding.

He saw farmsteads carved into hillsides with roofs of sod and no tree about for as far as the eye could determine. The ground was dry and parched, and the raggedy families stood in doorways waiting for the rain which never came. But still they stayed and waited. It was their lot, and they had cast their fate to it.

Some would hold their hand up to him, and he to theirs, but he rode without stopping, and he wondered if they knew what lay beyond, would they pack up and leave or hunker down and wait for the rain. He knew they would wait.

One evening, between sundown and darkness, McCall turned his horse toward a brilliance of lights that rose from the dark prairie with great authority, and the horse hurried to it.

LAWRENCE, KANSAS, the sign read.

He stood his horse where the sign was, then touched the horse with his heels and rode to the far end of the street where two saloons dominated opposite corners. Yellow light filtered through dirty windows cast into the street, long shadows of the horses tied at the posts out front. He heard a piano, and he heard loud laughter, and he heard the sounds of loud whisky voices coming from both places.

McCall rode by. Too crowded for his taste. Too high a price for the hot bath, the big steak and the cool beer upon which he had his mind set.

Then the sweet laughter of a woman's voice lifted across the soft evening air, and he turned his horse around.

The next morning McCall sat for breakfast in the hotel dining room. He took a table where no one else sat and watched a portly man approach the desk clerk. Together they checked the register, then the portly man walked over to McCall's table and introduced himself as the mayor. McCall listened as the mayor explained that the town was looking for a new sheriff. In the last three years four men had held the job. All four lay side by side in a small cemetery just outside of town.

The mayor recognized McCall's name and knew him by reputation from the Texas Rangers. Before he could finish his breakfast, three other city council members joined the mayor at McCall's table. They made him a generous offer, and by the time he had finished his coffee, Brady C. McCall was the new sheriff of Lawrence, Kansas.

The United States of America was a country on the move. The railroads inched westward, and with every mile of new track came a lawless following of land grabbers, con men, and those who lived and died by the gun. Lawrence attracted them all.

It was a frustrating task and, even though McCall did make a difference, for every outlaw he locked up, two more appeared in his place. McCall's hands were tied by the restrictions of due-process-of-the-law, and a circuit court judge who was controlled by the illegal financial structure of the town.

McCall's frustration peaked, and he issued the city council an ultimatum. Either he be given full authority to enforce the law without political restrictions, or the town of Lawrence could find a new sheriff.

Desperate not to lose the only real chance they had to bring honest law enforcement to Lawrence, the city council agreed to give McCall the authority he needed and further agreed to replace the corrupt judge who sat on the court's bench.

McCall went directly from the meeting to his hotel room, where he unwrapped his big Sharps buffalo gun. He ran several patches through the wide bore and oiled the exposed hammer and set triggers. He loaded a heavy fifty-two caliber round into the breach, put a handful of extra ammunition in his coat pocket, and loaded up two extra cylinders for his revolver. McCall slid the pistol from its holster and clicked the hammer back and let it drop several times.

Satisfied that he was as ready as he was going to be, McCall shoved the pistol back in the worn, leather holster. He picked up the Sharps and walked down the stairs to the hotel lobby. As he passed the front desk, the clerk spoke up.

"You going hunting, sheriff?" he asked.

"In a manner of speaking, Abe," McCall responded, as he let the front door close behind him.

Ten minutes later McCall walked down Front Street, headed for the Longmont Casino. The thirty-six caliber Colt's Navy revolver hung at his left side, and he carried the Sharps on his right shoulder with his finger resting lightly on the trigger.

The owner of the Longmont and his three partners had previously been brought to trail twice on murder and extortion charges. A key witness was killed the first time, and during the second trial the intimidated witnesses refused to testify. McCall entered the casino alone and ordered all four men out of town. He gave them two hours to pack up and told them he would be back.

When McCall returned the outlaws were armed and ready. They refused to be told what to do in their town. Other sheriffs had tried, and they were all buried in the same cemetery. The four men refused to leave. McCall asked them one more time, and again they refused.

Townspeople, who had gathered in the street, fled for cover when a barrage of gunfire opened up on McCall from inside the building. McCall heard the cutting sound of flesh and fabric before he felt the searing pain of the stray bullet that creased his leg.

He rocked back from the recoil from his Sharps rifle as the blast blew a gaping hole in the door, and the bullet that shattered the door killed the two gunmen behind it.

McCall rushed through the door, surprising the other two killers waiting inside. Before they could react, muzzle fire from the Colt's revolver sent two rounds into each of the two men waiting inside. The impact sent them both reeling off their feet. One was dead when he hit the ground, the other lay on his back, his gun held tightly in his paralyzed right hand.

As blood pumped through the holes in his silk vest, the dying owner of the Longmont looked up at McCall.

"What happened?" he asked, his voice gurgling past the fluid filling his throat.

"You should have left," McCall said quietly.

McCall killed two more men that day, and the following day the unlawful men of better judgment and weaker conviction began to leave town. The citizens of Lawrence, Kansas had their first taste of law enforcement, and for everyone who applauded McCall's efforts, an equal number of disapproving citizens condemned his violent ways.

The new sheriff quickly learned that law enforcement was the small end of the task when it came to keeping a town safe and lawful. The big end was the political end, and he managed to succeed there as well, without compromise or acquiescence. The experience was as good for him as it was for the town.

By the summer of 1860 Lawrence, Kansas was a long way from becoming a sleepy little town, but McCall had placed control back in the hands of its citizens. He had hired two deputies, and after that the new judge's docket remained full.

In early August, McCall was summoned by the United State's Marshal's office in Kansas City. They asked him to accept a special assignment to transport a federal prisoner from San Francisco to St. Louis. He accepted, put his deputies in charge, and two days later he was on a train headed west, his mind filled with thoughts of Allison Granger.

CHAPTER FORTY-FIVE

Eastern Kansas: August 20, 1860

McCall gazed out at the flat land from the open window of the train. He was deep in thought as the wheels clicked over the steel rails and black smoke billowed back from the heavy-breathing engine.

He had neither heard from nor tried to contact Franklin, Kincaid or Allison. Allison's daughter would be five or six years old, he calculated. He thought of Allison often and wondered how she was getting along. Probably had two or three more kids by now. He could even envision a little Waddell Jr. He smiled to himself at the thought of it.

He had no false hopes, but he did allow himself the liberty of keeping Allison in his thoughts. The train car rocked and creaked its way toward the end of the rails, where McCall transferred to the Butterfield Overland Stagecoach for the long, bumpy ride to California.

McCall arrived in San Francisco in the late evening. He climbed down from the coach and stretched his cramped legs. He hoped he could finish his business early enough to give him time to locate Allison and maybe pay her a visit. The prospect of seeing her again excited him, and he refused to think she wouldn't receive him gracefully . . . at least as old friends.

He decided to go directly to the U.S. Marshal's office rather than waiting until the next morning.

At the marshal's office he was informed that the plans had changed. The schedule was moved up, and the prisoner was to be secretly taken out before dawn the next morning to protect him from those he was to testify against.

That left McCall with barely enough time to get something to eat and to get a few hours sleep, before he had to be back on the road with his prisoner. He was disappointed and walked through a drizzling rain to his hotel.

Maybe it's just as well, he thought to himself. Allison was settled into her life, and as much as he wanted to see her, it would only make things worse for both of them.

He remembered the time they had together in San Gregorio and how rapidly and intensely their love had grown. Thinking back, he could no longer even remember why he left. Now, it didn't matter.

Somewhere close by she must be lying in her warm bed next to her husband. McCall stared out through the rain-streaked hotel window at the flickering lights of the city, trying not to imagine that.

It was a restless night for McCall, and before dawn he was up and out of the hotel. He crossed the last street and walked up the stairs to the office of the U.S. Marshal. It was surprisingly noisy inside, and there was an unusual amount of activity for that time of the morning. At the top of the stairwell a voice called out.

"Sheriff McCall. Glad you're here. Come into my office, please."

It was agent Thompson. He looked distressed and worn out.

"What's going on, Thompson?" asked McCall, as he stood in front of the federal agent's desk and nodded toward the activity in the hall.

"They tried to kill your prisoner last night, sheriff," said Thompson. "He's not hurt bad, but he won't be going anywhere for a week or so. I hate to do this to you, McCall, but you're going to have to wait here in San Francisco until he can travel. I hope that doesn't inconvenience you too much."

McCall was elated. He smiled, and Thompson looked confused.

"No, no inconvenience at all," McCall said with a grin.

The marshal stood up, and McCall said, "You know where to find me if you need me." Then he touched his hat and left.

There were no doubts in McCall's mind. He would see Allison and set everything straight with her. He knew she had her own life, and he knew he would never be a part of it, but he wanted her to know how he felt about her.

When the mercantile opened he bought himself a new suit with a high-button vest and a string bow tie. And, while the store clerk protested on behalf of good taste, McCall refused to trade in his old hat for a new one to top off his stylish suit of clothes. The next stop was for a haircut, a shave, and a long overdue bath.

That evening he splashed on a generous handful of lilac water and headed for the Waddell Stuart residence. Polished and dapper, he strode proudly across the uneven cobblestone street. His jacket bunched up awkwardly where it hung on the protruding bulge of the Colt's Navy revolver. The sweat-stained hat he wore as a ranger drew odd stares from the civilized citizens he passed on the street, but McCall couldn't have been more pleased with himself as he gazed approvingly at his handsome reflection in the store windows.

He found someone who was vaguely familiar with the Stuart family and was able to locate an address, and he was on his way.

McCall paused at the gate before proceeding up the long walkway leading to the massive pillar-supported front porch of the Stuart house. He started to knock with the back of his knuckles but noticed the ornate brass knocker, and gently lifted it and let it fall softly against the backing plate. It elicited no response, so he tried again. Again no response, and the third time he banged it forcefully and began to repeat the action when the door was promptly swung open and a formally attired, elderly gentleman stood before him.

"Yes?" the gentleman asked stiffly.

"My name's Brady McCall. I'm here to see Allison Granger. Excuse me, I mean Allison Stuart," Brady said, as he removed his hat.

"I am terribly sorry sir, but the Stuarts are no longer in residence here."

"They're not?" McCall asked.

"No sir. Mr. and Mrs. Garrison bought the entire estate more than a year ago."

McCall looked questioningly at the gentleman.

"The house and the property," the doorman said smugly.

"Oh, I see. Well, can you tell me where the Stuarts went?" McCall asked.

"I am sorry, sir. I am a recent resident here myself and, quite frankly, I have no knowledge of the whereabouts of the previous owners."

McCall was crushed. He returned to his hotel room. He was angry, restless and unable to sleep; he could not calm his thoughts. He knew Waddell Stuart was a successful banker and an important man in financial circles. He also knew Stuart would not leave San Francisco unless it was for a bigger opportunity somewhere else, the kind of opportunity that lures ambitious men to odd places all over the world. They could have gone anywhere.

He may never see Allison again, but wherever she was, McCall had to know. He pulled on his boots, and with the night half over, he set out for San Gregorio.

The sun was high in the sky when McCall rode through the familiar town square in

San Gregorio. As he approached the store he saw Mrs. Hayes sweeping off the wooden walk out front. Nothing seemed to have changed much. Mrs. Hayes was a little heavier but still looked trim. Her hair was mostly gray, and she showed her age. She glanced up at McCall sitting silently on his horse and, not recognizing him, shifted her eyes back down and continued sweeping.

McCall stepped down, wrapped the reins around the hitch rail, and then walked up behind her.

"Mrs. Hayes," McCall said apprehensively.

Recognizing the voice, she spun around and stared at McCall with a stern look.

"Brady McCall," she finally said. "My word, what are you doing back here?"

"Ma'am, I don't mean no harm," McCall said defensively. "I just came to see how Allison and her family are doing. I stopped by their place in San Francisco and found out they don't live there anymore."

Mrs. Hayes' expression softened and she put her arm around McCall and led him into the store.

"Please come inside, we must talk," she said, as she closed the door behind them.

She looked up at McCall, and for several moments did not speak. McCall shifted uncomfortably from one foot to the other.

"Brady, you broke my daughter's heart," she finally said. "She waited for you and sent letters everywhere she thought you might be and never heard a word back from you."

McCall lowered his head.

"Ma'am, I'm truly sorry for that. I always meant to write but never seemed to be in the right place at the right time, and never was in one place for very long. Next thing I knew, a lot of things had got away from me."

"Brady, I never saw a person hurt for someone like Allison hurt for you. It took a long time, but she got over it. She started her own life. She has a beautiful daughter and just doesn't need any more complications in her life right now."

"Mrs. Hayes, I know you're right, and I sure don't want to do anything to make anyone feel bad, but I just want you to know, I never meant to hurt Allison."

"I'm sure you didn't, Brady, but I think it is for the best that you forget about her so she can get on with her own life."

Mrs. Hayes hugged McCall, and there was a sad look on her face.

"She always loved you, Brady. I'm so sorry things didn't work out differently. You better go now."

She kissed him on the cheek, and McCall

turned and walked out the door. McCall stood with the reins in his hand as he slumped against the hitch rail, staring vacantly down the street that led out of town and out of Allison's life. He stepped up into the saddle and moved his horse slowly along the dusty street.

In the middle of the square an old Mexican man leaned over the large, round fountain and splashed cool water on his face while his burro drank. Several small children played near the water. Their laughter and squeals caught McCall's attention, as he found a spot to water his horse. The sorrel gelding thrashed at the water with his muzzle before settling in for a long drink.

McCall watched the children play while the mothers busied themselves under the shaded arbor at the edge of the square. A little golden-haired girl stood out from her dark-haired friends as they chased each other around the adobe-edged fountain. When she passed in front of McCall, he saw that she wore a silver and turquoise bracelet on her left arm. At the same instant he recognized the bracelet, he heard a familiar voice call out from the arbor.

"Elizabeth. Come on, sweetheart, it's time to go."

McCall's heart pounded, and he looked

away to avoid being recognized. He hesitated, aware that Allison was looking at him and slowly walking his direction. An eternity passed and McCall turned his face toward her, as she approached with uncertainty. When their eyes made contact, his throat tightened. He watched her, but could not speak.

"Brady? Brady McCall, is that you?" she asked, in disbelief.

McCall stepped down and dropped the reins. Allison continued walking toward him.

"It's me," he said, barely able to get the words out.

He took an unsure step in her direction and she ran to him with her arms outstretched. Brady wrapped his arms around her and swung her off the ground. He buried his face in her sweet smelling hair and held her tightly. Their faces touched and her tears wet his cheek. They held each other without speaking and, finally, Allison pushed herself away from him. She touched the tears away with a ruffle-edged handkerchief and looked up at him.

"Damn you Brady, why did you have to come back now? I needed you so many times and you were never there. Why now?"

Brady looked down at her. The expression

in his eyes was confident, but uncertain. All he knew was how he felt and he tried to tell her.

"Because now is all I got, and seeing you one more time was all I lived for."

"But you knew I was married. Why did you come back?"

"I have so much I need to tell you," he said. "I did everything wrong, and I see that now. I just couldn't leave it like that between us."

Allison turned and walked over to the wide glazed-tile edge of the fountain and sat down. Brady followed and sat down beside her. She looked at McCall a long time before she began speaking. McCall could tell she was weighing her thoughts carefully, and he gave her time, as he waited in silence.

"Brady, I married Waddell and we were very happy together. He did everything for me, but I always felt so guilty because I thought of you so often." Allison dropped her gaze and looked at the ground. Her voice was almost a whisper.

"When we made love I was never sure who I was with, because you were always in my thoughts, and afterwards I would feel so ashamed. Eventually I put you out of my mind, but when my daughter was born I named her Elizabeth after your mother . . . just so you and I could have some unbroken connection between our lives."

Allison held her head down and took a slow, deep breath as she gathered her thoughts and tried to bear up under the embarrassment of confessing her private thoughts to McCall. McCall ached to hold her in his arms.

"A little over a year ago," she continued, "Waddell was thrown from his horse. He hit his head on the cobblestones and spent almost two months in a coma before he died. Then things got worse. He and his partner had borrowed heavily against all their personal and business assets to invest in a mining operation in South America. After he died the deal went bad, and we lost everything. It was terrible, but Elizabeth and I have our lives back together now. Brady, I loved Waddell and I lost him, just like I lost you earlier. I can't go through that again."

Brady pulled her close to him, and she wept. With his hands cradling her face gently, McCall kissed her on each closed eye, then softly wiped the tears from her cheeks with the back of his finger. McCall felt another presence and looked past Allison to see the old Mexican still sitting there, tears running down his brown, wrinkled face. The old man looked over at McCall, and he nodded his approval, as though he somehow had the final say in the matter.

McCall flushed. He held Allison's hand. She laid her head against his chest.

"If you think you could put up with someone like me, I promise you no one would ever love you more than I do. I know I could never take Waddell's place, but I'd be a good father to Elizabeth. We won't ever be rich, but we could have a good life."

Her face shone, and her smile was radiant.

"McCall," she said. "What are you trying to tell me?"

She laughed as he fumbled around with the words.

"Well, I'm trying to tell you I want you to be my wife . . . if you'll have me."

Allison looked up at Brady, and she wiped his cheek dry. She wept and couldn't answer, and McCall waited. Finally he put his finger under her chin and tilted her head up, and his eyes asked the question again.

Allison trembled, and the tears continued to fall.

"Yes, yes of course I will," she said, half laughing and half crying.

CHAPTER FORTY-SIX

McCall stayed in San Gregorio long enough to help get Mr. and Mrs. Hayes accustomed to the idea that he would be their new son-in-law. It was not an easy adjustment for either of them and, when Allison announced that she and Elizabeth would be leaving for Montana, it became a time of serious counseling. Allison reassured her mother, and while nothing Allison could say would ease her mother's trepidation, her daughter's rekindled happiness convinced her she must give her blessing. With great reservations, she conceded. Privately, she promised McCall she would personally track him to the end of the earth if he ever hurt her daughter or grand-daughter, then she hugged him and welcomed him to the family.

Brady and Allison shared their wedding vows at the foot of a massive, carved crucifix in the old Spanish mission in San Gregorio, and when the padre told them their marriage would endure throughout eternity, they never doubted him.

Allison prepared for the journey to Montana and waited while McCall returned his prisoner to St. Louis and resigned his position as sheriff of Lawrence, Kansas.

McCall and his new family made it to Montana. They moved into the old cabin Brady and Franklin had helped Kincaid build years earlier. With Kincaid's help they got it patched up the best they could before the snow fell.

That winter of 1860 would always be remembered fondly by Brady, Allison, and Elizabeth. Many nights they listened to the raw wind whistle through the cracks in the walls. In the evenings the wolves howled at the frozen moon, while Allison read to Elizabeth before the warm light of the fire. McCall would smile contentedly as he watched Elizabeth's innocent eyes when she asked her mother to explain the words she didn't understand.

McCall was as happy as he had ever been, and if he had any second thoughts about being a father, they were forgotten the first time he tucked Elizabeth in for the night. A brutal storm slashed through the valley, and the wind moaned loudly as it hammered the window with driving snow and ice. Elizabeth was frightened, and McCall sat with her by the fire and told her Indian stories. When she felt better and her sleepy eyes would no longer stay open, he laid her gently in her bed and covered her with a soft, warm buffalo robe.

McCall bent over to kiss her goodnight. She hugged him around the neck and, when she lay back down, she smiled with sleepy eyes and looked up at him and said, "Thank you for the story, daddy."

That was the first time she had ever called him daddy, and he never remembered a time when he felt more important.

When spring arrived, Allison announced that she was carrying McCall's child. In the fall, John William was born. John for her father and William for Brady's father.

News traveled slowly in this part of the country, but when South Carolina announced its secession from the Union and Jefferson Davis established the new capitol of the Confederacy in Montgomery, Alabama, word spread into the Gallatin Valley with awesome swiftness. By June of 1861 the capitol of the Confederacy was moved to Richmond, Virginia, and the Civil War was brought to the doorstep of the Mc-

Calls. Brady was certain his kin in Virginia would rally beneath the Confederate flag, not so much in support of slavery, but rather in defiance of any political imposition of Yankee will on southern morality. Montana Territory was not a part of the United States, and McCall outwardly refused to feel any responsibility toward the fight between the north and the south. Inwardly, McCall was torn.

Allison continually reassured Brady that it was not his war, but he was unable to convince himself, and he grew more and more restless as the army of the Union took the battle lines deeper into the south.

On a pleasant fall evening Brady returned home from the upper summer range of the Triple Dot. Allison's hand shook when she handed him the wrinkled letter from Virginia.

Dear Captain McCall,

Having resigned my commission in the Union Army, I have, in good conscience, pledged my support for Jeff Davis in defense of the new Confederate States of America.

Our Virginia brigade, under Col. Thos. Jackson, soundly defeated McDowell's army at Manassas, and we look forward to an early victory over the Yankees, who we believe have not the will to wage neither a lengthy nor a vigorous war.

We do, however, have a great need for your services to aid in the protection of the capitol in Richmond and to assist in the preservation of the Virginia homeland, which is constantly under threat by persistent Union forces.

Col. Jackson has authorized your services, with full officer's pay, as a civilian scout and reconnaissance leader and requests your presence, under special signed order of Pres. Davis, in Richmond.

The letter was signed by Lt. Col. Clayton Parmelee, and countersigned by Col. Thos. Jackson.

Brady looked up from the letter. Allison's feelings waged their own war within her. She knew Brady had no choice. She took his hand and held it to her breast.

"Brady, please don't let anything happen to you," she said.

CHAPTER FORTY-SEVEN

Parmelee was wrong. The Union had not only the will to fight, but the resources and manpower to wage a brutal and devastating war.

In the winter of 1861 McCall joined with Jackson's Virginia brigade. It was a shattering experience for McCall to see his boyhood memories of the rolling green hills of his home state laid to waste by the ravages of military battle. The tranquil beauty of the Shenandoah Valley had been desecrated by the litter of war and the irreverent presence of thousands upon thousands of Union and Confederate soldiers. It was a madness engaged in by both sides.

Parmelee died in battle only days before McCall arrived. He had taken a direct hit from a ten-pounder Union Parrott rifle and, according to the young private who had been entrenched next to Parmelee, "They wasn't enuff of him left to bury."

By August of the following year, McCall had been in more skirmishes and pitched battles than he could even recall. The smell of death followed him everywhere, and there was no relief from the suffering and devastation. Blue and gray uniformed bodies in various stages of decomposition cluttered the roadways and lay stacked like cord wood for burial details who may be force-marched to another front before they had time to dig the graves.

Nothing about the war made sense to McCall. Dysentery and exposure killed more men than enemy Minié balls. The short range of the weapons made each battle a face-to-face confrontation that unnerved men to the point that any sign of fearful panic in the ranks could cause entire companies of soldiers to turn tail and retreat.

McCall watched two young companies face off just before darkness fell one evening. The ineffectiveness of each volley brought them closer and closer, until one line could almost touch the other. In their haste to reload, both sides gave in to the fear, and a wave of panic washed out any remaining courage. One man yelled out in terror, and both sides broke ranks, running helter-skelter away from the battle.

Every engagement resulted in the loss of

thousands of lives, and the braver the soldiers, the greater the losses on both sides.

Robert E. Lee's Army of Northern Virginia was scattered from Gainesville, on the Manassas Gap Railroad, all the way up to Jackson's camp at Sudley Ford on Bull Run.

Jackson's brilliant victories in the Shenandoah Valley campaigns earned him a promotion to Major General, and his unwavering battle line at First Manassas had earned him the nickname, "Stonewall."

By late August the battle lines were once again drawn at Bull Run, as Federal forces referred to Manassas, and McCall reported back to the Major General with information that General Pope and his Union forces had entered the battlefield on several fronts, heading toward the Confederates from Centerville.

Jackson was calm and methodical as he deployed his troops near Stony Bridge. General Lee was anxious to move the lines forward but refrained under advice from General Longstreet, who was waiting for a report from General Jeb Stuart. Jackson took his men and departed. McCall fell in with the movement and watched as Lee grew impatient and wheeled his big, gray horse to the right to go investigate for himself.

Later, McCall would write in a letter to his wife:

Virginia Dec. 19, '62

My Dearest Allison,

I trust this letter finds you and Elizabeth and John William all fine and in good health. I myself have no complaints. Compared to most I have been fortunate. The reports you must hear on this war cannot adequately describe the awfulness of it all.

I have never seen men so poorly outfitted for battle as most of the Johnny Rebs on our side. They wear every manner of gear, and some have no shoes. Their spirit for fighting is strong, but sickness and disagreeable weather kill more of our men than the Yankees, and they are easily disheartened.

Last August we had a sweet but costly victory over the Federals at Manassas. Lee and Jackson are great leaders, and the Blackfoot would say they have powerful medicine, but I fear the Confederacy cannot win out over the Union anymore than the Indian can overcome the white man. I now know for certain Franklin Stilwell is somewhere in Virginia, and I believe I see him every time we face the enemy. It grieves me that any day I may face him in battle.

Mostly the weather has been fair. The wind blows more than I remembered, and now it is beginning to storm again. The boys will spend another cold, wet night, but the Yankees will look for shelter and we won't worry about an attack tonight.

You are always in my thoughts, and everyday I think about the day this war is over and I return to you.

Your loving husband,
Brady C. McCall

After their decisive victory at Second Manassas, Lee's Army was buoyed with confidence, and when Jefferson Davis predicted an early end to the war there was a renewed energy among the rebel soldiers. Their anticipation of walking off the battlefield with their heads held high soon gave way to the realization that defeat grew nearer with each new battle.

McCall was masterful in his ability to move undetected in and out of enemy lines. He quickly learned the back trails and woodcutter roads that provided Lt. Gen. Jackson with mobility and cover in the heavily guarded area of Northern Virginia, where the Confederates imposed a threat on the capitol in Washington.

On April 30, 1863, McCall reported to Jackson after spending six days behind enemy lines scouting Union positions and strength. They sat together on wooden boxes outside Jackson's tent as the bearded general laid out a stained and tattered map. The general hung his hat on the corner pole of the tent and wiped the gray sleeve of his jacket across his forehead. His receding hairline and hawkish nose drew McCall's attention to his intense gaze, as the general studied the map.

"McCall, the look on your face tells me the Federals have moved into position. How bad is it?" asked the general.

McCall sensed that, once again, Jackson had already calculated where the main enemy forces would be and was only looking for confirmation before committing his own strategy. As the general's head scout, he had reviewed hundreds of battle plans with Jackson, and each time he was awed by the general's clear ability to assess the enemy's movement and plans.

"The way I see it, sir," said McCall. "The Federals have established a line from the Rappahanock down Mineral Spring Road and into Chancellorsville. The Eleventh Corps is here," he said pointing to the map. "They're on the Old Orange Turnpike. The Third is right here, and right here, between Old School and Fairview, is the Twelfth Corps. If you don't mind my saying, we can't take them head on, sir."

"I suspected as much," said the general. "Tell me, is there any way we could move our men around, through the wilderness, right here, without using any of the main roads? If we can flank them, here," said Stonewall, punching the map with his finger, "Anderson can hit them here. McLaws can hit them here, and our men can cut them off here."

"Yes sir, there is," said McCall. "I found a woodcutter's road that will bring us in to the west of them on Culpepper Plank Road and up across the Turnpike."

Jackson's eyes traveled back and forth across the map, following his finger as he mentally went through the options and countermoves, trying to determine exactly where the enemy would be, and where they would move in response to any shift in the position of his own forces.

Finally, Jackson looked up.

"McCall, it will work, but we must get through the wooded area, here, without being detected. Are you sure you can find the way?"

"General, I can find the way," McCall said. "I'll get them through."

Jackson finalized the details of the movement with his generals. On May 2nd, while the Union forces were convinced the rebels were in retreat, Jackson's troops fractured the Eleventh Corps in a massive surprise attack that left the Federals in a confused panic. The battle of Chancellorsville raged on, and McCall fought side-by-side with the foot soldiers of the Confederacy.

The rebel armies aggressively pursued the Federals, and numerous, brave counterattacks by Union forces were ineffectual. By nightfall there was a confused clamor in the Confederate ranks as companies and regiments were inextricably mixed. Enlisted men and officers wandered through the chaos, attempting to reform with their own units in the dim moonlight.

Jackson sensed his strong advantage and asked McCall to ride forward with him on the Turnpike to assess the situation nearer the Federals' position. Several other aides rode with them in the darkness. In the path of their retreat, the Union forces had abandoned several important pieces of artillery, and the large number of personal items left strewn along the roadway suggested the Federals had incurred great losses. Muskets, ammo packs, headgear and canteens littered the narrow road.

Eager to get back to camp to organize for tomorrow's march, Jackson turned his horse and led the way at a fast trot with, McCall riding at his side. Unknown to the returning party, Jackson's Eighteenth North Carolina Regiment had already reformed and was positioned along the Turnpike, braced for a surprise attack from the Union cavalry.

Unaware that Jackson and his aides were on the road, they readied their muskets at the sound of the advancing horses and, when the general was in range, they opened fire. Every man in the North Carolina Regiment was energized from the earlier fighting, and when the general approached, they were prepared for another attack.

The volley was deafening and before Jackson's party had identified itself, the two aides at the rear of the entourage he had been killed instantly. McCall went to Jackson's defense, but he was too late. The general had been hit three times. The first shot shattered the upper part of the general's left arm, a second shot went through his left forearm, and a third shot broke two fingers on his right hand.

Jackson's arms went limp, and he was crippled in the saddle but remained upright. The smoke and noise panicked Jackson's wild-eyed horse, and he bolted. The horse was caught a short distance down the road, with Jackson still mounted but in great pain. As they lowered the general to the ground, artillery fire shook the road, and Jackson was moved to the rear.

On May 3rd, they amputated the general's left arm below the shoulder. He was convalescing and was moved to Guiney's Station for further recovery. On the tenth of May, his lungs began filling with fluid, and by three in the afternoon he was dead of pneumonia.

In the meantime, McCall reported to Maj. Gen. A. P. Hill, who took over Jackson's command. They had the Federals on the retreat, but on several fronts resistance was intense. McCall fell in with a company of young Georgia recruits of the remnants of the Twenty-third that had been captured earlier by the northern armies.

On the third night of non-stop battle, a lull in the fighting gave both sides a moment of relief. McCall lay back in exhaustion. His rest was disturbed by the sobbing of a boy who didn't look to be more than sixteen or seventeen years old.

McCall sat back up. The boy sat cross-legged, rocking back and forth. He cried, but there were no tears. McCall put his hand on the boy's arm.

"Son, are you hit anywhere?" he asked.

The boy shook his head from side to side.

"Can you tell me what's wrong?"

The boy nodded.

"Go ahead, son. Tell me what it is."

Something in Brady's quiet calmness soothed the boy and he looked up at Mc-Call.

"Sir," he said. "I don't think I can do this no more. I'm so tired I can hardly move. I'm scared all the time, and I don't want to keep on killing people."

He sobbed and pointed to the bodies of gray uniformed soldiers lined out for burial.

"My big brother is layin' over yonder with his belly shot out, and I just can't tell my ma and pa I let him die."

McCall put his arm around the boy's shoulder.

"What's your name, son?"

"Jubal. Jubal Sayler. My brother was Robert."

"Well, listen, Jubal. This is a bad war, and every man here is tired and scared, just like you. We'd all like to go home. It don't make

454

it any easier for you, but don't blame yourself for feeling the way you do. We gotta take it one hour at a time. If you can find the strength to get through the first hour, you can worry about the next hour when it comes. Do you hear what I'm telling you, Jubal?"

"Yes sir, I think I do. My momma always told me to trust in the Lord and He would provide. I 'spect that's what you're sayin'."

"Something like that. Come on over to the other edge of the woods. We can keep a better eye on the clearing from over there," said McCall. "You can tell me about your momma and daddy."

Jubal followed McCall and he seemed relieved and less troubled. They talked, and McCall liked the strong innocence and straight-forward manner of the boy.

Then it started again. In the bright moonlight, he saw the tidal wave of blue uniforms advancing toward them, light playing off their shiny coat buttons and fixed bayonets. Jubal set his jaw and prepared himself. Before the rapidly moving army was within rifle range, the green company of young rebels started firing. McCall shouted to those nearest him.

"Hold your damn fire. Wait 'til they get in range."

Jubal waited. His eyes filled with fear, but he overcame the compelling urge to run. The blue uniforms advanced, and their ranks stretched forever back into the darkness from which they marched. It gave the impression of an army of unlimited proportion. When the outline of the enemies' facial features shone clearly in the moonlight, McCall stood up and called out.

"Fire at will."

The ensuing battle was a nightmare. The darkness gave everything a feeling of shapes with no depth, no color, only the sulfur smell that hung like a fog. Frantic cries of agony and the deafening volley of gunshots filled the woods. Everywhere there was confusion. Soldiers from both sides became disoriented as blue and gray crossed together into a massive killing mob at the peak of desperation, and in a chaotic frenzy that looked like an artist's conception of hell. It was no longer a question of courage. With no time to reload, soldiers began slashing indiscriminately with their bayonets. Men started running, only there was nowhere to go.

It was impossible to know who was winning and who was losing. Jubal fought at McCall's side. All his fears and frustrations were unleashed on the enemy. He fought bravely.

"On your left, sir," Jubal yelled, as he stood to come to McCall's defense. The Union infantryman lunged with his outstretched bayonet, and McCall sidestepped him. Off balance, and with too much forward momentum to correct himself, the bluecoat slipped past McCall. Jubal met him in full stride, and with a powerful upward stroke with the butt of his rifle, the young rebel soldier from Georgia shattered the jaw of the attacker. McCall nodded to Jubal in appreciation. Jubal smiled and nodded in return.

Then Jubal lurched forward and the smile was replaced with a look of surprise. He dropped face-down at McCall's feet, a widening circle of blood spreading across his back.

McCall bent down and gently turned him over. He was still alive, but losing blood at an alarming rate. McCall held the boy's head in his lap.

"Jubal, can you hear me?" McCall asked.

"Yes, sir." The boy sounded clear-minded and McCall prayed he would survive.

Then the boy's eyes closed and a peaceful look came over his face. He began to speak softly of his childhood, his home, and his family. He spoke to each of them as though they were there with him. He rambled on for a few minutes, then his eyes opened. He whispered to McCall.

"Sir, please tell my ma and pa their boys died proud."

His chest rattled and his last breath escaped in a slow, relaxed hiss.

McCall held him closely, ignoring the battle raging around him. He put his hand gently to the boy's face and closed his eyelids.

"Go on home to God now, Jubal Sayler. You got nothing to be ashamed of," McCall said.

CHAPTER FORTY-EIGHT

Massaponox Creek, Virginia: July 1863

The battle continued into the night, but by dawn the fractured Federal armies had withdrawn. There was no pursuit. There was no victory. There was no rejoicing.

In the dim, gray light the landscape had taken on definition once again. The acrid, thick layer of smoke hung in the heavy morning air. Only the wounded and delirious made any sounds. Hundreds of survivors sat gazing as in a stupor, while others stumbled aimlessly about.

McCall gagged when the darkness lifted and he saw the staggering numbers of dead around him. Bodies in gray and blue uniforms, bloody and torn, lay twisted and deformed. He thought he had grown accustomed to the death and suffering, but this morning it was completely incomprehensible to him.

The dead lay about in massive numbers.

Young boys, some no more than children, gave up their lives right alongside the veterans. McCall was struck by the absurdity of it all. In a few days, the ground they fought to win would be abandoned as the battle front moved to other locations, and this place would once again become an insignificant mark on a military map somewhere. The wooded battleground was strewn with so many bodies it was impossible to walk through it without stepping over one dead soldier after another.

For as far as he could see, every tree was pockmarked by the direct hits of thousands of minié balls that had been discharged throughout the night. In the early morning haze McCall pushed his way past the shattered battalions and through the fragmented companies of soldiers who were lost and detached from the real world. Like all good soldiers, they simply waited for someone to give them their next orders.

McCall located Jubal Sayler and made sure the young boy from Georgia had a fitting burial. He put the boy's name and address on a scrap of paper and stuffed it into his pocket. McCall would be sure to let Jubal's parents know their sons died bravely. He said a short prayer for the young Georgia soldier, then set out for Chancellorsville to regroup with his company.

He forded Massaponox Creek and swung to the northwest to pick up a woodcutter's trail that would take him back to the Turnpike. He made his way through a thickly wooded area and followed a ridge that paralleled a narrow creek, twenty-yards below. McCall calculated that he was still in Confederate territory, but he proceeded cautiously and kept himself concealed as he traveled the backwoods toward Chancellorsville.

The horses that weren't killed when the fighting broke out had run off in the night, and McCall was afoot. He moved silently through the trees and heard voices coming up from the direction of the creek. He stopped and waited, as the sound came slowly closer.

Judging from the distance of the voices, they would cross the clearing directly in McCall's path. Like the stalker, he waited. Within minutes, McCall made out the uniforms of three union soldiers through the brush. One of the soldiers limped along on a badly wounded leg, and supported himself with the aid of his two companions. The bloody limb hung limp and useless, and all three Yankee soldiers hobbled along, arm-in-arm.

461

McCall shifted undetected to a position that would allow him to out-flank his quarry. As they passed by, McCall came in behind them on the trail. With his pistol leveled at their backs, he spoke up calmly.

"Hold it right there and don't turn around," he ordered. "You are now prisoners of General Lee's Army of Northern Virginia. Welcome to Chancellorsville, boys."

The bluecoats stopped without turning. McCall noticed the officer on the right slowly reaching for his sidearm.

"Don't make me put a hole in that blue coat of yours," McCall said.

The officer paused, then dropped his hand. He steadied his wounded comrade and turned his head slowly to look back at the voice. He looked across at his two companions who stood with ashen faces, and all hope drained from their eyes.

"It's okay," he said to his men. "It's just some dumbass cowboy lost from his company."

Franklin T. Stilwell turned and looked at McCall.

McCall's eyes widened and a big grin shone on his face. He shook his head and holstered his weapon.

"Damn," he said. Then he approached

Stilwell and wrapped his arms around him, and they slapped each other on the shoulders, and the two soldiers stood speechless and watched, not knowing whether to run or stay.

It was an improbable reunion by all counts. Brady and Franklin couldn't get over the unlikely odds of meeting, particularly under such remote circumstances. They discovered that they had both been in the same area for the past four months and, while they had never faced one another in battle, their paths had crossed closely several times.

Brady's first concern was for Franklin's condition. Franklin explained that he and his men hadn't eaten in a day and a half, and they had no medical supplies or ammunition except for the unspent rounds in Franklin's revolver. Their company had been trapped in a cross-fire, and as far as they knew, they were the only survivors.

McCall treated the wounded soldier and fed all three men from his own ration pack, then he and Franklin sat down to talk.

"I never thought I'd be happy to see another Johnny Reb again if I lived to be a hundred, but that sorry face of yours is one of the prettiest sights I seen since I been down here," Franklin said.

"All the same, Franklin, you are my prisoners," McCall said.

Franklin looked up at Brady, and Brady wasn't smiling.

"No we ain't," he said back.

"You damn sure are."

"No we ain't."

"Are too."

Franklin shook his head as if to discount Brady's argument and said, "Look, I seen you sneaking around up in them bushes like you was getting away with something. Why do you think I let you get the drop on us the way you done?"

"Maybe because you never knew I was there. You three were talking and carrying on like school girls going to a picnic. Hell, you were walking right into the middle of half the damn Confederate army and didn't even know where you were going."

"Well, just so you'll know, look here on this map and I'll show you where we was going, if you can keep from telling it all to that barefoot, farm boy army of yours out there," Franklin said.

He folded out his map and showed McCall where he was trying to rejoin his forces. They both became very serious, and McCall pointed to the spot on the map just ahead of their present position.

"Franklin, your armies have retreated all the way back to here. The last I heard, they were moving their artillery across the Rappahannock. You do know you're in the middle of Confederate lines don't you?" McCall asked with grave concern.

"Yeah, I do know that much," Franklin said. "And I also know we ain't your damn prisoners."

McCall pointed through the brush into a clearing up ahead where a company of rebel soldiers was bivouacked.

"You'll be mine or you'll be theirs," he said, and as he said it the other two soldiers began to move as if to make a break, but Stilwell stopped them.

"What are you thinking, B.C.?" he asked.

"Well, you can't travel at night, and this place is thick with Confederate armies. You give me your weapons, and I'll march you through our lines at gunpoint. We get to federal territory, and you and your boys can slip on in on your own. Anybody stops us, I'll just tell them I'm delivering my prisoners, and nobody will be the wiser."

Franklin nodded in agreement. "It's the only chance we got," he said.

"But, just so you know . . . you didn't really capture us . . . we was baiting you."

Brady pulled out the Gros Ventre knife

and drew it flat-edged slowly across his trouser leg without looking up.

"I been following you since last night . . . could have taken you in your sleep," he lied.

Franklin shook his head, and they laughed. They talked and rested until early afternoon. After they got caught up on all the news, McCall looked over at Franklin.

"I been thinking," McCall said, then he paused.

"I don't need any more of your ideas. Do you remember the last time we had this conversation? You said, 'Wouldn't it be a good idea if we just joined the army?' Well, I did but you lit out for parts unknown, and that was the last I heard from you." He settled back and looked off across into the trees.

He turned back towards Brady. "Why is it every time you get an idea I end up getting shot at?"

"It's your nature to get shot at, Franklin. People like shooting at you."

"Not that I'm interested," Franklin said. "But what's your idea this time?"

"Well, I think you and me should get out of this war as quick as we can and get back in the cattle business," Brady said.

Franklin laughed a sarcastic laugh. "Now who doesn't want to get out of this war? I still got eight months to go on my commission . . . and besides, where are we going to get enough money to get back in the cattle business?"

"We still have a share in the Triple Dot . . . not that we have any claim to that, but we got the land. We can go down into Texas and Mexico and gather up a couple thousand head of those free-running, longhorn range cows. They'd make us a good start," Brady said.

"Are them cows easy-picking or do we have to hunt them down one at a time?" Franklin asked.

"They're easy picking."

"You sure about that?"

"I'm sure."

Franklin thought about it a minute. "Alright, let's do it," he said, then he smiled as though they could pack up that evening and go get it done.

But neither man had any way to know the war would drag on, but it did, and they fought through the hot stifling summer and the unmerciful cold of winter. Every time a rebel soldier fell, Franklin prayed it wasn't Brady. Confederate victories came less frequently and soon the Union forces dominated battle after battle. The price of victory was dear, and when the final count would someday be tallied, they would find more than six-hundred thousand soldiers had died.

With their supplies of food, ammunition and clothing depleted, the Confederate armies fought on sheer determination, but it wasn't enough. In the spring of 1865, General Robert E. Lee brought an end to the suffering and relief to both the North and the South when he surrendered with honor and dignity at Appomattox. And two men, one wearing gray, the other blue, threw down their packs and saddled their horses and rode west.

CHAPTER FORTY-NINE

Shenandoah Valley, Virginia: April 14, 1865
McCall paused at the summit as he crossed the Appalachian Mountains on his way back to Montana. He turned his horse and looked down into the Shenandoah Valley. He would never again be able to think of Virginia as home.

He followed the sun west and rode straight through the first two days, stopping only to feed and water his horse. At night his mind spun with thoughts of Allison. He wondered how much Elizabeth and John William had grown, then hours before sun-up he was back on the trail.

Col. Franklin T. Stilwell resigned his commission in Washington, D.C. the day the war ended. Throngs of people crowded the streets and it seemed that all of humanity was on the move. It was a glorious time of rebirth for a nation whose heart had been cut out by the very men who fought for her well-being. There was hope and excitement in the air, and young and old alike celebrated, not the end of a war, but the beginning of a new country.

Franklin ached to breath the sharp, cool, Rocky Mountain air and to wake up to the quiet stillness that he always remembered in the unending loudness of war. Somewhere east of Kansas City, Franklin thought about the deal he had made with McCall. He chuckled. "I don't know," he said out loud, "how the hell he thinks me and him are going to run four-thousand head of cows out of Mexico, but I'm damn sure ready to give it a try."

Well, they did it. Not once, but three different times. McCall and Stilwell pioneered cattle drives, set new trails and joined the ranks of better known cattlemen like Goodnight, Loving, Chisholm, and a handful of others.

They operated on the fine line that separates the questionable from the illegal, but they never made a dishonest deal and never put an iron on a cow they knew belonged to someone else. That was not a quality shared by many cattlemen, but Kincaid was immovable on the subject. He swore he would hang any man caught altering a brand and would shoot any man he found marking calves with an iron that didn't match the brand its momma wore.

The beef industry went through hard times, and the Triple Dot Ranches swung dangerously close to failure, but each time Kincaid, Stilwell, and McCall were able to readjust and survive.

Over the years, McCall resettled his family on the northernmost ranch of the Triple Dot on the Sweet Grass River. Franklin stayed on and built up the original place in the Gallatin Valley, while Kincaid and his wife ran the big ranch at Ennis Lake.

In 1876, Kincaid made the last drive. He was sixty-nine years old, and they had just delivered over three-thousand troublesome longhorn cattle to the railhead in Abilene, Kansas. Water had been scarce, the cattle disagreeable, and the weather unpredictable. They watched a quicksand bog swallow a young wrangler and his horse, lost two good cowboys to a stampede that happened for no apparent reason, and were plagued by a lightning storm that struck a horse right out from under one of the night riders.

The drive of '76 would be talked about and remembered by the Triple Dot crew and the drovers who rode with them as the toughest drive any of them had ever experienced. Those who survived it would collect their pay and turn themselves loose on the eagerly waiting town of Abilene. They would drink heartily in honor of those they buried on the trail.

Kincaid sat high on the back of his big dun-colored mare and spoke to the cowboys bunched around the horse corral at the feed lot.

"Boys, I just want to tell you two things. Number one, I don't believe I ever rode with better. Number two, you'll draw your pay at the hotel at three o'clock. Well, I said two, but the truth is, I do have a few more things to add."

Kincaid shifted in the saddle and looked over the collection of drovers before him. Most were young. Age showed through on a few. They were tired, dirty, and just plain worn out, but Kincaid knew he could tell them they were going to cover the same trail back the next day, and every one of them would be saddled up at daybreak. Kincaid was proud of his men, and it showed when he spoke.

"There's a permanent job waiting for everyone of you that wants to ride for the Triple Dot. The food's good. The winters are too damn long . . . and the pay will just barely cover it . . . be here tomorrow morning if you're interested. To those of you with better sense . . . I wish you my best and hope our trails cross again someday."

The air exploded with whoops and hollers, hats flew in the air and, when the dust settled, it was a cowboy foot-race to the nearest bath house and barber shop. Kincaid laughed as he watched his good trail hands disappear around the corner. He turned the mare out in the corral with fresh hay, hung his saddle over his shoulder and picked up his rifle with his free hand.

He paused when he read the inscription etched into the barrel just behind the buckhorn sight of the Winchester. One of One Thousand, it said. He smiled. The rifle was a Christmas gift from the McCalls. It was special for that reason alone, but additionally so because it had been designated by the Winchester company as a specially selected rifle of superior accuracy.

He liked the heft of the long, twenty-eight inch octagon barrel and, in spite of its weight, he kept the '73 with him where ever he went.

Starting out toward the hotel, he felt uneasy. John William would be with the cattle buyer picking up the cash from the sale of the herd. It would amount to fifteen or twenty-thousand dollars, Kincaid calculated, as he replayed the situation in his mind. He did not want to make John William feel like he was watching over him, but he knew Abilene attracted more than its share of thieves and outlaws. Maybe it was nothing, but it just didn't feel right to him.

He decided to stay clear and let John William handle this himself. The First National Bank of Kansas was a short walk from the buyer's office, and John William would have the deposit made, and they would be drinking a cold beer in less than fifteen minutes.

Kincaid waited out of the way, near the hotel on the opposite side of the street from the buyer's office.

John William came out of the building, followed by the deputy who was to provide security until they got to the bank. They stepped into the street, casually talking as they walked in the direction of the First National.

Kincaid positioned himself on the sidewalk where he had a clear view of both sides of the street. His nerves were on end. He unconsciously turned the latch screw to free the lever on the Winchester, then he methodically chambered a cartridge as he watched the two men near the center of the street.

Then it happened. Without warning, two

men rushed out from the alley alongside the Empire Saloon. They fired their pistols at almost the same instant, and the deputy dropped to his knees. Another blast of gunfire, and the unsuspecting lawman was slammed backwards to the ground.

John William drew his gun and fired as he went to the aid of the deputy. The boy's shot caught one of the attackers in the throat, and he spun him off his feet, dead.

Kincaid raised his rifle and fired a quick shot in the direction of the bandits. His bullet whined harmlessly off into the air, deflected by a wagon that had lurched into the line of fire when its startled team broke loose. Kincaid moved across the sidewalk and into the street, as he started to close the distance between himself and the shooters. When he cleared the wagon he noticed that John William had downed one of the men, but the other had quickly disarmed him and now held the boy in front of himself as a shield. A third outlaw, who Kincaid had not seen earlier, stood at the entrance to the alley with his rifle trained on Kincaid.

It was a standoff, and John William's captor threatened to kill the boy if they were not allowed to ride unharmed out of town. Kincaid was certain they would kill John

William at the first opportunity, and he stood his ground with his rifle pointed at the man holding Brady's son. It would be an impossible shot, more than a hundred yards, and only inches separated the outlaw from John William.

Kincaid was rock steady, and he squeezed the trigger. The bullet screamed by John William's ear and shattered the forehead of the outlaw, who never even heard the shot. At the same instant, Kincaid whirled the rifle to his left as he levered in another round. He squeezed the trigger again, and in unison two shots rang out. The outlaw tumbled from the alley entrance and crumpled dead in the dirt.

The outlaw's bullet ripped into Kincaid's chest and tore a massive hole through his ribs. For a moment, he just stood there, and it appeared he was unhurt. He smiled at John William. The bloodstain spread rapidly across the front of Kincaid's shirt. John William started for Kincaid. Before he reached him, the old cowboy had dropped to one knee, supporting himself with the butt of the rifle.

John William steadied him, then sat him down and held him and screamed for someone to get a doctor.

"Are you okay, Travis?" John William

asked, his voice cracking.

Kincaid shook his head slowly. "I don't think so," he said weakly.

John William tried in vain to stop the bleeding. Kincaid was alert but fading, as he gathered his thoughts and his strength. He smiled thinly and slowly shook his head.

"I believe this is it for me," he said in a raspy whisper. "J.W., I want you keep this in the family."

He handed John William the Winchester, then exhaled a long, deep sigh. Travis Kincaid was dead. John William gently laid the old cowboy on his back and wept openly.

At the first sound of the shooting, Brady and Franklin knew instinctively that something had gone wrong. Fearing the worst, they spurred their horses from the feedlot at a gallop. When they turned the corner at the end of Commerce Street, a crowd had already gathered in front of the hotel.

Brady leaped from his horse. He pushed his way through the spectators and shouted. "Where's my son?"

To his relief, he heard John William call out from the other side of the crowd.

"Over here, Pa. I'm okay, but they shot Travis."

Franklin was at Brady's side, roughly pushing the crowd aside as they hurried to the spot where John William knelt beside the fallen cowboy. Brady dropped to his knees and looked at John William questioningly. The boy restrained him with a hand on his shoulder.

"Pa, it's too late. Travis is dead. He saved my life."

Brady didn't speak. He reached over and closed the old cowboy's eyes, then he took Travis's gnarled hand in his own, and he looked up at the soft clouds in the sky. He imagined a gray-haired cowboy in ragged leather chaps and run-down boots, standing at heaven's gate with his thumbs hooked in his front pockets and his battered old hat pushed back, politely waiting his turn to enter.

Brady tried not to weep, tried to hold back the tears. And he prayed a short prayer in a voice that shook and failed as he spoke.

"Lord, this here is Travis Kincaid. We thank you for him and even though we don't understand why you called him now, we pray you'll welcome him in heaven and give him a warm place to sleep."

Then he reached down and touched Kincaid's cheek.

"God be with you, Travis," he said quietly.

CHAPTER FIFTY

In 1881, John William McCall married Anna Martin, the daughter of a miner from Butte, Montana. The following year their son was born. In honor of Travis Kincaid, they named the baby Miles Travis McCall.

Franklin never married. As much as the ladies liked being around him, none of the women he knew was willing to take on the task of trying to rehabilitate his tumbleweed nature. The thought of domesticating Franklin T. Stilwell humbled even the most determined of them.

He had pretty much given up on the idea of marriage by the time he met Jenny Kendrick. Jenny was a preacher's daughter from Bozeman. She was dark-haired and strong-willed and fell completely in love with Franklin the first day she met him.

Franklin met his match in Jenny and the two of them talked of marriage, but when he was ready, she had reservations, and when she was ready, he procrastinated, and so it went year after year and, in spite of their indecisiveness, no two people could have been happier together.

Elizabeth McCall grew up loving the Montana wilderness. She was Brady's girl, and he taught her everything he knew about horses. She was as good with a colt as any man on the ranch. She even bucked out a few, which made Allison nervous and Brady proud. She put her trademark on every horse she finished. Each one was gentle and responsive. Never a misfit in her string. Her ponies would work cows all week, then take you out for a quiet ride on Sunday.

She eventually established a reputation among the local cowboys and even the rough-stock riders would come to her for advice. Brady would shake his head and laugh every time he saw his little girl show some raw-boned cowboy how to get over a problem he was having with a new horse. There she would be, barely over five feet tall, hanging on to a rope with a snorting bronc at the other end, while some big cowboy stood by listening to every word she said.

Elizabeth left the Triple Dot when she

married a cattleman from the Billings area, where she lived and raised a family of her own.

Travis Kincaid and his wife Laura never had children, and after Kincaid's death, Franklin and Brady managed Laura's ranch for her, along with their own. Laura was family, and when she grew too old to get by on her own, Brady and Allison moved her in with them.

Laura was Allison's best friend. She was grandmother to the children, mentor to Allison and Anna, and Aunt Laura to Franklin and Brady.

It was a time of change in the West, and the speed with which the land and the people gave in to it was incomprehensible to Brady and Franklin. They dug their heels in and resisted. They fought the barbed wire and the railroads. When other cattlemen began switching to the stockier Hereford and Angus breeds from Europe, they stayed with the Texas Longhorns. Some of their decisions were good ones, and others proved to be costly, but they held on to their land while others sold theirs off in parcels. The land was their strength.

CHAPTER FIFTY-ONE

Madison River, Montana: June 1891
Brady McCall's body lay amidst the blood-stained rocks and dirt of the dry creek bed where he had made his last futile attempt to climb the steep embankment. The struggle had ended quietly.

If and when they found the body, they would shake their heads and wonder why he had given up so easily. They wouldn't understand the helplessness, and they would think it unlike McCall to accept such a fate with so little resistance.

Birds returned to the trees from which they had been startled earlier in the day. Their sharp calls and warbling songs gave no suggestion of the struggle for life that had that had gone on here. Nature adjusted quickly, and neither a birth nor a death made any lasting impact.

Flies gathered on McCall's bloody hand and buzzed about the fleshy socket that had once held his thumb. A line of black ants marched across his out-stretched leg, which had become a new obstacle in their path as they went about their daily business.

Buzzards who had circled above for the last hour watched, and one circled lower and landed awkwardly near the body. It arched its head and watched the body with first one eye, then the other. It hopped closer and eyed the body again. It pecked at the boot, then at the trouser, and eyed the bloody hand hung across the man's chest.

The bird hissed, then flapped its scruffy wings and came to rest on the man's out-stretched legs. It cocked its terrible head, then reached forth and tore a piece of the raw flesh from the still bleeding hand, and when it did so a fearsome sound emanated from the body, and the man sat bolt upright, and the buzzard scrambled back to safety and took flight.

McCall reeled back at the sight of the yellow eyes in his face, and the stench of the bird made him turn his head and lash out with his good hand. McCall screamed again as though he had just awoken from a nightmare to a reality more frightening than the nightmare itself.

He rose to his feet and was standing before he knew it. He turned and took a desperate leap for the ledge, pushing with his legs and grappling with his hand. The momentum carried him up the embankment, and he crawled and scrambled towards the branding fire. His lungs burned and his eyes were heavy, and when he reached in and took hold of the branding iron, he was unable to hold it. He kicked the hot handle with his boot and spun the hot end around, placed a willow branch between his teeth, then ran the bloody wound up against the hot iron, and the smoke that rose from it was putrid, and the pain slammed him back and he lost consciousness.

When he awoke, the afternoon sun was on his face, and the pain from his hand seemed to extend to every part of his body. He looked at the hand, and it was black and swollen, but the bleeding had stopped. He sat up. His head ached, and he was thankful to be alive.

McCall rose slowly to his feet, staggered, then stopped and listed from side to side until he regained his balance. He needed water, and he stumbled toward a small creek and floundered through berry bushes and over river rocks and lay with his face close to the water and the coolness of it soothed the hand, and he drank.

And when he could, he stood and walked back to the dry creek bed. He retrieved his hat and followed the tracks of the horse and bull. His ribs hurt when he took a deep breath, and the throbbing hand had to be held high to keep the pressure off of it. He felt light-headed.

The horse and bull left a clear trail, and McCall followed it through the trampled brush and into a small clearing where he found the horse tethered to a tree, the rope held fast around the saddle horn and wrapped around a stout sapling, with the bull lying choked to death on his side at the far end of the rope.

McCall approached the horse slowly, caught up the reins, and cut the rope loose. The horse stood, and McCall led him to a downhill slope and mounted from the uphill side, then slumped in the saddle and gave the horse his head as he nudged him forward with his heels.

CHAPTER FIFTY-TWO

McCall rode for a long time, and the last of the daylight was fading when he rode up on a brush corral and waited. Deacon Rounder, the ranch foreman, was the first one back, and he led in a heifer on a rope and turned her in the pen and rode out to meet McCall.

"Hey, boss," Deacon said, not noticing the wounded hand.

McCall tilted forward and nodded, and let his hand drop from inside his jacket.

"What the hell happened?" Deacon asked, as he swung down from the saddle and caught McCall just before he fell out of his own saddle.

All McCall could do is nod toward the bloody hand.

"My horse jerked down. My rope fouled."

The cowboss untied his canteen and offered McCall water, and McCall drank most of it.

Where's the rest of the boys?" he asked.

"Franklin and J.W. is set up just north of Widow Creek there where that old cinnamon bear got into the remuda last spring," Deke answered, pointing out across a ravine that opened into a broad meadow.

"We better get you back to the ranch," Deke said. "Can you ride?"

"Yeah, Deke . . . I've had better days, but I'll make it."

Deke got him back up into the saddle and steadied him. They rode together and, when they arrived at the ranch, McCall had no recollection of the ride at all.

When McCall woke up, his eyes opened to the familiar wooden cross-beamed ceiling of his own bedroom. He tried to sit up, but the pain in his chest sent him reeling back. He tried again, only more slowly this time. Finally he succeeded in getting upright. As he adjusted himself t a more comfortable position he noticed his ten-year old grandson, Miles, standing at the other side of the bed, watching him.

"Here Grandpa, you can have this," Miles said, picking up the pillow he had on the small bed he had made up for himself on the floor next to his grandfather. Miles stuffed the pillow behind McCall.

"Are you okay, Grandpa?" Miles asked.

McCall nodded. "I'm okay Miles Travis. "How's my boy doing?"

"I'm doing good," Miles responded.

The boy folded back the covers of the makeshift bed on the floor and brought out McCall's Gros Ventre knife.

"I was taking care of this for you," he said.

McCall smiled. "You been sleeping down there?" he asked, tipping his head toward the blankets on the floor.

"Yeah, I have. You been asleep a long time, grandpa."

It was mid-day McCall judged by the slant of the sun where it crossed the room. He watched Miles as the dark-haired boy padded barefoot about the room, putting his bed in order and busying himself with McCall's things, which hung on a chair near the window.

"Boy, can you bring me my pants and boots? It's time for me to get out of this bed and get back to work before your daddy and Uncle Franklin think I'm taking advantage of a good thing here," McCall said, as he swung his legs tentatively over the edge of the tall bed.

As McCall sat there letting his head clear, Miles stood next to him.

"Hey, grandpa . . . how come you had a

finger in your pocket when you came home?"

"What do you mean, son?"

"When uncle Franklin took off your vest to put you in bed, he found a finger in it."

McCall laughed. "Oh, I remember now," he said. "I guess I couldn't figure out what else to do with it, and it didn't seem right to just throw it away, so I stuck it in my pocket."

"It was pretty ugly, grandpa."

"Well, which was it . . . pretty, or ugly?"

"It was ugly!"

"Where is it now?" McCall asked.

"Uncle Franklin buried it by the barn," Miles said, with a disgusted look on his face. "But one of the dogs dug it up, and we couldn't get it from him."

With the help of the boy, McCall managed to get dressed. He was a bit unsteady, but determined. With his good hand on Mile's shoulder, the two rounded the corner to the kitchen, where Allison intercepted them.

"Good Lord, Brady! What are you doing out of bed? Sweetheart, are you all right?"

McCall walked over to a chair at the table and sat down.

"I'm fine Alli. A little tender in the ribs and a little concerned about how I'm going to count past nine. But, yeah, I'm just fine. Me and Miles here are so hungry we could eat a horse," he replied as he tousled the boy's hair.

Miles laughed and pulled up a chair next to his grandfather.

"Brady, I've been so worried about you. Do you know you have been sleeping for two days? You were so groggy you couldn't even tell us what happened," said Allison.

She walked over closer and kissed him on the cheek. McCall put his arm around Allison's small waist and pulled her nearer.

"It wasn't much, thinking back on it," McCall explained.

"My horse jerked down and I had a big yearling bull on my rope. I hit the rocks, and that was enough to ruin my day. Then the rope fouled my hand and the bull took off . . . and so did my thumb."

"Between you and Stilwell, I feel like I've spent my whole life mending the two of you," Allison said, as she laughed. "Sweetheart, I'm just so glad to have you back safe and at least half-ways sound." She put her arms around his neck and kissed him.

"Miles you go out there on the porch and sound the dinner bell," she said, as she carried more dishes to the table.

Almost before the last ring faded, boots

were clomping around on the wooden porch and lining up at the wash basin. Franklin strode through the door first and behind him John William and Deke Rounder.

"Well, look who finally got hisself out of bed now that the branding is about finished," Franklin chided, as he hung his hat on the hall-tree near the door.

"We'd about give up on you this time B.C.," Franklin added.

Brady smiled.

"In fact, Deke and J.W. here was just arguing over which one would get your .44-40 and which one would get your new watch if you didn't make it." Franklin laughed and sat down across from McCall.

John William and Deke looked at each other and grinned, both shaking their heads.

"It's good to see you up and around again, daddy. How's that hand?" John William asked, as he gave his father a pat on the shoulder.

"It don't look too pretty, but it's just fine, son. By the way, you and Deke can forget about collecting my handgun and my timepiece for awhile, though," McCall said.

Deke spoke up as if to clear the record.

"Boss, for what it's worth, I didn't say nothing about your timepiece." He glanced over toward Franklin, as though he had been offended by the suggestion of any callousness on his part. Then he shifted his eyes back to McCall.

"I had my eye on the .44-40."

Franklin laughed, and John William smiled.

Brady laughed. "Allison, throw them all out. It hurts too much to have to take this."

The door swung open again, and three more Triple Dot cowboys found their places at the table. Pete Caldwell was in the lead. Next to Deke, Pete Caldwell was as good a man with a horse and a rope as any that had ever ridden for the ranch. He was steady and reliable on the job, but a hell raiser in town. Pete wore a black Stetson with a wide brim and a high crown creased down the front and pinched on the sides. He was slightly built and barely five-and-a-half-feet tall. People tended to underestimate Pete, and that invariably proved to be a serious mistake for anyone spoiling for a Saturday night fight.

Sebastian Bell entered behind Pete. He was lanky and easy going, and as long as he could remember only his mother ever called him Sebastian. Everyone else called him "Get Wood." The name, he explained, was a gift from his father. From the time he was old enough to walk, those were the only two words the sullen old man ever said to him. By the time he was old enough to understand, the boy thought Get Wood was his name, and that's what he told everyone it was.

Get Wood stood well over six feet tall, and while he towered over Pete, Get Wood looked up to his short friend like Pete was his big brother. Get Wood ambled to the table and sat next to Pete. The two made an unlikely pair. Pete was quick-witted and volatile. Get Wood, on the other hand, was slower and easy going. He was good-humored and easy to get along with, and his mood never varied regardless of the time of day or the circumstances.

The last man through the door was Walter Crow Child, a Blackfoot from northern Montana. Walter was about John William's age and was the son of a medicine man who had been a friend of Travis Kincaid. There was an air of intensity and seriousness about Walter that caused most people to approach him with caution and to pay him the kind of respect things of danger tend to command.

Only Franklin seemed unaware of Walter's reserve. While the others made an effort not to offend Walter, Franklin disregarded his privacy as readily as he ignored the privacy of the other men. Franklin sat with his back to the door. Without looking over his shoulder, he said loudly.

"Watler, I know it's you sneaking up on me, 'cause I smelt you coming." Franklin made the same joke every day since Walter hired on. And every day the boys roared with laughter like they had never heard it before. Franklin laughed and pulled the chair next to him away from the table.

"Come on an' sit down here right next to me, where I can keep a eye on you."

Walter knew about Franklin from things his father had told him. He admired and respected the old ranger and excused his sharp-edged manner. None of the others attempted to cross that line with the Indian.

Walter slid into the chair. Looking down the table, he ignored Franklin's remark and said to McCall, "Good to see you back, Brady." Then he said something to McCall in Blackfoot. McCall nodded in agreement and they both looked at Franklin and smiled. They continued the guttural dialogue with no regard for Franklin.

Franklin watched back and forth as the two men spoke, then he lost his patience and blurted out rudely, "Are you two heathens gonna have a tribal meeting here, or are we gonna eat? Even if you don't have nothing important to say, the least you and Watler could do is talk like civilized folks."

Deke did his best to choke back the laugh stuck in his throat. Get Wood and Pete stared down at their plates, while Walter and Brady just smiled.

Franklin began calling the Indian, Watler, two years ago. He had instructed Get Wood to paint the names of each of the permanent hands on the storage boxes assigned to each of them in the bunkhouse. Get Wood had misspelled "Walter" and no one but Franklin had ever noticed the error.

Franklin never considered pointing the error out to anyone, and it never occurred to him to correct it. Instead, he just started calling the Indian Watler. The rest of the cowboys figured that "Watler" was simply further evidence of Franklin's inability to master the English language.

Franklin took great pleasure in believing that he was the only one who was aware of the mistake, and he never missed an opportunity to flaunt his discovery. Franklin had his moments, and at one time or another he managed to get under the skin of each one of them but, like his rangers, there wasn't a man at the table who wouldn't ride through the fires of hell for Franklin T. Stilwell.

CHAPTER FIFTY-THREE

Sweet Grass River Ranch, Montana: July 1891

Sunday afternoon Brady and Franklin sat on the front porch of McCall's house. McCall's ribs had healed, and he was getting by just fine with nine fingers, although he claimed he had to get up earlier each morning just to get his shirt buttoned. Talk was slow, and Franklin was in a reminiscing mood.

"B.C., you remember when we could ride out from here and go for a week in any direction and never see a fence?" Franklin asked. He turned his chair to put his back to the sun.

"It sure ain't like it used to be," he added.

McCall nodded in agreement, but didn't say anything.

"I'm telling you . . . it ain't natural. Hell, me an Watler rode up to Butte this past spring. They're smelting copper up there and digging so many holes under the town that the whole damn place is going sink away some day. Besides that, not a damn thing will even grow around there. We was in the post office and heard a sound like something inside the earth exploded. The men in there told us it was miners blasting away in a tunnel nineteen-hundred feet right below where we stood." Franklin explained, in a mixture of amazement and disgust.

"You know, if you didn't see it with your own eyes," Franklin continued, "you wouldn't believe it. I asked Watler if he ever seen a man-dug hole nineteen-hundred feet deep. He says he hadn't . . . so we goes on up to the mine at Anaconda. When we gets there, we seen some old boys with a big white mule all trussed up with rope and wrapped in a canvas sheet. They had him on pulleys hanging over the shaft where the men go down into the mine. When we asked what the hell they was doing with the mule, they tells us he's going down to pull the ore cars from the side tunnels to the main shaft, so's they can get the ore out of the ground.

"I seen Watler a eyeing the mule, and he asks them boys how does the mule get back out. You know what they told him? They says the mule don't come back out . . . they work that damn jackass until he dies or until the they give up on that tunnel, then they leave him there. If the mule is lucky, some sombitch shoots him in the head when they leave . . . otherwise he wanders in that old, dark tunnel until he starves to death or steps down another shaft and gets himself killed."

"They call it progress, Franklin," said Brady. "Three years ago, when they voted for Montana statehood and it won . . . it was like a sign that nothing would ever be the same again. It's not just the fences and the mines and more people . . . it's the idea that they're all so ready to give up them things that men like us value. I sit here and look down at them good horses, then I remember what it was like to ride from the northern Rockies down into Old Mexico and never see a cabin or a fence. To take what I needed to live each day from whatever the earth had to offer, which sometimes wasn't much. It wasn't always easy, but it was always free."

Franklin shook his head, and his expression was clouded with doubt and concern.

"You don't suppose we're like those old mine mules, do you, B.C.?"

Brady waited and Franklin continued.

"We just keep on doing what we're doing,

and the rest of the world is leaving us behind."

McCall was surprised at the reflective insight coming from Franklin. He looked over at his friend. Franklin's dark eyes still had that devilish sparkle in them, but the black hair had long ago given way to the silver thatch that now showed beneath his hat. His hands were big-knuckled and rough. They showed strength and a lot of hard work, with only the brown spots of age giving any suggestion that they were the hands of a man almost seventy-years old.

The thought of the mule dug into McCall's sensibilities. The more he thought about it, the madder he got.

"Well, I'll tell you one thing," McCall said. "I don't want to end up like an old miner's mule, do you?

He walked over to the edge of the porch and spat. He stood there looking out over the treed meadow, and Franklin watched him without speaking. He spat again and turned to look directly at Franklin. A smile creased the edges of his eyes, and Franklin stood up and raised in hands in protest.

"No. Whatever it is you're thinking, the answer is, no," Franklin said.

He looked seriously at McCall. "B.C,. I want to get old. I want to sit on this damn porch and tell lies and do the things old men do. I want to take Jenny for buggy rides, and I want the kids to bring me coffee or a beer when I want one. And you know one more thing? I'm done getting shot at. It was never my intention to get shot in the first place. So I guess that's clear enough . . . I ain't listening to any more of your ideas."

Brady withdrew his knife and walked over to the table. He set the point down on a spot in front of Franklin. He looked up, and he bent over the table.

"This here is the Triple Dot," he said. "And this here," he said, making another spot southeast of the first one, "is Nevada."

Franklin laughed his most sarcastic laugh. "Nevada?" He shook his head in disbelief.

"Do you know what they got in Nevada?" he asked.

Brady looked at him, waiting for the answer he was sure was coming.

"Nothing . . . that's what they got in Nevada. No grass, no water, no trees, no people . . . nothing."

"They got horses in Nevada," Brady said.

"Horses?"

"Yes, horses . . . and lots of them."

"B.C., look around. Do we look like we need any more damn horses?"

Brady leaned forward, and his expression was solemn. "No, we don't, but Walter's people do." Then Brady stood up straight. "We'd be doing it for them."

Franklin looked away and shook his head and muttered under his breath.

Brady continued. "You know the mustangers are taking those horses out of there and selling them for waste . . . those they don't trap, they shoot. We'd be doing it for the horses too," Brady said, hoping to add weight to his argument. His voice got quiet, and he played his trump card.

"It's about time we paid back for all we got," he said.

"You know, B.C., I never liked doing business with you . . . ever. You are so, so . . . I don't even know what the word is, but you're it all over."

"So, you'll do it?" Brady asked smiling.

"Why don't you just shoot me now and be done with it?" Franklin asked. "You been trying all our lives to get me killed."

Brady laughed. "Good. I knew I could count on you."

"Well, you might as well fill me in on the plan," Franklin said.

Brady explained the plan. He knew where seven or eight-hundred mustangs had been run into a canyon and cut off there while the mustangers picked them out as they wanted them. All the boys had to do was to ride in, break out the horses and drive them north. It was Franklin's kind of plan, and before they got back to the barn to work out the rest of the details, it had become Franklin's plan, and he rallied up all the enthusiasm it took to convince the others to go along with it.

As they walked back from the barn that evening, Brady looked down at his thumbless hand, then back at Franklin.

"This could be dangerous," he said.

Franklin smiled. "Yeah, could be," he said.

"Mustangers won't give them horses up easy," Brady said.

Franklin nodded. "But what's a few shitters among friends?"

Brady smiled back. "That's what I was thinking."

Franklin cleared his throat. "I never liked getting shot," he said. "But it beats dying in a mine shaft."

CHAPTER FIFTY-FOUR

For the next two weeks every activity at the Triple Dot was focused on the mustang rescue. John William and Walter were headed north and Deke had already returned from Bozeman with Laird Bingham, the new cook.

Laird insisted on his own list of supplies and, for his name and occupation, he was built thin and tall and looked to be in his fifties, although he had looked like that since he was thirty and would probably still look that way at seventy.

He limped from an old Civil war wound, wore a bowler that he never took off, and handled the chuck wagon team like he may have been a top hand in his day. Laird had mothered cowboys on the trail for a long time, and every year his foul disposition got worse. Talking to Laird was an exercise in frustration, and only Franklin seemed oblivious to his sarcasm, impatience and intolerance.

But Laird Bingham was the consummate camp cook, and getting trail hands to sign on to a job was substantially easier when they found out he was cooking. He double-checked his list as supplies were loaded on the wagon. The horses' feet had been trimmed and shod, and at first light the next morning the Triple Dot outfit would roll out for the Medicine Lodge. Then, into Nevada.

Whoops and hollers filled the air as the cowboys down at the corrals took the kinks out of the green horses each had in his string. This was going to be a long, hard and dangerous trip, and everyone knew it. There was no secret about that, but every man going felt privately privileged to be included, and it showed. Walter Crow Child's people caught up the spirit of it along with the Triple Dot crew and by early evening, what started out to be hard work and careful preparation, turned into a celebration.

Laura Kincaid watched from the window inside the house with sad eyes that remembered a time when Travis would have been right out there with them. She imagined that he looked down approvingly at what she had always considered to be the work of little boys acting out their play in old men's bodies.

It warmed her heart to watch Brady and Franklin, and she looked upon the two aging friends as she always remembered them, still boys, still full of mischief and unpredictable behavior. She looked past the gray hair and the lined faces. She never saw two old men; all she saw was the boys, Travis' boys. And she saw him in everything they did and said, and she approved.

Elizabeth and her family came over for the send off. Allison tended Elizabeth's two young ones while Elizabeth and her father walked arm-in-arm toward the barn where the broodmares were brought up for foaling. The sweet smell of fresh hay greeted them when Brady pulled the big wooden door open. The mares nickered and stuck their heads over the top rail of the loafing shed fence. Brady and Elizabeth leaned against the rail to look in on the mares.

"See that dun mare over there with the dark stripe running down the middle of her back?" McCall said to his daughter, as he pointed out a well-muscled horse with bulging sides.

Elizabeth beamed. She loved to hear her father talk of horses, and she loved the look in his eyes when he did so. She never stopped admiring his knowledge of horses, and she liked that she learned something new from him every time they spoke of horses.

She looked at the mare then back at her father.

"Perfect top line," she said. "Well sprung ribs, good hips, good slope to the shoulders, thick in the stifle with strong legs and substantial bone." She smiled up at her father. "And that nice soft eye we like so much," she added.

"Which bloodline you make her out of?" McCall asked his daughter. He always tested her this way, and she loved the challenge.

She furrowed her brow in mock concentration the way she always did to tease him when she knew the answer.

"Well," she said slowly. "If I had to say, I'd say she's all Morning Star on the bottom side and strong Buffalo Dancer on the topside."

Her father grinned. "It's in your blood, isn't it?" he said.

She smiled back at him. "Has been for as long as I can remember," she said, then she put her arms around the old man and didn't say anything for a long time.

When she did speak, she looked over at

the mare. "I'll bet you a dollar she has that baby tonight," she said.

McCall looked over at the mare himself. "Based on the pure unpredictability of a mare, I'll take that bet."

They shook hands, and Elizabeth held her father's hand, and her expression was serious.

"Is there any way I can talk you and Franklin out of this trip?" she asked.

"Why would you want to do that?" McCall asked.

"I just feel better having you and Uncle Franklin close to us," she said, trying to avoid any references to age or danger.

McCall held her at arm's length. "You really don't want us to go?" he asked.

She shook her head from side to side.

"Sweetheart," McCall said. "Your uncle Franklin and I are at a point in our lives where we may never get another chance like this again. The world is closing in on men like us. Just understand, nothing is more important to me than your momma and you and your brother and them little grandchildren of ours. This may be our last go-round. You wouldn't want to see us sit it out, would you?"

Elizabeth looked up at her father. His eyes were full of love and concern, and they had the look of a little boy pleading for something he wanted more than anything else in the world. She bit her bottom lip, then smiled and said, "Well, you and uncle Franklin just go and give 'em hell, daddy." She smiled big with tears of pride running down her cheeks and hugged her father, and he held her tight.

She spoke into his shoulder. "And when you come back I want to sit up all night on the porch with the two of you and listen to all your stories and try to figure out which of you tells the worst lies." Then she laughed, and he laughed, and he knew it was all right.

The dinner bell sounded and Miles Travis stuck his head into the barn and yelled, "Come and get it before the flies do," and he was off.

Every seat at the table was filled. McCall said grace over the food and asked for a safe journey. He prayed for good weather, asked for easy river crossings and the Lord's hand in helping them with the horses. Then he asked the Lord's blessing on those present, and those who were away. Amen.

Franklin looked over at Brady with a serious expression, and said, "B.C., I ain't at all sure it was appropriate for you to ask the Lord to help us steal horses."

"Are we stealing them horses?" Get Wood asked Pete quietly. "I thought we was just moving them."

"We are just diverting them, Sebastian," Pete said mockingly. "It's just that there may be a few folks what don't approve of where we're diverting them from."

"Is that true, Franklin?" Get Wood asked, looking confused.

"Well, do you think a sawed-off little shit like Pete would lie to a big sombitch like you?" Franklin snapped back.

Get Wood shook his head, now more confused than ever. "No, I guess not," he said.

"Who you calling a sawed-off little shit?" Pete shot back to Get Wood.

Get Wood looked startled. "Pete, I never said you was . . ."

Pete cut him off. "Well, don't you never."

Allison carried a huge platter of beef to the table and the conversation ceased when she cleared her throat to speak.

"Unless you boys want to eat out in the barn, you best keep your profanities to yourselves in front of these children," she said, scolding the men collectively.

Franklin started to speak, but Allison pointed a finger at him and shaking it said, "And that goes double for you, Stilwell."

"Yes, ma'am," he said obediently.

Miles sat at the head of the table next to his grandfather. His mother, Anna, sat at the other end of the table with Allison and Elizabeth. Between bites, talk slowed down. The women held their private conversation at one end of the table. The men talked with their mouths full, knowing it would be a while before they ate this good again.

McCall and Get Wood speculated on how far they would travel the first day, while Pete and Franklin talked about the new singer at the Prairie Dog Saloon in Bozeman.

Sitting up straight and as tall as he could, Miles spoke out. "I'm going with you tomorrow, grandpa."

Suddenly the room was silent, and all heads turned Brady's direction. Anna's face went ashen as she reached over and grabbed Allison's arm for moral support.

"Son, I figured you to stay here and take charge of the ranch," McCall said calmly.

"They don't need me here grandpa, and I may never get another chance to ride on a important job like this with you and my dad, and uncle Franklin," Miles argued.

"You simply are not going and that is final," Anna said, hoping to end the discussion right then and there.

"Miles, your momma is right," McCall reaffirmed. "You're a mite too young to be thinking about crossing that much territory on horseback with no one to look after you."

The boy set his jaw and stood up, and looked McCall directly in the eye.

"Well, I damn sure ain't," he blurted out in anger. "You did it."

His mother's mouth fell open in astonishment. She started to speak, but Allison calmed her with a firm, gentle touch of her hand. "Better let Brady handle this," she whispered.

Miles fought the tears that threatened and, through gritted teeth, he defended his position.

"Grandpa, I'm ten years old. I can shoot, and I can ride. I can take care of my own gear. I ain't too young. I remember all them stories you and uncle Franklin told me about when you were my age. I don't care if I never killed an Indian, and I don't care if I never do, but I should get a chance to go, just like you had. I even have a knife that aunt Laura give me that used to belong to uncle Travis," he said resolutely.

Miles sat back down and laid the knife and its old worn leather sheath out on the table in front of him. Brady and Franklin looked at each other as they both recognized the knife Kincaid had used the night he

rescued them from the Comanche renegades. A wave of emotion ran over both of
the old cowboys, but neither spoke. McCall
looked down the table at Anna and Allison,
but saw no approval in the eyes of either of
them.

Franklin shrugged his shoulders in a, let's-
let-him-come, gesture.

"Miles," Brady began in a slow, deliberate
manner. "What you say is true, and I can't
think of a better partner than you, but son,
you got to understand this is a different time
and a different set of circumstances. It just
isn't like it used to be."

"It's progress," Franklin muttered to himself.

To Anna's great relief, Brady finally settled
the matter.

"It's best you just put it out of your mind.
When we get back we can pack back into
the Absarokies and get us a deer or two for
the winter," he said, patting the dejected
boy consolingly on the back.

"Uncle Franklin, please tell him it's okay,"
Miles pleaded.

Franklin was torn. He looked at McCall.
"B.C.?" he said weakly, not wanting to make
the matter worse.

"Grandpa, please don't take my only
chance away from me," the boy said, as he

stood with his hand on McCall's shoulder.

"Son, I'm sorry . . ."

Miles was devastated. He ran from the room, swinging the front door open violently and letting it slam against the inside wall without closing it.

There was a long period of silence. Brady knew how the boy felt, and it hurt him to tell him he couldn't do things that in his heart he knew the boy could do.

Laura Kincaid, in her soft voice, broke the quiet and, at the risk of going counter to Anna's wishes said, "Brady, do you ever remember Travis telling you there was anything you couldn't do? And you Franklin, he always treated you boys like men. I can't remember how many times Travis told me how young and green you two were then, but it never stopped him from treating you like men. Now you got a chance to return the favor to your own grandson. Are you two so old you can't remember what it was like to be a boy getting ready to be a man?"

"Aunt Laura, that was different," Brady said, in feeble defense.

Laura's mind and memory were sharp and unfailing, and everybody was thinking what only she had the gumption to say. The problem was, no one else could get themselves up to say anything for fear of upsetting Anna, who still thought of Miles as her little baby.

Brady got up from the table and walked toward the door. He took his hat from the hall tree and pulled it down tight on his head.

"Where are you going, Brady?" Allison asked.

"I think I'll take a walk down to the broodmare barn. There might be a young cowboy down there who is feeling a little low right about now," Brady answered.

McCall sidestepped in through the partially opened barn door and saw Miles sitting in with the mares. When he approached and looked over the rail, he saw Miles sitting and helping the dun mare clean off her new baby. McCall watched quietly, and Miles looked up at him and smiled. Finally, the new colt stretched his long, spindly legs out in front of him and pushed his front end up off the ground. Then he made one quick lunge, and he was up on all four feet.

McCall climbed over the rail and stood beside Miles. He put an arm over the boy's shoulder, and Miles put his arm around his grandfather's waist. Together they watched as the foal found the mare's udder. The colt's legs were still shaky, but he drank his fill then began to explore. At first he stayed close to his mother's side, but soon he ventured out in larger circles. The colt walked confidently up to Miles and sniffed the boy's fingers with his soft muzzle. He nibbled at the buttons on the boy's shirt then whirled to return to his mother.

"Looks like we got us a stud colt there, Miles," declared McCall. "Judging by the way he looks, I would say he is going to be a buckskin. Nice straight legs, good angle to his shoulder. Look at that front end and that butt on him. He's going to be a mover."

"Do you think he likes me grandpa?" Miles asked.

"Well, I'd say he likes you just fine." McCall paused, and watched the boy's eyes as they followed the colt.

"Seems like every man ought to have him a buckskin horse at least once in his life. What do you think?" McCall asked.

"I'd like to have a buckskin someday," Miles said, looking back up at his grandfather.

"It takes a heap of hard work to bring on a colt," Brady said. "It takes someone who is understanding and willing to put in the work."

"Grandpa, I'm a hard worker," Miles said, with excitement building in his voice. "And

I understand real good too."

"A man's got to be strong to handle a big colt," McCall added.

"I'm strong, grandpa. I lift those feed sacks all by myself all the time, and I clean out stalls, and nobody helps me," Miles exclaimed.

"I was just thinking," said the old cowboy. "Did you ever own any buckskin horses when you was a kid?"

"Grandpa, I am a kid," Miles said as he laughed. "But I never owned no buckskins yet," he added quickly.

"Well, maybe when you're ten," McCall said, like he was contemplating some long-range plan.

"Grandpa, I'm already ten," Miles said, with his impatience starting to show through.

"Well, damned if you ain't." Then McCall looked up as though he were doing some complex mental calculations. Finally, he looked back down at Miles.

"You know, the way I figure it, you're the next one in line for a buckskin horse around here," McCall said.

"I am?" Miles asked, his eyes lighting up and an uncontrollable grin stretching his face back to his ears.

"You are for sure. That skinny-legged little

fella over there must be yours then."

"He is? Really, Grandpa?"

Brady nodded and Miles hugged the cowboy before he inched his way back to the colt. The colt watched the boy through soft, brown eyes. His short bristle-brush mane gave him a carousel-horse appearance, and he stood quietly as Miles touched his soft nose and talked to him in a low voice. Miles touched the foal on the cheek then returned to sit on the fence with his grandfather.

They sat there for almost two hours watching the colt master his small universe as he grew stronger and more confident. He nuzzled his mother, then nursed until the mare became impatient with his head-butting. He found a spot in the clean hay and stretched out on his side and slept.

Brady stepped down from the rail and Miles jumped to the ground next to him. He put his arms around his grandfather and said, "Grandpa, I love my new horse. Thank you for giving him to me."

Late that night after everyone had gone to bed, McCall got up and quietly made his way through the dark house and out onto the porch. The air was cool, and the moon was full. In the silver light McCall saw Miles sitting on the front step watching the mare and her colt, standing in the corral.

McCall put his hand on the boy's shoulder and sat down beside him without speaking. The cowboy couldn't remember how many new foals he watched run by their mother's side, but still there was an excitement about it that made it impossible to sleep the first night. He knew Miles would have the same problem, and he understood just how the boy felt.

"Grandpa," Miles said quietly after a long period of silence.

"What is it, son?"

"I got a name for my colt."

Miles turned to his grandfather, and in the moonlight Brady thought he saw a little of the man showing through on the boy. Brady looked down at the boy and saw his own father looking down at him.

"So, what are you going to call him?"

"I named him Buffalo Dancer."

McCall turned away. The sound of the name brought back so many feelings, so many memories. An image of the battle-scarred, buckskin stallion flashed across his mind. A flood of emotion swelled up in the old cowboy's throat and he was unable to speak.

"Grandpa, that's okay, isn't it?" Miles asked, after the uncomfortable, long silence.

McCall put his arm around the boy's shoulder and remembered how it felt to be ten-years old and the new owner of a buckskin stallion. The lantern light reflected in McCall's eyes, and Miles thought he saw a tear when his grandfather replied.

"Miles Travis, you couldn't have picked a prouder name."

CHAPTER FIFTY-FIVE

It was an hour before sun-up. The dogs barked and a fat, red rooster stood on the top rail of the fence, crowing and flapping his wings. The horses at the hitch rail pawed the ground and shifted positions back and forth, as they nervously watched the activity going on around them.

Laird Bingham was already up on the seat of the chuck wagon, one foot on the brake and both hands on the reins. The team was anxious, and all four horses were a bundle of pent-up energy waiting to explode. Just about the time Laird had the team under control, Pete whooped and hollered as the fresh horse he climbed aboard humped up and bucked all the way from the barn, past the chuck wagon, and on his way around the back of the house.

Laird cursed Pete as he went by.

"Keep that jug head the hell away from my team."

Pete was hanging on for his life and looked back just long enough to glare at Laird and reply through clenched teeth as he bounced past the wagon.

"Why don't you chunk one a your biscuits at him? That ought to quiet him down."

Before either one could get another word out, Pete and his horse bucked through a cloud of dust and disappeared around the side of the house.

Laird turned in time to see Deke with one foot in the stirrup as his horse went straight up in the air with a twist and a grunt. When the big gelding came back down, Deke was still half in and half out of the saddle. The gelding spun his direction, and Deke managed to get his free leg over, but never found the other stirrup. The horse sunfished back up, and a full-grown man could have walked under the space between its belly and the ground.

When the horse came back down Deke was ready. He shortened up a rein, jerked its head around and buried the rowels of his spurs into its sides. The horse stuck out its nose, pointed himself south, and his feet barely touched the ground as he flew down the road. When they shot past the chuck wagon, Laird fired a biscuit at them and cursed something unintelligible about

Deke's mother.

Laird managed to hold the team in check, but by now they were so charged with nervous excitement that all four horses were in a lather. The cook watched suspiciously as Pete rode his horse quietly out from behind the house and to the barn. Pete looked as calm as an undertaker as he gathered up his bedroll and tied it on behind his saddle.

Deke trotted his horse back in from the darkness and, even though it was still high-headed and snorty, he had ridden all the kinks out of it, and it was ready to go to work.

The family gathered on the front porch. The children still wrapped in blankets and the women with shawls held tightly about their shoulders. Allison shivered, but didn't know if it was from the chill or the excitement.

Over the ridgeline of the mountains to the east, the sky began to take on the hopeful colors of dawn. Allison watched Franklin riding back and forth, waving his arms and shouting orders at everyone. She could see Brady's beaming expression as he sat tall and proud on the bay gelding. A chill ran down her back. In all the excitement, it had never before occurred to her that she may never see him again. She forced the thought from her mind.

She and Brady never said long goodbyes, and this time was no exception. They had taken care of that earlier and now a final wave would do it as they pulled out. As Brady rode toward the wagons, he suddenly turned his horse and trotted back to the porch. He felt the same thing Allison did, and he wanted to make sure nothing was cut short this time. He leaned down from the saddle, gathered her up in one arm and kissed her.

"We'll be back before the snow flies," he said, as he gave her a reassuring wink. "Remember how much I love you," he said.

The ground shook and a rumbling sound like thunder preceded the remuda as the bell-mare clanked by, leading the charging horses down the road. Get Wood whooped it up as he galloped by with the thirty, stampeding horses he jingled from the lower pasture. He grinned and waved his hat, then spurred his horse on faster when he went past Laird, who shook his fist in a fit of obscenities.

Laird let out a shrill whistle and turned the team up the road and followed the remuda as they lined out for the Medicine Lodge River.

Pete fell in behind the chuck wagon and was joined by Deke. It was a magnificent sight. The cowboys on horseback tended to their early-dawn duties. The chuck wagon creaked and clattered behind the remuda of well-bred horses. Even the small cootie wagon, heavy with bedrolls and equipment, seemed like part of a bygone time, brought to life for this occasion.

It was just a handful of cowboys with high hopes and a thinly devised plan to rescue eight-hundred horses for what seemed like a good cause. And, at this point in time, there was nothing more important in the world than these men and this particular Montana morning.

Allison watched with great pride as Brady and Franklin trotted up on their strong, young ponies and fell in with Pete and Deke. The two old cowboys sat tall in their saddles and they rode with great authority. They talked and laughed and their hands made great and wild gestures.

Aren't they a handsome pair, Allison said to herself. *Just like two kids.* She smiled and held her arms wrapped tight about her.

She looked over at Laura who stood beside her. There was an eternity of history in the lines on Laura's face. Laura's eyes were wet. She looked at Allison. "For as long as I can remember, those boys have always ridden good horses," she said with a hint of pride in her voice. "Wouldn't Travis be proud?" she asked, but it was not a question.

Allison nodded, and just watched as the procession rolled out the gate. The two old men would forever remain the two young men who changed her life.

The horses pranced and jigged down the road and the riders stood up in their stirrups waving their hats in a glorious salute. Brady and Franklin grinned at each other. Franklin leaned over towards Brady.

"If we run across any Gros Ventres this trip, you're on your own, cousin," he shouted over the noise of the horses and the creaking wagons.

Brady laughed.

"Well," he shouted back. "I'll keep that in mind."

Franklin looked over at the old Indian knife at Brady's side. He reached down and touched his own knife then the pistol. He smiled and sat straighter, then settled into the saddle for a long ride.

The rapid clatter of shod hooves upon the dry road behind them caused both old cowboys to turn in their saddles at the same time. A fifth horseman galloped up and reined in between them as he jerked his horse down to a walk. He looked first at Franklin, then at Brady.

"It's me, grandpa. I'm coming with you," Miles said.

McCall turned quickly in the saddle and looked back questioningly at the house. Anna stood in the yard with her hand to her mouth and tears streaming down both cheeks. She waved and nodded her approval. McCall looked across at John William and John William smiled.

"Takes after his grandpa," J.W. said, smiling.

Miles grinned and waved a hand at his father.

McCall smiled broadly, then turned back to Miles and stuck out his hand. Miles grabbed it and shook it hard.

"Welcome to the outfit, cowboy," McCall said.

ABOUT THE AUTHOR

They Rode Good Horses is **D. B. Jackson**'s debut novel. His second book, *Unbroke Horses,* according to a review by Mile Swarthout, Screenwriter for John Wayne's *The Shootist,* ". . . brands him as a coming talent in this classic old genre."